PUSHKIN PRESS

The OTHERWHERE POST

'An epic dark fantasy tale of love, justice, the delicate magic of finding connection, and the complex art of scribing... thrilling, gripping and thoroughly enjoyable'
Kirkus, starred review

'Inventive worldbuilding... witty banter and reluctant romance... inject levity and depth'
Publishers Weekly, starred review

'With delicious layers that readers will love unravelling, this fantastical piece will positively whisk you away'
Booklist, starred review

'A high stake, deliciously dark tale of a young woman risking it all for the truth. From its brilliant magic to the torturous slow burn romance, *The Otherwhere Post* mesmerizes'
Lyssa Mia Smith, author of *Revelle*

'Unique, whimsical and utterly spellbinding'
Jessica S. Olson, author of *A Forgery of Roses*

'This dark academia fantasy features masterful worldbuilding, a wildly interesting new magic system, and a loveable cast of characters'
School Library Journal, starred review

The OTHERWHERE POST

EMILY J. TAYLOR

PUSHKIN PRESS

Pushkin Press
Somerset House, Strand
London WC2R 1LA

Published by arrangement with Razorbill, an imprint of Penguin Young
Readers Group, a division of Penguin Random House LLC

The Otherwhere Post was first published in the United States of America by
G. P. Putnam's Sons, an imprint of Penguin Random House LLC, 2025

First published by Pushkin Press in 2025

Hardback ISBN 13: 978-1-78269-442-7
Trade Paperback ISBN 13: 978-1-78269-546-2

A CIP catalogue record for this title is available from the British Library

The authorised representative in the EEA is
eucomply OÜ, Pärnu mnt. 139b-14, 11317, Tallinn, Estonia,
hello@eucompliancepartner.com, +33757690241

Offset by Tetragon, London
Printed and bound in the United Kingdom by Clays Ltd, Elcograf S.p.A.

Pushkin Press is committed to a sustainable future for our
business, our readers and our planet. This book is made from
paper from forests that support responsible forestry.

www.pushkinpress.com

1 3 5 7 9 8 6 4 2

For Rogue and West

Maeve always carried the love letter with her. She knew every ink stroke by heart, that it took twenty-three seconds to unsheathe the brittle paper from the envelope and read the tender words penned by her mother to her father ages ago. It was all she had left of her parents.

Today, however, it sat like a weight at the base of her right pocket.

Tucking her rust-red braid into her coat collar, Maeve hurried up the rain-slicked cobblestones of Widdick's Close until she crested the hill near her flat.

Autumn air clung like wet leaves to her tongue. Bleak ocean winds beat her cheeks, and the city of Gloam spread out before her: blackened stone university buildings tangled between steep roads that ran together like an ink spill. The city of Gloam in Leyland.

It was such an ugly world.

Maeve imagined she could see the two other known worlds of Inverly and Barrow wrapped over this one like the translucent sheets of tissue she used to package quills. The three known worlds appeared identical if you squinted, but truly comparing them was the same as searching for similarities between a fresh apple and a lump of hearth coal.

Unfortunate, considering she happened to be stuck in that lump of coal.

She pulled out the love letter, along with a train ticket she'd purchased just yesterday. The ticket took her ages to save for. It granted passage to the south coast of Leyland in exactly one week. In seven short days, she would kiss this decrepit city goodbye for good.

A smile tugged at her lips. She tucked the precious ticket back inside her pocket, then dragged a gloved finger along the love letter's tattered corner.

She dearly wished she had a single memory of her mother, but Aoife Abenthy had died from a wasting sickness when Maeve was a mere babe. Her father was a different matter entirely.

She'd discovered this letter in his things the week before she lost him, back when she wouldn't let him walk out the door without slipping her hands over his wiry shoulders and forcing him to hug her twice. Before she learned he was a twisted murderer.

She was only eleven years old. Now, at eighteen, she had lived with that knowledge for too many years.

Her fingers tightened, straining the envelope until it was on the verge of ripping. This love letter might have been written by her mother, but it belonged to *him*.

"Guess what, Father? I finally saved enough to buy a train ticket. I'm leaving your favorite city in one week's time. After that, I hope to never spend another minute of my life thinking of you."

A burst of lightning lit up the gray sky, as if her father were laughing at her. He'd perished in another world, but Maeve was half convinced his spiteful ghost resided here nonetheless, haunting her every step.

Trembling, she tucked the letter down into her pocket, beside the train ticket. Out of sight.

As much as she wanted to love something her mother wrote, she hated that letter. But she didn't dare get rid of it. The constant feel of the envelope against her hip bone served as a necessary reminder to be careful to never use her real name. To never speak it. If anyone discovered who she was, they would call the constabulary. Unless the families of her father's victims came for retribution first.

Maeve took a strangled breath, feeling the sickening weight of his crimes pressing against her lungs—the shame of having to live in a world that he had tarnished.

At least she was leaving in a week. It might prove difficult to run away from the blood in her veins, but she would certainly try her best.

More lightning cracked across the sky, followed by rain. Maeve tightened her scarf. It was a long trek to the Alewick Inksmithy, a quaint, quiet establishment in the southernmost neighborhood in Gloam. Maeve's eyes watered as she finally entered through the front. The heated shop air was scented with lampblack ink, powdered blotting papers, sealing waxes, and solvents: all the tools one required to pen a letter.

"Is that you, Isla?" Mr. Braithwaite called from the back.

It took Maeve a full second to answer; she still wasn't used to her latest alias. "Yes, I'm here! And drenched, I'm afraid."

His cane knocked against the rough-hewn floorboards as he hobbled into the front. A thick scowl deepened the wrinkle lines in his brown, freckled cheeks. "You're awfully late again."

She wouldn't be surprised if her employer had a ticking pocket watch instead of a heart. "Only twelve minutes."

"Late is late. I thought I would be forced to hunt you down and make you feed Bane."

3

The old nipping mare had a countenance as charming as her master's. Maeve avoided Bane. She avoided all horses.

Peeling off her gloves, she caught her reflection in the front mirror and frowned. Her damp coat pulled against her wide bust—where the tarnished row of brass buttons almost never remained in their holes—but she was too chilled to shrug it off. The mole above the right corner of her lip stood out like a point on a pallid map. At least with a pinch to her cheeks, she appeared slightly less like a blanched onion.

Maeve came around the counter, pausing at the locked valuables cabinet that had stood empty yesterday.

"Those came in late last night." Mr. Braithwaite gestured to three left-handed quills hanging inside, their fletching dyed exquisite shades of indigo and violet.

The quills were crafted from molted right-wing feathers, which made them enormously expensive. Most feather merchants gathered right-wing feathers for other uses besides left-handed quills, and the few they sold were usually snapped up by university faculty long before they arrived in Alewick.

Maeve ran a finger over the blisters along her left-hand thumb, dearly wishing feathers weren't as costly as train tickets.

Tearing her eyes from the case, she took out her favorite quill knife, a small, rusted blade that got the job done faster than most. She tested it against a fingertip. When a bead of blood welled, she licked it off.

"So?" Mr. Braithwaite said a whole half a minute later. "Why were you late?"

Meddlesome man. "I forgot my hat at home and had to go back for it," Maeve lied, then reached for a box of molted swan feathers.

"Back for a hat?" Mr. Braithwaite said with a disagreeable grunt.

He pushed his reading spectacles to his forehead. "Doesn't seem such an important thing to me, but I suppose I can't understand the importance of fashion to a woman." He glanced toward the aged sepiagraph hanging behind the counter, of a pretty young woman, her dark cheeks stained pink. "My Una loved shopping for hats, and I never understood it," he said, then dabbed tears in his eyes.

Maeve fidgeted, uncomfortable at the sight of him weeping.

A job posting brought her here eight months prior. Mr. Braithwaite had been trying to hire a stockist for weeks; his demeanor likely sent all other applicants fleeing in terror. It was the perfect opportunity, until he confessed in a gut-wrenching tone that Una had passed away.

Lonely people were the ones Maeve watched out for, who recognized the loneliness in her and thought it an invitation. She had almost walked out, but then he offered her the job, and she needed the money more than she cared to admit.

"Una was in Inverly the day it was destroyed, shopping for a new hat," he said quietly, still staring at the portrait.

Maeve jolted at the mention of Inverly—one of the three known worlds—and dropped her quill knife. She scrambled to pick it up.

He had never told her how Una died.

Mr. Braithwaite didn't seem to notice her reaction. His eyes were lost in his wife's face. "Una preferred the Inverly haberdashers, with their colorful spools of thread. She had an appointment to visit one two blocks from Blackcaster Station that very afternoon. I've always wondered if she tried running for Leyland and simply didn't make it."

Blackcaster Station was no train station. It once housed the two great Written Doors—doors people used to travel back and forth between the three known worlds. Once, you could leave a university lecture in Gloam in Barrow, have dinner in Gloam in Inverly, then visit a tavern here in Gloam in Leyland, all in a single evening. Until one terrifying afternoon seven years ago.

"I'm so sorry," Maeve managed through a tight throat.

She had been in Inverly that afternoon as well, and thinking of it never failed to send her back to the moments of terror she'd experienced—people screaming, everyone running to escape. She was one of the lucky ones—close enough to Blackcaster Station to dart inside and make it through to Leyland before it was too late.

Minutes after she escaped Inverly, the Written Door between the two worlds was burned to cinders, obliterating its magic. Then the fire spread to the other Written Door connecting Barrow and Leyland, burning it as well, stranding thousands on either side. By the time the smoke cleared, everyone had learned the truth: that Inverly was destroyed and everyone inside of it was gone forever. Just like that. Barrow and Leyland were both spared, but with the doors burned, all travel was cut off instantly, stranding everyone wherever they happened to be. Trapping Maeve in godforsaken Leyland all by herself.

In the wake of Inverly's destruction, the House of Ministers recruited specialists to try to repair the Written Door connecting Leyland and Barrow. The effort was intended to help those stranded in the wrong world to return home, but nothing came of it. Now the only people able to cross between Leyland and Barrow were couriers trained in the magical art of scriptomancy, delivering precious letters to those desperate to hear from their loved ones.

Maeve never hoped for a letter herself. Everyone she loved had been in Inverly.

Tears burned the backs of her eyes, and the memories of that afternoon threatened to swallow her. When Mr. Braithwaite failed to stop his weeping, Maeve couldn't stand it anymore. She unwrapped a sheet of tissue from around a quill and tossed it to him, then turned to face the wall.

Breathe, she told herself.

Mr. Braithwaite didn't mention Inverly again, thankfully. He wiped his cheeks, then stepped to his worktable, where he proceeded to open today's copy of the *Herald* and give Maeve a rundown of the news, along with his delightfully pessimistic commentary.

Professor's Row was being repaved—*two years too late!* The Leyland campus of the university hired new faculty—*but they were all snobs with wallets bigger than their brains*. A tavern in Old Town caught fire, but no one was hurt—*a miracle considering the festering buildings*. On and on it went.

"Ah. There's actually something interesting from the Otherwhere Post," he said.

Maeve glanced up. The paper was opened to the back page, where Postmaster Byrne's newsletter was printed weekly.

"Would you look at this. Old Byrne has announced that the backlog of letters from the months after the Written Doors burned are finally being sent out. My sister wrote me from Barrow some twenty times all those years ago. Wouldn't it be something to get her letters now?"

"Without a doubt." At least Maeve knew that none of those old letters were for her.

"It's good the Post finally sorted out their disastrous infrastructure. God knew how hard it was for Byrne to find enough couriers he could teach to scribe. I heard it's one in a hundred that can pull off the magic."

It was one in three hundred, but she didn't correct him. The talk of scriptomancy caused her palms to sweat.

He flipped the page. "One of these days, I'd like to see exactly how scriptomancy works."

"It would be a sight to behold," she said, hoping Mr. Braithwaite would drop it. Already, images of her father with a quill between his fingers poured across her mind.

Scriptomancy is the art of enchanting any piece of existing handwriting, from a penned novel to a scribbled grocery list, he always told her with a twinkle in his eye. He was a skilled scriptomancer, and had promised to teach her the art "one day soon," whatever that had meant. Then he'd given her journals and asked her to fill them, said that scriptomancy required a deep understanding of linguistics and chirography before you were ever allowed to practice. She'd listened fiercely because she'd loved him more than anything in the worlds. Things had certainly changed.

Maeve shoved her father from her mind and set about carving quills. A few minutes passed, and the shop grew strangely silent. Mr. Braithwaite hadn't made another peep. It was unlike him. Worried something had happened, she turned to find him regarding her with a bewildered frown.

"What did I do now?" She hadn't cracked a feather or spilled any ink. The front counter was as neat as a pin.

"You're leaving in a week."

"Yes, I know. We discussed it yesterday."

His expression turned grim. "I won't be able to replace you, and I don't like it."

"Sure you will. You'll hire a brawny stock boy who likes to smile and can name more parchment substrates than I can."

"They won't be half as capable."

"That's utter nonsense." She had neat writing, certainly, and above-average organization, but she couldn't upsell a customer to save her life. She always tried, though, rather awkwardly.

"Ill-tempered as you may be, you have no idea of the treasure you are to me."

A treasure? Maeve glanced at his worktable to make sure he hadn't accidentally inhaled anything, but there were no uncorked solvents.

He called her a treasure, but the reality was, she was a liability. Her father's legacy made sure of that.

Her eyes dropped to the fine blue veins threading the inside of her wrist. She often wondered if the potential for murder was passed through blood, if evil lurked inside of her now. Even if it didn't, she was still a risk to Mr. Braithwaite. Her father's crimes were so disgraceful that everyone in Leyland had reason to hate him. If anyone discovered her identity, this shop would be tainted by association, and nobody would come in. Mr. Braithwaite would lose the shop, the flat above it, even the shirt on his back, and it would be her fault for not quitting sooner. The past eight months had already been too long.

The front door opened, and the grocer's wife, Mrs. Findlay, bustled inside with a steaming loaf for Mr. Braithwaite tucked beneath her homespun cloak. She dusted a drop of rainwater from the tip of her pink nose. Her inquisitive eyes pierced Maeve. "Ah, Isla. I spotted you from my shop window running in late. Did something happen?"

Half the neighborhood was too nosy for their own good.

Maeve held up her quill knife. "Would you look at how dull this is? I'll need to sharpen it in the back straightaway."

Mr. Braithwaite retired to his upstairs flat at six o'clock sharp, leaving Maeve to lock up at seven. By half past six, rain lashed the windows. Maeve doubted any customer would brave a storm for a dram of ink, but she'd been asked to stay, and she needed her final week's pay.

Shucking off her boots, she sidled into the stained shop chair and opened her latest journal until the spine made a satisfying crack.

She drew a contented sigh through her nose.

Regardless of her complicated feelings toward scriptomancy, Maeve kept up with journaling. At first, she used it to record the black thoughts about her father that wouldn't let her sleep at night. But she eventually grew to need the calming feel of parchment against her palms. Now it was the only piece of her past that she wasn't willing to part with. Her life often felt like a violent ocean tossing her about, but writing gave her a foothold. A moment to catch her breath.

Mr. Braithwaite thought it strange she had so much to say with ink, considering she volunteered so little with her mouth, but on the page, her words always spilled out in a torrent of meticulous lettering.

Maeve dipped a quill into a thimbleful of lampblack ink, then filled pages with her hopes for her trip south, including a detailed description of her future perennial garden—nestled against a sloped yard, like her aunt's garden in Inverly, with each flower carefully chosen to attract bees and butterflies. The outside world faded as if she were in the clutches of a spell, her presence trapped between quill and parchment.

Her eyes snapped up at a rumble of thunder. The sky had darkened to pitch. Time to go. Maeve locked the shop, then started the long walk back to her flat.

Clouds smothered the moon. The dim gas lamps lining Alewick's main avenue barely illuminated the streets. She flipped up her collar to shield her neck from the wind off the ocean.

"You there!" someone shouted.

Maeve spun to face a hulking silhouette carved by lamplight. A man with a saddlebag slung across his heart. His grizzled beard twisted in the wind, and his black cloak billowed around him, a storm made corporeal.

There was nowhere to run—they were alone together on the street.

The man strode toward her, and Maeve backed away until her heel caught on a cobble. She braced herself, expecting him to pull a knife.

He held up an envelope instead.

Maeve blinked in surprise. "You're an otherwhere courier."

"I am," he said in a voice half-swallowed by the wind. "This is for you. It's one of the letters from after the doors burned. Seven years late, but hopefully it will still mean something."

The envelope was old and tattered and entirely blank.

But it couldn't be for her. "Are you positive you have the right person?"

He grumbled and forced the letter into her hand. She tried to give it back, but he shook his head. "Like I said, it's for *you*."

Maeve nodded in disbelief. Everyone knew otherwhere couriers never delivered a letter to the wrong person. It simply was not done. Regardless of the facts, it seemed impossible that the letter was for her; she'd thought everyone who knew her had been lost in Inverly. This envelope, however, meant that she might be wrong.

She paused at the thought. All the letters posted after the Written Doors burned were from lost family members trying to find one another.

Tears sprang to her eyes, and a confusing tide of emotions moved through her: surprise, pain, then a sharp longing that caught her off guard. It slipped beneath her breastbone, pressing like a blade against her heart.

A black wax seal sat on the envelope's fold, embossed with a bead-eyed pigeon holding a scribing quill in its sharpened talons: the emblem of the Otherwhere Post.

"Goodnight, miss," the courier called, then slid into the night.

Not wanting to waste another second, Maeve severed the seal, cracking the pigeon at the neck. She scrambled to unfold the letter.

Dear Maeve,

I'm a childhood friend of your father's. He visited me in Leyland in those final days and told me a secret that changes everything. Meet me at the mouth of Edding's Close on the first of the month. Your father was innocent, and you deserve to hear the truth.

—an old friend

Maeve ambled along the cliff path the following morning with a splitting headache and two letters tucked inside her pocket. One with her real name scrawled across the top.

Couriers could use scriptomancy to deliver letters with just a first name, but the fact that it was done on her felt unsettling. That courier had found her. All the way in Alewick. She'd stayed up far too late last night worrying about it all, unable to pry her eyes from that letter.

It was indeed seven years old, dated six months after the Written Doors burned—one week after she turned twelve. Edding's Close was a covered alleyway near Professor's Row—three blocks east of the Sacrifict Orphanage, where she had lived all those years ago. Only three blocks! It would have been simple to meet with her letter-writer then. They probably waited for hours, and she never showed up. It was cursed luck that she didn't receive this letter until now.

You father was innocent.

The words felt impossible.

Maeve inhaled stark ocean air and tried to dredge up a good memory of her father—something that didn't make her want to retch. It was difficult.

His soft features came to her first: a mess of chestnut hair that never stayed put, wheat-colored skin that smelled of the herbs used in scribing pigments. He had her wide hazel eyes, and callused fingers always ink-stained from hours spent scribing.

She had watched him do just that on their last night together, while she sat tucked like a kitten to his side. Halfway through a scribing, he'd rolled his shirtsleeves, revealing a paragraph of what looked to be notes scribbled along his forearm. Maeve had grazed a fingernail over a word, then pushed her index finger through a moth hole near his elbow. "You have a tear in your shirt," she'd said.

Her great-aunt Agatha had clucked her tongue from across the room. "See? Your own daughter is noticing how shabby we've become." Aggie came to stand beside Maeve, her knobbed fingers knotting together. "Jonathan, you could be a steward and make twice the pay you do now. You could afford new shirts for yourself and a better school for Maeve if you only spoke up."

"I have spoken up, Agatha," her father had said softly. "They offered me a promotion last week, but I decided to turn it down."

Aggie drew back. "You did what? If Aoife knew . . ."

Her dead mother's name caused a painful ripple in the room. Her father looked down at his crow quill. He never angered, always went about the world as gently as a lapping lake, but there was a firmness to his next words. "I told the stewards that I wish to remain in my current role as a scriptomancer. And they agreed, so long as I teach the occasional class. I'm relieved about it all, and I had hoped you would be as well."

Anger simmered across her great-aunt's features. "I can't say that relief is what I'm feeling, Jonathan, but congratulations, I suppose," she said, then stormed off.

Her father turned to her. "Don't listen to your aunt. Save for you, darling, I would give it all up to practice scriptomancy. When you discover what it is you love, you must clutch on to it with your whole heart and never let it go." His ink-stained fingers then turned liquid, dancing over the toothy vellum as if to prove a point. Maeve watched him write until her eyes grew heavy and she fell asleep against his chest. She woke the next morning already hoping her father would visit again that night.

The same day the Written Doors burned. The day he was lost to Inverly.

In the seven years since, Maeve had gone from the Sacrifict Orphanage to a life of moving between vacant rooms across Gloam, picking up whatever odd job she could find and then leaving before she could catch her breath. Her rules kept her safe: never stay anywhere for too long; never start conversations that couldn't be ended quickly; never speak to anyone outside of work. All to keep her identity a secret—her father's identity. The rules were easy to follow, save for that time a boy at a job asked her to drinks at the neighboring tavern. He had clear blue eyes and an easy grin that made her heart skip, but she'd turned him down and quit the next day.

Maeve faced the gray ocean. Already, ominous clouds leaked across the sky like runnels of sealing wax against a crisp envelope. It would be fifty minutes, give or take, until the storm hit.

She pulled out her new letter and drew a finger over the last line. *An old friend.*

This friend had likely made a mistake by sending her this letter. Or maybe they hadn't.

Maeve tucked her bottom lip between her teeth, considering

the possibilities. The letter was probably a lie, and she was likely better off to forget all about it. But now that it was in her possession, would she ever be able to forget about it?

If this stranger could somehow prove her father's innocence, it would change everything for the better. Heavens, it could change her life.

For a breathless moment, Maeve let herself wonder *what if.* What if she searched for this old friend? What if she discovered the letter was true? What if she told others? The answers were enough to send her to her knees, and she knew without a doubt that she had to find a way to speak with this person. Whoever they were.

Tucking the letter down her pocket, Maeve started at a clip toward the center of town, until she stood before the sleek black letterbox on Main Street with a bead-eyed pigeon clutching a quill embossed across the front.

There were thousands of these letterboxes scattered throughout Leyland. Once, they were all sunny yellow and painted with the initials L.L.S. for the Leyland Letter Service. After the Written Doors burned, a company came around with gallons of black paint, turning them into the frightful little coffins they were today.

Eight tiny words were etched below the seal:

Postage must be fully paid before depositing letters.

A door rattled.

A middle-aged woman scurried from Alewick Grocery & General with a stack of letters in hand. Maeve stepped back, watching as the woman slid each of her letters through the mail slot before dashing off.

Maeve peered into the general store.

Nosey Mrs. Findlay sorted a display of shaving soaps at the front counter beside a large sign listing postage fees. Four shills to merely send a letter wasn't too obscene, but a whole hallion to commission an otherwhere courier to come out and enchant one felt like robbery.

Our menu of specialty enchantments is vast, the sign read. *Using scriptomancy, our couriers can add emotions to a letter that your loved one will feel in their hearts, scents they can smell, or memories for the letter to conjure.*

There was more tiny writing. Maeve squinted but couldn't read it from outside. She waited for Mrs. Findlay to walk to the back room, then slipped through the door.

The shop smelled of lemon water and tasted like fresh soap. Maeve ducked past a rack of cooking herbs to a display of mirrored arcthiometers. Their floral packaging promised the wand-shaped contraptions could make use of arcane magic to cure everything from feminine hysteria to fits of the vapors.

It was all a lie. Her father used to complain about how arcthiometers were junk, meant to prey on superstitious people. Arcane magic was real, of course. It was an invisible element that existed everywhere like the air one breathed—but *only* scriptomancers could harness it. And they created their enchantments by writing, with extensive training and special pigmented ink. Not by waving wands.

Maeve scanned the front counter. Mrs. Findlay popped out, and Maeve ducked down, covering her mouth.

"Is that you, Isla?" Mrs. Findlay called. "What in the worlds are you doing here this early?"

Maeve considered running out the door, but she needed answers. She looked around and quickly snatched a bar of soap from a display. "I was looking for one of these," she said, bringing it to the counter.

Mrs. Findlay's brow wrinkled. "You wish to purchase shaving lather?"

So it was. The pale violet woman's soaps were all perfumed and cost more than she could afford at the moment.

"It's for a dog," Maeve said quickly, then pulled a shill from her pocket and set it on the counter, hoping it was enough.

Mrs. Findlay took the shill. "Do you need anything else, dear?"

Maeve hesitated. "Do you know how someone might find the sender of an anonymous letter?"

"Why? Did you receive one of the old letters?" She leaned forward. "Mr. Braithwaite will be pleased to hear it. He worries about you all by yourself."

Did the two plucking hens spend all their free time gossiping about her loneliness?

"Can I see your letter?" Mrs. Finlay held out a hand.

Maeve caught the flutter of a black cloak from the corner of her eye. Outside, an otherwhere courier stood beside the letterbox, emptying everything into his saddlebag. He would be able to answer her questions better than ten Mrs. Findlays. He shut the letterbox and began walking away, turning a corner off the road.

"Isla, now don't rush away from me!" Mrs. Findlay shouted as Maeve fled the shop. She ran down the side street, searching all directions. Where had he gone?

Turning in a circle, she spotted him standing before a strange black door that hung a foot off the ground on the side of the Alewick Apothecary. She had never seen a door there before. It was a courier's door, she realized. One that would take him directly back to Blackcaster Station on the north end of Gloam the moment he stepped through it.

A door only *he* could step through.

"Stop!" Maeve shouted above the wind, but the courier was half a block away and couldn't hear her. She lifted the bar of shaving lather and threw it as hard as she could manage, aiming for the wall to get his attention. It hit him square in the back of the head.

Heavens above.

Maeve raced over puddles to the man, then realized just how much she loathed running when she doubled over with her hands fisted against her knees. She fixed her gaze on the hideous tassels of the courier's expensive shoes, biding her time before she had to face him. "Are you all right?" she asked between pants.

"As good as can be expected, considering someone attempted to murder me with a bar of soap," he said in a flat tone.

Maeve's neck burned hot with embarrassment. She considered apologizing, but then bit her tongue; she could never admit to it and expect him to help her.

"I saw it happen," she said. "A terrible crime."

The courier was silent for a long moment. "You mean to tell me that you merely *witnessed* the soap being thrown?"

"I did." Gathering courage, Maeve stood and faced her victim: a tall young man, no older than twenty. His heavy-lidded eyes were bruised from lack of sleep and hidden behind rounded spectacles that sat crooked across his nose.

He straightened them and raised a dark eyebrow. "Interesting. I could have sworn I heard a frantic *woman* shout for me a moment before the soap hit."

So he had heard her. And yet he didn't bother to turn?

"Yes, that was me. I shouted because I needed your help. But then a man came out of nowhere and threw the soap. He ran off quickly." She shrugged. "I'm afraid I failed to get a good look at him."

The courier gave her a searing look, then pushed his spectacles up his nose, smudging what Maeve had thought were freckles. But no—they were ink splatters. More ink splotched the brass-buttoned vest peeking from beneath his cloak.

He was filthy. Perhaps she should have offered him the soap instead of flinging it at him.

"Now, what was so important that you felt the need to chase me down the alley?" he asked, still rubbing his head.

She touched the outside of her pocket. "I received a letter from someone who lives in Leyland," she said, then realized her *old friend* might very well work at the Post. Her father used to live on the grounds, after all. But then why wouldn't they simply admit to that? Maeve set the idea aside for the time being. "It's one of the old letters from seven years ago, but the sender didn't leave their name. I need to speak with them most urgently."

"And you believe that I can somehow help you?"

"You are an otherwhere courier, are you not?" There were other types of couriers, but none wore black cloaks or took letters from letterboxes.

"Yes, I suppose I am." He dragged in a long sigh. "Let's see this mysterious letter of yours, then."

"Certainly not." It was addressed to her real first name, and she could never let anyone see it. "I left the letter at home."

"Well, that complicates things a bit, doesn't it?" He considered her for a moment. "I'm afraid that even with the letter, there isn't a lot you can do." He looked toward the door. "I should be on my way. Busy day ahead."

He was leaving? But he couldn't—not yet.

"Wait," she said, studying him. He was almost handsome be-neath the ink splatters, with large features that were likely disarming if he ever decided to bathe. She wished she had been born with the charm to coax information from him, but the mere thought of flirting with anyone made her decidedly queasy. She still had her wits, however. They'd brought her this far. "You said there isn't *a lot* I can do."

"Yes, I know what I said. And?"

"That implies there is something."

His mouth pulled flat.

"How does one find the sender of an anonymous letter? Please. I must know."

He tugged a strand of brown hair badly in need of a cut. "There might be a scribing to track down someone who doesn't leave their name."

Commissioning a scribing was all it would take? If she combined her shills, she had just over a hallion. It was everything she'd saved to go south, but she would pay it in a heartbeat to get her *old friend*'s name. She rifled through her bag. "Let me gather the coins."

"Oh no. I believe there's been a little misunderstanding."

Her head snapped up. "How so?"

"There's only a small handful of people who practice that level of scriptomancy, but the stewards of the Otherwhere Post don't exactly take scribing commissions. And I'm not even positive a scribing exists that would do precisely what you're asking. I only said there might be."

"Then is there some other way to find the sender?"

He ran his thumb along his full bottom lip. "There could be old records of who paid for the postage, but it's impossible to know without digging."

"Records?" Maeve stepped closer. "How do I dig?"

"You can't, I'm afraid. If you were a courier, with access . . ." His eyes traveled from the popped buttons on her too-small coat to the fraying lace edging her sleeves.

Her fingers curled under reflexively. She was obviously dressed for shabby stockist work, and not as someone who spent their days in an expensive upper school toiling over their writing, hoping to gain enough skill to be selected for the prestigious courier apprenticeship at the Otherwhere Post. She couldn't even afford a left-handed quill.

He must have realized it, because his eyebrows drew together. "Forget I said that. Access to those records is difficult to come by these days." He squinted up at the darkening clouds. "Oh dear. It's going to rain soon, and my shoes are brand new. It would be a crime to ruin them in a puddle."

"But it rains constantly. I just—"

"Good luck and all with that letter of yours." He opened the courier door and stepped through.

"Please wait," Maeve said, but the door shut with a snick. The handle disappeared before her fingers reached it, along with the door.

She beat a fist against the cold stone wall.

MR. BRAITHWAITE WAS in the midst of helping customers when Maeve ducked into the shop and headed straight to the back room. She dug through soiled blotting papers in the waste bin until she found yesterday's newspaper, covered in coffee stains. Flipping to the back page, she skimmed through the Postmaster's newsletter until she found the large paragraph that appeared every year around this time: the listing for the courier apprenticeship. All writing students interested in trying out were instructed to bring their writing program completion certificates to one of the testing locations on September seventh.

Less than a week away.

It was unfair that you had to complete a writing program to test. All the programs Maeve knew of were absurdly expensive. There were a handful of city-funded programs, but those grew to have years-long wait lists after the Written Doors burned and people realized the only way to cross worlds was to become a courier.

She pushed her feelings aside and continued reading about how you could only test within the two years after graduating upper school, otherwise you forfeited your opportunity—the House of Ministers' rule. They only had so many trained scriptomancy instructors and refused to waste a spot on anyone whose career might be stifled by old age.

It seemed money, youth, and a burning penchant for writing were the requirements. Maeve had two and could easily fake the third with the right clothing and snobby attitude.

It could work. Except for the fact that she didn't have a writing program completion certificate.

Maeve walked past the tall chest of drawers filled with blotters, to where a piece of paper hung in a dusty frame. Mr. Braithwaite's completion certificate for an upper school merchant program. It was handwritten, with a pair of stamped seals at the bottom that she could easily recreate in a few days with all the inksmithy's tools at her disposal.

She could make her own certificate in no time—for a writing program somewhere far away.

Maeve stepped back to the newspaper and quickly scanned the remainder of the paragraph. Her mouth pulled into a frown at the last line.

All those who pass will be immediately brought to the Otherwhere Post to begin a year-long instruction in the scriptomancy needed to deliver letters.

The idea of learning scriptomancy brought to mind the image of her father, hunched over his notebook at their old kitchen table.

She took a long breath through her nose. Maybe scriptomancy was a necessary evil. If she could win herself a spot in the apprenticeship, she would have all the access she needed to track down her *old friend*. That courier had said as much.

She chewed on her cuticle, thinking through logistics. The past seven years had taught her how to keep her identity a secret. After Inverly, the newspapers all reported that she had perished with her father and Great-Aunt Aggie. Most of her father's old scriptomancer colleagues probably worked for the Post, but she'd never met them. Even if someone had seen the old sepiagraph of her that her father used to carry in his coat pocket, they wouldn't recognize her now; she used to be stick thin with a gaunt face and shorn hair that Aggie would style into ugly pigtail ringlets.

Her unwieldy braid had lightened over the years to the pale orange color of cast iron rust. Her hips and face had filled out, and her hairline was freckled from hours spent journaling at the Alewick cliffs without a proper hat.

That pigtailed girl was long gone. Maeve had gone by Isla Craig for the past eight months. What harm could a few more weeks do? She had paid a handsome sum for her forged paperwork so no one would question it.

It was perfect, save for the unsettling fact that she would have to try out for a spot in the godforsaken courier apprenticeship.

At least she could write. It was her greatest asset, aside from knowing when to run.

Maeve read over the Postmaster's announcement a second time. A third. A fourth. Then she opened her journal and scribbled across the top:

There has been a change of plans.

Maeve returned her train ticket and used a portion of the money to purchase a sturdy new skirt and blouse from a secondhand store, then a smart writing case made of oiled cowhide that she filled with expired inks and used quills from Mr. Braithwaite's waste bin. The morning of the examination, she dressed by candlelight. She folded the love letter into the anonymous letter and tucked them both down the pocket of her new skirt, then grabbed her suitcase and shut the door of her flat, sealing away yet another chapter of her life she would never return to.

The nearest testing location was an hour's walk north up Gloam's narrow, twisting streets. Her heart pumped inside her chest as university buildings loomed overhead—buildings hewn centuries ago, just after the Written Doors were created and the University of Gloam was founded, spanning all three known worlds.

The Barrow campus used to house only natural and applied sciences, whereas Leyland used to be the hub of all language arts.

When the Written Doors burned, the Leyland campus scrambled to add in all the missing disciplines so it could function independently as a full university, but Maeve could still feel the history of language arts everywhere she looked. It had shaped this city, from the grubby, handwritten store signs that read like novellas to the inksmithies that stood on every street corner. Even the buildings themselves were shades of black and white and parchment. They leaned haphazardly against one another as if built as an afterthought by someone who passed their days with their nose buried in a well-worn book.

Gloam in Inverly had felt entirely different. It was where all the other humanities were once taught, with neighborhoods that bled together like watercolors, awash with painting and poetry and music—all long gone now.

Maeve rubbed away a stray tear, frustrated by thinking of Inverly when she had a writing test to take. She picked up her pace. A thick fog rolled in by the time she reached Galbraith Hall. The southernmost testing location was an imposing cathedral-like building situated in the university's College of Rhetoric. A dozen black carriages perched along the gravel drive, all marked with the Post's pigeon, likely here to take all the apprentices who made the cut to their new home.

Maeve wove around the first few carriages then halted at a commotion.

Protesters gathered near the building's entrance. Men and women in plain winter coats and homespun skirts and trousers carried banners emblazoned with bold slogans calling for more apprenticeship opportunities, for reformation in the writing programs. Three constabulary officers in stark gray jackets guarded the main door.

Maeve searched, but there was no other way inside. Her fingers touched the letters in her pocket, and she forced a deep breath through her nose.

Holding her writing kit tight to her waist, she made her way to the nearest officer, a large man with a patch of razor burn spilling from behind his decorated coat collar.

He turned to her, and she felt eleven years old again, at the Sacrifict Orphanage while Headmistress Castlemaine's ruler cracked down on her left hand. *Never tell anyone who you are again, you foolish girl! And stay far away from the constabulary.*

"If you're here to test, I'll need to see your official paperwork," the officer said. When Maeve failed to move her lips, his chin tilted. "Are you well, miss?"

She was far from it, but she pulled out Isla Craig's identification along with the completion certificate she'd painstakingly forged from looking at Mr. Braithwaite's. It appeared perfectly legitimate, and yet her heart thrummed behind her ribs while the officer glanced over everything.

Taking his time.

"I need to get through as well," someone said. An older woman in a ragged tweed coat shoved Maeve aside, waving a leather ledger at the officer. "My paperwork, sir."

The officer took the woman's ledger, flipping through it. "Are these tenement agreements?"

"Yes," she said, lifting her pale chin. "All by yours truly. Written as well as anyone from an official program. Let me have a chance to test," the woman begged.

"You'll have to step back," said the officer.

"But my mother and sister are in Barrow. *Please.*"

The officer gave an exasperated sigh, then handed Maeve her paperwork. "You can go," he said, and nudged her around him, then turned to face the woman. "You, on the other hand—"

Maeve rushed inside before she could hear the rest of his sentence.

As soon as the doors shut behind her, she fell against them and dabbed at perspiration with the back of her gloved hand, staring wide-eyed at a grand entrance hall. Young men in oilskin hats and finely tailored jackets chattered away with women in fitted blouses and bustled skirts. So many people, and nearly all of them carried suitcases and small personal effects.

Maeve did some quick calculations. There were several other testing locations. Most here would never make it to the Post. Those who didn't were likely fated to become barristers or academics, or perhaps do nothing at all; their family fortunes meant they would never have to lift a finger for anything if they didn't wish to.

That woman with her tenement agreements should have been given a chance.

A few groups on the fringes wore similar attire to the protesters out front, probably from a city-funded writing program.

A girl in a peach-colored bonnet stood by herself. She looked pleasant enough.

"Are we all supposed to wait out here before we take the writing test?" Maeve asked her.

"Oh, yes. I think they'll call another group soon," she said, pointing to double doors at the back with a banner above them that read: EXAMINATION ROOM. She fanned herself with a stack of papers with some official-looking seals that bore little resemblance to Maeve's forged completion certificate.

"What are those papers?" Maeve asked.

"You mean my transcripts? We're supposed to have them out and ready to present."

"Transcripts?"

"To prove your upper school writing scores," the woman said, her smile faltering at Maeve's expression. "But don't worry a bit. I've heard they take all sorts of scores into account. It's the writing test that matters the most."

As soon as the woman finished, Maeve muttered an excuse and darted to the nearest lavatory, locking herself inside. Bracing one hand on the sink, she peeled off her gloves and splashed water on her face.

Why hadn't she thought of transcripts?

"You're woefully out of your league," she said to her reflection, feeling quite the uneducated fool.

She had sold her train ticket and walked all this way. This couldn't be it. Surely there was another way inside one of those carriages waiting along the drive.

Determined to find it, Maeve left the lavatory and wandered past the entrance hall, into a bustling student lounge flanked by blazing hearths and scattered with leather chairs. Several people held black folios on their laps, stamped with that bead-eyed pigeon.

"Pardon me," Maeve said to one young man who sat hunched over a folio. He squinted up at her with a sour expression. She gestured to the folio. "What is that for?"

"It's what you're given when you pass. To keep your transcripts together with your admittance letter and any paperwork you might have brought."

He tucked the folio away, then took out a journal and a well of pale blue ink.

Maeve knew the shade. It was named Raven's Tears, imported from a forested island off the southern coast called Gol. A bottle cost twenty-eight shills; Mr. Braithwaite swore to have her head if she broke one.

"That's a fine color," she said.

His thin eyebrows furrowed to a line. "Not really, but I ran out of lampblack, and it was the only bottle I could find. It's difficult to see against parchment."

Because you dried Raven's Tears in sunlight to deepen the color to true sapphire.

He scribbled some words, then shook pounce powder over them, which would only *lighten* the ink. Heavens, he had no clue what he was doing.

Scriptomancy demands an expert knowledge of writing tools. You have to become an encyclopedia of ink and pigment, her father had told her more times than she could count.

Turning in a slow circle, Maeve surveyed all the people her age—young men and women with horribly expensive educations. But she probably knew more about ink than many of them and had certainly written as much.

A young woman walked by with a curtain of auburn hair bobbing against birdlike shoulders. She sidled into a chaise, fiddling nervously with the black folio in her lap. At first glance, it would be easy to mistake her for Maeve, given their similar coloring. The woman even had a mole near her upper lip. Maeve shut her eyes and imagined herself sitting in the woman's place, with the black folio filled with transcripts on her lap.

She turned the dark thought over in her mind. If she were able to switch places with this woman, she would have everything she needed.

But no. Maeve knew how much this apprenticeship meant to all the applicants here—especially to those who had family trapped in Barrow, on the other side of the now-burnt Written Doors. She couldn't take away someone's chance to see long-lost family again. The thought was appalling. She didn't even know how she would attempt such a thing.

As soon as she gave it a moment's thought, however, ideas rushed forth on exactly how to accomplish it. A plan formed in her mind that would even give her a chance to speak with the woman, ask her some questions, before making any regrettable decisions.

Maeve chewed on her lip, considering.

If she left now, it would be weeks before she might have enough saved for another train ticket. Mr. Braithwaite would ask too many questions if she suddenly begged for her job back. She didn't want to go back, anyhow. The thought felt like a sliver in her thumb.

Moving swiftly to an empty hall, Maeve popped open her old suitcase. Her cowhide writing kit sat snugly beside a change of clothes.

She took off her coat and pushed it inside, then pulled out her journal and ran her fingers over the leather. Leaving her suitcase beneath a sideboard, Maeve held her journal in front of her and walked to where the redhead sat, while her stomach churned.

The woman, it turned out, wasn't much younger than Maeve, with stockings the color of summer sunflowers peeking from an ankle-length crepe skirt. She tugged her earlobe, pulling at a lustrous pearl earring that must have cost a handsome sum.

Her black folio rested against the floor.

"I beg your pardon." Maeve tapped her journal, then ran a gloved finger to a spot on the blank page. "Are you the incoming apprentice Neve Baird?"

She spoke the name slowly, as if reading it for the first time.

The woman dragged in a sigh. "I'm afraid I'm not. I'm Eilidh Hill." She spoke in an elegant albeit dismissive voice.

Nodding, Maeve tapped a spot toward the bottom of the page. Hard. "Yes. Miss *Eilidh* Hill. Here you are." She snapped the journal shut and smiled. "You must bring your things and come with me."

"This instant?"

"Yes, of course," Maeve said, not giving her a moment to argue. It worked. Eilidh followed her until they were alone beside the sideboard where Maeve had left her things.

"What is the purpose of this?" Eilidh asked.

"I'm Miss Erskine, an understudy steward at the Otherwhere Post." Maeve raised her chin, summoning a hint of Headmistress Castlemaine's disdainful demeanor.

Eilidh looked her over with a sneer. "But you're . . . young."

"Is that a problem?" Maeve squared her shoulders, managing to keep her composure.

"No. Of course not. I didn't mean—"

"It's quite all right. The reason we're speaking is I've just received some news from our testers. Confidential news. As such, I'll need to see your paperwork before I speak any more," Maeve said, rather convincingly.

She was quite good at this. She didn't know whether to feel horrible about that fact or cheer.

Eilidh riffled through her leather satchel, digging out an official Leyland identification paper.

It seemed that Eilidh *Pretoria* Hill was seventeen and hailed from Almsworth, a small hamlet in the far south. "Did you come here all by yourself?"

Eilidh gave a hesitant nod. "Mother took the train halfway

up Leyland and would have come farther, if not for my younger brother. He's quite the handful." A sheen of moisture filled her eyes, and she dabbed at tears with her lace-gloved hand.

Eilidh's family might have all the money in the worlds, but they were likely missing her as well. Perhaps it wouldn't be such a bad thing to give them a little more time with each other.

Maeve carefully placed the identification on the sideboard, then took out her journal, along with a few papers from her own writing kit. She set them on top of Eilidh's identification, forming a neat stack. "I'll also need the folio with your admittance letter and transcripts."

Eilidh gripped the folio with spindly fingers, hugging it to her stomach for a flinching moment before handing it over.

Fine silver thread wove along the edges. Maeve cracked open the black leather and scanned a letter, written by one of the stewards themselves, an Eamon Mordraig. It congratulated the admitted on successfully completing the writing examination, then went on to explain logistics, mainly how carriages would begin to leave at eleven sharp for the Post grounds just north of Blackcaster Square. Eilidh was to present this very letter and her paperwork to a driver to secure her seat. There were no other instructions.

Maeve dropped the letter on the growing stack of papers and rubbed her freezing hands together, feeling nauseated. It was time. If she was going to commit to this scheme, she had to do it now or give up.

"What is this about?" A tremor ran through Eilidh's voice.

"It's rather unpleasant tidings, I'm afraid. I know the journey from Almsworth must have been strenuous, which is why it is *difficult* to deliver the unfortunate news I've been tasked with relaying."

Eilidh's thin lips parted. "Unfortunate?"

"I'm afraid so." Maeve gave a withering smile. "Through a testing error, we've accidentally passed more people than we have room for. I've come to break the unlucky news to a handful, and you're the first."

"You mean I didn't make the apprenticeship?" Eilidh looked on the verge of tears.

Maeve's breath caught in her throat. "Do you have any family in Barrow?"

Eilidh shook her head. "My family was lucky. They're all in the far south."

Thank goodness for that.

"At least you'll be with them soon. And because of the mix-up, we want you to come and test again next fall."

As far as Maeve knew, that wasn't against the rules. Eilidh would have a year with her family before getting another chance, and Maeve would get inside the Post. It was a win for them both.

Maeve was about to bid her farewell when another thought struck. If Eilidh had a classmate at the Post who knew her, they'd realize Maeve was lying. "Is there anyone else here from your writing program that I might inform?" she asked.

"I'm the only one who made the trek north this year."

"How about last year?"

"I don't know."

"The year before?"

"I wasn't close with anyone from those classes."

But would they remember you? Maeve nearly asked, but saying it aloud might come across as odd. This conversation had already taken far too long.

She fished through the papers on the table, folding one and handing it over. "Your identification."

Eilidh tucked it down her own bag without realizing it was Isla Craig's identification. Eilidh's lay buried in the stack.

She reached for the folio, but Maeve stopped her hand. "I'll need to confiscate your folio."

"What about my transcripts?"

"I'll make sure they're filed away for future reference."

Eilidh nodded, then looked to the floor for a long moment. When she finally looked up, Maeve's heart lurched.

The girl's bottom lip quivered. Glistening tears leaked down each of her cheeks.

"What's the matter, dear?" Maeve took her hand.

"My mother paid for the train ticket and I—I spent the six hallions she gave me for the return trip shopping yesterday." A blush rose to her cheeks.

"*Six* hallions?" It was a despicable amount to spend on anything.

"I assumed I would get in," Eilidh said, sniffling, and Maeve had to school the revulsion from her features. "And now I'm afraid I don't have the means to get home. Is there someone from the Post I can speak with about contacting Mother?"

Blast it all. "Dear me, I've gone and forgotten! We're awarding everyone involved with enough funds for a train ticket home."

Maeve dug inside her suitcase, furious with herself as she pressed her small purse to Eilidh's hand quickly, leaving no room to second-guess. All the shills to her name.

Eilidh managed a smile and walked away with the last of Maeve's money.

Maeve found an empty hallway on the second floor of Galbraith Hall and hid there for several long minutes, scanning through what she could of Eilidh's paperwork, but there was more than a novella's worth of information, and her eyes couldn't tear themselves from the window—the officers below. As soon as they left, Maeve rushed outside, where she stood in the swirling fog beside the wet hedges, her eyes locked on the row of the Post's carriages. The young men and women with black folios soon joined in a slow trickle. Then a whistle blew, and liveried drivers, alongside otherwhere couriers in sweeping black cloaks, filed outside.

A deep voice shouted, "Line up with your paperwork out!"

Clutching her things in one hand and Eilidh's folio in the other, Maeve stepped to the very end of the line, hoping to give herself time to gather her wits. But when she got to the front, there was only one carriage left.

She tried to hand Eilidh's folio to the otherwhere courier driving the carriage, but he held up a hand. "You won't be going."

A cold knot formed in her stomach. "Excuse me?"

"This last one is my carriage, and eight's my limit." He motioned to the cab, where two figures were pressed against the fogged windowpane, the center piled high with suitcases.

It was merely full.

Maeve's breath returned to her lungs in a rush.

The courier checked a wristwatch and peered into the thick fog, but you couldn't see more than ten paces ahead. "There's one more carriage due, and they should be here any moment. Are you all right to wait by yourself, miss? The Post is a two-hour ride north this time of day, and I want to get moving before the rain sets in."

With little choice in the matter, Maeve nodded. As the carriage rolled away, she kicked at stray rocks, anxiously listening for any sound of horse hooves or wheels coming down the drive but hearing nothing. Minutes passed. Worried the final carriage had missed her, Maeve started down the drive. Fog snaked around her ankles. Holding her hand in the air, she wiggled her fingers, watching as they wavered in and out of the haze.

She stilled at a pop of gravel.

"Hello?" she called out. A moment later, the hollow clattering of horse hooves beat the ground from somewhere nearby. Maeve turned in a circle, searching the fog.

"Watch out!" someone shouted.

A massive black horse reared above her, strapped to a carriage. Maeve twisted, stumbling. She lost her balance and fell, her head hitting the gravel with a sharp thump. Pain split across her temple.

In one fluid motion, the carriage's driver leapt off. A dark cloak flooded her vision as he knelt over her. The billowing fog made the man appear wraithlike. For a long moment, Maeve wasn't sure if this was real life or a dream, or perhaps she had taken a step into the afterlife. Her eyelids fluttered, and she parted her lips in an attempt to say something, but her head felt plugged with sealing wax.

A warm, wet sensation filled her right ear.

The stranger looked to the sky and muttered something that might have been a curse. When he brought his attention down to face her, he seemed . . . vexed. As if she were causing him a great inconvenience after nearly being run over by *his* hell horse.

"Leaping in front of oncoming carriages is a disastrous habit that you should break immediately," he said.

Leaping? "But I didn't leap."

"I don't believe you're in any state to debate the definition of a verb."

Squinting, she could make out a bespectacled face, ghostly in the gloom, head topped with nut-brown hair that hung in damp clumps around pale ears. The contrast reminded her of lampblack ink on fresh parchment.

She pushed herself to sitting, and the world tilted, wavering. Her head smarted.

He took her in, and his eyes narrowed. "I believe we've met before."

Indeed they had.

It was the otherwhere courier she had spoken with. *Bespectacled, messy young man with a penchant for hideously expensive footwear.* She'd recorded the description in her journal the night after her encounter.

Today, the ink smears on his face were relegated to the cleft of his chin.

"You're that girl from Alewick, who caused me to get caught in a storm and ruin a perfectly good pair of shoes."

Maeve swallowed down a wave of panic. "I was *visiting* Alewick," she corrected, in case he discovered that Eilidh Hill was from the south.

She quickly thought through their previous conversation. She didn't remember telling him anything specific about the letter that might give herself away. She had been wearing worker's clothing, but she could make up some excuse for that.

His clothing, however, was as ink splattered as she remembered it. His gloves were covered with metallic silver and copper splotches, and more was speckled on his cloak. It was a wonder he had the audacity to accuse her of ruining his shoes.

He flung off his saddlebag, spilling sodden books and papers on the drive, but he ignored the mess and came toward her. "Are you able to stand?"

She wasn't entirely sure. Gulping her breaths, she managed to push herself up on wobbling legs.

The courier peeled off his gloves.

"What are you doing?" Maeve shrank away as he lifted his bare fingers toward her head.

She never let anyone touch her; it went against her rules.

"I'm fine, truly."

"That might be the case, but I would rather inspect your head now than risk you expiring in my coach. If you want to be stubborn about it, I can take you to the infirmary once we arrive. Although our sadist of a head doctor might force spirits down your throat with a copper tube." He made a face.

She swiped at her forehead. Her glove came away with a smear of blood. "Oh dear."

"*Oh dear* is right," he said, then touched her temples with cool fingertips, tilting her head gently.

40

Maeve kept her eyes downcast during the examination, stealing close glances at him through her lashes. He had a sturdy albeit slightly crooked nose, and large gray-green eyes hidden behind his spectacles that appeared more tired than when she'd clocked him with soap.

His gaze flickered down, catching her staring.

Startled, she squeezed her eyes shut, and could have sworn she heard him laugh under his breath. She didn't dare look at him after that. As it was, it would be a miracle if she wasn't bright pink from blushing.

"I think you'll live," he finally said, releasing her and replacing his gloves. "I'll need to see your folio with your transcripts and admittance letter."

Maeve handed over Eilidh's folio. She was far from devout, but she uttered a silent prayer that everything was in order.

The courier scanned through the first few papers quickly, then flipped to a section in the back—a part she hadn't had the time to read.

"What section is that?" she asked.

"Just some things your former instructors had to say about you."

"What does it say?"

"Don't you already know?"

Her heart thumped. "It—it was packed away, and I never got an opportunity to read through it."

"Maybe you should have," he said, then flipped another page. "How fascinating."

Panic struck. Maeve tried to peek, but he tilted the folio away— on purpose? Irritated, she pushed up on her toes, closer. Right when she could finally see a smattering of printed words, he shut the folio abruptly. "Everything seems to be in order."

Maeve pressed her lips together before she might say something she'd sorely regret.

Next, he knelt and dug through his saddlebag, making a stack of items next to his foot: a soiled writing kit, crumpled papers, three broken quill feathers, and an apple with one bite out of it. Maeve wouldn't be surprised if he pulled out a potted fern next. But he slipped the folio between some books and tossed everything back on top save for a large turkey quill that he tucked behind his ear.

"Now that's all settled, I'll need to check the horse." He left her, busying himself with the front of the carriage. After a moment, he muttered something and waved at her. "I need some assistance. The horse cast a shoe."

Maeve bristled. The horse snorted and stomped, and the sound alone made her short of breath. No matter how innocent they might appear, horses were dangerous.

"Apologies, but I don't think I could go within five paces of that thing."

He gave her a strange look, then patted the horse on the flank. "This *thing* is called Butternut, and she's a dear."

Maeve would beg to differ.

"Do you not like horses?" he asked.

That was putting it mildly.

"Horses, sir, do not like me." And Butternut had already tried to kill her once. It was bad enough that she was forced to ride behind it in a carriage.

"It won't take long."

"Please don't make me help," she said, then winced at the desperate note in her voice.

The courier pushed up his spectacles, regarding Maeve with a strange expression that she couldn't decipher.

"Very well, then. No re-shoeing for you today," he finally said, and she let out a long breath.

He came around and pried open the cab door to a disastrous mess. Ribboned packages from various tailors and cobblers were piled high on the seats. Past them, crates were heaped with letters.

It was the most cluttered cab Maeve had ever laid eyes on, but she'd take a mess over a horse any day. She moved boxes then wriggled into a small spot by the door, yelping as something sharp poked her backside. She dug it free. It was a thick green book with glossy black type across the cover that read: *The Scriptomancer's Companion.*

"That's yours," he said. "Steward Mordraig requested each apprentice get a copy before the coach ride. It's required reading, written by an academic who loved a good run-on sentence. It takes about three hundred mammering pages to get across anything useful, but there are a few good points at the end." He moved to shut the door. "If you need anything during the ride, my name's Tristan."

"Your given name?" She never liked to be on a first name basis with anyone. It made things too casual—too easy to slip up and say something she shouldn't. "Isn't it a bit soon to forgo formalities?"

"I don't think so."

"But we hardly know each other."

"That's not true." He looked her over. "Already I know that you have a propensity for getting your way, a strange trepidation toward horses, and an impressive disregard for your own safety. Not to mention a wicked throwing arm." He rubbed the back of his head. "Still bruised."

Maeve's eyebrows shot up in shock.

"If you're still concerned about formalities, you're perfectly free to call me Mr. Tristan," he said with a wry twist to his mouth, then shut the door and locked it from the outside.

As the coach set off, Maeve's blood pounded in her ears. Tristan was far more observant than she'd bargained for, and it made her ill. She pinched her temple. When the sickening feeling didn't subside, she grabbed *The Scriptomancer's Companion* and flung it open, then spent the next hour paging through a twelve-chapter introduction that made her eyes glaze over, mostly because she knew the material already from her father.

It brought up a memory—of the day he had placed her great-aunt's grocery list in front of her.

"This spot right here is a scriptomancer's canvas," he'd said, tapping the empty space below the last line of her aunt's handwriting. "If a trained scriptomancer wanted to enchant this list, they would dip their quill in special pigment, then jot down a single sentence right here called a scribing."

"It sounds so easy."

"Indeed, darling, but a scribing is the most difficult sentence in the worlds to write. If done correctly, the words in the scribing pull in arcane magic, then disappear immediately, leaving Aggie's grocery list all by itself, enchanted to do something marvelous when you read it."

"Like what?" Maeve had asked. Her father merely answered with one of his secretive smiles.

The memory was small, but it made her mind wander to other, heavier thoughts.

She slammed the book shut and forced her attention out the fogged window. The ride was bumpy, and the carriage jostled to and fro as they crossed over the river Liss, passing through the claustrophobic streets of Old Town, where university buildings were pinched together like wax melts beside blackened smoking taverns and boarding houses. They soon rolled through Edding's Close, then up the narrow road bordering Blackcaster Square.

The wrought-iron perimeter fence stood tall, topped with sharp spikes. Mourners paying their respects wandered around the fence, where the ground was littered with a river of candles, bouquets of flowers, and little sepiagraphs of lost loved ones, all waterlogged from the rain. They passed an older woman as she placed a sepiagraph beside a bouquet of tulips then collapsed to her knees, bowing over the memorial, her face contorted in anguish.

Maeve's heart lurched, but she couldn't do anything with the carriage rolling. It didn't take long, however, for a flurry of Leylish clinicians in long gray robes to rush to the woman's aid.

The clinicians were courtesy of the House of Ministers and stationed at makeshift tents around the square, in case of incidents like this woman—or worse. They were put into place after two men gored themselves trying to scale the fence because they believed in conspiracy theories that the Written Doors were never burned, that scriptomancy was a hoax dreamed up by the ministers to control communication, that Inverly still thrived.

Maeve wished it were all true.

She peered past the fence, across the sea of ancient cobblestones, to the small building in the center of the square.

Leyland's Blackcaster Station.

Salt from ocean winds streaked the station's verdigris walls, coating the two turnstiles in front that once led inside to each Written Door. Two turnstiles long chained.

The last time Maeve stood inside that square was the day the Written Doors burned, when a stranger dragged her away by her shoulders. The memory tasted like a flash of ash against her tongue.

Things were much different now. A long line of couriers waited to enter the station through the small employee entrance on the north side. A pair of university couriers in flowing plum robes stood at the front, chatting away with a group of constabulary couriers in dove-gray officer's coats.

There were vicious stories of constabulary couriers in action. A courier's ability to track people to deliver letters came in handy when you needed to hunt down a criminal. Fortunately for her, the only kind of courier who lived at the Post were otherwhere couriers. All other types still went through the apprenticeship program, then were recruited afterward to train in the specialized disciplines and made to live closer to their respective organizations.

Maeve squinted but couldn't see any minister couriers in deep scarlet raiment, but there were fifty or so otherwhere couriers, black cloaks billowing, mail-filled saddlebags strung across their hearts.

The most common type, given the enormity of their task.

Maeve knew a little of how it worked. Couriers went inside that station and used scriptomancy to somehow create a courier door that took them close to their deliveries—the same type of door Tristan had disappeared through in Alewick.

Entering that station was a part of the job. But after narrowly escaping Inverly, Maeve doubted she'd ever be able to step foot inside that building again.

The carriage rounded the north corner of the square, where a sea of protesters filled the road between the north gate leading into Blackcaster Square and the large gate across the street that led into the Post's forested grounds.

Maeve recognized the same types of banners she'd seen in front of Galbraith Hall, calling for more apprenticeship positions, more equality in the writing programs, quicker delivery times, more news about the repair of the Written Doors.

As they rolled toward the crowd, Maeve tensed. But the protesters parted, giving the carriage a wide berth. The reaction surprised her, but then she remembered how a few months after the Written Doors burned, a line of coaches was set ablaze by an angry mob, destroying all the precious letters inside. After that, everyone still made a fuss, but they allowed otherwhere couriers to do their jobs.

The carriage lurched to a halt at the Post's gate, throwing Maeve against the seat.

She scrambled up and pressed her forehead against the cold windowpane, straining to see.

The gate was propped open, but a pair of officers blocked their way through.

Tristan hopped down and began arguing with them. He gestured at the coach, furious.

Was this about her? She gripped the seat while one officer walked around the coach, then back over to Tristan. They exchanged more words, and Tristan kicked the ground. After what seemed like forever, the officers stepped aside and waved them through.

Maeve ripped off her gloves and splayed her blue-tinged fingers. They were shaking, but she was past the gate, rolling up the forested drive. Gnarled, autumn-bare branches scraped the wheels. Then the trees parted for an ancient stone archway carved with quills and inkwells and overrun by dead ivy. Two stone statues of ancient scriptomancers stood on either side, carrying globes, baring their teeth to all who passed. THE COLLEGE OF SCRIPTOMANTIC ARTS was carved across the top.

It was a wonder nobody had chiseled those words away.

Right after the Written Doors burned, Leyland's House of Ministers founded the Otherwhere Post. They built a new office in Barrow, but here in Leyland, they took over the crumbling buildings of this old college, repurposing them for the Post's new headquarters. For centuries before that, this was simply an underfunded program at the University of Gloam, set back in the woods because scriptomancers insisted the art was dangerous.

But they weren't called scriptomancers anymore.

Beyond the archway, cloaked otherwhere couriers walked in groups along winding pathways lit by gas lampposts glowing a luminous white.

Her father's home, where he lived in a residence hall so he could send the entirety of his academic's salary to her and her great-aunt. She half expected "Jonathan Abenthy" to be carved on that stone archway for how much he adored this place. Now here she was, Maeve Abenthy, being driven right inside.

She'd hated this place for so long, wanted nothing more than to see it burn, along with everything else that reminded her of her father. Tears clouded her eyes.

Of course, Tristan chose that exact moment to stop and unlock the carriage door.

"I was just—" he began, staring at her.

Maeve blinked. "Dust in my eye."

He pulled out a crumpled handkerchief. She took it and dabbed her eyes, then tried to return it.

"How about you keep that," he said.

Her fingers tangled in the powdery material. The edge was embroidered with the initials T.B.

"What does the B stand for?"

"I'm not falling for that." He reached past her and stacked the shopping parcels into a tall pile, then attempted to carry them out. But the stack was too tall, and he lost his grip, sending clothing and shoes spilling across the drive. He stood there for a long moment, staring.

"Do you want help cleaning it up?" Maeve offered.

"Perhaps. If the gate officers hadn't taken up every spare minute with their nonsense." He kicked a box. "I'll have to come back for it," he said, then started at a furious pace down a stone pathway.

"What exactly were you arguing with the officers about?" Maeve asked, catching up with him.

He glanced at her. "We weren't arguing. They were simply making things difficult for me like they usually do."

At least it wasn't anything to do with her. Her nerves, however, remained on edge as they skirted an ancient building with a sign that read: HENBANE HOUSE. They passed Pricklesweet Hall next, then Wolfsbane Residence.

"They're all named for herbs," Maeve said.

Tristan nodded. "An old scriptomancer thought it would be fun to name the buildings after the sacred herbs we use in scribing pigments. Be grateful they don't smell like the herbs as well." He wrinkled his nose, then wove her past a few more herb buildings. One was left to ruin, but most appeared refurbished.

Her father always complained about leaky windows and cracked foundations, how the university board didn't care a whit for the College of Scriptomantic Arts. Back when the Written Doors were in place, there was no need to use scriptomancy for traveling between worlds, and most other uses were either deemed too dangerous to practice or considered nothing more than parlor tricks. There were rumors the House of Ministers even asked the university board to archive the scriptomantic libraries and shut down the college permanently, leaving only a small team in place to help track criminals for the constabulary.

The past seven years had changed everything.

A piercing chill cut into Maeve's coat. She tucked it tight around her as they came upon an oak-filled courtyard, a fountain in the center.

Black liquid sprayed from a spout on a top tier, raining down the sides. Lampblack ink. The stone figure of a woman in robes was perched at the top.

"Molly Blackcaster?" Maeve asked, wandering to the fountain's edge.

Tristan came up beside her. "The magnanimous founder of the College of Scriptomantic Arts herself. This fountain was carved nine hundred years ago, right after Molly finished scribing the Written Doors into existence. It was filled with ink to commemorate the day she banned travel outside of the three known worlds."

Molly's small mouth was carved into a smirk. A monstrous quill hung from her hip to her knee, as large as a knight's scabbard.

The greatest scriptomancer to ever live.

Maeve inhaled, tasting loamy soil and pungent fumes from the lampblack ink. "I wanted to be just like Molly once," she said, staring at the statue's face.

Tristan lifted an eyebrow. "Then you'll be pleased to know old Molly was also gifted at throwing soap."

Maeve cut him a glare, then fixed her eyes on Molly's cloak, covered in a pattern of spirals, circles, outlines of eyes, and triangles, some overlapping. Her father would often draw those same symbols when he scribed but never explained them. "What are those symbols?"

"Dangerous," Tristan said. "But I still like the statue." He placed both his hands on the rim. "The House of Ministers wants to have the whole thing removed to put the money spent on the lampblack toward more pressing things."

"They can do that?"

"They've done worse. They approve everything here now, down to what we eat for breakfast. Prepare yourself for some delectable government fare." He grimaced. "They think that if they can put enough money into the right places and keep it out of the wrong places, we'll somehow sprout extra arms and deliver more letters." He patted the fountain and turned to her. "So? Where's your empty inkwell?"

All the inkwells in her writing kit were already topped off.

"I don't need any ink."

"Is that so?" He cocked his head. "All new apprentices stop here to fill a well from this fountain for good luck. It's tradition."

Her pulse fluttered. "I've never heard of it."

"That's strange. All writing programs give out an empty inkwell in case you make it here."

"Then mine must be behind the times," Maeve said. "Shouldn't we get going?"

Tristan gave her a searching look. His brow furrowed, and his eyes narrowed for a long moment. Then he finally—*finally*—nodded.

Maeve thought she might have a few minutes to calm her skittering nerves, but Tristan led her inside an adjacent building with cold, stale air and cracked stone floors. They turned down a tight corridor that emptied into a massive lecture hall lit by a single, shuddering gasolier. It hung like an octopus from a coffered ceiling, illuminating sharp rows of seating that descended to a pit in the front—a stage, a lectern pushed off to one side. People sat along the first row of seats. There were at least fifteen, all holding clipboards against their laps. All gray-haired and straight-backed.

"The stewards," Tristan whispered.

The scriptomancers who ran the Otherwhere Post.

Maeve's hand scrambled for her right pocket, hoping the feel of the letters might help keep her together.

An elderly man stopped them on the steps, his blue-veined hands clinging to the top of a pitch-black wooden cane. His pink face sloped forward to peer at Tristan through spectacles as thick as a milk bottle. "Is that you, Tristan? God's nose, boy, you're late! Did you bring the last of them?"

Tristan nudged Maeve forward. "She's all yours."

The man's glittering eyes raked over her. "Have you used the lavatory recently, madam?"

"I haven't, I—"

He waved his hand. "Never mind. It's much too late anyhow." He looked toward the people with clipboards. "Those are my colleagues. I'm Steward Eamon Mordraig, in charge of the apprenticeship."

The man who penned Eilidh Hill's admittance letter.

He touched Maeve's elbow, and she flinched. "You come with me," he said, tugging her down the steps.

Maeve shot a nervous glance at Tristan. He merely smiled and tumbled into a seat off to one side, kicking his feet up.

Steward Mordraig brought her to stand in the center of the stage.

She hugged her sides and dared a look at the row of stewards, immediately wishing she'd kept her gaze down. Over a dozen pairs of eyes scrutinized her. They were all older and had probably worked for the college before the Post was established. They would have known her father.

But you don't look anything like him, she reminded herself. She had never met any of these people. Even if she had, they wouldn't recognize her now.

She searched the faces for Postmaster Byrne. She knew what he looked like; his portrait hung in most government buildings. But he wasn't here, thankfully; he had a brutish reputation, especially toward apprentices.

Steward Mordraig turned to Maeve. "Now listen carefully, because I don't like to repeat myself. The House of Ministers thinks that they can give us all the money in the worlds in hopes that we might churn out couriers faster, but it doesn't work like that."

He motioned for one of the stewards to stand. And stand he did, stretching nearly half a foot taller than all the others. He looked like a willow branch, with spindly brown limbs and a head of curling gray hair.

"This here is old Tallowmeade, the Steward of Inks and Pigments, and the meanest knucklenook player this side of the river Liss. Don't say I didn't warn you," Steward Mordraig said.

"Welcome." Tallowmeade spoke in a voice as smooth as a skipping stone. He bowed his head, sending the corked inkpots he wore around his neck jangling. Then he pulled something from his pocket and handed it to Steward Mordraig. A blank envelope.

"This envelope contains a piece of paper with a written, first-hand account of events that have been enchanted with a memory scribing," Mordraig explained. "Both the Leyland and Barrow

Houses of Ministers have dictated that all new apprentices read this particular memory in order to understand the danger of what we do. And since they pay for all our quills, you have to do as they say." He handed her the envelope. "Go on, madam. Crack open that letter, and give it a nice little read."

As far as Maeve knew, memory scribings allowed a reader to picture whatever memory was written about in a letter as if they were remembering it themselves. She glanced over at Tristan. He gave her a forbidding smile.

The envelope felt heavy in her hands, but she opened it and pulled out the paper inside. A page of lampblack ink began:

It happened on a summer afternoon . . .

Her ears popped.

"W-what is this?" she stammered as her vision clouded. The lecture hall winked away, and she now stood on the cobblestones outside of Blackcaster Station.

There was no perimeter fence, no mourning candles or water-logged bouquets. People were coming and going from the station's shining turnstiles.

Maeve wasn't herself; she stood much taller than her normal height. She tried to step but found she couldn't control her legs; they were moving of their own volition. Running, then skidding to a halt.

She was somehow *inside* someone else's memory, looking out through eyes locked on Blackcaster Station, where a strange green vine grew along the north edge of the roof. A vine that had over-run most other worlds; a vine that had caused Molly Blackcaster to ban travel outside the bounds of the three known worlds all those centuries ago.

The Aldervine.

A scream tore through the crowd, and Maeve knew which memory this was. She was standing in Inverly right before the Written Doors burned. In the moments before Inverly was lost forever, along with everyone trapped inside.

People grew frantic around her. The body she inhabited raced toward the station, halting as a sweet scent wafted through the air. It stung her nostrils.

Across the square, a woman sat beside a baby's buggy, her long fingers entwined through the handle while delicate green tendrils coiled around her ankles, their thorns drawing rivulets of blood. The woman's chest rose and fell, as if she had fallen asleep, save for her eyes that remained wide open, the irises pure white from the Aldervine's poison.

A single prick from the Aldervine's thorns sent its victims into an endless nightmare of sleep. It didn't kill them outright but left them unconscious and unaware of the world around them, growing older but never waking. It might sound like a fairy tale if it weren't so horrific.

More dark vines grew from behind the station, threading over a nearby building.

"Keep your head down!" a woman shouted.

Maeve knew that voice.

Her stomach lurched as her great-aunt Agatha stepped into her field of vision, heading with the crowd toward the station, her arms wrapped around an eleven-year-old version of Maeve. She'd forgotten how scrawny and pale she was back then.

A riderless horse tore through the crowd, bounding toward her aunt.

Maeve tried to scream, to tell her aunt to run. But this was a memory—there was no changing it, she realized. She was forced to watch as the horse reared its legs. Aggie tossed the younger Maeve out of the way just in time for the horse's thick hoof to crack down on her great-aunt's neck, snapping it like fragile porcelain. The horse left blooms of red hoofprints against the wet cobblestones as it fled.

Eleven-year-old Maeve tucked her knees to her chin, staring at her aunt's lifeless body, shuddering. A moment later, a man ran over and hoisted her younger self up, walking her to where armed officers stood on either side of the turnstiles, shouting and shoving people through, panicked.

Maeve could never remember what the man who saved her looked like. But there he was, standing a few paces away, his back to her.

Turn around, she willed, hoping to see his face, but he disappeared inside the station with her younger self before she could make out any features.

The body she was stuck inside then turned to gaze out at Inverly, or what was left of it.

Dark green vines covered nearly every building in a filmy sheath as fine as a bridal veil. It was eerily silent; most everyone left in the square had fallen into the poisoned sleep.

They were gone. Inverly was left to ruin.

Maeve's eyes snapped open. She was on her knees, gasping and breathless. Blood leaked from one of her nostrils, dripping to the floor—of a stage. The lecture hall at the Otherwhere Post. The memory was over.

She stared down at her reflection in the gleaming wood—at eyes as wide as hallions. A drugged sensation rolled through her as she lifted her head. The memory-scribed paper was now on the floor a few feet away. She caught Tristan's eye. He watched her with a furrowed brow.

Steward Mordraig hobbled across the wood to help her up. "That's one hell of a memory, isn't it? The account of the last man to escape Inverly alive. Our very own Postmaster Byrne."

Maeve wasn't expecting that. Onrich Byrne had lit the fire that burned down the Written Doors before the Aldervine could get through, which saved both Leyland and Barrow. He had been the hero of that day, promoted from a fledgling steward to the head of the Otherwhere Post because of it. But she had no idea he had seen her in Inverly.

The Postmaster had watched her being carried away, along with every person who viewed this memory scribing. What if he recognized her? No, he wouldn't; she looked too different now. Besides, everyone assumed she was long gone. There was no way the Postmaster would connect her with that scrawny little girl.

"You are now officially a courier apprentice in the Otherwhere Post's Program for Scriptomantic Arts." Mordraig clapped her on the back. "You will receive lodging, meals, a uniform, supplies, and six shills a week as payment for your time during the length of the apprenticeship, which continues until next spring. Make it through to the end, and you will become an otherwhere courier."

Maeve drew in a long breath, trying to push Postmaster Byrne out of her mind. This scheme would work. She would find her answers without speaking to anyone besides the occasional steward. It wouldn't be much different from sorting pounce powders in Mr. Braithwaite's back room.

She felt a measure of relief, until Mordraig turned to Tristan and said, "You can now take her to meet the Postmaster."

Tristan led her down a dark wood corridor of an adjacent building. The walls were lined with portraits, including one very large painting of Postmaster Byrne himself, a severe-looking man with a pointed beard and a shock of dark silver hair the same hue as a new-formed axe blade.

"You look rather green," Tristan said.

"I'm fine," Maeve lied. She had to somehow calm herself down, so she pictured her journal on her lap and a quill in her hand, a fresh bead of ink at the nib, then writing about the rosebushes her aunt had planted from seedlings against the side of the house in Inverly, that blossomed into pink roses the size of her head each spring.

It helped, until Tristan opened a door, and they entered a freezing office that smelled of mushed peas and stale coffee. A sideboard held a few half-eaten platters of food in shades of brown and muddy white.

Two men stood as she entered. Maeve recognized the deep scarlet minister's uniform on the first man, decorated to the gills with medals, along with a large letter *L* denoting that he served the Leyland house. The man beside him wore a simpler version of the same uniform—a minister courier's raiment, she realized. The third man was Postmaster Byrne.

He sat behind a large desk and barely spared a glance at her or Tristan. "Gentlemen, I believe we're done for the day. We'll pick up our talks tomorrow."

The minister nodded, while his courier gathered together stacks of official-looking paperwork.

Tristan leaned close to her ear and whispered, "That's Leyland's Minister of Communication and his private courier. Both are far too codheaded for their own good."

This particular minister had the difficult task of relaying everything the government was working on to help people after Inverly. He was a powerful public figure, but then so was the Postmaster.

After the two men gave formal goodbyes and left through a side door, the Postmaster pulled out a sheet of paper and a quill, dipping the nib into a well on his desk.

"You're late," he said without looking up.

Tristan's mouth pulled flat. "I hope you're ready for an unpleasant few minutes," he murmured to Maeve under his breath, then stepped forward and cleared his throat. "There was an accident involving Butternut," he said to the Postmaster. Tristan didn't mention that she had been the other half of the accident. "We lost a bit of time."

"I suppose I shouldn't be surprised. You are your mother's son."

Fury flickered on Tristan's face. "That's very kind of you to say, Father."

Maeve drew a palm to her throat, noticing the resemblance between the two men for the first time.

Tristan was his *son*. Heavens, she'd spent the entire day with the Postmaster's own son without knowing it.

Tristan brushed a lock of hair from his glasses. "This is Miss Eilidh Hill," he said. "She passed her arrival exam, then had the misfortune to wander directly into my carriage," he said dryly, an attempt to poke fun.

He could have pressed a pie to his face, and Maeve wouldn't have laughed. How could she when she was standing on the edge of a knife? But then the Postmaster turned his attention to her. It was the briefest look, but she nearly swayed with relief; there was nothing in his face that indicated he recognized her.

He held out a hand. "Her papers."

Tristan fumbled though his saddlebag and pulled out Eilidh Hill's black leather folio. He handed it to his father, who rifled through it.

"Eilidh P. Hill, from the far south," the Postmaster said.

Maeve nodded. "Yes, sir."

He flipped through pages and stopped at one at the end, scanning it slowly, then flipping to another. Thunder sounded in the distance, followed by the shriek of birds. This was taking too long. Eventually the Postmaster lifted a silver eyebrow in a gesture identical to his son's. "It says here that you hail from a family of equestrian experts. That you were the head of the horse club at your upper school. Is that true?"

Every single muscle in Maeve's body went taut.

"Well?"

What could she say? She forced herself to nod.

"Then you can teach the other apprentices what you know. We sometimes use coaches to cart back mail from Blackcaster Station. You could help with the horses in your spare time if you want."

Maeve stole a glance at Tristan. Their eyes met, and his mouth twitched terribly.

He *knew*.

Tristan knew she was an impostor before she ever stepped foot inside his carriage—from the moment she professed to loathe all horses. It was why he had acted strangely when she refused to help him with Butternut. Probably why he made a point to ask after her inkwell at the fountain. Yet he didn't say anything that whole time, when there were plenty of opportunities to turn back.

"Now." Postmaster Byrne turned to his son. "I have decided that you will be Eilidh's mentor this season. You can show your apprentice to her quarters. It's late, and I'm sure you have early duties in the morning."

She would be Tristan's apprentice?

Tristan seemed even more startled than her. He shot forward. "But, Father—"

"Was I not clear?"

Tristan grew panicked. "But . . . I thought that I would be working as an otherwhere courier. Alone."

"You will not," the Postmaster snapped, and Tristan drew up. "Nearly all couriers volunteer as mentors in the two years after they apprentice. This is your second year post-apprenticeship."

His jaw tightened, and something dark flashed in his eyes. "True, Father. But after what happened last year, I don't think it would be wise for me to mentor anyone again."

"You don't get a choice in the matter," the Postmaster shot back. "The House of Ministers would like for us to shorten scribing times by half, which means we need more capable couriers, and *you* need to spend more time in the Scriptorium."

Tristan's throat bobbed. "I've already told you that I won't scribe anything above letters for delivery."

The Postmaster lurched from his chair. "You don't get to decide what you want. It's been a year. It's time to stop wasting your potential! You will sit with this girl and help to teach her scriptomancy by showing her how it's done," he said, then settled back behind his desk.

Tristan's eyes grew glassy for the briefest moment, but then he blinked and schooled his features, seeming to bury whatever Maeve had just witnessed deep within himself, leaving nothing behind but a simmering anger beneath a blank stare. His gaze flickered to her, and she felt it beat against her like a branding iron.

"Now that that's settled, you can show Apprentice Hill to her room at Hawthorne House." The Postmaster gave his son a dismissive wave.

They were excused, and Maeve was forced to follow Tristan out a side door.

The silence between them rang sharp, slicing into her.

"If you're considering running, don't," he said flatly, all hint of amusement from earlier gone. "The entrance gate is leagues away and you won't be able to find it in the dark through the misting woods. It would be locked by now anyhow."

He turned and headed in the direction of the ocean—away from all other buildings.

Gusting wind tore at Maeve's sleeves. She hugged her arms around her body. "You're not taking me to my room?"

"No."

"Then where are we going?"

"Somewhere where we can speak privately, Eilidh P. Hill."

Gray slivers of moonlight pierced the grounds as they crossed an ancient graveyard bordering the eastern side of the office building. Headstones kissed one another, their markings rubbed away from centuries of battering wind. Scriptomancers of old were buried here, bones turning to dust. As Maeve's skirts scraped against stones, she wondered if the truth about her father was worth this suffocating feeling of dread that grew heavier, weighing her down with each step. At least the Postmaster didn't recognize her. It was only Tristan she had to worry about.

Tristan Byrne, the Postmaster's son.

He wove her diligently around gravestones, the blank expression from his father's office shifting to a clenched jaw, probably mulling over whether he should turn her in. The thought kept her on guard.

Past the graveyard, the bare oaks thickened, then opened for a circular clearing, a dark pit in its center. Hundreds of sharpened metal spikes lined the edges of the pit like the yawning mouth of a beast.

A howling gust came up from within that mouth, misting Maeve with salt spray.

She licked it from her lips. They must be very close to the

ocean ledge, probably perched on a cliff above it now. This hole likely emptied to sharp rocks below.

Her heart slammed into her throat. "So now what? You're going to throw me in?"

"You underestimate me. If I was planning to kill you, I think I could come up with far more creative ways than shoving you down that."

"Then why did you bring me here?"

He lifted a rock and tossed it down the hole.

Maeve listened, but the howl of the wind wrapped around her ears and made it impossible to hear if the rock landed anywhere.

"It's called the abyss. They used to bring scriptomancers here centuries ago to toss down for violating the most important of rules. Fascinating little hole, isn't it?"

Maeve would rather feed a horse with her naked fingers than hear another word about that little hole.

She tightened her arms across her chest as a new gust of wind grabbed the edges of her coat, her braid. It stung her eyes, and she cursed herself for getting into this situation to begin with.

Tristan stared at a spot beyond the trees. "My father and I might not be the chummiest, but I know him well. He's beholden to the House of Ministers. Because of it, he runs a tight ship. He doesn't take kindly to people breaking any of the Post's rules. If he learns about what you did, he'll bring you here and hang you over the edge until you tell him everything about yourself, down to the color of your knickers. Then he'll deliver you straight to Stonewater."

The Leyland prison was infamous for feeding its prisoners rats, among other delicacies. Maeve had no desire to pay it a visit.

Perhaps if she wished it hard enough, the ghost of Molly Blackcaster would appear to give Tristan a healthy shove down that hole.

Tristan turned to face her. "I don't care much for the Post's rules, but I'm also on a stipend that I'd rather not forfeit by harboring a swindler, no matter how innocent she may look. We both know you're not Eilidh Hill. Either I'm returning you to my father, or you can tell me who you are and why you're here and we can go about our merry way. I don't suppose you have a preference?"

He only wanted answers? She could certainly give him some answers.

"You already know why I'm here. I told you that day in Alewick," she said.

"The letter?"

She nodded.

"You mean to tell me that you would impersonate an apprentice and lie your way inside the Post to find out who sent you an old letter?" Disbelief was written on his face.

"The letter is important to me."

He seemed truly perplexed. "Nothing is that important."

"It is. If I can find the sender, it—it could change my life," she said, praying he would understand. But he still appeared skeptical. "If you could reverse the worst thing that's ever happened to you, wouldn't you risk everything to try?"

"The worst thing that's ever happened to me is irreversible," he said, then held out a hand. "But let's see it."

"My letter?"

"No, your knickers. Of *course* your letter."

She shuffled backward. "I misplaced it."

"Ah, yes, of course. A letter that's so important it has you sneaking inside the Otherwhere Post—risking going to *prison* over—and you simply misplaced it." He sighed. "Do you honestly expect me to believe that?"

She straightened her shoulders, bothered that she only came to his chin. "Believe what you want."

He nodded to himself. "Very well. Even if you're not here for some odious purpose, you've somehow cheated your way into the most selective apprenticeship in the worlds. The stewards will figure you out in minutes." He looked her over with an eyebrow raised. "Can you even hold a quill?"

The way he said it made her hands curl to fists. "I know how to write."

"Of *course* you do. How *dare* I suggest otherwise?"

Maeve's nails dug into her palms. She had never understood the desire to punch someone in the face until now.

"I assume that you know perfectly well how to scratch out a few garbled sentences," he went on, "but apprentices can craft paragraphs as if ink is their lifeblood and parchment is their very bones. If you haven't been to a writing program at an upper school, which I can't *fathom* that you have, you'll never be able to trick anyone that you're up to snuff. Only a fool would try. You didn't strike me as inkbrained at first, but perhaps I was mistaken."

Good heavens, Maeve wanted to prove him wrong. Perhaps more than she'd ever wanted anything before. Then an idea struck her, and she held out a hand. "Writing pad."

"What?"

There was no way she would pull out her own journal in front of him, and he needed to watch her write.

"Do you have a writing pad, or is your saddlebag merely chock-full of garbage?"

He grumbled and rifled through his bag, handing her a rumpled pad, along with an inkpot and a gorgeous hawk quill covered in globules of melted wax. Its fletching stuck to her fingers as she opened his pad and uncorked the ink. She penned four neat rows of text, then handed him the pad before the ink had time to fully dry.

"Read it."

He glanced at it, then back at her. "It's written in Old Leylish."

"Yes, it is," she said. Her father had made her learn the runic language as a child. Scriptomancers had used it for centuries, even after the modern tongue had replaced it in common use, because it had descriptive words missing from the modern tongue—words used to hone scribings. It fell even further out of favor after Molly Blackcaster revolutionized scribing, but Maeve's father still found it useful. "Aren't you going to read it?"

"Not many people can read Old Leylish," Tristan said simply. "Most here can only write a few words with the help of a guide-book."

That nearly made her smile. "Now do you agree that I can do more than merely scratch out a few sentences?"

"That depends." He handed her the pad. "I think I would really need you to read me what you've written in order to believe in your ability."

Her stomach dropped.

"Go on," he said, crossing his arms.

He was truly going to make her read it? Very well. "Translated it says: These words prove me capable to stand beside anyone from an upper school. If you refuse to see that, then you are no better than . . ." Maeve let the words trail off.

His left eyebrow arched dramatically. "No better than . . . ?"

"An animal combined with a body part," she said quickly.

Tristan covered his mouth with his knuckles. "Fascinating. Which animal and which body part would that be?"

"Don't you dare make me say it."

They stared each other down for a long moment, then his mouth quivered. His shoulders began to shake. He was laughing at her.

"This is not a laughing situation!"

"Oh my. Now why did you have to go and say *that?*" he said, gasping for breath.

Her embarrassment swiftly boiled into anger. She opened her mouth.

He put up a hand. "Stop it, I beg you." He slid his fingers beneath his spectacles and wiped his eyes. "I read what you wrote the instant your nib hit the paper, and I thought it was a brilliant insult."

She blinked at him. "You could read Old Leylish that whole time?"

"Of course I can. My father made me learn it. It pains me to say this, but I'm thoroughly impressed that *you* can. I was telling you the truth that most here would never be able to string that many runes together. Where did you learn it?"

"From an old book." *And the scriptomancer who made me read it.* "Now do you think I'll be able to join the apprenticeship without being noticed? I only need to stay long enough to investigate my letter."

His gaze hung on her for a prolonged moment—longer than anyone ever bothered to look at her. It felt as if he were taking detailed notes on each of her eyelashes. It unnerved her, and she tugged the tangled clump of her braid to keep from squirming.

Finally, he tipped his face to the night sky and muttered, "Common sense be damned." He met her eyes. "I don't believe you're being truthful about your letter, but then I've never been so curious in my entire life, and I'm a curious person by nature. I'm also fairly certain that if I don't turn you in, someone else will within the week, and that will prove much more entertaining to watch."

His words chilled her more than the wind, but she felt a small measure of hope. "Does this mean I can stay?"

He shoved the writing pad in his saddlebag without bothering to close it, smearing wet ink on his gloves. He wiped them across his cloak without a care. "You can stay, but do anything to jeopardize me or anyone here and we'll pay a swift visit to my father."

TRISTAN BROUGHT MAEVE back through the Post's grounds, pointing out the various buildings inhabited by famous scriptomancers of old. When Tristan wasn't threatening her life, he had a steady and somewhat pleasant demeanor. It could be genuine, but it could also be an act to get her to relax her guard—and give away secrets about herself.

Just as he finished up a story about Molly Blackcaster's pet crow—who liked stealing quill feathers and nipping at other scriptomancers—they arrived at an enormous yet slightly crooked stone building with a sharply steepled roof called Hawthorne House. Maeve's new residence hall. Its tight, twisting corridors were lined in moth-eaten tapestries and overfilled bookcases. Tristan plucked a few old books as he wove her through, tucking them beneath his arm.

He halted when a group of couriers came toward them. One of the couriers spat as he passed, the glob of spittle landing on the toe of Tristan's tasseled shoe.

Tristan's expression tightened, but he didn't say anything to the man.

"Why did he do that?" Maeve asked after the group had left.

"For the same reason the gate guards made us late; they're all jealous of my wardrobe." He gave a humorless smile.

He wasn't telling the truth, but given her own tangle of lies, Maeve decided not to press for answers.

The encounter put him in a worse mood. She sensed it as she hurried behind him up a spiraling stair to a third-floor hall where more old books sat in tipping stacks against walls yellowed from pipe smoke. The chill air smelled of floor polish and moldering tea.

"This is the corridor for apprentices," Tristan said. "Or those impersonating one, I suppose."

Maeve tensed up. "Must you say that so loudly?"

"No, but your reactions are lifting my spirits." He pulled a clipboard off a side table. "Eilidh's room should be listed here." She reached for it, but he took a step back. "You haven't told me your real name."

"Miraculously, here it is." Maeve took the clipboard from him and ran a finger down the side. "Eilidh Pretoria Hill. Room 403."

He wasn't amused, but he held her gaze. "Who are you?" he asked.

The question carved its way into the pit of her stomach. "Nobody interesting."

"Fine, *nobody interesting*. If you're still here tomorrow, you should speak with someone in the Hall of Routes."

That came out of nowhere. "Why?"

"Because they keep records of everything from paid postage to our librarians' dietary habits. I can't promise you'll find out much about your mysterious letter—the clerks could all be replaced with gilded doorstoppers and nobody would notice—but unless you want to go speak with the stewards about it, it's somewhere to start."

Maeve stared at him, dumbfounded. He was helping her, and she had no clue what to say.

"Now go before I change my mind and drag you to my father's office."

She wouldn't argue with that.

She started down the hall, where sepiagraphs cluttered the spaces between chamber doors. The nearest depicted an apprentice class gathered beside the ink fountain at springtime, budding leaves erupting from surrounding oaks. All the other pictures seemed to be of more classes. Many more than seven years' worth. Some sepiagraphs had to be of scriptomancy students from when this was part of the university.

"Jonathan Abenthy is in the twenty-fourth one down, if you're curious," Tristan called out.

She froze in shocked disbelief at the sound of her father's name spoken so casually.

He pointed to a sepiagraph along the hall. "All new apprentices usually want to see it."

Right. Of course they would all be curious.

Maeve counted the class portraits as she walked, all the way to twenty-four—a larger sepiagraph, its silver frame tarnished from age. It showed at least fifty students in antiquated hairstyles and long university robes. She knew which one was him because his face was blotted-out with a thick scribble of lampblack ink, the word "murderer" scratched beside it.

Her father. The man who unleashed the Aldervine in Inverly.

The story went like this: Jonathan Abenthy was a brilliant young researcher with untamable curiosity and a penchant for scriptomantic travel. He used it to visit a world infested with the Aldervine, outside the bounds of the known worlds, which was already the highest crime. But then he brought the Aldervine back to Inverly, where it spread more quickly than the morning fog, leaving unfathomable destruction in its wake.

In the weeks that followed, there was a lengthy, public investigation. Journals were discovered in her father's room that showed an obsession with Molly Blackcaster and the scriptomancers of her time. But the most damning piece of evidence came in the form of a statement put out by the College of Scriptomantic Arts itself, explaining how all scriptomancers were taught about the dangers of the Aldervine. It said that Jonathan Abenthy might have not traveled outside the known worlds with malicious intent initially, but he still made the decision to return to Inverly, knowing full well the risk.

There was no denying it was her father's fault. In the span of days, every paper in Leyland ran his likeness, calling him a murderer, a vile criminal who deserved to rot. Maeve's name was printed in several of the articles, saying she perished in Inverly.

She still remembered the moment she'd seen that first article. Headmistress Castlemaine had dragged her to her office at the Sacrifict Orphanage by the earlobe, then swatted her with a copy of the *Herald*. She called Maeve a bad omen and threatened to turn her out, which she never followed through on. Why would she when the woman received a tidy sum of hallions from the Leylish government for each orphan?

"You will never speak of your father again," Castlemaine had snarled, pointing to her blackboard. "Now write it in chalk one thousand times."

"One thousand?"

"Or until your fingers bleed."

Maeve barely made it to seven hundred before her skin broke. Seven years later and she still had a scar from the blisters.

She picked at it now as she brought that finger to the blotted-out sepiagraph, picturing the dimples that dotted her father's smile, that hole in his shirtsleeve on their last night together.

The College of Scriptomantic Arts didn't allow children, but before Inverly, he'd inquired about a pass for Maeve to visit. He wanted her to love this place as he did, to work here beside him and make the name Abenthy as famous as the name Blackcaster.

Now it was, she supposed.

After Inverly, it took a whole month before she began to hate her father for what he'd done. And now it had been seven years—seven years of being alone, of hearing her father's name spat from strangers' lips like a curse. Her hatred felt like it was etched with a rusted quill knife into each of her rib bones.

Would proving his innocence ever change that? Perhaps not. Perhaps coming here was a mistake. But then if she wasn't here, she would be sitting in her sad, lonely flat in Alewick listening to laughter bleeding through the walls while she packed her shoddy suitcase with items from a life she despised. Then she would have fled Gloam, and nobody would have cared, because she never let anybody get close enough to care.

Maeve groaned and pinched a spot on her forehead. There was only so much feeling sorry for herself she could take in one night.

Footfalls echoed. Three young men passed by in the tight hall, the last with a wine bottle tucked beneath his arm. He caught Maeve's eye and his lips slipped up, showing off an attractive smile.

"You must be one of the new apprentices. We're heading to the central courtyard." He patted the bottle. "Want to join us?"

Maeve could say yes. She could follow this boy to his party, drink his wine, maybe even slip into the shadows to whisper secrets in each other's ears. And maybe, with the wine loosening her tongue, she would whisper the kind of secrets that would make him call an officer of the constabulary. "I can't. Sorry."

"Perhaps another time," he said as he and his friends disappeared down the hall.

"Perhaps."

Maeve found Eilidh's room without any more hallway propositions, a dark space dappled by moonlight. She managed to light a candle without singeing off her fingertips, then swept her gaze around the room.

A bed was pushed into one corner, another small bed beside it. There were two dressers and two old writing desks covered in ink splatters. One of the desks was stacked with papers. In fact, that whole side of the room was already stuffed full of books and suitcases, with a pair of lace knickers hanging from a dresser knob. Maeve stepped to the desk and grazed her fingers over the rim of an uncapped inkwell spilled over a copy of the *Herald*.

It seemed Eilidh P. Hill had a roommate.

Maeve collapsed on the opposite bed, her head in her hands. Her flat in Alewick had been her sanctuary because she had it all to herself. How was she supposed to exist living beside another person?

As she thought it, the door opened, and a tall woman wandered in and flung herself onto the other bed, propping her head in her hand. A waterfall of thick black hair spilled onto the pillow. "Hello there. I'm your roommate, Miss Ferro, but do call me Nan. I can call you Eilidh, right?" she said in a smooth, fashionable voice, then fished a small pot of rouge from her pocket and smeared the bright paste over her lips. "I suppose you're dying to know all about me."

"I really don't—" Maeve started.

"My grandfather was from Barrow," Nan said, checking her nails. "A sourpuss of a man. It's why my father moved to Leyland before the doors burned. That's where my mother's family is from, though old Mum spent most of her time in Inverly before meeting my father. She used to sit as a model for some of the great painters there. It's where I got my cheekbones." Nan fluttered a hand at her face.

Maeve didn't care where she got her cheekbones. "Please don't take this the wrong way, but . . . do you think I might be able to switch to a single room?"

Nan's eyes flew wide. "Have you seen any of them? They have closets the size of two kidney beans squished together, and they're all already assigned." She rolled onto her back and put her hands behind her head. "Besides, I think we're going to be great friends," she said, smiling to herself.

"I'm not here to make friends."

"Dear me, you're a load of fun, aren't you?" Nan pushed up and adjusted her blouse, then the waist of a pair of men's wide-leg trousers that looked fashionable on her slim form. She wiped her teeth on her sleeve, then tied a silk scarf around her neck.

"Are you leaving?"

"I'm heading to the Groggery here on the grounds. It's mostly for couriers who go to have a pint and play knucklenook and barter tools. They don't like to let in apprentices, but I happened to make friends with the barkeep this afternoon. It sounds like the perfect place to get gossip and forget the fact that my nose will be trapped inside dull books for the foreseeable future." She stepped to the door, then motioned for Maeve to follow. "Come on."

Surely she wasn't serious. "It's late, and we start classes tomorrow."

Nan rolled her eyes. "Don't be boring. I want to introduce you to a few people. You don't have to say anything. You could sit across from me and stare glumly at the ceiling if you wish."

She couldn't believe that Nan was pressing the matter. "I'd rather not sit across from anyone or meet anyone new. I meant it when I said that I'm not here to make friends."

"Fine. Be a sad potato if you want. But if we have to room together for the next two terms, I'm going to make it my mission to become your good friend, whether you like it or not." She tossed her hair over her shoulder and ducked out.

Maeve pressed her palms to her eyes, thankful that was over.

She wanted nothing more than to let sleep take her for a few hours, but she dragged herself up to survey her side of the room.

A dresser was stocked with a single uniform skirt, a blouse that looked too small, then a camisole fit for a ten-year-old boy. Squeezing her breasts inside would take strategic creativity. She lifted a pair of regulation knickers, wrinkling her nose at the rough-spun wool that conjured images of her life at the orphanage.

Maeve moved to her writing desk. A few packets of sealing wax granules sat on top, along with a quill knife, a bone letter-fold stamped with the bead-eyed pigeon, and a stiff right-handed goose quill that would give her blisters for months. There were drawers filled with papers and a few pots of ink. Maeve uncorked and re-corked all of them, looking for god knew what.

She set the pots aside and pulled two printed sheets of paper from a bottom drawer. The first was titled *A letter written by Molly Blackcaster to the first ever apprentice class at the College of Scripto-mantic Arts.*

It read:

On the morrow, thou shalt begin instruction in the five scribings. A form scribing to produce illuminations in ink, a sense scribing to twist perception, a memory scribing to ignite the mind's eye, a seek-ing scribing to find a friend most dear, and a traveling scribing to bring a door to call. Taketh heed and mind thy ash, scriptomancer.

Maeve knew a few things scribings could do, but her father had never categorized them so eloquently. She slid the paper into the drawer, then lifted the second sheet, a curriculum for the fall ap-prentice term.

She would take four classes during weekdays: History of the Known Worlds, Pigment Lab, Fundamentals of Scriptomancy, and Methods of Chirography. Her nights were reserved for practice in the Scriptorium—the beating heart of these grounds, where her father had spent most of his days and many of his nights.

According to this paper, she was to report there tomorrow at eleven for an introductory lesson.

Tomorrow, she would have to walk into that building and pretend she hadn't spent the past seven years hoping the place would spontaneously burn to the ground.

Bracing her elbows against the desk, Maeve put her face in her hands, breathing through her fingers from the pent-up nerves. It felt like a river of water was filling her lungs and she was drowning in the very air she breathed. The sensation grew worse when she thought of her life leading up to now—the hiding, the lies, the torturous years of solitude. A life she hated.

A life she could *change*, so long as she didn't let her wretched feelings get in the way.

She forced her gaze up. If her *old friend*'s name was somewhere in this place, she had to find it, no matter the cost. Yes—she would find it. She would dig the truth out with her teeth if it came down to it.

But what was the truth?

The question lingered in her mind. Was her father a good man? Did he love her until the bitter end? Did he regret what he did? Perhaps none of the articles were true, and he never even made it to Inverly the day the Written Doors burned. Perhaps he was framed—

Maeve's hands dropped to her sides.

Up until now, she'd been so focused on the exact wording of that letter and whether or not her father was indeed guilty that she hadn't given much consideration to anything else—or *anyone* else.

The idea rolled on the surface of her mind like a fresh drop of ink, and a new thought struck her—something that hadn't occurred to her until this very moment. If her father didn't destroy Inverly, it meant that someone else was guilty of the crime. Someone else released the Aldervine, destroying an entire world and decimating its inhabitants, then framed her father—an innocent man.

And they got away with it.

Maeve woke in the chill predawn hour, when the shaded light was barely enough to see by. Her fingers weren't used to her new uniform, and she prayed that Nan was a heavy sleeper and wouldn't hear her bustling about, trying to wiggle into an ill-fitting camisole and plucking at unruly buttons. The courier's cloak was the only item she adored; its dark hood slipped easily over her head to cover it completely, the thick waxed material muting her curves until she couldn't tell her hips from her elbows. She sighed at how secure it made her feel. Venturing outside, however, was a different matter.

Clouds of silver mist pooled between the bare oaks, and their spindled branches gave little cover from the morning rain. Maeve was thoroughly soaked by the time she reached Tristan's suggestion of the Hall of Routes, a gray stone building on the north edge of the grounds. Its imposing, unwelcoming facade gave her pause, but she nudged away her reservations and stepped inside to a bustling open chamber with soaring ceilings crisscrossed with elaborate brass sorting chutes. Rows of enormous bins the size of carriages lined the floor beneath the chutes, brimming with envelopes.

Maeve had read about this building in the Postmaster's

newsletters—where all mail was brought after being collected, to
be sorted for scribing.

A reception desk stood amid the chaos. Maeve's heels clicked
along the stone floor as she made her way to a clerk at the far end of
the desk, a mustached older man, fully engrossed in today's *Herald*.

"What is it?" he barked.

Maeve fidgeted. "I'm in need of help."

"Of course you are," the clerk said, and returned to reading his
paper.

Gilded doorstopper indeed.

Maeve swallowed and crept closer to the desk. "I need to find
the sender of an anonymous letter. It's one of the old letters from
right after the doors were burned. It was delivered with no name.
And the recipient would dearly like to know who sent it."

The clerk yawned. "Afraid I can't help you there."

"Why not?"

He gave her a disdainful glance. "There aren't records in the
Hall of Routes for letters that old."

"You could try the tracking office," someone said from behind
her. The deep voice resonated through every one of Maeve's bones.
She turned slowly.

Steward Tallowmeade towered beside her, carrying a large
bundle of letters.

"Undeliverables," he said to the clerk, and the man scrambled
to take the letters from the steward's hands. Tallowmeade turned
to her. Earthenware pots jangled from his neck, scents of cedar-
wood and clove drifting to Maeve's nose. The spiced scents would
normally be soothing, but they had an opposite effect. "You're Apprentice Hill?"

Maeve nodded, focusing her attention on the desk.

"Look up, child," Tallowmeade said.

She forced her eyes to the base of his bearded chin.

"Much better," he said in that deep, meandering voice. "A scriptomancer must always keep their gaze level with the horizon, paying attention to their surroundings. It's one of Molly Blackcaster's rules for traveling, written in the *Ideals of Scriptomancy*. There should be copies floating around the apprentice hall. It might serve you well to give it a read."

"I will," Maeve said.

"Good. Now, about that letter of yours . . ." he started, and she tensed instinctively at the mention of the letter, then forced herself to take a breath. "Someone at the tracking office would know exactly how to help you. They have special methods of tracking old letters, even ones from before our current postage records."

Maeve tried to keep her voice even. "Thank you for the advice, Steward Tallowmeade." As he began to turn away from her, she risked one more question. "Is the tracking office nearby?"

"It's in Barrow, Apprentice Hill. You could give it a visit once you're able to cross worlds."

Her newfound hope withered on the spot.

He nodded to her, then lumbered away, walking as slowly as he spoke.

Maeve waited until he was out of sight before she, too, headed outdoors, circling buildings for a few minutes before finding the courtyard, the ink fountain. She braced her hands against the fountain's edge, staring at her reflection in the black ink.

She had no way to visit Barrow to find the tracking office. That was a dead end. And worse, now Steward Tallowmeade knew that she was searching for the sender of a letter. If he mentioned it to others—

Stop it, Maeve told herself. She was only being paranoid. People received letters all the time.

She squeezed the fountain's stone lip until her fingers were chilled through her gloves, then shook out her hands, looking around her.

If she couldn't go to the tracking office, she'd simply find another way to investigate from Leyland. There had to be something she could do from here—the place where her father had lived for so much of his life. Surely if she could uncover more about her father, she might be able to guess who his *old friend* was.

The misting rain darkened the gray buildings that her father had spent his days inside. He must have filled countless journals here—journals that never seemed to wind up in their home in Inverly. She had learned her own journaling habit from him, after all, and she rarely saw him without one.

Last night, she'd noticed a few journals were stuffed between the books in Hawthorne House. The shelves seemed to have no clear order, and were organized simply at the whims of the couriers living in the halls. There would be no easy way to search them besides sifting through shelves by hand. But if she knew which residence hall her father had lived in, it would be a start.

If she found just one of his journals, it might mention the names of people he was close with. A name would give her a lead.

A group of stewards walked into the north end of the courtyard, including Tallowmeade.

Before anyone might wonder what she was doing, Maeve darted into a nearby building. Her stomach clenched from hunger as heavy smells of breakfast meats and stale coffee assaulted her. She followed the scents to a loud mess hall filled with otherwhere couriers. Hanging at the edge, she watched them sip from steaming cups and slather beans onto bread crusts. A worker carried a basin filled with mush to a sideboard covered in opened canisters of gray jelly and a brown sauce that nearly stifled her appetite.

The food budgets set by the House of Ministers must be minuscule by the look of it. But then they probably didn't care if otherwise couriers ate well, only that they bruised their fingers scribing letters for delivery.

This place must be a shock for someone from an expensive upper school, who was used to oysters and prime rib on silver platters.

Maeve stuffed four slices of soda bread down her saddlebag to take with her, then spotted Tristan. He sat at a nearby table in the corner by himself, reading. The bruises beneath his eyes were darker this morning. Did he sleep at all? He ruffled his hair, then he flipped a page in his book. An untouched plate of food sat beside him.

She knew it. He was one of those disturbing people who could pick off morsels for hours, whereas she tended to lick her plates clean. He probably hated all sweets as well.

Maeve was about to leave, then halted when a courier stood up from the table behind Tristan. A large fellow with a thick neck and bunching shoulder muscles. He carried a full glass of milk, then raised it above Tristan's head.

Tristan flipped another page of his book, oblivious.

Maeve once had a glass of water tipped down her back at the Sacrifct, and knew intimately what it felt like to be whispered about, targeted. Hated. A sharp burst of anger struck her at the painful memories, and she pointed to the courier with the milk. "Tristan, watch out!"

Tristan was seated close enough to hear her and looked up, then leapt out of the way a moment before the milk splashed onto his chair.

The room fell to silence.

The courier's gaze shot to her for a heated moment, and Maeve's scalp prickled. Then he took Tristan's entire plate of food and flipped it onto the open book, mashing it into the page, then walking away as if nothing happened.

Tristan stared at the mess for a long moment, his back to her. He must be scalding with anger. Maeve braced herself for an outburst, but it never came. Tristan gave his book a brisk shake, then tucked it down his saddlebag and turned to meet her eyes.

To her surprise, it wasn't anger she saw. Her mouth slackened at the sorrow plainly etched in every line of Tristan's face.

He gave her a curt nod of acknowledgment, then exited through a back door.

Outside, Maeve tried to make sense of what just happened. Tristan seemed intelligent and friendly enough to those who weren't apprenticing at the Post under a false identity. He didn't strike her as someone who people would despise. Even if she had calculated wrong and his peers did loathe him, she wouldn't expect them to spit on his shoes or pour milk on his head. That went far beyond the bounds of reasonable behavior, even if he hadn't been the son of the most powerful man at the Otherwhere Post. But it was Tristan's reaction that confused her most of all. She'd expected him to be furious, to lash out at the brute. Not look at her as if his entire world were falling apart.

Nan interrupted her train of thought, popping up beside her with a wispy young woman trailing a step behind.

The woman twisted a strand of white-blond hair around a finger. A vein in her pale forehead stood out as she fixed her large, pale blue eyes on Maeve.

They were both staring at her. "Is something the matter?"

"I was calling your name for a full minute," Nan said, and Maeve tensed. "Didn't you hear me?"

At this rate, she might as well turn herself in. "Heavens, no. I didn't hear anything. I was lost in thought."

Nan didn't seem convinced, but the blond woman stepped forward before Maeve could think of an excuse. "So this is your roommate, then?" she said to Nan, then smiled at Maeve. "I'm Shea Widden, Nan's mentor."

A Widden—Maeve took a reflexive step backward, steeling herself. The infamous Widdens owned buildings across Leyland and Barrow. Their family was as rich as the central trust, and their drama filled gossip columns. They were always in the spotlight. Maeve didn't want anything to do with Shea Widden.

"Nan tells me that you're interested in attending all the Post's social functions," Shea said.

Maeve cut a scathing look at Nan, who merely shrugged.

"I have something for you." Shea dug through her saddlebag and handed over a flyer. It was for the annual Scriptomantic Exhibition.

The flyer boasted of a weekend of events: an opening reception, various demonstrations of scriptomantic talent, and talks by prominent scriptomancers. It was used as a platform to give the public more information about everything from repairing the Written Doors to scribing times—put on by the ministers for transparency, so protesters didn't feel the need to storm the Post.

A knot thickened Maeve's throat as she scanned through it. Her father used to help plan the annual exhibition when it was put on by the College of Scriptomantic Arts.

"It goes for a full week in Barrow, right after Midautumn," Shea said. "I'm showcasing a few new types of scribing commissions later in the week. You and Nan could go together if you're crossing worlds by then."

That was weeks away. If she were still here then, it would be because Tristan's father had thrown her to the bottom of the abyss.

She tucked the flyer down her saddlebag. "I'm not sure I'll be up to snuff, but I'll see what I can do."

"Who's your mentor?" Shea asked.

"Tristan," Maeve replied shortly, desperate to escape a longer conversation.

"Tristan Byrne?" Shea's already wide eyes grew a size larger. "You're Tristan *Byrne's* apprentice?"

"Is there something wrong with that?"

"Of course not," Shea said hastily. She patted the letters in her hand. "I have to get delivering. If you two need anything, don't hesitate to find me."

Once Shea was out of earshot, Nan turned to Maeve. "Is this Tristan related to Postmaster Byrne?"

"It's his son."

Nan whistled. "And I thought I lucked out getting a Widden as my mentor. I can't imagine the gossip the Postmaster's son must have about this place."

Nan looked like she wanted to press Maeve with more questions, but a clock rang out from across the grounds.

Maeve froze. "Aren't we supposed to be in the Scriptorium now?"

"Blast it, I think you're right. Let's hurry," Nan said. She took Maeve's arm, and they rushed down the stone pathway that led south from the central courtyard. The path hooked eastward.

"Are we almost there?" Maeve asked, out of breath.

"I think that's it." Nan pointed through the trees, to an enormous old building set back from the path.

Maeve expected a columned mausoleum after the way her father spoke of this place, not a crumbling facade hidden under dead ivy.

They walked slowly to the main entrance. Nan pulled open the front door and held it as they went inside.

The space was chilly enough that Maeve kept her cloak on. Daylight barely seeped in; the darkened windows looked covered in layers of coagulated ink. Her steps slowed, eyes adjusting.

"It feels sinister, doesn't it?" Nan whispered into the darkness, taking Maeve's arm.

Maeve was too nervous to push her away. This was where centuries of scriptomancers had learned their trade—and it hadn't always gone well. Early scriptomancers read scribings here that infected their minds. Her father told her of one man called Howling Thomas, who didn't leave his worktable for twelve days, then removed his clothes and ran out screaming all the way to the river Liss, where he dug his own grave with his fingernails.

As they wandered past oaken scriptomancy worktables, Maeve braced herself, waiting for the familiar burst of anger when she remembered old stories of her father's. But the scratch of quills filled her ears, and something long buried seemed to flicker to life inside of her. She took a deep inhale of the parchment-scented air, sensing the energy of an open journal, a fresh well of lampblack. Sinister lighting or no, she liked the feel of this place.

Perhaps learning scriptomancy wouldn't be so terrible. She could compartmentalize it like she had her journals, make it something separate from the tangled feelings about her father.

"Are you coming?" Nan called.

Maeve realized she'd wandered to a stop and hurried after her roommate, to where a large group of apprentices gathered between worktables.

The young man with the blue ink from the writing exam was there, along with several more men and women with Maeve's same coloring. At least she wouldn't have to worry about standing out with her red hair. A handful had Nan's dark hair and deep tan complexion, some darker. A few apprentices glanced her way, and she felt their eyes like knife tips dragging against her neck.

Steward Mordraig rifled through drawers at a worktable, pulling out stoppered wells, a handful of carved quills, and a large abalone inkwell.

Apprentices leaned in as he placed a letter in the center of the worktable, addressed to a *Dear Miranda*.

"I'm guessing you're all here because you want to learn how to get to Barrow, right?" he asked everyone.

There were nods, excited murmuring.

"Good. I like it when apprentices are eager. Makes things speedier. Today, however, is all about the basics." His small eyes glittered. "This is a scriptomancy worktable." He ran fingers over gouges thick with yellowed wax. "The tabletops are treated so scribing pigment will not stain them permanently." He tapped a dark blotch. "But blood will. So if you're going to stab yourself, go do it somewhere else."

An apprentice in front gave a chuckle, and Mordraig silenced him with a grunt.

"Now, most people think of a scribing as a mere sentence, but if all a scriptomancer had to do was scribble a sentence, we could strap quills to babies and hire them for the job. It would certainly get the House of Ministers off our backs." He looked across everyone. "Can one of you strapping youths tell me how a sentence *becomes* a scribing?"

Maeve knew the answer from her father. It might be good to answer a question here and there, so as not to stand out.

She raised a hand, then put it down when she realized that she was the only one.

"Apprentice Hill?" Mordraig pointed to her.

All eyes trained on her.

Her neck grew hot. "A sentence becomes a scribing through the process of Arcane Infusion," she said quietly.

Mordraig leaned on his cane, staring at her for a sharp beat that made her neck prickle. "Which upper school did you attend?"

"One in the far south. In Almsworth, sir."

He nodded and looked away.

Maeve pressed her lips together, vowing to never speak up again.

"Apprentice Hill is correct," he said. "Arcane Infusion is what we call the reaction that happens when you perform a scribing, and it takes—pulling in arcane magic."

He clamped a magnifying glass with a telescoping arm to the side of the worktable, enlarging *Dear Miranda*'s letter tenfold.

"The infusion is the hard part, though. It's a combination of perfects. A scriptomancer must select the *perfect* words and order them in the *perfect* way, using the *perfect* combination of tools, pigments, and chirography, then seal them *perfectly* using the symbol corresponding with the type of scribing they're performing. Only then will arcane magic flow into your sentence, attuning to the command you've written. In other words, the magic will do exactly what you've told it to do. Your sentence will then disappear, leaving only the original text, which can be anything from a handwritten book to a word scrawled onto a pair of knickers."

Or a grocery list, Maeve thought, imagining her father lecturing beside Mordraig.

Mordraig sighed. "But since the House of Ministers now dictates our days, we're only allowed to perform scribings on letters."

"Only ever letters?" someone behind Maeve asked.

"Yes. Unless you're one of the select few to interview with a government agency after graduating. Though I'd much rather scribe letters all day and night than carry the folios filled with bureaucratic nonsense the minister couriers are made to deliver."

He made a disgusted face, then pulled a matted swan feather quill from a tin cup. Without any attempt to be careful, he flung the cap off a pot of silver liquid and dumped it into the abalone well.

Scents of red honey and humid earth hit Maeve's nose, and she stiffened. The pigment—it smelled exactly like her father's clothing.

"Are you all right?" Nan whispered beside her.

Maeve realized her fingers were clenched into fists at her sides. She shook them out. "I'm fine," she said, then turned back to Mordraig.

He held up a vial of silver liquid.

"This is pre-mixed scribing pigment." He dipped his quill and wrote down a flurry of tiny silver words at the bottom of the letter. Wisps of black smoke rose from them. "Now for the seal." He drew a silver triangle that encompassed the silver sentence he'd just penned. "The Divine Triangle is the seal for all form scribings. Form is one of the five scribing types, along with traveling, tracking, memory, and the ever-wondrous sense! Most of you will only ever perform the traveling and tracking scribings, given those two are needed to deliver letters. A handful of the most talented, who aren't snatched up by a government agency first, will be assigned to scribing more advanced commissions onto letters, where the other three types come into play."

He drew a line, closing the last corner of the triangle.

All of the silvery writing dissolved into the paper, leaving the original letter penned to Miranda by itself on the page.

Nan leaned toward the paper.

Mordraig snatched it away. "For god's sake, don't read the text unless you want to trigger the enchantment." He waved the letter in the air. "All enchantments trigger when you read the original text, and trigger to a stronger degree when you read it *aloud*. You may be tempted to read the letters you scribe to test how you've done. Don't. Each read weakens the scribing's effects, not to mention it'll make you look like an inkbrained fool. Some scriptomancers even learn to blur their eyes while they work as a precaution. Try it if you want, though don't come crying to me if you accidentally spill your ink." He folded the letter and placed it on the table, the words hidden from view. "Now, everyone follow me!"

Nan hung beside Maeve as Mordraig led them down a narrow stone stair to an underground chamber lit by archaic torches.

An incongruous wooden sculpture stood in the center of the room. It looked like a piece of furniture had bent in on itself, then twisted at impossible angles through the air. Four large spindles shot from one side like jagged spears, while human rib bones protruded from the front in a grotesque arc.

"Morbid," Nan whispered.

The crowd of apprentices moved cautiously around it. On the back side, a corroded magnifying glass and the remains of a large quill were embedded deep in the wood, along with a handful of little white stones. No, not stones—teeth.

"A scriptomancy worktable," Mordraig said, then pointed to the protruding ribs. "And the scriptomancer it was assigned to."

Everyone grew silent.

Mordraig held up an iron box engraved with the same five symbols from Molly Blackcaster's statue, including the Divine Triangle. They all had to be scribing seals.

The steward gave the box a firm shake, and dust leaked out.

"This table is proof of what can happen if you finish a scribing without applying the contents of this box to the reverse side of the letter first."

He set the box on the ground and pulled out fistfuls of tiny gray satchels. Each apprentice was given one to string around their neck. Maeve opened hers to a thumbnail's worth of dust that smelled of winter's frost.

"It's crematory ash," Mordraig said.

Maeve choked and shut the satchel.

Other apprentices coughed.

"Ash from bodies?" Someone asked.

"Wouldn't that be something?" Mordraig chuckled. "No, no. It's made from rare white elm trees that have matured and died, then slightly decayed. The trees are native to Leyland. We've tried to grow them elsewhere, but they never do as well. We think it's why Molly chose to establish the College of Scriptomantic Arts here in Leyland. Once we locate downed trees, we gather the wood, then fire it in the old crematorium below the Hall of Routes. The process gives the ash a miraculous chemical composition."

"What does it do?" Nan asked.

Mordraig dipped his finger inside a satchel. "The ash repels arcane magic. If you're in a pinch, dusting a letter will instantly null most scribings." He held up the letter for Dear Miranda, then dusted some ash over the top. The sentence he'd penned in scribing pigment reappeared, along with the triangle.

Maeve hadn't known that was possible.

She brushed her hand over the letters tucked away at her hip. There might be something in the courier's scribing that could give her a clue to her *old friend*'s identity.

Mordraig lifted a satchel into a shaft of torchlight. "I won't give you another satchel until a month and a day from now, so don't lose it. The ash is used to coat the back of each letter *before* you scribe it. Unless you've been given permission, your scribings are only to be done on letters backed with a coat of crematory ash. To scribe on any other surface without it"—he knocked on a protruding rib—"can have ill effects. It's the result of the arcane magic sinking deeper without the ash barrier. You'll use it on everything you do except for the traveling scribing, and that's because the traveling scribing is not done on paper."

"What is it done on?" someone asked.

"Your wrist," Mordraig said with a grim twist to his mouth. "It's the *only* skin scribing we allow. If you try scribing anything else on your body, and it doesn't kill you, you'll get a swift kick out the front gate. Understand?"

Everyone nodded, and that was that.

Maeve's brows knit together. Her father would write on his arms on occasion. She watched him do it the night before the Written Doors burned, and a number of times before that. But if skin scribing was as dangerous as Mordraig made it out to be, her father must have been merely writing, not scribing. As it was, she wrote on herself all the time at the inksmithy when she couldn't find paper.

She nudged the thought away to focus on the lecture. After a lengthy speech on the importance of inkwells, Mordraig dismissed them. Before Nan could say a word to her, Maeve raced up the stairs and locked herself inside a lavatory, then took out the letter from her *old friend*, dusting it with crematory ash. A small sentence appeared below the text in dark blue pigment.

This letter will find its way to Maeve.

That was it? She grazed fingertips along the scribing seal in the shape of an eye—another symbol from Molly's cloak.

This sentence must be a tracking scribing, considering a traveling scribing was written on a courier's skin. A generic tracking scribing given that it didn't tell her anything new. She slipped the letter in her pocket then bent to grab her saddlebag.

The pale edge of an envelope stuck out from the flap.

Maeve hesitated only a moment before tugging it free. She ripped it open, and a crisp letter slipped out.

After what Mordraig had shown them, there was no way she would read a mysteriously placed letter without crematory ash. She pinched some between her fingers and unfolded the paper.

Four words were penned in a deep red ink that glimmered with an inner fire. She'd never seen the shade before.

I'm watching you, Maeve.

As she stared in horror, the inked words grew glossy. Wet. Ink beaded against the tail of the *g* and dripped down the paper, splashing against the floor. More ink dripped down, until a river bled from the words, obscuring them. Maeve dusted crematory ash, but the ink had already claimed the entirety of the page. It covered her fingers like a slick of blood.

It's just ink, she tried telling herself, sucking in ragged mouthfuls of air.

But it was so much more than ink; someone knew who she was. Her worst fear had come true, and on her second day here, no less.

She threw the letter into the sink and flipped the faucet on high.

M aeve peered through the dense fog outside the Scriptorium, half expecting to see a flash of eyes catching hers through the branches. Her bare fingers were stained red and trembling badly. She rubbed them together and tucked them beneath her cloak before a courier could stop to ask her what was wrong. What would she even say? *Someone left me a letter that bled all over me, and now I'm a shaking mess because of it.*

But why leave her the letter? If someone knew who she was, why not turn her in instead? It would be easier than *watching* her—whatever that meant.

If this had been any other situation, she would rush back to her room, pack her suitcase, and run. She wanted to run, to be honest, but she had already given away all her money and risked everything to come here. And the letter wasn't threatening to turn her in. She couldn't let it scare her away.

She was here to investigate, after all. Now she simply had a second mystery to solve. Somebody here knew her real name, and she had to determine who.

Maeve instantly thought of Steward Tallowmeade sneaking up on her during her trip to the Hall of Routes earlier that morning. He could have suspected who she was and made the effort to speak with her. He would have known her father, of course—but then so did every other steward and courier her father's age. Still, she should take extra precautions around him until she could rule him out as this mysterious watcher. She should be extra cautious around everyone.

When a large group of couriers filled the pathway, Maeve wanted to be anywhere but near them. She wandered down a narrow stone footpath that led into a heavily wooded section of the grounds, until she found herself surrounded by nothing but bare oak trees. Then she noticed that many of the tree trunks were covered in small carvings. Initials.

She had heard of this place from her father. Scriptomancers used to carve their initials into the hardened wood after performing their thousandth scribing.

Stepping off the path, she picked her way around trees, searching. Some carvings were as faint as lace against thick bark, others were carved deep and dripping with hardened sap. Then she noticed one set of initials in the foot of an oak tree that dripped with ink.

She knelt and ran her fingers over the initials J.O.A. Jonathan Owen Abenthy. Above the initials, the word "monster" was penned beside the words "world killer."

"I want to believe you're innocent, but it's still so hard," Maeve whispered.

Just yesterday, seeing his scribbled-out sepiagraph had felt as though something was eating away at her soul, and she still felt that desolation with every inhale.

How could she live here feeling like this? Would she even make it another week?

The feelings threatened to overwhelm her. This time, she shoved them down. If she planned to remain here, she would need to push past the persistent fear that had ruled her life and learn to fight.

She dug her fingernails beneath a corner of the black ink, picking it off, scraping until she was peeling bark from the tree like an animal. A new determination burst to life inside of her, filling that desperate hole that had been slowly widening from the moment she stepped foot on these grounds. If someone thought they might scare her with a letter, they were wrong.

When the wretched words were gone and only her father's initials remained, she took a step back, breathing hard. Feeling much better. She tried to find the footpath she had taken into the woods but must have gotten turned around, because she didn't see it anywhere.

"The impostor is still here, I see."

Maeve spun. Tristan sat sprawled along a large oak branch that jutted out waist-high over a patch of bracken, reading his soiled book. One of his feet was propped on the branch and only clad in a stocking.

"What happened to your shoe?"

He pointed to where it sat toe-down in mud ten paces away. "I was rash and kicked it off a little too eagerly," he said, never taking his eyes from the book. "You probably think I'm a catastrophe."

She absolutely did, but she sensed there was a reason for how he acted that bothered him deeply. "I don't believe in forming firm opinions of people I haven't spent much time with. You could have used the shoe to chase away a bear, for all I know."

The corners of his mouth lifted. "I threw the shoe because I was angered, and throwing a shoe into mud is far less painful than punching a tree." He flipped a page.

This had to be about what happened in the mess hall, and now he was wallowing. Maeve had wasted enough of her life doing the same and had little patience for it anymore. "It must be nice to have such a disregard for expensive things," she said.

"It was just a shoe."

Her eyebrows rose. Heavens, he could stand to be reminded of his privilege a little more often. "A shoe costly enough to pay for a month of my rent."

She expected a grimace. Instead, his mouth curved. "You're refreshing, you know?"

For goodness' sake.

She turned westward, where the Post's stone buildings stood out through the bare oak branches. She should leave Tristan and get back, but a niggling idea came to her.

"Is there a reason you're still standing there like a pigeon begging for a breadcrumb?" he asked.

Maeve took a deep inhale. "Someone told me the tracking office could help me find the sender of my letter."

He tore his eyes from the book and pushed his spectacles up his nose. "In Barrow?"

"Yes."

"I suppose it could be worth a visit."

Her fingers twisted together. "Is there any way you could speak to someone in the office for me—to see if it's even possible?"

He considered it. "It wouldn't do any good. They would need to inspect your letter or ask you questions at least. If memory serves, haven't you misplaced the letter somewhere?"

"I have," Maeve said instantly. "It's very much still misplaced."

He looked back down at his book, chewing at a smile. "You could just give it to me, you know. Even though I'm highly tempted, I promise you that I won't read it. I'll take it straight there."

She could never believe that. "I can't do that, but," she started, and swallowed, "I have another thought."

He shut his book and pivoted, facing her while still balancing his stocking foot on the branch. At least he was curious. "Does it involve soap?"

She sent him an exasperated look. "I know that it takes a traveling scribing to cross worlds. What if you taught me how to do one quickly? Then I could go to Barrow myself."

"No."

"You wouldn't have to show me any other scriptomancy, I swear it."

"*No.*"

"It could help get me out of your hair sooner."

"Very tempting, but it doesn't change my answer."

"But I thought your father wanted you to help me with scriptomancy?"

It was the wrong thing to say. All amusement leached from his features. "My father has misguided intentions. I'm not helping anyone with scriptomancy ever again. End of discussion."

Again.

Something terrible must have happened to make him this opposed to doing his job.

Was this the reason for the wallowing? If that look on his face in the mess hall was connected to his reluctance to teach her scribing, then it was cruel to press the matter.

"Forget I asked," she said, wishing she could take everything back. Not knowing what to say to make amends, she picked her way over to where his shoe lay in mud. It made a sucking sound as she tugged it free. She wiped the mud off with her cloak and placed it beside him on the branch, sensing his gaze on her the entire time.

She turned to leave.

"Wait," he said, staring intently at his freed shoe. "No, I'm not teaching you scriptomancy ever, so please get it out of your head. But I can show you something else today that I think you'll find helpful." He met her eyes. "So long as you don't mind me bending a few rules."

TRISTAN'S SPIRITS HAD vastly improved when they met up an hour later. He wouldn't tell her where they were going, merely led the way southeast through the damp woods, whistling a tune that Maeve recognized.

"'Sheep in the Fields of Brin,'" she said. Students at the College of Song in Inverly would busk for money in the summertime, belting out the quick-paced stanzas.

"You know how to sing it?"

"I don't know the words." She knew them by heart, but she would sound like a beached porpoise if she attempted such a thing.

Tristan started singing the lyrics. He had a pleasant voice, and she let herself get lost inside of it, then held her breath when he came to the verse she loved the most—about the shepherdess sleeping beside her sheep through a long winter. But his lyrics weren't the same as she remembered. In his version, the sheep ran themselves off a cliff.

"Those poor sheep don't die," Maeve said. "They spend the winter with their mistress, then lead her to her true love."

Tristan raised an eyebrow. "That's a bold statement from someone who doesn't know the words."

"Fine. You've caught me."

His mouth curved. "Then will you sing it?"

"Absolutely not." She grabbed a broken branch from the ground and tossed it at him. "I think you would be tempted to jab your ear with that if I attempted it."

"Surely you're not that bad."

He had no idea.

"I like listening to music only, so long as the music is *not* about suicidal sheep. I love listening, actually," she said, almost to herself. She turned to find Tristan stopped a few steps behind, watching her with his brow furrowed in a frown. "Is something the matter?"

"There's an old book in one of the libraries that the stewards believe was written by a very early scriptomancer. It says that partaking in other arts takes focus away from scribing. Aside from me, you'll be hard-pressed to find music at the Post. Nothing is official, but my father generally forbids it."

"But that's ridiculous. If anything, songs help you remember things."

He nodded. "I don't think I could live without music. It would feel like locking a part of my soul inside a box and tossing it into the ocean."

Maeve agreed with every word. "Don't you think that's a touch dramatic?"

"It's the truth." He continued past her and swatted a tree with the stick, then turned suddenly. "So? What do the Brin sheep help you remember?"

Only the spring sunlight on her face and taste of paint in the air and her great-aunt's fingers weaving through her unruly curls. "Nothing much."

"That's it," he said. "You've exceeded your caginess limit for the day. Now that I'm officially hiding you, I think I should know a little more about you."

"That's not part of our bargain, I—"

"Do your parents live in Leyland?" he asked pointedly.

She wanted to lock her lips together, but she knew from experience that if she didn't give any information, it would only make him more persistent in digging up the truth. "My parents are both dead."

"Siblings?"

"I'm an only child."

"Me too, if you're curious."

"I wasn't."

He laughed. "Very well. Then I won't tell you about what happened to my mother . . ."

He let his words dangle. He was insufferable! "All right. Out with it. What happened?"

"Absolutely nothing that makes for a good story," he said with a flicker of a smirk—teasing her. Maeve's mouth pinched, but before she could think of a witty retort, he said, "If you must know, my mother died."

Oh. "I'm so sorry."

"Don't be. It was long ago, and I've survived well enough. And if my mother were still alive today, she'd be married to my father, and I wouldn't wish that particular suffering upon anyone." He swatted another trunk with his stick.

"Your father does seem like a rather dogmatic sort," Maeve said, then bit her lip. She wanted to understand their relationship, and how easy it might be for Tristan to run to the Postmaster the next time she angered him.

"He can be."

"And you hate him?"

"Hate is a strong word. My father and I disagree on a few things. But frankly I'd rather talk about anything else. We could sing about sheep again, or talk of the weather, or how terribly these cloaks are cut, for that matter."

"Our courier cloaks?" Maeve ran her fingers over the thick material that covered her from shoulder to foot. "They're wonderful."

He halted, gaping.

"What? They're far more sensible than whatever it is you're wearing under there." She poked her finger at his chest.

"This *vest* is made from finely woven silk brocade. It has hand-hammered buttons."

"You say that like I'm supposed to be impressed."

"You're not?"

Was he serious? Oh dear; he was. If he expected the type of girl who fawned over cloth, he was in for a disappointment. "Fine. It's a handsome bluish vest with a nice spotty pattern and shiny round buttons. Are you happy now?"

For some odd reason, that made him grin at her with a disturbingly handsome smile.

Her gaze lingered on it, then she realized she was staring and flipped around, her cheeks blazing. "I think it's about time you told me where in god's name we're going."

They had to be near to the ocean by now or going in circles.

Tristan brushed past her, to where the Otherwhere Post's perimeter fence cut through the foliage. He led her along it, then stopped where two bars were bent wide enough for a person to squeeze through.

"It's a secret way out of the Post," Maeve said.

"Or in. I found this spot a couple of years ago and use it when I don't feel like mincing words with any of the Post's gate guards, which is more often than not these days." He pointed south through the foliage, where Maeve could make out Blackcaster Square. "We're going there."

Maeve turned to him. "You're taking me to Blackcaster Square?"

"I'm taking you inside the station."

Her pulse skittered. "Wouldn't it be easier to just tell me what it is you want to show me?"

"Am I to believe the criminal who lied her way inside the Otherwhere Post is nervous about going inside a little station?"

"I'm not." She was terrified of bursting into tears before she ever got that far.

But she wanted whatever information he had.

Tristan didn't give her a chance to consider anything. He slipped through the fence, and she was forced to follow. A moment later, they came to a steep embankment that led out of the trees, to the road along the north side of the square. Tristan took her hand and helped her down to the cobblestones, then wouldn't let go of her. He turned her hand over, inspecting her palm. "Left-handed," he said, running a finger up her calluses. "You don't use a proper left-handed quill, do you?"

"I left mine in Alewick, along with my chest of brocade vests and diamond-studded ballgowns." She jerked her hand away, ashamed of what it must feel like. "Let's just go."

He took her elbow as they wove through the protesters, then got behind another group of couriers heading into Blackcaster Square through the north side gate.

"Keep your cloak hood up, and don't look suspicious," he whispered. "Apprentices are only allowed to come here once they're crossing worlds, so I'd rather not get stopped."

Maeve felt an officer's eyes on her, and her pulse ratcheted. Tristan took her hand again and squeezed it, then pulled her briskly alongside him through the gate, until they stood in the line of couriers waiting to enter the station.

The sight of her feet planted inside the square shook her to her core. She caught the two chained turnstiles from the corner of her eye, but kept her gaze down for fear she wouldn't be able to go through with this.

When they reached the front of the line, she sucked in a breath, holding it as she stepped through the narrow employee entrance to a dim, gas-lit space. Inside. Memories slammed into her—a stranger's arm around her shoulders, the screaming. This very room had smelled of blood and paper smoke and the thick cologne that man had worn.

Tristan wove her around iron benches beside the old ticket counter. The station looked like any other train station, but instead of platforms along a train track, there was only a black stone wall that ran the entire length—a wall ancient scriptomancers erected centuries before Molly commissioned this station to be built around it. It marked the spot that worked best for scriptomantic travel.

Maeve's eyes wandered along the wall, stopping at the charred remains of the two Written Doors. Each was the size and shape of a large, peaked church door.

One for Barrow. One for Inverly.

The frames were made from hundreds of layers of paper filled with original text, all finished with thousands of individual scribings done by Molly Blackcaster herself. The doors were said to sing with magic, once. For nine hundred years, they were never closed, always propped open. You could see inside to Barrow and to the lushly painted streets of Inverly if you stood where Maeve was and simply looked.

Now, however, scaffolding surrounded one door. A group of government workers stood beside it in long coats and gloves. One worker held a vial, flaking off pieces of the charred frames with surgical tweezers. Tables were strewn with tools that looked straight from an archaeological dig: tiny brushes, magnifying glasses, canisters of sloshing liquids.

As soon as Barrow and Leyland were deemed free of the Aldervine, the House of Ministers ordered a team of scriptomancers to repair the Written Door between the two remaining worlds. They worked for weeks, until three of them were killed trying to recreate Molly's layered scribings. There was nobody alive with Molly's abilities, and the task was deemed too dangerous and abandoned. Leylish scientists now tried to understand the doors, but it seemed a fool's errand. Scientists weren't likely to understand anything made from centuries-old scriptomancy.

Tristan wove Maeve past a flurry of couriers emptying their saddlebags into bins labeled by neighborhoods in Gloam, then down a long hall where a plaque was lit by two burning torches, its corners chewed away by time.

The inscription read:

*If thou findeth thyself not in Leyland, Barrow, or Inverly, but in
another world, thou shalt surrender thyself to the Aldervine.
Scribe true and step swiftly, courageous one.*
—MOLLY MAEVE BLACKCASTER

Maeve stared at the middle name. It hadn't been fashionable to
name girls after Molly for years, but her father had insisted.

"That plaque was hung sometime during the two decades
that Molly spent scribing the Written Doors, when scriptomancers knew the extent of the Aldervine's corruption but were
still forced to use the traveling scribing to cross worlds," Tristan
said, then brought Maeve down the hall, to a room where couriers milled about beside more mail bins. They ducked behind one,
standing near the black stone wall. Tristan put a finger to his lips
and pointed.

A door materialized against the wall and flashed open. A courier glided into the room, cursing, his shoulders drenched from rain
as he clutched an overflowing sack of mail between wiry fingers.

"We empty letterboxes as we deliver and bring everything back
here to be sorted," Tristan whispered, nudging her arm. "Now
watch that woman over there."

The courier he pointed to stepped to the wall and adjusted her
saddlebag.

"All the letters in her saddlebag are scribed with tracking scribings. Each letter will physically tug her to its recipient, so long as
the courier is standing within a small radius of them. The traveling
scribing, on the other hand, is how she gets to that radius."

The courier poked the black stones with the sharp tip of her umbrella, then unbuttoned her sleeve, sliding it up. A dark scribble of ink shone against the inside of her wrist.

"To enact any scribing, you read it," Tristan whispered. "But when you use a traveling scribing, you must read it aloud, which makes the scribing trigger more powerfully. Otherwise, there's a chance you'll wind up somewhere that you don't want to go."

The courier said, "Alana Donall," in a clear voice.

The words written on her wrist.

A dark door materialized. The courier opened it and stepped through. The door disappeared as soon as it shut behind her.

Tristan's fingers moved to his wrist. He rolled his cuff to expose a lean forearm, then made a fist. Along the inside of his wrist were the handwritten words: *Tristan Byrne.*

His name.

He took her hand and turned it over, drawing his thumb along the inside of her own wrist, sending a current of nerves up her arm.

"Courier doors are specific to the person that creates them. It's made for you, and you alone. The traveling scribing requires you to write your full name in ink right here, then scribe after it with a sentence dictating exactly wherever it is you'd like to go." He spoke gently, meeting her eyes. "Then you step to that stone wall and read your full name aloud."

Which she could never do.

N an didn't return to their room after dinner. Blissfully alone, Maeve sorted the contents of her saddlebag into her desk, then stuffed the flyer for the Scriptomantic Exhibition in a back drawer so she wouldn't have the reminder of her father sitting out. Her fingers were too restless for sleep, and she found herself paging through her *Scriptomancer's Companion*, taking copious notes in her journal.

According to the text, the traveling scribing would only work with your full name, but there was no clarity on how loud you had to speak it.

If she got it to work, she could figure out a way to get inside the station when it wasn't busy, then whisper her name quietly. The scribing might take her to Barrow, but there were no guarantees.

Then there was the issue of performing a traveling scribing in the first place. It didn't sound too complicated, which likely meant it was near impossible. And she would also have to write her name—a name she hadn't spoken aloud in seven years.

Maeve put the book aside and crawled into bed, pretending to snore when Nan stumbled in and fell asleep fully clothed atop her coverlet. Fortunately, her roommate was still asleep when Maeve woke, and she was able to dress and make it outside without having to converse.

She stuffed a breakfast of dry biscuits from the mess hall into her pocket and found her way to Steward Tallowmeade's scribing pigment laboratory, arriving before anyone else.

The room smelled like the acidic solvents that clung to her fingers after a long day at the inksmithy. Scribing glasses sat in a heap against one wall. Hanging pots filled with milk thistle and winter violets dangled over glass beakers and burners. Dozens of small sepiagraphs were pinned to a cork wall below them.

Maeve wandered over to the pictures. Most were portraits of a much younger Tallowmeade in an upper school uniform she didn't recognize. One picture stopped her. It was taken beneath the same stone archway she'd walked under, with "College of Scriptomantic Arts" engraved across the top. Tallowmeade stood beside a younger version of her father—one that wasn't scribbled on.

Her *father*.

Her chest squeezed so tightly that she had to remind herself to breathe.

She hadn't seen her father's face in seven years, and there he was, with Tallowmeade on his left and . . . Tristan on his right. How?

Maeve leaned closer. It wasn't Tristan; his features were sharper, and he didn't wear spectacles. It was Postmaster Byrne. A few women she didn't recognize stood with them. Everyone had their arms tangled around one another. Tallowmeade carried a jug, her father a picnic basket. Postmaster Byrne was *smiling*.

"We all apprenticed together," Steward Tallowmeade said from a few paces behind her. Maeve shrank away as he came forward and wiped dust from the sepiagraph. "Well, not all were apprentices. Byrne was one year older. He was Abenthy's mentor."

Maeve took another step back. She didn't want Tallowmeade to read the shock on her face. "The Postmaster mentored Jonathan?" she asked, gritting her teeth at the sound of her father's name on her tongue.

"Yes. But after that year, we all grew apart." He gestured to the seats, which were now mostly full. "Would you like to sit, Apprentice Hill, or teach the lecture yourself?"

Maeve barely managed to walk to her desk and sit. She leaned heavily on her elbows, her mind spinning.

Postmaster Onrich Byrne had mentored her father. According to that memory scribing, he was the last to leave Inverly. Then afterward, he lit the flame that burned down the Written Doors before the Aldervine could get through. Onrich Byrne became a hero on the same day her father became a monster.

If anyone had something to gain by framing her father, it was him. He was promoted to Postmaster as soon as the Post was founded, right in the wake of Inverly. The position would have given him enough power to sweep evidence under a rug. To plant new evidence in its place. As her father's mentor, he probably knew her father well and had access to his room, his things.

Then was it the Postmaster who slipped that letter into her bag? Maeve thought back to that moment with Tristan in Postmaster Byrne's office. He didn't seem to recognize her, but then someone with the skill to pull off a crime as massive as Inverly probably excelled at keeping their composure.

Maeve didn't dare take out her journal in the middle of a class, but she made a mental note to write Onrich Byrne directly on the top of a list of suspects.

She jolted as Nan dropped into the seat beside hers.

Her roommate massaged her temples. "Remind me to never

stay at the Groggery for more than an hour," she said. Nan's tongue darted out, swiping at her upper lip. The scent of stale wine lingered on her breath. "Someone bought a bottle of wine to wash down a stale fruitcake from the mess hall. Its disgusting gelatin decorations are still stuck to my teeth." She dug at a canine then winced and grabbed her side. "And I think I pulled a muscle from laughing at Shea's stories."

Maeve felt an absurd twinge of longing. It had to be nice to eat cake and laugh without wanting to crawl beneath the nearest table. "I'm devastated I missed it," she said dryly.

"Just wait. You'll be begging me to go soon enough."

Maeve sighed. "I absolutely will not."

"You remind me of my father, you know?" Nan leaned against her desk and looked Maeve up and down, her mouth quirking. "You two are the only people in the worlds who won't cave to my whims."

"I think I may like this father of yours."

"You would hate him."

A bright shaft of light hit their eyes.

"Oh, for god's sake," Nan grumbled, squinting.

Tallowmeade finished drawing the curtains. "Good morning, and welcome to my scribing pigment laboratory."

Maeve tried her best to tune out Nan's grumbling as Tallowmeade waved a beaker of silver liquid. She might not have come here intending to actually learn scriptomancy, but if she was going to find her footing and uncover who wrote her that letter, she'd have to pay attention to the lessons.

"This is a pre-mixed scribing pigment base. In this room, you'll learn how to mix it, then add various ingredients tailored to whatever scribing you hope to accomplish. The right scribing pigment

works like a magnet for magic, making Arcane Infusion easier."
Tallowmeade held up a large book embossed with bundles of herbs.
"The *Pigment Almanac*. You'll find a copy in your worktables. This
book is divided into hundreds of recipes for each of the five types
of scribings. You'll all use the recipes for your entire career unless
you're one of those rare individuals who wishes to modify your
own recipes."

"Like Molly Blackcaster?" someone in the front row asked.

"No, not like Molly Blackcaster." Amusement flickered in the
steward's eyes. "Molly wrote half of the recipes in this almanac
herself during the year she served as an apprentice. You might
write a handful if you're lucky. I wrote six myself. But your Postmaster bested me. Old Byrne created a total of eighteen. All for-
mulated for form scribings—Onrich's specialty."

Form scribings.

Maeve pictured the rivulets of ink dripping like blood from that
letter. She hadn't read much about form scribings in her *Scriptomancer's Companion* yet, but the bleeding words did constitute a
change of form.

Tallowmeade moved between rows of desks, lecturing about
various herbs used in pigments. Maeve wrote everything down to
have something to do with her hands, but her eyes kept darting
to that sepiagraph of the Postmaster. The slow rumble of a storm
sounded outside the windows. She wrapped her chilled arms
across her body, unable to escape the sense that she'd stumbled
into dangerous territory.

A bell rang out. Apprentices shot up.

Tallowmeade raised his large hands, halting everyone. "If you
want, you can find your worktable in the Scriptorium this evening
and try some of the basic scribings in your guidebooks. I doubt

any of you will get them to work, but if one of you turns out to be adept, find Steward Mordraig and let him know immediately."

Maeve had never heard the term. Everyone appeared equally confused.

"Mordraig didn't explain what it means to be adept?" Tallowmeade asked, then sighed when nobody answered. "'Adept' is the term we use to describe a scriptomancer who can produce Arcane Infusion on their first couple of attempts without practice. We get a small handful with each apprentice class, but they tend to be uncovered during our writing tests."

She couldn't believe what she was hearing. There were people walking around Leyland now with the ability to scribe on their first try? What was the point of the apprenticeship? The House of Ministers was desperate to deliver letters, and people were even more desperate to get to their families. Why would they hide this knowledge? You would think they would simply have everyone in Leyland attempt a scribing and recruit all those who could. Or at least tell people. People deserved to know about this.

Others seemed to be wondering the same thing because someone asked, "Why go through all the trouble to set up this school if anyone might be adept?"

"I've misspoken. *Anyone* isn't," Tallowmeade said.

There were confused murmurs, but Tallowmeade put up his hands, shushing everyone.

"The ability only comes to those with an advanced understanding of language honed from years upon years in a writing program, along with an adept in their direct lineage. Some believe the abilities began when the scriptomancers of Molly's day practiced skin scribings that changed their physiology, then passed those changes down to their children, but there's nothing concrete written about it. And adepts only seem to ever perform one type of scribing instantly, which doesn't help with deliveries. The other four types will take them as much time to learn as the rest of you."

As the apprentices began whispering excitedly about what-ifs, Maeve's chest tightened with anger. But it shouldn't surprise her that wealth and breeding were requirements for this quicker way to scribing—to reuniting with missing family. Privilege seemed to be the only way to get anywhere these days. Unless you falsified your name and risked your life.

If one of the protesters got wind of this, it would be all anyone talked about.

Maeve waited for someone to bring up that point, but no one did. They were too busy asking Tallowmeade questions that only concerned themselves and their odds of being adept.

Tallowmeade answered a few, then splayed his spindly fingers against an empty table. "Also know this: an instant ability to perform advanced scriptomancy doesn't mean you should. It's the same as letting a toddler play with poisons. You can get yourself killed. And there are only so many of us with the desire to babysit."

Maeve glanced down at her hands and wondered if her father had been adept. He'd been skilled, she knew—she'd often heard him refer to scriptomancy as his "gift." What if he was adept at the traveling scribing? If he was and she'd inherited the ability to do it instantly, she could try whispering her name at the black stone wall, then sneak into Barrow and speak with someone in the tracking office this evening. Maybe find her *old friend* first thing in the morning and get answers. Then she could take those answers straight to the Leyland Constabulary, to the House of Ministers.

Tallowmeade dismissed the class, but Maeve didn't bother with the Scriptorium.

She ran to the ink fountain and scooped a thimbleful of lamp-black and made her way to a stone bench tucked behind a building. A pair of crows shook loose from a nearby tree, beating black wings against the faded morning mist. The cool air kissed her skin as she tugged off her glove and slipped her sleeve above her elbow, exposing the swath of pale skin on the inside of her wrist. Her quill trembled in her fingers.

Maeve Abenthy.

It was all she had to write, but it felt as if a blade dug against her knuckles, threatening to carve her flesh if she attempted it.

Headmistress Castlemaine's shrill voice came to her. She tried to shut out the woman's words, but they only grew louder. *Don't ever give anyone your name. Someone will lock you away. They'll hunt you and string you up because of him. They'll hurt you.*

It turned out to be true.

Six months after Maeve had arrived at the orphanage, she made a mistake. She whispered her name to another girl called Margery, her best friend. Margery took it upon herself to give Maeve's name to someone else, and that girl told someone else. On it went. Within hours, Maeve's secret had spread throughout the halls of the Sacrifct Orphanage like a bead of ink falling into water.

The three weeks that followed were a living nightmare. Several girls were orphaned because of the Aldervine, and everyone knew her father's name. They spit at her. They crushed milk bottles and scattered the larger pieces of glass beneath her pillow, saving the smaller ones for her only pair of shoes. They twined dead lengths of ivy though her bedpost to look like the vine and poured garden dirt inside her dresser drawers. They slashed her underwear—slowly. One or two cuts each day, until Maeve thought she was losing her mind. Until she snapped and ran to Margery's room and clawed it apart, screaming at the top of her lungs.

Headmistress Castlemaine had pulled her away by her scalp, but not to her attic room. The woman dragged her to the dilapidated barn behind the building and locked her inside. There were three old horses there that slammed their hooves and screamed into the freezing night. Rain swept through the gaps in the rotten boards, dripping onto her shoulders, but nobody came to unlock the door that night, nor the next day. Maeve shivered there, starving for three whole days, her knees tucked against her chin. She couldn't remember who finally unlocked the barn, but the moment a sliver of daylight hit her eyes, she ran outside, then away from the orphanage for good.

She spent a day wandering the freezing streets of Gloam before she slipped inside a warm hall in the university's College of Book-keeping and curled up and fell fast asleep. An elderly professor woke her the next morning. Maeve was only twelve, but she told the professor she had nowhere to go and begged the woman for a job. When the woman asked her name, Maeve didn't hesitate to give a false one.

That night, seated in a new room in the quiet attic of a university office building, Maeve vowed to herself that she would never speak her name to anyone again. Never think it. Never write it down.

She dipped her quill then pressed the tip to the inside of her wrist.

Write your name. If you're adept at the traveling scribing, you can leave for Barrow right now.

It was only two little words, but her fingers juddered and turned to ice. The nib scratched her skin, drawing blood. The letter M came out looking like a misshapen N. The tip snapped in a splatter of ink.

She couldn't do it.

She abandoned the broken quill to the damp ground.

MAEVE SPENT THE evening seated on rocks overlooking the ocean, writing in her journal about the happier times—with her aunt in Inverly at first. Then she decided it might do good to write about her father, so she allowed herself for once, jotting down little memories like how horrible he was at cooking anything besides fried eggs, but she would always ask for seconds of whatever he made. More good memories of her father flowed from her nib—things she never allowed herself to dwell on. Eventually, stars pricked the sky, and her breathing evened out.

Her fingers were stiff as boards by the time she returned to her room. Nan was gone again, of course. This time, she'd left a note on Maeve's desk explaining how she was heading to Old Town with the other apprentices. That Eilidh should join them to "uncork a bottle and powder a bit of her hair."

Maeve crumpled the note and tossed it into the wastebin.

Her braid was tangled from the salty wind, but she could ignore it until tomorrow. Stripping off her skirt and blouse, she changed into her nightgown and pulled out the letter from her *old friend*, her fingers stretching the wrinkled page. If she wasn't brave enough to write her own name, then she would simply find another path to answers. Maybe the tracking office in Barrow wouldn't be of any help anyhow.

She put her letter away and crawled into bed, vowing to come up with a new plan the next morning. But when she tried to close her eyes, sleep evaded her. Then a chorus of piano music drifted to her ears from somewhere outside her room. Strange that someone would play music after Tristan told her it was forbidden.

Maeve stuffed her pillow over her head and tossed. Maybe the

Postmaster was right. It should be a high crime to play piano so late when everyone should be sleeping. But when the music didn't let up, she lit a chamber-stick, hissing when a flame caught her fingertip. Cold seeped into the soles of her feet as she padded down the darkened hall, the music growing louder. It poured from a room at the very end, the door cracked.

Maeve nudged it open, then froze.

Tristan sat at an upright piano. Candlelight guttered from a number of lit taper candles along the piano top, while his fingers moved deftly across the keys.

Her feet rooted themselves as the music built, turning haunting. Moonlight poured in from the window, seeming to dance along with the melody.

It gave the same feeling as his whistled song in the woods, but the piano music added a new dimension. Maeve could almost imagine she was back in Inverly.

But Tristan's music felt different than the songs she remembered from her childhood. His notes grew melancholy, slowing, until a single, hollow note rang out that seemed to catch in her throat. She brought her hand to her face and was surprised to find tears on her cheeks.

"I hope that was an improvement over suicidal sheep," Tristan said without turning around.

"A vast improvement," Maeve shot back, swallowing. "You told me your father doesn't allow music here."

"He doesn't."

He lifted a wine bottle beside his foot and took a long swig, then turned to her, his mouth stained a deep red. His usual vest was gone, and his buttoned undershirt hung open to his collarbone, where a crematory ash satchel rested in the dip of his throat.

In the dim room, Maeve couldn't see Tristan's eyes behind his spectacles, but she felt them like fingers dragging from the top of her head down her nightgown until they brushed against her feet. His throat bobbed.

It startled her out of her stupor. "Has anyone ever told you that it's wildly improper to stare at a woman's bare feet?"

He swung his legs over the bench to face her fully, elbows resting against his knees. "Not that I'm complaining, but I believe that you're the one standing in my bedchamber, in your nightclothes no less."

That she was.

She backed away, prepared to bolt.

"Don't go yet," he said. He stood and dug through a chest beside the piano, pulling out more men's silk scarves than she'd seen in her life, tossing them to the floor like rags. He came toward her holding a long box. "I have something for you."

She eyed it warily. "I don't need anything."

He gave her an admonishing look. "Yes, you do. Besides, I owe you a great deal for warning me earlier about the glass of milk that narrowly missed my head. Here."

He opened the box and pulled out a swan's molted right-wing feather. A left-handed quill. A drip of pure silver ran down one edge of the creamy fletching, ending in a teardrop shape with a red ruby encased in its center.

It was beautiful and must have cost a small fortune.

Maeve blinked at it, both horrified and deeply touched that he wanted to give it to her. It took a long moment to rein in her emotions. And when she spoke, her voice was rougher than she would have liked. "There's no way I can accept that."

"Why? It's bad manners to refuse a gift."

"A gift would have been a turkey quill. That, sir, is the equivalent of a dowry where I come from."

"Well, where I come from, it's the equivalent of one of my used shoes. I bought it on a whim last month, and now it collects dust in the bottom of my trunk. I think we can both agree that's a terrible fate for such a feather."

He spun it between his fingers.

It really was the loveliest she had ever seen—ever heard of. The silver edge caught moonlight as he placed it back inside the box then shut the lid. Before she could protest, he pushed the box into her hand. She flinched and almost gave it back, but hesitated. It would sell for more coins than the purse she had given away to Eilidh Hill. Enough coins to escape Gloam if it came down to it.

As long as she never carved it.

"Thank you," Maeve said, but Tristan wasn't looking at the box.

His brow creased, and his hand slid to her wrist. He ran a finger over the rough scab with the misshapen M. "What's this?"

"It's nothing." She ripped her hand away. Thank goodness the M was botched enough to be unreadable.

"This scab is from an inked nib." His eyes flicked to hers, his mouth drawing flat. "I've never seen anyone accidentally stab themselves while attempting the traveling scribing. It's impressive."

"I wasn't attempting anything."

"Your wrist says otherwise."

This conversation was over.

"Thank you for the quill," she said, taking a few steps down the hall.

"Wait just a moment," he called out.

Maeve spun to find him leaning a shoulder against his door-frame. He ruffled his hair. "I'm going to play piano for another hour at least."

"Good for you?"

"No one here appreciates music." He fiddled with a silver button on his cuff. "You could stay for a while if you want. Listen while I play."

The offer was more than tempting. She could listen to his sad piano songs for hours. And wanted to. But then he stepped aside to let her back inside his room, and she froze at the implication. She had never dared spend any time in someone else's bedchamber, let alone a boy's, but she considered it for a blistering moment.

Except there was nowhere to sit. He had a settee against one wall, but it was stacked with unopened packages. And she certainly would never dare to sprawl out on his bed.

Although—Maeve didn't see a bed in the room. Only the settee beside his piano. She didn't understand it, but it seemed that Tristan Byrne had a bedchamber with no bed.

A bedchamber that she had no business setting foot in ever again.

"So do you want to stay?" he asked, crossing his arms. "It's not a difficult decision to make."

It wasn't. Luckily, she came to her senses and fled, stammering out an excuse about an early lecture as she went.

Tristan called for her, but she was already skidding inside her room, slamming the door before she could draw a breath. She fell against it, clutching the box with the swan feather to her chest while trying to understand what in the worlds she was feeling, and why on *earth* she had almost said yes.

"An advanced scribing is defined as one that cannot be recreated easily by another scriptomancer," Mordraig said as he walked across the stage of a lecture hall the following afternoon. "The Written Doors, for instance, are very advanced, considering nobody has a clue how they work. But that's an extreme example. Most advanced scribings simply use more advanced sentence structures and word usage."

"Does he have to speak so loudly?" Nan whispered into Maeve's ear, looking worse than she had the day before.

"He is the one standing up there, attempting to lecture," Maeve whispered back.

Nan grumbled and put her face in her palms. She'd made sure to sit beside Maeve yet again, determined to use every opportunity to woo her into some mythical friendship. But Maeve didn't need Nan, and she *certainly* didn't need Tristan.

Shame spilled through her as she thought of how ridiculous she must have looked while standing in his bedroom in her nightgown. But the most dangerous part was how he'd noticed the scab on her wrist. She touched it, hopelessly bothered that she couldn't write her name, and that Tristan had recognized her poor attempt instantly. She would have to be more careful if she attempted it again. More secretive.

Maeve jolted as Mordraig clapped his hands. "In the coming days, I would like you all to find the Scriptorium and start on a particular sense scribing that we call the coffee scribing. We've placed a practice stack of the original text on each of your work-tables. Once you get it to work, reading the text will have the same effect as a few cups of coffee. You'll have to redo the scribing each morning, since the arcane magic in any scribing diminishes after each use. But a word of warning: never read a coffee scribing later than noon. Nobody wants to hear you singing at the top of your lungs in the middle of the night."

He excused them all.

Nan tried to drag Maeve to dinner in the mess hall, but Maeve made a quick excuse and headed to the Scriptorium. She wasn't ready to try the traveling scribing again, but maybe if she could get another type of scribing to work, it could help her hunt down her *old friend*. At least it would tell her if she were adept, and she couldn't help but be curious.

Most couriers had already left for the night. It was dark as Maeve climbed to where her assigned worktable sat in a corner of the sixth floor. She dragged her fingers across the rough-hewn wood already stocked with supplies, including a pile of practice sheets with the same handwritten paragraph for what had to be the coffee scribing.

She scanned a note on the top of the stack from Mordraig. He explained that she was to use the pre-mixed scribing pigment in her top drawer, then scribe a sentence after the passage, com-manding the reader to wake up. That the paragraph was an ex-cerpt from an epic poem about a scriptomancer who wrote a skin scribing on his eyelids that left him unable to slumber for a year. He said this particular passage was used for the coffee scribing because of the Law of Intentions.

Scribing only amplifies the intention of the original text. You cannot command a love letter to make a reader feel hate. You can always try, but Arcane Infusion simply won't happen. Good luck and DON'T FORGET CREMATORY ASH!

There were no left-handed quills. The box with the swan quill sat in Maeve's saddlebag, but she didn't dare to waste it. Instead, she found a right-handed crow quill already sharpened.

Smoothing a layer of crematory ash on the back of the paper with the coffee scribing text, Maeve turned the page over and scratched a command along the bottom, then did the same to three more practice sheets, using variations of the sentence. She checked *The Scriptomancer's Companion*, then sealed each scribing with the circle used on sense scribings.

She waited. Her sentences looked perfect, but despite her best efforts, none of them disappeared into the paper.

Not adept at sense scribings, it seemed. That left four more types.

Maeve paged to the section on memory scribings. Done correctly, they showed the specific memory that was written about in the original text, but how the memory manifested depended on the skill of the scriptomancer. A simple memory scribing could plant an image, while an advanced memory scribing could do more, like show her the Aldervine as if she were living it.

Maeve flipped though her journal and ripped out a page—one where she'd waxed on about the Alewick cliffs. She dipped her quill and wrote a sentence at the bottom, then sealed it with the spiral used on all memory scribings.

Nothing happened.

She did it to three more pages, and still nothing. She opened the bottom drawer to discard the failed scribings and tensed.

An envelope rested beneath her worktable.

The sixth floor looked empty at first glance. A few gas lamps threw yellow light against the dark, cavernous corners, but many of the surrounding worktables were still bathed in shadows.

"Hello?" Maeve called out, but nobody answered.

She was only being paranoid. Anyone could have looked up her assigned table and left her the letter ages ago. It could be completely innocent. But she had a feeling it was from the same person as the bleeding letter.

I'm watching you.

A shiver raced through her. She held the envelope to the gas lamp on her worktable, letting the light seep into it. But the paper was too thick to read anything inside. She debated ripping it to shreds, but if there was a new message, it might be best to at least know what it said—so long as she was careful about it.

Maeve pinched a scoop of ash, then ripped the envelope and peeled the letter open to a paragraph of deep red writing that began with:

It rises from darkness . . .

That was as far as Maeve got before the paper grew too heavy to hold. It clattered to her worktable like a stone, face down.

Something moved beneath it. The back of the page rippled, then bulged into a large blister that grew. Red ink bled through, until the paper disintegrated, leaving a ball of writhing ink.

Maeve lurched backward and tossed her ash, but the ink *slid* out of the way, then over the side of her desk. Once on the floor, it rose on clawed fingers that began scrabbling their way toward her.

Her ash satchel sat on the desk, but the creature was in the way—too close. Not knowing what to do, she ran for the stairwell. The scrabbling sounds followed her down two flights, until she spotted a lit lamp in the corner of a deserted floor. A man hunched over a pile of letters.

She raced toward him, the scribing still chasing her.

"Please help me," she said, climbing onto his cluttered worktable.

Papers flew to the floor, glass rolled and broke as she crouched, looking around her, breathing hard.

Where was it? It had to be somewhere close. Maeve listened for the sounds of its claws against the wood but heard nothing. Then she spotted a small puddle of dark red ink three tables over. Unmoving. Its arcane magic must have run out.

A throat cleared.

She turned to stare across at Tristan seated behind the worktable. *His* worktable. And she crouched on it like a rabbit in a snare.

A new splash of ink soiled his vest. Her doing? His mouth twitched terribly, of course. She had to look ridiculous. Carefully, she slipped her shaking legs down, leaning against the desk.

"Now tell me," Tristan said. "Shall I call my father to berate you or a Leylish clinician to have a look at your head?"

"There was a mouse," she said without hesitating.

His eyes narrowed. "A mouse, you say?"

"A large mouse." She drew two fingers to her mouth. "With big yellow teeth."

"A large, yellow-toothed mouse," he repeated seriously, then chewed away a rather unserious smile. "And this creature chased you down from the upper floors?"

"It was fast. Probably rabid."

"Did it throw anything at you as well? A bar of soap perhaps?"

"You're poking fun."

"It's not very difficult when it comes to you."

She wanted to march him to the red puddle and splash it at him, then explain everything. But he would demand to know why she was suddenly receiving letters that tried to hurt her. He would question everything.

She rubbed her temples. That red letter must have been a form of scribing—the Postmaster's specialty. She'd read more about them since she'd received that first letter, but Tristan would know even more than her.

"How dangerous can a form scribing get? Could it hurt someone fatally?" she asked.

That got his attention. "Did something hurt you?"

"No, not me." *Not yet.*

He considered her. "A few years ago, a courier was dared to read a centuries-old form scribing taken from one of our libraries. The arcane magic had diminished over the years, but the scribing still managed to kill her."

"How?"

"Form scribings transmute the ink of the original text into whatever the scribing commands, no matter how dangerous. The ink in that particular letter transmuted into worms that crawled inside her through her nail beds, then chewed their way out through her eyes before dissolving into rivulets of ink down her cheeks."

Maeve grimaced. "Sounds like a fun way to go."

"I'm sure it was. And that's just one example. There are more gruesome stories out there. A form scribing can be as dangerous as a scriptomancer wishes it to be. That's why it's high treason to scribe anything but the mildest of them."

She nodded, feeling suddenly ill.

"Is that anonymous letter of yours form-scribed?" he asked.

"No," she said quickly. "This isn't about my letter." Not that letter, anyhow. It was about the claws on that creature that had sliced her worktable. It would have sliced her skin to ribbons if she hadn't run. Now that red puddle still stared at her.

A form scribing meant to hurt her. Maybe kill her.

I'm watching you.

Her watcher apparently didn't like whatever she was doing. Except she had done nothing but wander aimlessly! She hadn't spoken with her *old friend* or uncovered anything useful. Unless she counted growing weepy at every memory of her father. She didn't want to imagine what might happen if she started finding real answers.

Her stomach lurched at the thought. She braced herself on the worktable, cursing as a pigment soaked into her sleeve. "I've ruined everything, haven't I?"

Her voice shook, along with her hands.

"It's only a little mess. Let me help you." He placed his palm against her waist and guided her into a nearby chair.

The touch was only meant to help, but it sent a ripple of heat down her sides. She knew she should probably stay put, but she tried to stand and wobbled.

He nudged her firmly back down. "Try to stand again in the next few minutes, and I'll be forced to strap you to the chair." He unbuttoned his vest.

"What are you doing?"

"Cleaning."

"You know how to clean?" She didn't think he had it in him.

He threw her a halfhearted glare, then rolled his shirtsleeves and went to work dabbing spilled ink, wiping everything. When the table was clean, he pulled up a chair and took out a stack of handwritten letters from a drawer.

"Deliveries?" Maeve asked.

He glanced at her from the corner of his eye. "God, no. They're poems that I plan to form scribe so the ink manifests as a horde of evil mice."

She scowled at the side of his head, which caused him to laugh. He uncapped some pigment, pouring it into a fresh inkwell, mixing other ingredients. Then he dipped a quill and began writing.

At first Maeve watched him to take her mind off that puddle of red ink, but after a little while, she couldn't look away.

She'd thought he was a talented pianist, but he wrote as if his fingers were made for that singular purpose. He barely glanced at the words. They flowed out of him in a river as he penned fourteen detailed tracking scribings, finishing them all with the eye seal in less than ten minutes.

Her father was never that fast.

"I hope this doesn't go to your head, but you're good at that," she said.

Tristan's mouth curved a little. Only a little, though. He stuffed the scribed letters inside their envelopes and started on another stack.

His scribing was stunning. Impossible to look away from. After another few minutes, he glanced her way, and she realized she was staring open-mouthed. Her neck heated, and she tore her eyes away then scanned the area around them.

Tristan's worktable was in a corner beside a few overfilled

bookcases, ratty chairs, and a large mop bucket. There were other worktables on the floor, but none close by. "You're all by yourself over here."

He dipped his quill. "The steward who assigns worktables moved me here. I think they were sick of taking requests from people who wanted to be moved away from me."

He made it sound like it was normal to be so hated.

"Why is everyone like that around you?"

"I've already told you. Jealousy over my wardrobe," he said without looking away from his work.

He was obviously still hiding something, and she wanted to get to the bottom of it.

She waited a beat, then asked, "Does it have something to do with your last apprentice?" He'd alluded to it that first night in his father's office, then again in the woods when she'd rescued his shoe from the mud.

Tristan's hand stilled, silver pigment pooling beneath his nib. "Last year, my apprentice got herself in trouble and the whole situation angered a number of people. So yes, you could say it has something to do with her."

So the glass of milk dumped on his chair was indeed because of his last apprentice. Maeve waited for him to explain what it had to do with scriptomancy—something he was clearly gifted at. To give any hint at why the bruises beneath his eyes seemed darker every time they spoke, his expensive clothing more disheveled. But Tristan remained tight-lipped, racing through his scribing like Molly Blackcaster's ghost had commandeered his hand.

Maeve had her own secrets to run from, but apparently so did he.

O n her way out the door the following morning, Maeve found another letter addressed to her. This one, however, didn't turn into a disembodied hand. It was ink-smudged, with a line across the envelope that made her grin.

In case of rabid mouse: open immediately

She scanned the letter inside.

Apologies for my silence last night. It's difficult to think about last year, and speaking about it aloud is something I'm still learning how to do. After you left, I did some digging and made a discovery. There are a few rooms of old postage sale records inside the Second Library, left over from the years right after the Post was founded. The names of both the sender and the receiver were required to purchase postage back then. Interesting, right? I thought so, too. If you've read this far, I'm guessing you're plotting your search already. The only hiccup is you're not allowed inside the libraries until you've earned your courier key, but I could always help dig things up for you. If you would let me.

Maeve read the letter over twice, more curious than ever about what happened to Tristan last year.

She ran a finger over the bottom few sentences. She didn't have a courier key—whatever that was—and she certainly wasn't about to give Tristan her name in order to do the search for her. Still, it was something to go on.

Bone-chilling sleet trickled down as Maeve rushed outside. She held her hood tight around her ears and ran at a sprint to the small, single-story building southeast of the Scriptorium. A crumbling sign over a stone lintel read: THE SECOND LIBRARY. ENTER WITH PATIENCE AND TIME.

She had neither at the moment.

A glass-paneled door opened to a narrow reception room lined in richly carved wood. Maeve breathed in, tasting decaying paper and leather. A long front desk sat opposite a glass display filled with library information that needed a good dusting.

The pinned postings inside were faded and disorganized. Maeve searched and spotted a sheet listing all the various scriptomantic libraries on the Post's grounds and the years they were established. The newest library was over three hundred years old. There was no First Library, but there was a Third Library, a Library of Scribed Books, the Library of Teeth, and the Library of Forgotten Things, among a handful of others with equally enigmatic names. A map beside the list showed the Second Library's twenty-three floors descending below her, deep underground, connected by a spiraling stairwell with corridors and rooms spiderwebbing from it. Some rooms were labeled on the map, but with nothing concerning postage records.

Her heart sank. Even with a courier's key, it could take a month or more to search every corner.

Past the glass case was the entrance door to the library, set with a glass window. Behind it, shelves disappeared into darkness.

Maeve tried the handle, but it was locked. A small sign above the knob read: COURIER KEY REQUIRED FOR ENTRANCE.

A throat cleared.

She spun on her heel to face a tall, frail-looking woman standing at the front desk. Her delicately veined hands smoothed the front of a long gray apron. She stared at the curve of the woman's oval face, how the tops of her small ears stuck through her hair.

She had seen this woman before, in Tallowmeade's picture, standing near her father beneath the archway of the College of Scriptomantic Arts. She looked far older now, with strands of gray woven throughout her wispy brown hair and crow's feet wrinkling the light brown skin around her eyes. A nameplate on the desk read: MISS SIBILLA CREEL, HEAD ARCHIVIST.

Sibilla tilted her head to one side in a motion that reminded Maeve of a bird. "Can I help you?"

"I need to check a postage record, and I forgot my key." Maeve forced herself to smile. "Would you mind letting me inside this one time?"

"Of course," Sibilla said. She walked around the front desk and took out a ledger. "Your name."

Right. Maeve swallowed. She could give someone else's name. But she barely knew any other women besides Nan and Shea, and couldn't have anything get back to either of them. "I'm Eilidh Hill."

Sibilla flipped though pages for a full minute. "I don't see your name listed in here. Are you sure you have a courier key?"

"How does one come by a key again?"

"I believe that apprentices are awarded theirs when they complete their first scribing."

Maeve hadn't heard that yet, though nobody in her class had come close to completing anything.

"Well, I just completed my first scribing yesterday," Maeve said with as much confidence as she could muster. "They must not have recorded my name yet."

Sibilla's forehead wrinkled. "I'm not allowed to let anyone inside that isn't listed in this ledger. Even if you had a key, I would still confiscate it. And so would all the archivists you would find though those doors." She pulled out a yellow pad and tore off the top sheet, handing it to Maeve. "That's a request slip. You can fill out the top part, and I can find the materials for you. Then they'll be waiting for you when you receive your key."

Maeve muttered a thanks, pocketing the useless request slip. She left swiftly and walked the perimeter, searching for another way in, but the building was solid stone.

⌒⌇⌒

AFTER LECTURES THE following afternoon, Maeve stole a few slices of soda bread from the mess hall and headed to her worktable in the Scriptorium. If she needed to scribe to get a courier key, she could at least give it another try.

It didn't take long for her to discover that she was not adept at form scribing or tracking scribing. Since she wasn't eager to attempt a traveling scribing again, her only option was to learn scriptomancy the hard way. But within a few hours, she had broken three perfectly fine quills and given herself a fresh set of blisters, then called it a night before the sun had a chance to set.

The next day went much the same, as did the next and the next, until a week drifted by. With each passing day, Maeve felt as if she were splitting in two. During lectures, she was that scared girl from the Sacrifict Orphanage, forced to spin her fear into a tight knot and lock it away deep within herself. While at night, hunched over her worktable, she was a woman possessed.

She worked until her fingers were callused and ringed with blisters, until her clothes stunk of parchment and crematory ash, until the words themselves bled together and began to lose all meaning.

Maeve was spiraling, and the days were passing by far too quickly. But if scribing was her only path forward, she couldn't allow herself to pause—couldn't breathe.

She stayed in the Scriptorium one night until she was the last person left. Her muscles felt like taut strings, and she decided to take an unfamiliar path back to Hawthorne House to stretch her legs and suck in some crisp autumn air before she went out of her mind. But in the dark of night, the paths twisted, and she got turned around, then caught the distant sounds of laughter in the woods. She hesitated, but then decided to creep closer, hoping to ask someone for directions.

Through the press of trees, Maeve caught sight of a flame. People were huddled together around a bonfire, their breaths visible in the chill night air. Laughter mingled with the crackling wood. She recognized several of the apprentices warming their backsides, the necks of wine bottles dangling from their fingers. A party.

She searched for Tristan. She'd seen him in passing over the last week, but hadn't spoken to him. A wave of disappointment hit her when she realized he wasn't there, though he was probably as allergic to parties as she was.

"Eilidh, is that you?" Nan waved ferociously from beside the fire, then rushed over holding the front of a double-breasted coat closed over men's striped pajamas. She pressed a kiss to each of Maeve's cheeks. "Oh, how I've missed you."

"You saw me in Tallowmeade's lecture a few hours ago."

"Did I?"

Maeve leaned closer. Her roommate's pupils were the size of shills. Enlarged pupils were a latent effect of a strong sense scribing. "Have you figured out the coffee scribing?"

If it were true, it was horribly unfair; Nan barely spent any time in the Scriptorium.

"God, no. I can't scribe yet. None of us can." Nan took Maeve's arm. "Come, you must see this." She tugged Maeve toward the party.

Maeve braced her feet against the hard ground as panic set in. "I really shouldn't."

"How can such a pretty thing be an absolute curmudgeon?" Nan looped an arm around Maeve's shoulder and half dragged her to a canvas mail sack strewn over dead leaves, brimming with battered envelopes. Nan plucked one out and handed it to her. "Give it a go."

"A go?" Maeve turned the envelope over. It was blank and filthy, with the Post's wax seal flaked from age. "What is this?"

"An undeliverable. There are whole rooms of them floating around, but a couple mentors gathered only those that were scribed with an extra sense scribing." Nan slurred her words. "The recipient probably died, or the sender didn't get their name right, or they were moving when the courier was trying to get to them. Who knows? No one claimed it, so here it is. Opening them is a new tradition for apprentices."

A great burst of giggling came from a young man slumped in a lawn chair, a letter covering the top half of his face.

If the undeliverable was scribed with something that loosed Maeve's tongue, it would be easier to fling herself in the fire and get it over with quickly. "No thanks."

"But you must," Nan insisted, listing heavily to one side. Maeve grabbed hold of her coat, hauling her roommate upright while she wavered on her feet.

Shea Widden rushed over, concern etched on every line of her delicate features.

"Is she all right?" She touched Nan's chin, hissing through her teeth.

"I feel sublime," Nan crooned, then shrugged them both away, spinning in place.

Shea turned to Maeve. "She drank half a bottle of vintner's reserve before opening a letter. I think it's high time she got to bed." She pointed toward something through the trees, where Hawthorne House's peaked turrets shone bone-white in the moonlight. Sharp relief swamped through Maeve, until Shea said, "Would you help Nan back and get her to bed? I promised to stay put and monitor letters before anyone else gets out of hand."

"But it's early, and I'm not tired in the least." Nan took Shea's hands and stroked the tops with her thumbs. "We could open some letters together."

Shea brushed a lock of Nan's hair behind her ear, then bent and whispered something that made Nan's breath catch. It was an intimate exchange, and Maeve shrank away to give them privacy. Eventually, Nan stumbled toward her, pouting. "Shea said it's high time to get home before I fall straight into the fire."

She didn't sound happy about it, but she tossed an arm around Maeve's shoulders anyhow.

"Make sure she drinks water!" Shea called as Maeve half carried Nan until they were moving swiftly through the woods.

Without any warning, Nan threw her hand skyward with a huff. "What was that for?"

"For being forced to leave the party. For all the insipid lectures I'll have to sit through tomorrow," she slurred with vehemence, then exhaled a misty breath. "Don't get me wrong, I love the Groggery and most things that happen *after* lectures. And Shea— Shea's become one of my closest confidants. She makes things just north of bearable." Nan kicked a pebble, sending it skittering across the path.

Maeve knew better than to pry into someone else's affairs, but Nan's words bothered her. There were countless people who would trade everything to be in Nan's position. "Then why did you come here in the first place?"

"Do you think I had much of a choice? I tried for something else first, and it didn't work out, and my father suggested the apprenticeship. He liked the idea of me here, toiling away, my nose eternally stuck in books." Her mouth twisted.

"But you don't?"

"God, no. I wanted to be a real writer."

"But isn't that what we are?"

"A real, *published* writer," she clarified.

"Of what?"

"Poetry."

"You want to be a poet?" Maeve didn't realize Nan read anything besides her textbooks and the gossip sheets in newspapers.

"I want to write things that get read by others. Not have my words vanish the moment I put them to paper."

Maeve had never thought about scriptomancy like that, but her roommate had a point. All these hopeful scriptomancers went to years of writing school to never write a single thing that people might read. To never be remembered for their writing. She didn't care a whit if anyone ever read a word she wrote—her writing was only ever for herself. But if she did care—if she wanted others to read her writing—she certainly wouldn't let a bunch of gray-haired men stop her.

She turned to Nan. "Why don't you write poetry for yourself, outside of scriptomancy?"

"How can I with Mordraig and Tallowmeade breathing down my neck? I've barely gotten a grasp on scribing pigments. There's still too much to be learned—"

"During the *days*. You've made it clear that the nights still belong to you."

"And I should just, what, write in secret?"

"Why not? You could do it at the Groggery. Publish under a pen name if you must," Maeve said, thinking of how her journal energized her, even after the longest days.

But for all Nan's devil-may-care attitude, she looked a bit fearful. Was she afraid of the stewards? Her father? A society that told her she had to fit neatly into whatever little box she was given?

"Promise me that you'll write what you want," Maeve said firmly.

Nan's eyes gleamed in the darkness. "Fine. I will."

"Good."

A moment of silence fell. Nan's mouth quirked, and she looked Maeve over. "Now it's your turn. Why do you hate it here?"

The question startled Maeve. "I—I don't hate anything. I love it here."

Nan laughed. "Well, whatever it is that's bothering you might be easier to bear if you accepted an invitation occasionally. Made some friends besides whatever imaginary ones live inside the Scriptorium."

Nan's words were slurred, and yet they cut straight through Maeve's heart. But before she could respond, Nan swayed, clutching her stomach.

"Oh, dear god."

"What is it?"

"Bees in my throat," Nan gasped out, then vomited into a bush. She lurched up and stumbled forward—toward her own sickness.

Maeve jerked Nan backward by the shoulder, and they both lost their footing, sprawling into the middle of the freezing walk. The situation was so utterly absurd that Maeve couldn't help herself and burst into laughter.

"I thought I was doomed," Nan said, holding her knees.

"I wouldn't have let you fall."

Nan stared at her in disbelief. "Truly?"

Good heavens. Did Nan believe she hated her?

But that wouldn't be too much of a leap, would it? Nan, with her parties and endless friendships, only served as a painful reminder of everything she couldn't have. She'd avoided Nan at all costs when she was the one with real issues. But Nan had proved herself to be harmless. And she liked Nan, for the most part.

She chewed on her lip. Perhaps it was time to stop shutting herself away from her roommate. She'd started to feel freer around Tristan, after all. Perhaps her rules didn't have to be so staunchly black and white anymore.

Or *perhaps* she simply needed to go to bed.

"Let's get you back to the room," she said, helping Nan up. By some miracle, she was able to drag her roommate the rest of the way to Hawthorne House, then up the stairs without more sudden throat bees.

Until they got inside their room.

"I'm so sorry." Nan kicked off her shoes and collapsed into a sweating heap on the coverlet, groaning into her elbow.

"At least you missed the rug."

It smelled horrific. Maeve cracked a window, then found a bucket and mop in a hall closet, cleaning everything without breathing through her nose. She brought Nan a tall glass of water, and her roommate drank it down in loud, sucking swallows.

"I owe you," Nan said with water dribbling down her cheek. "What would you like in return?"

"For you to go to sleep."

"I can't. Not until you tell me something I can do. I could help you find Jonathan Abenthy's room. I know several people I could ask."

It took a full second for Nan's words to register. Her entire body snapped to attention. "Nan, why did you just ask me that?"

Nan gestured to Maeve's writing desk.

Her journal lay open to a list of places to search that she'd scribbled on her first day here. *Find out which residence hall the monster of Inverly lived in* was written at the top. She couldn't bring herself to write her last name, so she'd quickly jotted down the moniker people often used to describe her father without thinking anyone would ever see it.

"I didn't read any more of the pages, I swear it," Nan said. "But it was opened like that all day, and I couldn't help myself."

All day.

But the journal had been snug in her saddlebag for the past

week. She had used it during her morning lecture and hadn't come back to the room since. That meant someone had taken it out and come into this room to leave it sitting there, waiting for her to notice it.

Maeve felt like she might be sick on the same floor she'd just mopped.

"Forget all about Jonathan's residence hall," she said, twisting her fingers together to keep them from going numb. "A childhood friend discovered I made apprentice and asked me to look up *his* room. But I've thought about it more since, and I don't think I could go. It would give me nightmares."

She peeled off her gloves and ran her bare fingers over the polished desktop. Her chair was pulled back, one of her drawers opened an inch. She opened it the rest of the way.

Everything inside was crumpled. Sifted through. A few feathers were cracked.

I'm watching you, the darkened room seemed to whisper.

"Everything all right?" Nan asked.

Not at all. "Everything is fine. I have to use the lavatory."

Grabbing her saddlebag, Maeve rushed inside and sank to her knees, upending the contents of her bag. Bottles clinked against cold tiles. Her fingers scrambled through them, searching, until she found her vial of lampblack ink and a well of pre-mixed scribing pigment. When her cuff wouldn't come unbuttoned quick enough, she brought her mouth down and bit off the last button, spitting it across the floor.

Exposing her naked wrist to the lamplight.

This was it. If she couldn't be brave, then she didn't deserve to stay here another day. Quickly—before she could second-guess or tremble more than she already was—she scrawled her full name across the thin skin, right below her scab. She licked the lamp-black from her quill tip until it was clean, then dipped it into the scribing pigment, writing the words her handbook instructed her to, directly below her name. The combined words read:

Maeve Abenthy would like to visit the tracking office in Barrow.

She sealed the silver part with the traveling scribing's symbol of two overlapping triangles.

Maeve stared at it, her breath hammering her lungs.

At first nothing happened. Then the scribing pigment tingled against her wrist. It disappeared into her skin, leaving nothing behind but her godforsaken name.

The next two mornings, Maeve walked to a spot against the Post's perimeter fence that gave her a good view of Black-caster Square, watching the flow of couriers coming and going, memorizing their patterns. The lines were busiest in the morning and after luncheon, then ebbed to a trickle, stopping entirely when the station locked up at ten.

On the third afternoon, Maeve went to all her lectures and acted like she normally would: ducking her head whenever someone looked her way, then rushing out before anyone had a chance to pack their things. She stuffed her saddlebag full of old newspapers, so it bulged like a bag full of letters, then raced through the woods, stepping nimbly through Tristan's gap in the fence, stumbling down the embankment.

The road bordering the square was filled with protesters. Maeve spotted a pair of couriers in the crowd and snuck in behind them, darting through the north side gate of Blackcaster Square, until the station was on the left.

Go inside, find an empty section of wall, and whisper your name where nobody can overhear.

It sounded simple, but executing it would take all of her nerves.

At least with the sun low on the horizon, there was no line.

Maeve lifted her chin high and entered the station like a courier might: as if she had every right to be there.

The remains of the Written Doors were covered with sheeting, the salvaging crew gone, save for an officer nibbling away at a dripping sandwich, chatting with a pair of constabulary couriers.

Maeve's pulse picked up, but she forced herself to hurry past, nearly running through the sorting room and down the hall with Molly's plaque warning of the Aldervine.

In the last room, couriers were still sorting letters into large metal bins against the far side, opposite the black stone wall.

Before she could approach it, a door appeared, and an otherwhere courier stumbled out in a whirl of blotchy cheeks and dripping hair. He shook his head, flinging droplets on the floor.

"Got caught in the rain because of a crier in Barrow. I stayed with her for an extra hour and somehow agreed to go check on her mother here tomorrow," he said, then wiped his nose with a handkerchief and tottered by with a large stack of letters in one hand. One of the workers rushed over to grab his letters.

Maeve didn't dare to speak her name with the pair in earshot. She took her time walking to the farthest section of the black stone wall, hoping the pair would go about their business and not come any closer.

A plaque she hadn't noticed the first time hung on the black stones, embossed with the Post's pigeon and a small quote that read:

WE ARE THE LOVED ONE WHISPERING IN THE NIGHT.
WE ARE PROOF THAT A PERSON IS NEVER ALONE.

The irony of the words struck Maeve. She had never felt so hopelessly alone as she did now, trembling before a wall.

Enough of this.

She stepped forward, fidgeting with her cloak, waiting for the others to walk farther toward the bins, for the people sorting letters to look the other way.

One of the sorters caught Maeve's eye, then glanced to her empty hands. "Where's your letter?"

Maeve's heart lurched. "My letter?"

"It's protocol to hold one in front of you when you cross over," the woman explained. "So people see what you're about, and don't try tackling you for appearing out of walls."

Right.

Maeve pulled out the anonymous letter, vowing to bring a small arsenal of letters if she ever had to do this again. She faced the wall and opened her mouth, but nothing came out. Sweat beaded beside her nose. Another pair of sorters looked her way, whispering.

She stepped closer to the wall until she could smell charcoal steam rising from the stones. The marking on the underside of her wrist began to tingle, and the feeling miraculously managed to calm her.

Don't be a coward. Do it now. You will never get this chance again.

"Maeve Abenthy," she whispered softly.

Nothing happened.

Maeve cursed herself and started to turn, but stopped when a door appeared before her on the black wall, its wooden front warped from age. A sinister handle formed in the center, shaped from matte black iron. Maeve wrapped her fingers around it, jolting at a shock of cold. It clicked as she turned it, then made a thin wail as the door creaked open.

A strange air brushed against her tongue. It tasted like the

149

beginning of a Gloam lightning storm, where the stars seemed to spatter the earth and the sky danced with orange light.

There were no stars here, only an eldritch blackness that resembled the pit of Molly Blackcaster's fountain.

She held her breath and stepped.

M aeve had swum in the ocean only once in her life, on a day trip with her aunt Aggie. She had stood in the shallows, fearfully plucking threads from the edges of her sagging bathing suit, until a wave snuck up, spitting sand into her mouth, up her nose. Walking into another world felt like the crack of that wave.

Her breath caught in her chest and made her cough, as if the air were thicker, her lungs too small to breathe it in. When she regained her breath, she looked around her at the empty woods and started to panic, thinking she had made a mistake and somehow wound up in a world with the Aldervine. But then she heard voices carried on the wind.

Maeve walked to a nearby oak tree and slowly peeked around it, to an iron fence a few feet away.

A tall city rose beyond the fence that looked like Gloam in Leyland if she squinted; all of Gloam's steep hills were in the same places, along with the twisting streets. But here, the buildings were straight and scrubbed clean of the black sediment that dripped down the building sides in Leyland. The sky still hung with brooding clouds, but the city beneath it gleamed opalescent in the gray light.

Gloam in Barrow.

She'd made it.

Just southwest of her was Blackcaster Square, looking exactly as it did in Leyland. Judging from the iron fence in front of her, she had to be standing just inside the Barrow campus of the Otherwhere Post.

Maeve turned to see the strange black door she'd just exited hanging a foot off the ground on the side of a tree trunk.

According to the *Scriptomancer's Companion*, a courier door lasted for twelve hours, give or take, depending on the skill of the scriptomancer. Not sure how long she had, given that this was her first ever scribing, Maeve tossed her hood up and hurried down a pathway that led her between two enormous new buildings, their squared entrances carved from cream-colored marble.

There were no crumbling eaves or broken tree stumps used as stair risers. Not a single paving stone was cracked. They were all squared off and laid out in neat rows and columns. Maeve imagined Molly's ghost turning her nose up at this place.

This campus was planned and built by the glut of architects and mathematicians who went to university here before the doors burned, when this city's colleges all taught the applied sciences.

A sign for the tracking office led her past several more pristine buildings before she found the one she wanted. She walked inside, passing offices dedicated to various ministers and government secretaries of Barrow—offices that didn't exist in Leyland. The stewards would likely put up a stink if any minister ever tried to work from the grounds there. Finally, Maeve spotted a small door marked TRACKING OFFICE at the end of the hall. Only a few paces before it, a pair of double doors stood propped open.

Maeve slowed as she heard muffled voices drifting from the open doors. She thought she recognized one of the voices. A steward?

She had to pass by that room to get to the tracking office. If a steward was inside and spotted her through the doorway, this trip would be over before she knew it.

Slowly, she peeked inside the room—a large drawing room where men were in the midst of a heated discussion. Some wore waistcoats with embellishments that marked them as Barrow ministers; a few others wore deep plum university robes; and then a handful wore the Post's raiment, including Postmaster Byrne himself. He sat with his back to the door beside Steward Mordraig.

None of them faced the open doorway, thank goodness.

Maeve tightened the hood of her cloak around her head and passed the doorway quickly, but halted just beyond when she heard a name she recognized. She tilted her ear.

The conversation inside the drawing room seemed to focus mostly on the Postmaster's announcements in the papers, until someone clapped their hands and said the name again. Tristan. But why were they discussing him? She crept closer, listening.

The conversation meandered for a moment, then someone said, "It would be nice to announce that we're actually attempting to fix the Written Doors again."

"No. Tristan needs much more practice before he attempts that," Steward Mordraig said, and Maeve's eyes flew wide. Mordraig beat his cane against the floor. "Tristan's nowhere near ready to experiment with that level of scriptomancy so soon after what happened to him last year."

Maeve edged even closer to the door.

"Then force the boy to practice!" someone said.

"It doesn't work like that. He must make the decision to practice again on his own. But he's mentoring again, thanks to our Onrich. It's a start," Mordraig said. They were referring to her. "And he seems in better spirits, too. I'd give it another year or two."

"A year or two?" someone echoed, frustration threading his words. There were grunts of disapproval. "But you told us that Tristan is a prodigy. That he could be the next Molly Blackcaster."

"And he will be," Mordraig snapped. "But you must give the boy time, especially after what happened to his last apprentice."

The room went silent, and Maeve found herself straining to hear.

"He should never have been paired with Cathriona," Mordraig said in a grave tone.

Cathriona.

"God rest her soul."

Maeve's hands flew to her mouth.

She thought through every moment she'd spent with Tristan, picking out clues that helped paint what might have happened: his fight with his father, his reluctance to scribe, and his flat-out refusal to teach her. Tristan's former apprentice was dead. Did scriptomancy play a part? Was that why Tristan was so reluctant to teach her anything?

Maeve blanched, remembering the story of the woman with chewed-out eyes. But Tristan said it was a courier who read the form scribing, not an apprentice. Still, if Cathriona died by scriptomancy, it would explain Tristan's ill feelings toward it perfectly.

That had to be it. And Tristan was still grieving, clearly.

No wonder he could barely stand to answer her when she'd asked him to teach her the traveling scribing. She wanted to run back and apologize to him, to beg his forgiveness. She put her face in her hands, feeling dreadful.

Then her mind went blank at a shuffling of feet.

The meeting had ended.

Without a second thought, Maeve rushed to the door at the end of the hallway, slipping through it before anyone might see her.

The tracking office was a stifling room filled with scriptomancer worktables. An incinerator chute hung beside a long reception desk, where a young clerk fanned herself with a copy of the *Herald*, the high neck of her blouse sheer from sweat. Her thick glasses slid down her fair, freckled nose.

Maeve fidgeted with her sleeves and approached the desk, her heart still pounding. "I'm a courier with the Leyland office," she said, trying to catch her breath and remember the speech she'd practiced for this moment. "I'm here because one of my deliveries turned out to be sent from someone who didn't leave their name on their letter, and the woman who received it has given it back to me to investigate. The recipient is beside herself. She thinks the letter might be from an ill relative. I promised to find the sender for her."

The desk clerk screwed her lips together. "I'm sorry, but there's no possible way to track down a sender if they didn't leave their name."

That wasn't what Tallowmeade had said. "I was told that someone here might be of help."

"I could take a look," someone called out.

A man stood up from one of the worktables. He ran his fingers over his close-cropped white hair, then adjusted the gray cuffs of his officer's coat.

Maeve's mouth went bone dry.

She braced her hands against the side of the desk. "You work for the constabulary?"

"Not technically. I'm a scriptomancer who only works along-side their couriers."

A bead of sweat caught on Maeve's lip. She swiped at it, unsure of what to do. It was far too hot to think.

"A name is always the best route for tracking, but I can some-times deduce things by studying a letter." The man held out a hand, and Maeve recoiled. He cocked his head. "I thought you told the clerk that you had the letter with you."

"She did!" the clerk piped in.

Maeve silently cursed herself. "Yes, I have the letter, but I've made a promise not to show it to anyone."

"Then you can tell your recipient that they've wasted a solid minute of my time."

Maeve chewed on her lip. This man knew nothing about her, and he worked in Barrow. She'd likely never see him again after this moment. But then this was the tracking office, and he worked with the constabulary to track down criminals.

"Could you tell anything from looking at the envelope?" Maeve asked, deciding that as long as he didn't read the letter, it would be all right. She pulled it out. "That wouldn't break my promise."

"I can try," he said.

She felt ill as she handed it over.

He ran his nose over the broken wax seal, then picked off a bit of wax and rubbed it between his fingers until it melted. "It was posted from Barrow."

"Here?" That was impossible.

"Without a doubt. I can tell by the faint blue tinge to the black wax. All letters collected in Barrow are sealed with this wax. The black wax from Leyland has a yellow cast to it." He turned the envelope in his fingers. "The envelope itself tells a different story. It's crafted from a special paper substrate made from yew, imported from the north. You can tell by the grit. The Barrow Campus of the University of Gloam used to order reams of this particular paper for faculty."

"Someone employed by the university sent that?"

"Yes—someone from the Barrow campus." He ran a finger over the fold, then ripped it open, pulling out the letter.

"Sir!" Maeve panicked and tried to grab it, but the desk stood between them.

He backed out of reach. "Unless I inspect the letter itself, madam, I can tell you nothing more."

She froze in place as he read through it.

He didn't remark on the contents, thank heavens. Instead, he placed the letter on the desk and held a magnification glass to his left eye. Then he took out a tiny metal measure used for typography, holding it between the individual words.

"Perfect leading. Masterful command of chirography." He clicked his tongue. "This letter was written by a highly trained scriptomancer once employed by the College of Scriptomantic Arts, as evidenced by the style of writing. A scriptomancer who probably became a university courier after the Post was founded, with access to this paper substrate . . . Or perhaps they're simply another type of courier who stole the paper and posted the letter from Barrow. This letter is written in a clandestine manner, after all." He handed it to her. "Tell your Maeve that she can visit the office of the House of Ministers in Leyland and open an official inquiry if she wants any further investigation, but her old friend was indeed a courier once. And given the scarcity of couriers these days, I'd wager they still are."

MAEVE FOUND HER courier door still waiting for her on the tree trunk. She used it to cross worlds and made it back inside the Leyland campus just after dark. Her feet stumbled through the woods, while her fist clutched her skirt over her hip bone, where the letters were tucked.

This whole time, her *old friend* was a courier.

The idea had popped into her mind a few times, but now that she was certain of it, the grounds took on a different feel—as if she might lift a paving stone and find hidden secrets buried beneath. Although, if they were still a university courier, they wouldn't live here. They'd have their own residence somewhere in Gloam proper. But that man in the tracking office said they could easily be an otherwhere courier who happened to steal the paper from Barrow. They could live on the Leyland campus. Be close by.

But there were hundreds who could have written the letter and no way to narrow it down. And she couldn't avoid the thought that the person sending her the threatening red letters was also part of the very same group. The two letter-writers might even know each other.

Maeve's thoughts spun in a wild tangle of possibilities as she climbed the stairs inside Hawthorne House. She halted on her landing. Piano drifted from the direction of Tristan's room.

The melancholy notes caught in her chest. He would probably be shocked if she beat on his door and asked to come inside, to listen.

She considered it, then quickly dismissed it. It was a terrible idea. As it was, he was probably poring over memories of Cathriona.

Curious, Maeve stepped to last year's apprentice class portrait hanging in a dusty wormwood frame. Names were jotted beneath each row of couriers. She ran a pinky along the names, stopping at *Cathriona Martin.*

"There you are," she whispered, then followed the name up to the image of an absurdly stunning young woman. *That* was Cathriona? It was hard to imagine someone so lovely toiling over a scriptomancy worktable.

A curtain of dark hair parted for angelic features and a complexion as bright as a pearl. Cathriona's lips curved into a wicked smirk. Perhaps she wasn't so angelic after all. This young woman had secrets, certainly, but Maeve doubted any were as big as hers. Now she was dead.

"I found it!"

Maeve jerked so violently, she stumbled and caught herself on the wall.

Nan raced toward her, then skidded to a stop. Her face was mapped with a sheen of sweat. A trickle of blood ran across her dark brow. "I found Abenthy's room."

Maeve was too stunned to speak at first. When she regained her composure, her voice came out high-pitched. "I told you I wasn't interested in him anymore."

"Yes, but you say the same thing about breakfast and the Groggery and speaking to anyone at all, for that matter. I may have been ill the other night, but I could tell there was something more to that scribble in your journal. I'm right, aren't I? You're dying of curiosity."

"I'm not."

She rubbed her palms together. "This is going to be fun."

"There will be no fun! We're not going to his room." They couldn't. As it was, Maeve could barely wrap her mind around what Nan was offering.

"Oh, don't be such a sourpuss. You helped me when I was sick, and now I'm returning the favor because that's what friends do."

"We're roommates, not *friends*."

Nan ignored her. "I was just outside the building. It's not far from here."

She motioned for Maeve to follow her.

"You expect to go right now?"

"Either now or another late night. The building is boarded up, but I found an entrance—sort of. The only problem is that it's right off the main path, and someone might see you during the day."

Already, the thought of visiting one of the last places where her father graced this world made Maeve want to curl up on the stone floor. But her roommate was looking at her like she would physically drag her down the stairs if she said no.

Maeve considered it. What if she went? Already, she could feel her time here slipping through her fingers. Her attempts at getting inside the Second Library were fruitless, but answers might be waiting for her inside her father's room. If Nan brought her there now, she could make up some excuse to not go inside, then return at dawn to investigate everything alone.

"Very well. Show me," she said before she could stop herself.

Nan's lips curved. "Then we need lights."

Portable oil lamps would be too bright. Maeve grabbed a pair of candles, and Nan led the way east across the grounds to a derelict building. A rush of dead vines clung to the ancient stone, and a large elm tree filled the front courtyard with dripping branches that clattered in the bitter ocean wind.

Nan picked her way to a weather-beaten plaque. Maeve lit a candle and cupped her hand around the flame as she held it up. ELDERMOSS HALL was carved onto the plaque in blackletter.

"Jonathan Abenthy lived in the easternmost room on the second floor," Nan said.

Maeve scraped her fingers against the ancient etching. There were answers inside this place—she could feel it.

When another gust rattled the elm tree, Maeve knew that she couldn't leave until she at least explored inside. "Where's the entrance?"

"I heard that nobody wanted to live here after Inverly, so they shuttered the building and nailed the main door shut," Nan said, then left Maeve to walk along the choked bushes to a garden-height window near one corner. The glass was shattered, and a board hung over the gap. "I went in through here before I came to get you, then saw a mouse and hopped right out."

Maeve was beside her in an instant, shoving the board aside, propping her foot on the window ledge. "I'll meet you back at Hawthorne House."

"You're going in alone?"

"Of course I am."

"It's as dark as pitch, and some floorboards are thoroughly rotted. What if you fall through them and break something vital?"

"I have the candles." Maeve hauled herself over the ledge, then hopped down, holding up her flame. Cobwebs covered the ceilings, and slicks of black liquid dripped down what was left of the peeling wallpaper. A rotting scent wafted up from the floorboards. The candlelight reflecting against the wall began to ripple. Maeve looked down at her shaking hands, feeling like she was disturbing her father's grave. Other graves.

There was a noise behind her, and Nan came over the sill, then stumbled over a buckling board, into her. Maeve nearly groaned with relief that her roommate was here.

Nan tilted back her chin. "Is that a glimmer of joy I see at my presence?"

Maeve choked out a laugh. "I think it is."

Nan shuffled past her and looked around them. "Did you honestly expect me to miss this? It took me all day to figure out where this was."

"How did you figure it out exactly?"

"Well, my father always told me that he got to his station in life not by sitting complacent, but by grabbing every opportunity by the throat. And I was in the dining hall and happened to be seated at a table over from the stewards, and—"

Maeve tensed. "Please tell me you didn't ask a steward after Abenthy's room," she said, her last name coming out in a choked whisper.

"No. I asked the Postmaster."

Maeve dropped the candle. It snuffed out, and she scrambled to grab it before it rolled away in the dark. "Nan, what were you *thinking?*" she said, struggling to light the wick again.

"Don't worry your pretty head," Nan said. "It was after the stewards left and the Postmaster was all by himself. I went about it innocently enough, and I'm certain he had no idea I was planning to come here. I'm sure he gets questions like that all the time, besides."

True, but not from the roommate of someone he'd like to do away with.

"You should never have approached him." And she should never have referenced her father in her journal.

Nan stepped closer. "This is about Tristan, isn't it? You're worried this might get back to him."

"This has nothing to do with Tristan."

"*Of course* it doesn't."

"What is that supposed to mean?"

Nan picked her way across the hall, brushing away cobwebs with her fingertips. "I've heard gossip about the two of you."

"People talk about us?"

"Don't worry," Nan said. "People like to talk about everything. Most of the gossip is about Cathriona anyhow."

The name echoed in the darkness.

Maeve knew she should change the subject, but if anyone

knew what had happened to Cathriona, Nan would. "I heard that she died."

"It's disturbing, really."

"You know how it happened?"

"Of course I do. She performed an advanced skin scribing on herself that boiled her blood."

Nan said it as if she were rattling off this week's scribing assignment, and it took a moment for her words to sink in. Maeve's limbs grew cold, and she pictured that beautiful woman in that class portrait and swallowed back a wave of nausea.

"There happens to be more," Nan said.

"I'm not sure that I care to hear more."

Nan came around to face her. "Tristan was the one to find her."

"What?"

"Dreadful, I know. Cathriona was well liked, and the last year's entire apprentice class is still in a tangle about it. Some believe the stewards handled it badly, but most are convinced that Tristan had something to do with it. I haven't been able to get to the bottom of any of the rumors. Has Tristan told you anything?"

"No, but he would never hurt anyone, if that's what you're implying," Maeve said, wishing Tristan were standing here now to defend himself, to tell Nan that none of it was true. It couldn't be. Could it?

Tristan wasn't only the Postmaster's son, but a valuable fledgling scriptomancer. Powerful people wanted to use him to repair the Written Doors. They needed him to scribe. What if Nan was right? What if he had a hand in Cathriona's death and the stewards simply made his troubles go away?

No. He couldn't have killed anyone. He was the kindest person she'd met here. He helped her when she did nothing to deserve it.

But what if he did something on accident? If he killed Cathriona without meaning to . . .

Maeve pinched her temple, hoping the thoughts of conspiracy would disappear, wishing she'd never brought up Tristan to begin with. She lit the second candle and shoved it in Nan's hand. "No more gossip. Let's get this over with so we can leave."

There were no lights inside the building, only their flames casting yellow halos against the moldering wallpaper. A tangle of debris littered the floor. Maeve picked her way over a tarnished candelabra, stepping over the remains of a wooden divan, its silk fabric hanging in soiled rags and covered in spots of mildew. She held her nose to keep from gagging at the scents of decaying animal.

Nan clutched a fistful of Maeve's cloak, huddling close.

They walked together through an abandoned foyer, the elaborate stone hearth stuffed with coarse boulders. Nan yelped when something rustled from behind them.

"Hush." Maeve raised her candle. There were pictures along the walls covered in thick layers of grime. A bookshelf still held a few books. Maeve lifted one, and the entire thing fell apart in rotted clumps. Nothing salvageable. So much for looking for her father's journals.

An old, curving stairwell lay beyond the parlor. Nan laced her fingers through Maeve's as they made their way up it, tiptoeing around a rotted section. Maeve's heart lodged itself inside of her throat as they turned down the short hall, facing the easternmost room. Her father's room. She knew it was his instantly because thick scribbles of lampblack ink covered the warped door.

BASTARD! TRAITOR! MURDERER!

She still didn't have concrete proof that any of it was false, but she didn't need proof to know how she felt, and those words were not her father. She stepped forward and placed her palms against them and shoved the door open.

"Welcome to the monster's lair," Nan said as dramatically as she could with a shaking voice.

Her father's bedchamber.

Where he slept and read his books and filled his leather journals and wrote pages and pages of love letters.

It was hard to picture him seated amid the rot, reading the very love letter that now rested at her hip, but he had. Her father penned countless letters to her mother, Aoife, in this very room. Then after her mother died, he was so stricken that he barely left this chamber for seven months and didn't visit Inverly at all. Her aunt told her that she had never been more furious. By the time her father finally showed up groveling, Aggie had already burned all the love letters he'd ever sent to her mother.

"What's this?" Nan held a candle to the wall.

"There used to be a dresser there, I'm guessing. And a headboard there." Maeve ran a finger over the discoloration from years of furniture once pushed against the peeling paint.

Maeve lowered her candle and walked the perimeter, shining it against more outlines. A writing desk. Another dresser. A shelf. A doorway.

She slipped through it, into an adjacent room with a rotted sofa and plugged hearth. A sitting room that had another door on the opposite wall. Nan opened it, and Maeve followed, into another bedchamber identical to her father's.

"I've heard of these larger suites with shared sitting rooms," Nan said. "They're common in many of the older residence halls. They usually get snatched up by senior couriers because of how spacious they are. I never realized that Jonathan Abenthy lived in one himself."

"Neither had I," Maeve said, her pulse fluttering wildly.

Her father had a roommate when she lost him to Inverly. A roommate she had never heard about, who was never mentioned once in any of the countless news articles about her father.

Maeve touched the letters at her hip, going over everything she'd uncovered so far. That the *old friend* was likely a scriptomancer turned courier. How in their letter, they spoke of a secret about her father that nobody else knew.

Her father's roommate would have watched him come and go and noticed things that her father never spoke of. He could easily have stumbled upon a big secret. A roommate might have also known about her. But why was his name erased from all the news?

Maybe Postmaster Byrne wiped the roommate's name from the records. He certainly had the authority.

Maeve looked around the bedchamber. She felt in her bones that this was something big. Everyone who had known her father had given public statements in the few weeks after Inverly was destroyed—but not his roommate. She couldn't think why, unless they knew something they shouldn't. Maybe even the truth of what happened in Inverly.

Whoever this room belonged to had to be hiding something.

"Look at this," Nan said, running her finger over a section of wall.

Maeve picked her way through debris and crouched down beside Nan. A few lines of faded words were inked on the wallpaper right beside the outline of the writing desk. Maeve recognized the long list of herbs used to make scribing pigment base.

"That's genius. I'm writing the same tomorrow beside my

worktable." Nan turned to Maeve. "Do you think Abenthy's room-mate wrote this?"

"Who's to say?" Maeve said, even though truth stared right back at her. She knew exactly who wrote it—the same person who wrote the letter in her pocket. Her *old friend*. The penmanship was identical.

It was him. Her father's roommate.

The revelation staggered her, but she made sure to not let it show on her face. She pulled her spine straight, feeling a renewed determination. After all this time, she was finally on the right path.

"What is that?" Nan asked.

Maeve looked up and jolted at a flickering light. At first, it looked like moonlight glinting off the cracked windowpane, but the light was coming from the trees. It bobbed and guttered. Lantern light. She caught a silhouetted face directly behind it. A person in the woods, watching them.

She snuffed out her candle.

The person began moving, their light bobbing as they headed west through the trees. Maeve darted to a nearby window, then another, keeping her eyes on the moving lantern.

"Watch it!" Nan called out.

A second later something shuddered then cracked beneath Maeve's feet. The floor gave.

She dropped, her back scraping the broken edge of boards as she fell, landing hard somewhere below.

Pain shot across her temple, hot and sharp, while a ringing started in her left ear. She choked, tasting metal and dust against her tongue.

Yellow candlelight sputtered above her, and Nan's face poked through a hole. "I'll get help."

"Don't. I'll be all right," Maeve croaked.

The world went dark.

Maeve didn't know where she was, only that everything hurt. She moved her arms and legs, taking a quick survey of her bones, but nothing felt broken. Cracking her eyes open, she stretched her neck until her temple throbbed. Her braid had come undone, her hair tumbling around her like mattress fluff. A violent shiver rolled through her, and she felt for her cloak, but it was missing. Where was she?

Her muscles barked in protest as she sat herself up against a worn leather settee and looked around her.

A long wall that seemed to be comprised of poorly stacked books sprawled out before her. Beside it, a piano was strewn with empty wine bottles encased in melted wax. Fringed scarves and polished shoes and towers of unopened boxes lay scattered about the floor in a mess that only one person could have made.

A door creaked open.

Tristan pushed his head through, balancing a tea service on one hand. He leaned a shoulder against the doorframe and looked her over, and she felt herself turning pink.

"It seems the impostor is finally awake."

His spectacles were crooked, and a smudge of something gray

streaked across his cheek. He was filthy, but at the sight of him, a bright feeling of relief struck Maeve between her ribs.

He arched an eyebrow. "You're smiling."

She flattened her mouth. "And you're covered in cobwebs."

"From when I extracted you from that ruin of a building then carried you across the grounds like a sack of lifeless mail three hours ago. It's the middle of the night."

"You carried me all the way here?"

"Aside from calling for help, there was no other option." He came closer. "The rain managed to wash much of your dirt away. Though I'm afraid the day has finally come to light your cloak on fire and toss it over the nearest cliff."

He gestured toward the puddle of fabric by the door.

"Don't you dare touch it," Maeve said as everything came back to her: the trip to Barrow, her father's roommate—the *old friend*.

She needed to find him.

Bracing her hands, she tried to push herself up, but it was too fast, and her head felt like it wasn't screwed on properly. A wave of dizziness rushed over her, and she fell against the cushions, shivering. Her teeth chattered together painfully.

"Don't move." Tristan placed the tea service on the table in front of her, then fished through a nearby dresser, tossing out gloves by the handful. He returned with a cream-colored wool blanket and tucked it around her shoulders. It smelled like pounce powder and old books and days spent inside sipping tea. She took a deep inhale then buried her face in the wool, hoping to disappear into it and wake up five years from now. But then the settee compressed beside her, and the scent of fresh Earl Grey had her mouth watering; she was horribly thirsty.

She opened her eyes to a tendril of steam weaving its way

around Tristan's spectacles and through his damp hair. He offered her a chipped cup.

"Thanks," she said, taking it from him. Their fingers brushed.

It was the slightest touch, but her breath caught. She looked up to find Tristan watching her intently. Heat rose to her cheeks, and she glanced down, focusing all her attention on her teacup.

Why did he have to sit so close? At least the cup was hot. Warmth seeped into her frozen palms, and she stopped shivering.

"Nan told me everything," Tristan said suddenly.

Oh, dear god.

"Don't look too frightened. She made me swear upon my future offspring that I wouldn't yell at you."

Maeve's fingers tightened against the porcelain. "What did she say exactly?"

He shifted. "That she wanted to see Jonathan Abenthy's room and dragged you there."

Nan took the blame for it? Maeve couldn't believe someone would do that for her. She would have to thank Nan later. Profusely.

"I've decided to not say anything about it as long as neither of you *ever* do it again," Tristan said, then brought his arms over his head, stretching. His shirt came untucked, a sliver of taut skin poking from the top of his waistband.

Maeve forced her eyes to her cup for the second time in a matter of minutes.

"So?" he asked, oblivious to his untucked shirt. "Find anything to make that fall worthwhile?"

His words made her pause. She needed information about the roommate, but didn't want Tristan suspecting anything. But she had to say something, and she could use that to her advantage.

Though if she worded things wrong or pushed him too hard, it would make him wonder about her motives, and why she was suddenly so interested in Jonathan Abenthy.

"We discovered that Abenthy had a roommate," she said cautiously.

His brow furrowed. "I always thought that Abenthy lived alone."

"Is there any way to find out who it might be?" Maeve asked, then added, "Nan is very curious."

"Official room records are kept inside the Second Library. Nan can search through them once she gets her courier key."

"But what if you helped her look the roommate up?"

"I'm not about to help anyone dig up information on Abenthy." Tristan sounded annoyed by the idea.

Maeve didn't press him. Her palms were already slick from uttering her father's name out loud. She rubbed the throbbing spot on her head, trying to think of something else to say.

Tristan, however, spoke before she could. "Nan mentioned something else that needs to be discussed."

Maeve's heart thumped at his grim tone. "What is it?"

"She said that she told you a few things about Cathriona, but wouldn't tell me what was said. And now I'm curious."

Maeve pictured boiling blood and grimaced.

"So she did tell you something." He leaned forward, his elbows resting on his knees. "What was it this time? By the look on your face, it must have been the tale of how I slit Cath's throat with a quill knife. Or the one where I strung Cath to a worktable and forced poison down her throat with a clinician's medicinal tube."

Maeve's eyes went wide. "No. Nothing like that."

"Then what was it?" he asked. "Nothing you can say will offend me. I've heard all the stories. Many times over, in fact."

"It was about a scribing," Maeve said, hoping that would be enough.

"And . . . ?"

"A scribing that boiled Cathriona's blood."

Tristan blanched. "I've got to hand it to Nan, at least that one's creative."

It wasn't true at all? Maeve's stomach sickened like it used to at the orphanage, when those horrible girls would gossip about her, because a large part of her had believed Nan—without a single speck of proof. Without confirming the story with Tristan first.

"Then will you tell me what happened?" Maeve asked. She wanted to hear the truth, and everyone deserved the chance to tell their own story.

He poured himself a cup of tea, then held it between his palms, rolling it. Liquid sloshed nearly to the edge. "Nan was right in that it concerned scriptomancy." His throat bobbed. "I used to love scribing so fiercely that I'd spend hours at it, but—but then I gave Cath pigment that was mixed too strongly for what she needed, and I didn't pay attention to *which* scribing she was attempting because I was too busy reading a scutting novel. I was careless, and too skilled at scribing. A lethal combination. Cath's scribing didn't boil her blood, but it killed her nonetheless."

The story made other things she knew about Tristan click into place. "That's why you won't help me scribe. You're afraid someone else will get hurt."

"Someone will."

"You think you're dangerous?"

His mouth curved into a bitter smile. "I don't think anything. I know exactly what I am."

She stared at him, open-mouthed. Cathriona was the reason

he'd looked wretched that day in his father's office, when he was assigned to mentor her. Heavens, the idea of teaching her anything must have horrified him.

What happened to Cathriona was an accident, and yet Tristan clearly blamed himself for everything, which wasn't fair. But he didn't hate scriptomancy. He'd just admitted that he loved scribing once. He was obviously gifted at it. A prodigy who now tormented himself for a mistake that wasn't his fault. Who held himself back from something that brought him joy.

"What if you started scribing again slowly, doing some of the things the apprentices are tasked with?"

He raised an eyebrow. "While helping you?"

"No, that's not what I meant. Shocking, I realize, but I've learned my lesson and this doesn't have anything to do with teaching me." The small writing desk beside the door looked stocked with several inks. "You could practice scribing here, away from the prying eyes in the Scriptorium."

"I see what you're doing," Tristan said. "It's disgustingly noble of you, but I'm not scribing outside of deliveries. I can barely bring myself to write anymore as it is. I wouldn't even know where to start."

"You start with a blank page and a single word," Maeve rattled off, then grew flustered when Tristan's gaze fixed on her. "My father used to tell me that whenever he gave me a new journal and I wasn't sure what I should write about."

"You mean, you don't fill all your journals with devious plots for sneaking into government facilities?"

She rolled her eyes and looked down at her lap, picturing her finger smoothing along the center of her journal. "Sometimes I don't know what I'm writing until I'm halfway down a page and the idea takes hold and won't let go. And in those moments, I feel like I can write forever. I know that scribing pulls in actual magic, but I think there's nothing more magical than filling a page with writing. It might be something you could try. To get used to writing things besides deliveries. To find joy in it again."

Maeve glanced up to find Tristan watching her intently. Heat rushed to her cheeks.

"Who are you really?" he asked.

"Please, not this again."

"What if you only told me your first name? I'd like to call you something other than an impostor." He leaned toward her. "I'd like for you to trust me with it."

Trusting him with her name was impossible, and yet Maeve let herself imagine what it might feel like to speak it aloud.

What was she thinking? If she said her name aloud, it would belong to Tristan Byrne, a scriptomancer who could track her down no matter where in the worlds she went.

A scriptomancer who waited patiently for her answer.

"I told you already; I'm nobody interesting."

"I think it's the opposite," he said. "I think you're somebody very interesting who has a lot to lose by revealing yourself to others. Most of all, I think you're scared of who you are."

"None of that is remotely true," Maeve said, but her voice came out much too high. Nerves flooded her, and she tucked her legs to her body so tightly that her calf twisted painfully. Shrieking, she pinched the muscle with her thumb, rubbing it lengthwise until it loosened. "It's just a leg cramp—probably from the cold," she said, then looked toward the door. She should make an escape before she made a bigger fool of herself.

Tristan took her heel.

"What are you doing?" She tried pulling her foot away.

He ignored her and tugged off her left shoe, then slid down her wet stocking, jerking it off as well. He did the same with the other foot, then dug through a trunk beside him and pulled out a pair of mismatched woolen socks, one the color of dried oatmeal, the other a deep burgundy. He put them on her, sliding them over her calves, to just below her knees. She sat frozen for the entire affair.

"Your skirt is wet as well." He fingered the hem.

"Don't you *dare*."

He laughed, his hands loosely clasped around her ankles. His fingers flexed. The small circles of pressure from his fingertips felt like embers catching on her skin. He sat close enough that it would be easy to lean over and kiss him. She imagined it for the briefest moment, then immediately banished the ridiculous notion, shifting away.

His hand brushed along her thigh.

They both stilled.

Her heart seemed to beat outside her body.

"You should probably get to your room," Tristan said, rather roughly.

Yes—yes, she should.

She slid her feet free, then stood on the warm socks and wiggled her toes. She considered removing the socks, but her feet were still cold. And even though the colors didn't match, they were nicer than all her socks, and he certainly didn't need another item of clothing. It would probably be best if she hung on to them for the time being.

She padded to the door slowly, taking in his room—such a small, ordinary slice of Tristan's life—then bent and gathered the damp puddle of her cloak. It wasn't ruined at all—only needed a good scrubbing. She balled it in her arms and halted at the writing desk beside his door. It was covered in uncarved quills and several expensive-looking bottles of ink. Too many for someone who barely wrote, but considering Tristan's shopping habits, it didn't surprise her. Maeve lifted a bottle in the center, then nearly dropped it.

The ink gleamed the exact fiery red as the threatening letters.

The black wax covering the stopper wasn't cracked, which meant the ink was unopened—never used, thank heavens. The elaborate gilt-foiled label was from Plume & Pen Inksmithy in Barrow, the color called Oxblood.

"I picked that up after deliveries yesterday," Tristan called out. "It's something, isn't it?"

It was indeed.

Maeve didn't sleep any more that night. She locked herself in her lavatory and reworked her traveling scribing, then changed without waking Nan. This time, she stole a handful of letters from the Scriptorium, stuffing them in her saddlebag. She made it through the gates and into Blackcaster Station by mid-morning, hurrying around couriers to the black stone wall.

The room was busier than the last time, but there was still an empty section in the farthest corner. Maeve walked to it, then made a show of waving a stolen letter. The sounds of sorting drowned out her voice as she whispered her name, calling forth the black door.

Feeling brave, she kept her eyes open. The moment her head passed the doorframe, a city appeared around her instantly. Her breath caught at the sight.

The last time, she could only see Gloam in Barrow from a distance.

As the strange, pristine buildings rose around her, Maeve marveled at their lack of ink-stained signs and cluttered windowsills. In fact, the leaded glass storefronts shone with a mirrorlike vibrancy. She turned in a slow circle.

Aggie had brought her here once before, but she didn't remember everything being so . . . perpendicular. All the buildings were crafted from sturdy stones that looked hewn by machines, not chipped away by hand, and the cobblestones were all perfectly square and symmetrical.

Maeve stared in awe. Until a pair of women in high-necked winter coats walked by, giving her strange looks.

She tore her eyes from the sights and found a signpost. The street names were the same in each world. She stood a few blocks south of Old Town, on a street she'd wandered down a hundred times in Leyland. It felt unsettling wandering down it now, but she made her way to the fanciful storefront on the corner, with a sign that read: PLUME & PEN. THE LARGEST INKSMITHY IN ALL THE WORLDS.

Inside, the shop floor spilled out in a river of glass cases, displaying inkwells shaped into animals and bone letter-folds swirling with gold tracery.

Maeve wove through the first floor, ducking through a room of molted feathers, where three clerks wielded quill knives, ready to carve on demand. She asked one of them where she might find the ink section and was directed to a wooden staircase that took her to a top floor with soaring shelves of inks in shades from deepest black to milk poppy. A long counter ran along one side of the room, with a single ledger book in the middle. It looked exactly like the purchase ledger that Mr. Braithwaite kept on the front counter of the inksmithy.

She quickly searched the massive display, then plucked off a bottle of the Oxblood ink.

A clerk popped over tugging her gold earring with fingers covered in dust gloves. "It's a beautiful color, isn't it?" She nodded at the bottle in Maeve's fingers.

"Yes. Lovely. I've never seen this shade of ink before. Is it new?"

"It is. The shipment came in last month. So far, we're the only store to stock it across both worlds."

Maeve tilted the bottle, watching as the ink caught the light. It seemed strange for the person writing her the threatening letters to choose such a rare ink. It was almost as if they wanted to be found. Or maybe this particular ink worked best with the form scribings in those letters; *The Scriptomancer's Companion* said certain inks paired better with certain scribing types. This color could have helped those letters bleed more, for all she knew.

"It's one of our more expensive bottles," the clerk said. "But with proper care it can last twenty years."

"What's the price?" Maeve asked.

"Thirty hallions and twenty-two shills."

Maeve nearly dropped it. "That can't be the real price."

The clerk plucked it from her fingers. "If you're looking for something less rare, we have this lovely burgundy for three hallions." She lifted a dark purple bottle.

Maeve glanced at the ledger book. "Actually, I must confess that I'm here because I was using a colleague's ink, and I spilled the entire bottle. Terribly clumsy of me, I know. I think it was Oxblood, but I'm not certain because the label was peeled off. Would it be possible to have a look at the purchase ledger to see if my friend bought a bottle?"

"I'm afraid customer information is confidential," the clerk said, then glanced at something behind Maeve.

"I never thought I would see an apprentice here, of all places," a bright voice said.

Maeve's stomach dropped. She spun around to stare into Shea Widden's wide blue eyes.

There was nowhere Maeve could run, no excuse she could think of to explain how she was standing in Barrow.

Shea grinned. Her keen eyes darted to Maeve's wrist. "Adept at the traveling scribing?"

Maeve's thoughts stumbled, but there was no way to deny it now. "Please. You can't tell anyone."

If Tristan found out, he would wonder which of her direct relatives was a scriptomancer, then he would wonder about other things.

"Don't fret." Shea took Maeve's hand and patted it. "I understand perfectly."

"You do?"

"Of course. There was someone in my year who hid it as well. They wanted to visit their grandmother in Barrow, but they couldn't do the tracking scribing to take deliveries yet."

"That's me exactly," Maeve said, then quickly thought through a story of a heartsick uncle in case Shea asked after her exact reason for visiting this world. "Thank you for understanding."

"Have you told Tristan?" Shea asked, and Maeve shook her head. Shea clucked her tongue. "Tristan should really know. Even though I don't particularly care for your mentor, he'll be able to walk you through all the rules, like what to say if you wind up in a cranky old man's bedroom." She quirked her mouth. "It's not pleasant, but every situation can be handled with grace if you know how to act. Promise me you'll tell Tristan soon."

"I promise," Maeve lied.

"Thank you—truly. It saves me from having to speak with him myself."

Maeve bit her tongue to keep from defending him. "I should really be going."

"Wait a moment," Shea said, tapping her bottom lip. "I came here to get supplies for my booth at the Scriptomantic Exhibition, but I suppose I could help you out. You did come all this way." She turned to the clerk. "How about I take a look at the purchase ledger for my colleague here?" She leaned toward Maeve. "It's what you wanted to see, isn't it?"

Maeve nodded slowly, while the clerk's cheeks reddened. "But, Miss Widden, I—"

"Do I need to remind you that my family owns this entire store?"

Owned? Maeve would never have come here if she knew that.

The clerk nodded and tripped over her feet, but returned with the thick ledger book, which she placed on the counter in front of them. Shea opened it before Maeve had the chance. "Whose name am I looking for?"

Blast it all.

"Mr. Braithwaite," Maeve rattled off the first name that came to mind. "But could you list off everyone who's purchased a bottle of Oxblood in the last month? Mr. Braithwaite might have been gifted the bottle from a family member."

Shea read the names. Only three bottles were sold. One bottle to a gentleman whose name Shea recognized, who owned a bank just south of Gloam in Barrow, one bottle to Tristan, and one bottle to the initials O.P.A.A.

"O.P.A.A.?" Maeve asked.

"My family has a supplies contract with the Post, and different departments use different initials," Shea said. "O.P.A.A. stands for the Otherwhere Post's Archivist Account."

"Like the archivists who run the libraries?"

"Of course. There aren't any others. Why? Is your Mr. Braithwaite an archivist? I don't recognize the name."

"No."

The only archivist she knew of was Sibilla, the head archivist of the Second Library. The woman in Tallowmeade's picture.

Maeve went over her last conversation with Sibilla, but nothing the woman had said or done seemed out of the ordinary. She was only one archivist, anyhow, and the Post had dozens. Besides, it would have been simple for Postmaster Byrne to sign O.P.A.A. to keep anyone from discovering that he purchased it. Perhaps the Postmaster chose such a rare ink because he wanted her to see O.P.A.A. and think it was an archivist writing the threatening letters and not him.

She thought of her father's roommate. He might be able to tell her if the Postmaster was behind everything once and for all. She had to speak with him, which meant she had to first track down his name in the Second Library.

She needed a courier key.

MAEVE DIDN'T RISK returning to Leyland through her courier door until the moon was high and the station was near empty. The temperature in Leyland was chillier than Barrow. The first flurry of winter's snow dusted her cloak as she made her way toward the Post's grounds. A bird shrieked from somewhere in the snow. The sound startled Maeve into a jog. She ran through the courtyard, then skidded on a new patch of ice, falling hard on her side. Her tooth went through her lip, and coppery blood slipped across her tongue.

She pushed herself up, hobbling the rest of the way to Hawthorne House. This time, she walked straight past her room and over to Tristan's, beating her fist against his door.

A lock turned, and the door cracked. He poked his head through the opening, buttoning the last button of his shirt.

His feet were bare, his hair a perfect mess. His face lit up at the sight of her. He smiled brightly, and for a moment, Maeve forgot why she was standing there. Then his smile fell when he noticed her split lip. "What happened to you?"

"The ground wanted to have its way with me, but I wasn't in the mood." She dragged in a breath. "I already know what you're going to say, but I need to get inside the Second Library. Can I please borrow your courier key? Just for an hour."

"If you already know what I'm going to say, then you know my answer is a resounding no."

"I'll be careful."

"You'll be stopped immediately. Probably by an irritable archivist with a fondness for screaming at the top of their lungs for help."

"I'll talk my way out of it before they make a peep."

"Doubtful." He took Maeve's hand, running his bare thumb across her palm. It was scraped up from her fall. "Did you get in a boxing match with a tree as well?"

She jerked her hand away.

"Why don't you let me look up whatever it is you're so keen to find?" Tristan offered.

It was tempting, but she had already asked him to look up her father's roommate for Nan yesterday. If she suddenly confessed it was for her, Tristan would spit back a thousand questions that she didn't care to answer.

"Thanks, but I need to go on my own," she said.

"Then you'll have to finish a scribing and show my father. He gives out the courier keys."

Of course it was the Postmaster. Showing him her true name on her wrist was out of the question, and she didn't have weeks to sit around until she figured out the other four scribing types.

She turned and started walking away.

"What if we made a bargain?" Tristan called out.

Maeve swung around. "A bargain?"

He leaned against the doorframe. "Tell me a secret, and I'll help you out."

He would trade his courier key for one of her secrets?

Then she understood exactly what he wanted. "I'm not giving you my name."

"You don't have to."

"I don't?"

"I only want a secret that nobody else knows, and as much as I'd love to know the material of your knickers, that won't do either." He took a step into the hall. "I want something big. Something that will help me understand you better. Something that you're afraid to tell me."

But she was afraid to tell him everything!

"Whatever you share will stay between us," he added.

She believed him, but it didn't make it any easier.

Maeve racked her brain for something good enough, then came up with a single secret that might appease him, that stood out from her vast sea of lies. It was certainly a big secret—hopefully big enough to fit his criteria without giving too much of herself away. It wouldn't endanger her to tell it, and yet the thought of giving Tristan a piece of her that she had kept buried inside for so long made her queasy.

She stepped toward him, checking the hall. They were alone, and she was terrified.

"All right," she said, measuring her breaths. She took another step, until she stood directly before him. "I'm from Inverly."

"What?"

"I—I was there when the Aldervine came."

His eyes narrowed, while his jaw slackened. Did he not believe her?

"I barely made it out," she said, hoping more details would help convince him. "I saw it wrap around a woman and prick her. I watched her irises turn pure white. A stranger grabbed hold of me and helped me escape into Leyland. The rest of my family was not so lucky."

Her heart pounded, but she held her breath, waiting for Tristan to respond.

His forehead creased into a frown. He stared at her but didn't speak.

It made her want to run away more than anything, but she pulled her spine straight. "Was that not a good enough secret?"

"I . . ." he started. He shook his head. "I mean—yes. It was. Of course it was."

"So where's your courier key?"

"Not anywhere nearby." He pressed his index finger to the space between his eyebrows, blinking, as if trying to compose himself. It startled her.

"Meet me in an hour on the north side of the Hall of Routes," he said without looking up. Then he stepped inside his room and shut the door in her face.

The winter moon cast a halo that shone from behind the night-time clouds. The frigid evening air felt like bitter frost and stung Maeve's nostrils as she made the trek to the north side of the Hall of Routes.

"I thought you might never show up," Tristan called out as she rounded the building.

He peeled away from a nearby oak tree like a flash of shadow, then lit a small oil lantern, handing it to her, while he carried a large leather writing case without explaining what it was for.

His courier's cloak hung open along the front seam, streaming out in the wind. Beneath it, he wore a deep sapphire dinner jacket buttoned to his neck. It was a preposterous thing to wear to go traipsing around at night, but Maeve found herself noticing how it fit him like a glove.

He caught her looking. "It's new. Do you like it?"

She tore her eyes away. "Not as much as my cloak," she said, then cleared her throat. "So? Where's your courier key?"

"It's a secret."

"I don't like secrets."

"That might be the most ironic thing I have ever heard come

from a mouth." He pointed to a spot northeast of them, in the middle of darkened trees. "We're heading that way."

"You keep your key in the middle of the woods?"

"It's inside a building that's impossible to see from here. I'll explain everything once we arrive."

They set off through the bare trees, dead leaves crunching beneath their feet. After he'd shut his room door in her face, Maeve expected the walk to be tense, but Tristan spoke easily. He told her how he first found this path through the woods right after he came to live at the Post. He didn't tell anyone about it until Steward Mordraig caught him wandering up it one day and pulled him aside, threatening to feed him to the crows if he didn't admit where he was going.

"When was that?" Maeve asked.

"Just after I turned fourteen."

Maeve halted. "You mean you've lived on the Post's grounds since you were fourteen?"

"Technically thirteen, but who's counting?" he said. "I came here after Inverly, where my mother and I lived up until the Aldervine came. That was how she died, unfortunately."

He said it so casually that it took Maeve a full second for his words to register. Shocked, she turned to him.

He gave a guilty nod. "Yes, I was also in Inverly that day. It was why your secret caught me so off guard," he admitted.

Maeve searched his eyes. She never thought she would meet anyone who shared her experience, let alone be able to speak freely about it. Her throat grew tight.

Tristan took her elbow, and they continued walking. "Cathriona was from Inverly as well."

"You knew Cathriona before you mentored her?"

"Long before. She and I were grammar school mates. She happened to be visiting Leyland the day the Aldervine came, whereas I was near enough to the station to run for it. Afterward, my father brought me to live with him at the Post, while Cath moved in with an incessantly chatty cousin in Old Town, near the Post's entrance. Cath spotted me one day and insisted we be friends. She wouldn't take no for an answer," he said with an exhale. "She and I were never more than friends, but we became close. She was bubbly and sweet—easy to be around, save for her annoying habit of constantly worrying about me."

"Why would she worry?"

He ran his fingers beneath his spectacles, rubbing his eyes, then turned to face her. "Surely by now you've noticed that I don't sleep very much."

"You don't say?" Maeve said dryly, trying to make light of it. As if that were possible.

He took a deep breath. "I have a severe form of insomnia that began immediately after the Written Doors were burned. It can be difficult, but I manage it. For the most part."

"I didn't realize."

"Not many know. But Cath did. She liked to bring me all sorts of despicable tinctures to try to cure it." A sad smile flickered on his mouth. "And I put up with all her antics because we understood each other deeply. We both knew what it was like to have your entire world ripped away in an instant. To be haunted by a life that no longer belongs to you."

His words stabbed between Maeve's ribs.

She never thought she would meet another person who could describe the feeling. Tears burned her eyes, and for a moment, she thought she might burst open from her own loneliness.

Tristan took her hand, squeezing it. But then he didn't let go of her hand. He threaded his fingers through hers.

Maeve shivered at the feeling, then scowled into the dark, angry at herself for letting him see how his story affected her. For allowing him to hold her hand.

She tugged her hand away, then folded her arms across her body. "Are we almost there?"

"Just about," he said with a sigh, then turned off the path and started jogging—heading eastward.

"Where are you going?" Maeve called.

"There." He pointed up, to a break in the tree line.

The sounds of ocean waves mingled with the howling wind.

Maeve squinted and could barely make out a circular stone tower rising like a fist from the ground, built on the edge of the cliff. It was topped with a round, peaked roof that reminded her of a witch's hat from a storybook.

"Molly's Keep," Tristan said above the roar of wind.

Maeve ran up beside him, breathless. "Molly Blackcaster lived here?"

"Not quite. That's only where she scribed."

Tristan led the way to a small door on the western side of the tower. It pushed open to a darkened room that smelled of books, damp stone, and ocean salt. He took the oil lantern from her and lit a torch beside the door. Light flared into the shadowed edges of an enormous circular room, the walls lined with wooden bookshelves. The column of a spiral stair shot up the center of the vast space like human vertebrae.

Maeve spun in a circle, taking in all the shelves. "So where's your courier key?"

"I'm not giving you my key."

She spun to face him. "But we had a bargain. You promised."

"My promise was to help you. Not give you a key."

"No, I distinctly remember . . ." Her words trailed off. He did say *help*, didn't he? But he'd also led her to assume that he meant a courier key. "You tricked me."

"If you want a courier key, the only way to get one is by learning how to scribe."

"And what—you're suddenly going to show me how to scribe?"

"I'm not. I'm going to tell you a story first, and then you can decide if you still trust me enough to stay here."

Maeve was thoroughly confused, but Tristan seemed determined. He pulled a book off a nearby shelf and handed it to her. A wolf's snarling face was embossed on the leather cover.

She flipped through it. It was written in what seemed to be Old Leylish runes too worn away to read.

"After Molly died, this building was eventually converted into storage for a collection of handwritten books," he said, then took the book from her and absently flipped through the pages. "Once upon a time, a sullen and stupendously foolish thirteen-year-old boy stole one of these books, then snuck inside the Scriptorium and tried a form scribing on the last page."

"Let me guess. That boy was you?"

"Sadly, yes. I had never touched scribing pigment before that moment, but my scribing took."

"How?" Tallowmeade said all adepts had to first spend years in a writing program before the talent would manifest.

"Hell if I know," Tristan said. "But by then, I'd heard how overly protective the stewards were of adepts. So when someone noticed me, I shoved the book in a bookcase and ran off, worried the stewards might lock me away and keep me from Cath. I thought I got away with it, but Mordraig came to find me two months later with the book. I confessed, of course. Then he sat me down and had me run through all the scribing types. I performed another form scribing and then a tracking scribing on the first try."

"You're adept at *two* types?"

"Three. I somehow managed a memory scribing on my second try."

"Oh, is that all?" No wonder they thought him a prodigy.

"The stewards decided I had potential but didn't tell me what for yet, then they ordered me confined to the Post's grounds for my own safety."

"They locked you up?"

"For the most part. I missed Cath every day. I wrote to her about asinine things like the books I'd read and Steward Mordraig's morning breath. She wrote me back at first—mostly worried letters asking about my insomnia—but then she started upper school, and her letters grew less frequent. Eventually they stopped altogether," he said as if it didn't matter at all, but the dark look on his face told a different story. "So I decided to put Cath out of my mind and focus on scribing, and that's when I grew to love it. When it became precious."

"An escape," Maeve said, thinking of her own writing.

His eyes flicked to hers. "Exactly. Then that winter, I was laid up with a bad flu and went to the infirmary. They put me in a cot beside a man who had been there for over a year. Part of his leg was missing. He couldn't speak; his vocal cords were damaged. Our head doctor wouldn't tell me anything about him, so I bribed a nurse. She told me the man had accidentally read a form-scribed book that he had found in the Scriptorium."

Maeve shot forward with a gasp. "It wasn't your fault."

"Ah, but technically it was." Tristan returned the handwritten book to the shelf. "I barely remembered what I scribed in that book—I'd done it when my insomnia was at its worst—but I confronted Mordraig and my father, and they confirmed the scribing that hurt that man was indeed mine. They said the characters from the book somehow came to life with ink and stalked the upper floor in the Scriptorium for a few hours before they were all doused with crematory ash. They'd never seen anything like it. Then Mordraig sat me down and said I could be the next Molly Blackcaster and repair the Written Doors one day and wanted me to start training."

He'd been earmarked so horribly young. What Mordraig did seemed especially cruel considering Tristan had just hurt someone and was clearly upset by it. "And what did you say?"

"I told them to go to hell, of course."

"I would have probably said the same thing."

"I think I'd pay good money to see that," he said. "And even more if you finished it off with a little ditty about sheep."

"Good heavens, no. I wouldn't want to kill anyone."

He burst into laughter. She hadn't heard him laugh like that. The sound echoed and wrapped around her and ended far too soon.

She considered singing so she might hear him laugh again, but he walked to the stairwell and knocked his knuckles against the banister.

"Up these stairs is a place that makes learning to scribe easier. It's where I used to come to practice, and it's where I'd like you to practice. But before we go up, I need you to hear the rest of the story, so you understand all the dangers."

Tristan's tone was grave, and Maeve nodded, despite her apprehension.

He searched his coat and pulled a quill from a pocket—a sleek hawk quill. The fletching caught the torchlight.

"Yesterday, I told you it was hard to write after what happened to Cath, but it started long before that. The truth is, I refused to touch one of these after learning about what I did to that man in the infirmary." He spun the feather. "My father felt pressure from everyone to somehow get me over what had happened—as if getting over nearly killing a man were possible—but he thought he could. He put me into the courier apprenticeship. I forced myself to do deliveries, but that was all I could stand. Then a year passed, and Cath appeared in the courtyard one day, bright and shining. I hadn't heard from her in three years."

"She came to apprentice?"

"Yes." His throat bobbed. "Later, I learned the stewards offered her the apprenticeship spot so I would agree to mentor her. They thought they could use her as a bribe to get me to love scribing again, and I was too thrilled to notice. It was instantly like old times between me and Cath. I didn't practice anything advanced myself; I was still too worried I would hurt someone if I tried. But it didn't matter because I taught Cath things that she never would have learned from another mentor. I showed her which Old Leylish runes worked better to amplify different scribing types, which quill feathers to use. I gave her scribing pigments I don't remember mixing because I was practically sleepwalking, and I think I threw in things I shouldn't have."

He lowered himself onto the bottom step. His head dropped into his hands and dark hair tumbled out between his fingers.

"A couple of months into the apprenticeship, Cath got her courier key. One day she showed me a journal she found in the Second Library, with notes about an advanced skin scribing called the Silver Scribing. She thought it might work better than one of her tinctures to cure my insomnia."

"Aren't all skin scribings outlawed because they're dangerous?"

"Yes," he said. "Extremely dangerous. I told her to get rid of it immediately. She promised she would, and I believed her because only a fool would try to recreate a historic skin scribing. A few days later, I was reading in the Scriptorium and heard something. I ran down the stairs and found Cath, face down in a puddle of pigment I'd mixed for her that morning. Then I turned her head—" He took a long breath. "I called for help. They found her body covered in writing mixed with Old Leylish runes."

"The Silver Scribing?"

"As far as I know. I never read it. That journal was confiscated, and I haven't seen it since. I hope I never see it again."

He sounded miserable.

Mr. Braithwaite kept a drawer full of expensive inks that had been dropped, their glass cracked beyond repair, held together with nothing but their sticky gilded labels. Precious, but a swift shake away from shattering. Maeve suddenly felt as if she were cradling one of those inkwells.

Tristan had just told her a timeline of the worst moments of his life. He blamed himself for everything. She felt deep sorrow for him, of course, but anger spiked alongside it.

That man in the Scriptorium was a mistake made by a lonely child who was hurting from losing his mother. Cathriona's death was not Tristan's fault either. Cathriona tried the Silver Scribing on her own, despite warnings, then snuck away and did what she wanted. It was a selfish decision, and yet Tristan thought himself dangerous because of it. Now that thinking held him back.

It struck Maeve how similar their situations were. What her

father did was not her fault, but she'd allowed it to hold her back as well, to rule over every aspect of her life.

"If you still want to go upstairs, I'll come with you. But I won't mix pigments or give you notes," Tristan said. "Or do any scripto-mancy myself, but I can explain things. I'll supervise you if you wish to try for your courier key." He pointed to the door. "But given everything I've just told you, I won't be offended if you want to leave."

Of course she wouldn't leave. It would validate this hatred he had toward himself.

But before she could say a thing, he shot up. "I should never have brought you here. This was a terrible idea." He raked fingers through his hair. "We should get you back to the grounds—"

"No," Maeve said. "I'm going to stay. We had a bargain, and I intend to get my end of it."

"But what if—"

"A blank page and a single word," she said. She took his hand and squeezed it, just as he'd done for her in the woods. Then she stepped around him and started up the stairs.

They were ungodly tall stairs, and Maeve's legs burned by the time she reached the top, but it was worth the climb. A window showed a perfect view of the ocean lit by moonlight. A cascade of light filtered in through the glass, illuminating the largest scriptomancy worktable she'd ever seen. She started toward it when something dark zipped by her cheek. It stopped, hovering in the air. Large black wings fluttered around a tiny body.

"Don't touch it," Tristan said, coming up beside her. He waved at the creature until it fluttered up to the ceiling, where more of them hovered around the rafters.

"Are they bats?"

"They're drear moths. Their ink stains everything."

"Ink?"

"They're all made from form scribings that the stewards believe Molly herself wrote. My father wants to be rid of them because he worries about them ruining the books, but the stewards won't allow crematory ash to touch them, given their historical significance."

"But I thought all scribings wear off when the arcane magic is used up."

"Nearly all do, but Molly's don't. She knew a way to write

scribings that continually pull in arcane magic. So Arcane Infusion isn't a single instance, but ongoing. It's how the Written Doors lasted until Inverly."

"Didn't she leave notes about how she did it?"

"A few, which is how we know it's possible, but they're not concrete enough to let us recreate it. The stewards have tricks to make the magic trapped in a scribing escape slower so it can be read multiple times, but nothing like the moths."

He riffled through his writing case and pulled out a long gadget that looked like a wand with a round glass sphere at the end that held a single mirror.

Maeve recognized it. "You brought an arcthiometer? I thought those were all junk."

"Most are. But my father gave me this one. It has paper at its center with a scribing that should still work, but it only lasts for a few minutes."

He flipped the arcthiometer over and pointed out a cavity with a piece of paper inside that held a tiny scribble of handwriting.

"You do the honors." He handed her the device.

"Show me arcane magic," Maeve read aloud from the paper.

The mirror inside the glass globe began spinning faster and faster, making a whirring sound. Then the globe began to glow like a gas lamp, but brighter. Maeve waved it through the air. The arcthiometer's light illuminated little particles of shimmering dust motes. They moved in a current like a river around her. Tristan ran his fingers through the motes, disturbing the current as if it were water.

They were everywhere. Maeve brought the device close to her face and inhaled, breathing in a stream of motes, but tasting nothing.

"It's arcane magic," Tristan said. "It seems to gather in certain places and flow away from others. There's a large amount around

Blackcaster Station. The stewards think the ancient scripto-mancers chose that spot to build the black stone wall because of it. There's slightly less of the magic in this tower, but there's still a great deal. Scribings always seem to take more easily here. I think it's why Molly chose this place to work."

The arcthiometer sparked and fizzed out with another whir, leaving them in the dark.

Tristan lit a few half-melted candles along the back side of the worktable, then unpacked the writing case, pulling out inkwells, pounce, dried herb bundles, a mortar and pestle, a large vial of sil-ver scribing pigment base, and a box Maeve recognized.

He opened the lid and took out the left-handed swan quill edged in silver and set with a ruby. Her quill. He looked at her. "You haven't carved it yet?"

Her face burned. "You took that from my worktable."

"Yes, because I gave it to you to use, and the right tools make everything go faster."

He set the feather down and sifted through his case again with a sigh. "I didn't pack a quill knife because I didn't think I'd need one. Do you have yours?"

The thought of carving that quill made Maeve feel ill, but she dug through her saddlebag. When she pulled out her quill knife, an envelope came with it. It sailed across the floor, stopping near Tristan's right foot.

A blank envelope.

Another Oxblood letter.

When Tristan bent to pick it up, she raced forward, but he'd already lifted it.

"I need you to give that back to me," Maeve said, trying to keep her composure.

"Is it your anonymous letter?"

"No. I—I don't know what it is."

His brows cinched together. "Then why are you terrified of me holding it?"

"I'm not."

"Fine. Then let me open it to see what it is." He took off a glove and dug a finger beneath the fold.

The ripping sound had her heart plummeting. If he was hurt because of her, she wouldn't be able to forgive herself. She ran around the table. When he tried to dart away, she crashed into him with such force that they were both knocked to the ground. She rolled on top of him, searching his shirt. "Where is it?"

He pulled the envelope out from somewhere behind him, holding it out of reach. "I'll give it to you if you tell me what's inside."

"You don't understand."

"Then help me to. You were honest with me about Inverly."

Yes, because her memories of Inverly weren't actively trying to rip her throat out.

She didn't know what to say.

He sighed and pulled a folded letter from the envelope.

"Wait! I think that's a letter scribed by someone who is trying to hurt me."

That startled him. "Why would anyone want to hurt you?"

Because they knew who she was and wanted her to leave. Or wanted something much worse. "I have no idea."

"We should tell my father. He'll start an investigation."

Her breathing faltered. "You know my situation. If there was an investigation, there's no way I would stay to see it through."

"Then at least let me open the letter with you and inspect it. I might be able to tell things about the intention of the letter-writer. Scribings can look like they're meant to harm when they're harmless. Others that look harmless can be much more dangerous." He held her stare, as if challenging her. "I won't tell anyone."

Of course he wouldn't tell anyone, unless her full name was penned in red letters on the inside. But she considered his offer. "How about I read it first, then if there's nothing specific, I'll let you look?"

"Done."

They both stood. Maeve carried the letter to the worktable, while Tristan tugged off his crematory ash satchel and placed it beside the paper. He looked the other way.

Maeve held her breath as she unfolded the letter.

"Well?" Tristan asked.

It wasn't written in Oxblood ink.

It was a simple letter, beginning with *My Sweet Deidre*, then going into torrid details of how the author longed to touch his Deidre—everywhere.

It was one of the letters Maeve had stolen from the Scriptorium and stuck inside her saddlebag before crossing over to visit Plume & Pen. And it was scribed with a bit more than a tracking scribing. Whoever had sent this letter wanted Deidre to feel the strength of his desire, and he had paid the extra commission to make that a reality.

"Well? Is it dangerous?" Tristan asked.

The sound of his voice reverberated deep inside her belly. "That depends on your definition of dangerous."

He snatched the letter from her fingers.

"Don't read it," she said weakly, but it was too late.

201

Tristan's face flushed when he came to the end. An overwhelming need to step closer to him washed over her, but she gritted her teeth against the sensation and focused on his forehead—at a speck of wax that must have splattered there at some point earlier today.

"It's a sense scribing," Tristan said in a strained tone.

"I'm aware."

The intense longing to touch him made that startlingly clear.

Maeve struggled to remember her lessons about sense scribings— she knew they were able to transfer the emotions described in the text to the reader, but she couldn't remember anything else. As it was, she could barely breathe. "Would crematory ash do anything?"

"Perhaps. If you ingested enough. But I don't recommend it; it makes you violently sick. And there are no guarantees it will work. Sense scribings are tricky. It's better to wait it out."

"How long?"

"I don't know. A few minutes?"

"Whoever scribed that letter should be tossed down the abyss."

Tristan nodded, then shifted to place the letter on the table and grazed Maeve's wrist. The touch was feather-light, but they both stilled.

A bead of sweat caught on Maeve's lip. She licked it away, and Tristan cursed beneath his breath. She wanted to kiss him. As soon as the thought entered her mind, it was all she could think about until she felt consumed by it. Then she wondered if it was all *he* could think about as well, and her body heated in a terrible blush.

Tristan's eyes dropped, focusing on her mouth. Then he seemed to remember himself and scooted backward a step. Only a step— as if that was all he was capable of moving. His spectacles slid down his nose, and he pushed them up.

She wanted to reach across and take them off, to press her mouth to the bruises beneath his eyes.

She gripped the edge of the table.

"What do you plan to do after you leave the Post?" he asked in a strained tone.

"Are you trying to distract me?"

"Of course. Now answer my question."

"I don't know exactly what I'll do," Maeve forced out. "Probably head south."

"And?"

"Work. Write. Plant a garden."

"What kind of garden?"

"A small one, like the gardens that grew outside the College of Landscape Arts in Inverly, but on a sunny slope of a hill. With a pretty view and the most colorful flowers I can find seeds for. Then I'll leave room in the center for a bench, where I can sit and write."

"And what would you write?"

"Anything that came to me." The cadence of his breathing notched up, and Maeve forced herself to picture the tangled, leafy flower beds, which her mind's eye populated with plump sapphire buds matching the exact shade of Tristan's blasted dinner jacket. "When I'm not writing," she forced out, "my hands grow restless, and I find myself picking at my clothing and straightening things that are already straight. I love writing in my journal because it's a release, and I've always thought a garden might be that as well, in a different way. But I haven't been able to have a garden yet."

Tristan's tongue swiped along his bottom lip. "Why not?"

"Because I'm afraid."

"Afraid of flowers?"

"Horribly."

He huffed a laugh.

"I am. You see, I'm afraid that if I plant some, I'll have to leave them suddenly. And I think leaving a garden to dry up and wither is sadder than never planting one in the first place." Her eyebrows drew together. "I don't think I've ever told anyone that."

"Thank you for confiding in me."

"You're welcome, but I don't feel any different."

"Neither do I." His gaze flickered to hers.

She trembled, and without realizing what she was doing—without truly thinking at all—she lifted her hand and trailed a slow finger up the right side of his neck and along his jawline.

"You should probably stop that," he said, and slipped a hand around her waist, pulling her against him, until she could feel the cold edges of his jacket buttons through her blouse.

"We'll both stop on the count of three," she whispered.

"Deal," he said, but neither of them counted. His other hand cradled her neck, his fingers playing in the curls at her nape, his mouth treacherously close. "I think you should step away from me this instant. If you don't, I'm fairly certain that I'm going to kiss you."

Oh, how she wanted to kiss him, but a part of her held back. *Kiss him, kiss him, kiss him*, her mind chanted.

But it was the scribing putting these thoughts inside her head. She didn't want this. How could she possibly want this? She clamped her lips together, determined to *not* kiss him. It didn't stop her, however, from dragging her fingers across his scalp.

He cursed and slid her backward onto the worktable. Bottles crashed to the floor as he craned over her and nudged up the hem of her camisole, his warm hand carving a slow path across her belly. His *teeth* grazed along the edge of her jaw.

It felt as if she were melting, like if she breathed too deeply, she would unspool into a thousand particles to mingle with the arcane magic floating around them.

This was dangerous. And yet—and yet she couldn't bring herself to stop.

She slipped her fingers beneath his jacket, gliding her hand up to the apex of his chest, frantic to touch him.

He tensed.

It was the slightest twitch of muscle, but felt like a bucket of cold water upended onto her scribing-addled mind.

Maeve pulled away, breath sputtering. "We need to stop this right now. We're *friends*," she emphasized.

"I think we're a little past being just friends," he joked, then looked at her.

Whatever he saw in her face had him nod and push off her.

Maeve blinked up at the drear moths circling overhead. A rush of cold air skated over the tops of her thighs. The cold cleared her head, and she sat up. She still felt the dregs of the scribing on the edges of her mind, along with the start of a terrible headache.

Tristan opened windows across the room, letting in more cold air. He glanced at her then turned away quickly. "Your shirt."

Maeve looked down at herself, horrified.

Her blouse was unbuttoned, her camisole rucked up above her navel, where his fingers had just been. A sharp pang of longing hit her.

Not real longing. No, it had to be another sensation brought on by that scribing. What they just did didn't mean anything. It couldn't. She would forget all about it the following morning, and they would go about their merry business as if it never happened.

"Are you feeling normal again?" Tristan asked as she fixed her clothing.

"I'm fine," she said, then stood and realized how *not* fine she was. A wave of nausea had her double over. Tristan rushed to help, but she held up a hand. "I told you I'm fine."

"Strong sense scribings can sometimes have a nauseating effect the first time you read one. You'll want to try to sleep it off for a few hours."

Hours? "I can't. I have to scribe."

He rolled his eyes and dragged her to a spot on the rug before the hearth. She pulled her knees to her chin and hugged her calves, shivering.

"I'll build a fire. Try not to freeze to death in the meantime," he said, then went to work at the hearth, stacking wood, kindling. He removed his sapphire jacket, setting it aside.

Of *course* his fitted shirt strained across the muscles of his back while he worked. Maeve forced her eyes to the rug, wishing Tristan was small and hairy, not built like *that*.

Once the fire was going strong, he sat down beside her. The space between them felt charged and awkward. Why did he have to sit so close?

"You're still wearing my socks," he said with a wry curve to his mouth.

"They're my socks now." She stretched her toes like a cat before the flames.

They were both silent for a long moment, then Tristan asked, "Do you regret it?"

Her neck burned.

"We were influenced by the scribing," she said, afraid to look at him.

"That's not an answer."

"It's the only one you'll get."

She tipped her throbbing forehead against her knees and felt the instant Tristan stood, like a hot tickle of air against her side. A moment later, something soft and warm pressed into the small of her back. A stack of pillows.

Curling against them, Maeve tried to shift all thought away from Tristan, and found it impossible. The letter wasn't their fault, but what they had done went far beyond anything she allowed herself. It was inexcusable and broke all her rules a hundred times over. And despite it all, she still wanted desperately to kiss him, which terrified her more than anything.

∼

IT TOOK MAEVE far too long to fall asleep, but when she finally did, she dreamed of dark vines weaving up walls, crawling over cobblestones and buildings. Of racing toward Blackcaster Station while bodies sank to the ground around her in a white-eyed sleep.

A shock of cold stabbed her finger.

She woke to a large drear moth perched like a hummingbird on her hand. It hung there like a silent shadow, then it fluttered its wings and took off toward the rafters, leaving behind a smear of centuries-old ink on her knuckle.

Maeve stared up, amazed, until something shifted to her left.

Tristan lay beside her, his hands tucked against the curve of her hip. One of his feet had woven itself around her leg like a curl of Aldervine from her dream. His spectacles were off, his blue-tinged eyelids shifting with each steady rise and fall of his chest. Sleeping soundly.

It felt like she was witnessing a small miracle.

He was still fully clothed in his shirt and trousers, but the neck of his shirt had come unbuttoned below his crematory ash satchel. The small sliver of his chest that was exposed had writing on it.

Maeve drew up. Was it a skin scribing or simply writing? She couldn't tell from where she lay.

Her nausea seemed to be gone. She untangled herself and rolled onto her knees to get a closer look, then froze when Tristan stirred. He shifted to his side—away from her.

Something jangled.

A small ring of keys lay on the floor near his right arm. They must have slipped from his pocket.

Maeve pulled herself up, then tiptoed around Tristan and lifted the keys with the hem of her skirt so they wouldn't make noise. Six total.

She pocketed them and left.

It was still dark when Maeve reached the Second Library. From the outside, the front desk looked deserted.

She tugged her hood up and entered the lobby. A sign on the desk read: ATTENDANT RETURNS AT EIGHT SHARP. ENTER AT YOUR OWN DISCRETION.

Sibilla was probably still asleep.

Maeve pulled out Tristan's key ring. It took a few attempts to find the right key, but eventually the library door clicked open, and she stepped into a dark corridor laced with the smell of stone and parchment. Guttering lamplight helped lead her to a massive chamber where bookshelves soared to the ceiling.

At the whisper of footsteps, Maeve kept moving and spotted a stairwell with a sign that listed out the twenty-three descending floors. It gave a broad overview of each, but there was no mention of where she might find old room assignments.

Maeve took the stairwell down one floor, passing a room of historical documents from when the university was founded. On the next landing, she found a sign that simply read: RECORDS FLOOR.

Promising, at least.

She walked down a long hall, then through a room lined with scribing pigment almanacs going back hundreds of years, then another room filled with the College of Scriptomantic Art's historic ink collection. No room assignments. At the distant sound of more footsteps, Maeve dipped into a long room with a sign marked: INCIDENT REPORTS.

She was about to walk through it when she noticed the words HAWTHORNE HOUSE embossed on the spine of every book on one shelf. They were all arranged by years. She pulled one out, flipping through reports of leaking faucets and busted dressers. One man complained of a sparrow that had flown in through a broken window and gotten into his scribing supplies. Listed below his name were the names of his two roommates.

Maeve put the book down, searching. Then she found a shelf with ELDERMOSS HALL marking the spine of at least a hundred books, their dates going back centuries.

She pulled out the volume for the year the Written Doors burned.

It was a heavy tome that sent a plume of dust in the air when she flipped it open. The writing inside was too tiny to read in the dim room, and she searched around for a candle—anything to brighten the space. She needed more light.

Carrying the massive book with both arms, Maeve hurried down the adjoining corridor until the light was brighter. She knelt and opened the book once more. It took her a few minutes of squinting over graying text filled with reports of broken handles and crooked bed frames until she found her father.

Jonathan Abenthy had filed an incident report complaining how his window was stuck. Listed right beside his name was his roommate, a Mr. Fion Claryman.

She'd found him.

A library cart rattled. Someone was heading toward her.

She ripped the page out and shoved it down her pocket, then ran deeper into the library, until she hit a hall that was cordoned off by an iron gate with an ancient-looking wooden door behind it.

Another cart rattled. Footsteps clicked along the floor.

Coming her way.

Maeve took out Tristan's key ring, fumbling through keys. Only one of his keys looked large enough for the iron gate's lock.

She pushed it in and turned. The gate clicked open. She shut the gate and raced through the wooden door beyond it, then softly shut the door before anyone could see her. She covered her mouth at the sound of the cart's wheels rolling closer. She heard footfalls. Whoever it was halted. The sound of the gate jingling sent a wave of terror through her. Her hands felt her pockets. Her letters were there, but Tristan's key was still in the lock.

The jingling continued for another few seconds. It eventually stopped, and the cart rolled away. Whoever it was had gone. Maeve was about to sink to the floor with relief, but something moved out of the corner of her eye, and her pulse leapt.

She took a survey of the space around her. The room was at least a story and a half tall and lit by a single torch. She walked over and pulled the torch from the wall, bringing it to the side of a large case made of thick glass welded together with what looked to be pure silver. Something shifted behind the glass. A dark shape moved toward her.

Maeve jolted and fell backward, dropping the torch. Her hand flew out to catch herself and slammed against something metal on the floor. It sliced her. Searing pain lanced up her arm.

She looked down to where her blood dripped against a rusted

plaque that read: ALDERVINE SPECIMEN, RETRIEVED BY MOLLY BLACK-
CASTER.

Maeve gripped her wrist and scrambled to her knees, her eyes
locked on the glass case.

Inside it, deep green tendrils uncoiled, slick thorns clawing for
purchase exactly as they had along the side of Blackcaster Station
in Inverly.

If the glass weren't there, she could reach out and run a finger
along a thorn.

Her entire body began to tremble. It felt as though she was beside
Blackcaster Station right after witnessing her great-aunt's death.

That entire moment came back to her. Maeve could practically
feel that stranger's arms grabbing her shoulder, dragging her away,
the soft give of his muscles as she inhaled the scent of pounce
powder and herbs wafting from him like cologne—just like her
father always smelled.

Her eyes widened in shock.

She'd felt comforted by that stranger because he had smelled
exactly like her father. She'd never realized it before this moment.

She still couldn't remember the stranger's face, but she could
picture his fingers gripping her arm perfectly. They were splattered with ink. He wore a necklace with a gray satchel that she
had focused on to keep from looking at all the people dropping
around her.

Maeve touched her own crematory ash satchel.

That man who had saved her had been a scriptomancer, and
she'd never put it together until now.

Then more memories slammed into her, one after the other:
screaming horses, her aunt's cry, the copper taste of blood rinsing
across her tongue. Her chest tightened like a fist was squeezing it,

like she was losing everything she loved all over again. She tried to scream but couldn't draw a breath. She couldn't breathe—

Someone gripped her shoulder, dragging her up.

It was Sibilla.

"Hurry," she said, forcing Maeve out of the room and through the metal gate, then past a blur of bookshelves, until they came around an aisle to a dim part of the floor. Sibilla's face rippled with fury. "What were you thinking?"

Maeve collapsed to her knees. "The Aldervine—how does nobody know about it?"

"Many people know about it. A team of scientists come to study it once a month, but there isn't very much they can test from behind the glass." She narrowed her eyes. "How did you get past the gate? Only senior officials have access."

Then Tristan must have somehow gotten a key from his father.

Maeve could still see the gate from where she stood. Tristan's keys were gone from the lock. Whoever rattled that cart must have taken them. "The gate was left opened," she said.

Sibilla's right eye twitched. "That's impossible."

There were footsteps a few aisles away.

"Get up!" Sibilla dug her fingernails into Maeve's shoulders, forcing her to stand. "If anyone asks, you were never inside that room, and you certainly didn't see me," she said in a shrill tone, then rushed away in the direction of the footsteps.

Maeve peeked around the shelves. To where Sibilla came up beside Postmaster Byrne and three other stewards. They spoke in hushed tones, then made their way toward a far stairwell. Sibilla glanced back once before following the group.

Sibilla had saved her. Maeve didn't know what to make of it, and she certainly didn't have time to stand around wondering.

Something warm and wet slipped down Maeve's fingers. She lifted her hand and gasped at blood weeping from where she'd cut herself on the plaque.

Thinking fast, she ripped a piece of fabric from her cloak and wound it around her wrist, then raced up the stairs, back through the main entrance. Freezing morning air sliced into her chest, and sleet pelted her shoulders, but she was outside—away from that vine. Tipping her face skyward, she sucked in a deep breath until she was dizzy.

She dug in her pocket and pulled out the page she'd ripped from the incident report, read the name of her father's roommate.

Fion Claryman.

She recognized the name.

Maeve started walking, trying her best to push all thoughts of the Aldervine from her mind. Her legs trembled badly, but the mess hall was nearby at least. She rushed inside, scanning along the postings hanging in the entranceway, until she found a flyer for the Scriptomantic Exhibition and held it to a light. Her blood smeared the paper.

When she was ten, her father dragged her to that year's exhibition. Back then, it was held in a shabby lecture hall in the north side of Gloam in Leyland. He made her sit on a stained chair while he gave a demonstration to four upper school writing students, hoping to recruit them.

This year's exhibition lasted an entire week, with a merchant hall where dealers sold supplies, and couriers from the Post, like Shea Widden, set up booths to scribe novelties and give speeches to ease everyone's minds. The flyer listed a litany of scheduled talks about everything from the Written Doors to the inner workings of the Post.

Maeve ran her fingers down the paper, past more details.

The weeklong event didn't start for another three weeks, save for a closed-door reception for the planning committee the week after next in Barrow.

It went on to list committee members, including Mr. Fion Claryman, Professor of Linguistics at the Barrow campus.

There he was. His name had been sitting right under her nose this entire time. And Postmaster Byrne had to know this man if he was involved in planning the exhibition.

Her father's roommate.

Her *old friend*.

"I'm coming for you," Maeve whispered.

"What do you mean he won't be back for another two weeks?" Maeve stared at the pretty clerk seated at the front desk of the university in Barrow's linguistics office.

"I meant just what I said. Professor Claryman is in the south meeting with a few prospective candidates." The woman picked at her rouged lip.

"But for two whole weeks?"

"Our college is only seven years old. I'm sure you know how hard it is to find anyone with a linguistics background in Barrow that isn't recruited by well-paying businesses first. It's a small miracle Professor Claryman found candidates at all." She pointed to a flyer for the Scriptomantic Exhibition hanging on the wall. "He'll be back in time for the exhibition. You can try him then."

Maeve fled the stuffy office, gulping in a lungful of the chill Barrow evening air.

Two weeks was too much time to sit around waiting to speak with Fion Claryman, but she didn't know how to do a tracking scribing to hunt him down. There was no option but to wait until he returned.

Maeve left the office, then turned south, maneuvering through Barrow's clean streets until she found herself beside the river Liss.

A young man with dark hair and spectacles passed her by, and she tensed, thinking it was Tristan.

She'd left him sleeping in Molly's Keep just this morning. He would have realized she stole his key by now. She frowned at the thought. Hopefully, it would make him angry enough to avoid her entirely for the next two weeks. She wasn't sure she could go another hour feeling like she had in the attic room with him. It would drive her mad.

Hoping to push a confrontation with Tristan as far out as possible, Maeve stayed in Barrow until well past suppertime, then returned through her courier door when the moon was high.

Leyland was freezing, a light dusting of snow coating the ground. A deep shiver rolled through her. Her cloak had a couple of small rips from falling through the floor in Eldermoss Hall. Even though she'd managed to salvage it, her favorite material in the worlds was barely enough to keep her warm.

Hugging it tight around her, she left the square, then found the secret opening in the perimeter fence and slipped through, looking forward to her toasty room. But by the time Hawthorne House came into view, she halted, then rushed behind a nearby oak tree.

Tristan leaned one shoulder against the entranceway, a bottle of wine dangling from his gloved fingers.

He wore the same sapphire jacket, but it looked horribly disheveled, and his cloak was nowhere to be seen. His hair was mussed, sticking up everywhere. She remembered how it felt against her palms and clenched her fingers into fists. For a fleeting moment, she simply wanted to be a girl, without the kind of secrets that drew blood.

Tristan scanned the footpath near where she hid.

Before he might see her, Maeve raced into the woods like a

coward. She picked her way around another residence hall, then through a copse of oaks. Snow coated her ankles. She had to get inside somewhere before her toes went numb. She could go to the Scriptorium, but it was straight east—clear across the grounds—and Tristan would come looking for her there.

Searching the trees, Maeve caught flickering lights coming from another building close by. She started toward it, then realized it was the Groggery. She'd avoided it up until now, but nobody in their right mind would think to look for her there.

Maeve picked her way through trees and over to the Groggery's quaint entrance. The scents of ale and sweat wafted through the wooden door. The sounds of voices and bawdy laughter spilled from inside, but she forced her fingers to grip the door handle and turn it. Blessedly warm air enveloped her. The interior looked like an old Gloam tavern, with a dappled walnut bar and small tables in the back made from stacked barrels and partitioned by meager wooden dividers. They were filled with couriers drinking and chattering, their shirt necks unbuttoned, cloaks puddling against the stained floor.

Maeve felt her spirits lift at the sheer merriment, as if every ill thought had been banned from entering the premises. Best of all, nobody looked her way. Instead of panicking at the amount of people, the noise and commotion calmed her. A courier clapped another on the back. A group in one corner whooped over the last move in a heated game of knucklenook. Even the old barkeep had a smile lifting the corners of his mouth.

It seemed a shame now, standing amid such innocent revelry, that she'd allowed herself to be afraid of this. It seemed almost absurd to her.

She scanned the crowd and noticed Nan hunched over a pile

of papers and books at a corner table, her back to the bar, tapping a quill nib against a well of ink.

"I thought that was you," Maeve said, gliding into the chair opposite her roommate.

Nan jolted. When she realized it was Maeve, her eyebrows rose considerably. "I must have hit my head on the way in here, and now I'm in some twisted reality. I'm dreaming, right? I can't believe my eyes. You're here. *You.*"

Maeve gave a sheepish smile. "Surprise."

"That's one word for it," Nan said, then gathered her mess of papers and books into a pile. Yellow slips stuck out from all the books.

They were the checkout slips from the Second Library, the ones Sibilla had shown her. "Have you won your courier key?"

"God, no. A friend checked all these out for me," Nan said, then leaned toward her. "I've taken up the advice you gave me after the bonfire and started writing again—outside of scribing."

"Poetry?"

She nodded. "And I plan to publish it. Under a pen name, of course. How do you think Murdina Stewart suits me?" She leaned back. "Or maybe Zelda Crawford? I've always thought I should have been named something brazen like Zelda."

Maeve couldn't believe Nan was writing. "Can I read it?"

Color bloomed across Nan's cheeks. "Not yet. It's not ready to share. Maybe in a week or two." She shoved all the papers and books into her saddlebag, then shot up. "Oh! Let me get you a drink."

Maeve didn't want a drink, but Nan was up and speaking to the barkeep before she could get a word in. She returned in no time with a tall glass of honey-colored liquid that foamed at the top and smelled decidedly sour.

"Mead" was all Nan said, placing the tall glass directly in front of Maeve.

She stared at it.

"It's not going to bite you," Nan said.

Oh, but it might. Everyone around her, however, was tossing the liquid back, and they all seemed happy enough about it. Maeve lifted the glass and decided to give it a try. She took a small sip and coughed. "It has the flavor of what I imagine a city puddle might taste like."

"But you're smiling."

Was she? Maeve took another sip. The second one went down easier. Her chest warmed pleasantly, and she let her limbs relax.

"So." Nan leaned forward on her elbows. "Are you going to tell me why you're here, or should I guess?" A coy smile spread across her painted red lips.

Her roommate was on the prowl for gossip. "I came because I didn't feel like going back to the room just yet."

"Does it have anything to do with this?" Nan pulled an envelope from her bag and placed it beside Maeve's glass of mead.

Key thief was scrawled across the front in handwriting far too elegant to belong to anyone but Tristan.

Maeve lifted the letter. "You spoke to Tristan?"

"I wouldn't exactly say that we exchanged words. He shoved that in my hand during luncheon in the mess hall. I tried to get information out of him, but he remained as mute as a statue, then stalked away rather swiftly." Nan craned forward. "What in the worlds did you do to him, Eilidh?"

"Was he very upset?"

"I've never seen a man so agitated or worried." Her eyebrow arched. "And dare I say, a touch heartsick."

"Tristan is not heartsick."

"If you say so," Nan said, and folded her arms in front of her. She nodded at the letter with her chin. "Aren't you going to open it? I won't peek. I promise."

Maeve didn't believe her for a second.

She drummed her fingers against the envelope. She didn't particularly want to open it, but then what if Sibilla returned the keys to Tristan and told him everything about dragging her from the room with the Aldervine? Perhaps that was why Tristan looked upset in the mess hall. Maybe this letter was a warning telling her that Sibilla had changed her mind and was planning to turn her in.

She was terrified of what she would find, but she cracked the seal and pulled it out, then braced herself for the furious words that she knew would be inside.

Dear Nobody Interesting,

I thought more about your advice on starting with a single word. After you fell asleep last night, I wrote for a while, which turned into three hours. When my hand cramped, I decided to try mixing a batch of scribing pigments that I haven't attempted since before Cath. The recipe came to me in a flash of inspiration, and I was able to craft the pigment without touching my almanac once. Honestly, it scared me to death, but it also felt exquisite, like falling into an old chair after years away from home and finding the leather still molded to me. What I think I'm trying to say is thank you.

—Your Faithful Sheep

P.S. I hope my key served you well. Now would you kindly return it, or I'll be forced to make you re-shoe a horse.

Maeve read it a second time, smiling to herself.

Sibilla wasn't mentioned anywhere in the letter, and Tristan seemed to be in good spirits—mixing scribing pigments of all things. She wouldn't believe it if it wasn't staring back at her in his own handwriting.

Now he was probably worried out of his mind, wondering what happened to her in the library. And she'd acted like a complete fool and run from him.

She should find him and let him know she was all right.

"What does it say?" Nan tried to look over the top.

Maeve pulled the letter to her chest. "Strangely enough, it says that Nan should learn to mind her own business."

A smirk grew on Nan's lips. "At least Shea will be glad to know that Tristan likes you too much to murder you. You've lost your heart, haven't you?"

Perhaps there was a way to seal someone's mouth shut with a scribing. "I assure you that my heart is firmly inside my own chest."

"Whatever you say."

"You're exasperating."

"I'm aware of that, and you like it. Admit it," Nan said.

Maeve couldn't help herself and laughed, then pushed off her chair. "I need to get back."

"Then I'll walk you. I've been here for hours, and my back is killing me."

Nan pried at Maeve endlessly about Tristan on the way to their room. Maeve didn't give an inch. She was determined to keep what transpired between them in Molly's Keep a secret—locked tightly away until some distant future moment when she wasn't such a coward.

Tristan was gone from the front of Hawthorne House. The

building stood stark against the moonlit oaks, the upper floors all lit up. Maeve checked Tristan's window to see if his light was also on, but his room was dark. Their room, however, was not. A light flickered from inside their window, silhouetting a figure.

Maeve stepped forward, staring intently at their window.

"Bees in your throat?" Nan asked, nudging her.

"Shh. Not bees."

Maeve counted the windows again, thinking she had made some error, but it was their room.

The light winked out.

Without hesitating, Maeve flew into the hall, then up the stairs, skidding to a stop in front of her door.

It hung open an inch.

A dull thudding sounded in her ears. She brought her fingers up and pushed the door the rest of the way.

The room was empty.

"What was that for?" Nan raced up behind her, out of breath.

"Someone was in our room." Maeve lit the stub end of a chamber-stick and sent a spray of candlelight to the dark corners, but there was nothing there.

As quickly as she could, Maeve checked her own side of the room, opening her dresser drawers, looking beneath her bed. It was all orderly. Nothing was out of place like the last time.

Nan made a choking sound.

Maeve turned, her eyes flying wide. Nan stood rigid over Maeve's writing desk, where a letter sat open. Ink spilled out from beneath the paper, rushing over the side of the desk and dripping to the floor. It looked like a river of blood. Above it, an arm had manifested from Oxblood ink, reaching up from the center of the paper, its liquid fingers clamped around Nan's neck.

The hand pushed upward, arm elongating in an unnatural column of churning red ink, taking Nan with it until her toes dragged along the floorboards.

She sputtered, gasping for breath.

Maeve ripped off her ash satchel and tossed a pinch of dust at the ink manifestation, the letter. The arm dissolved into a splash of red ink, soaking Maeve's desk and splattering the floor.

Nan stumbled and slipped in it, landing on her side.

Without a moment's hesitation, Maeve knelt beside her, feeling around Nan's windpipe. Nothing seemed broken. "Are you hurt?"

"I don't think so." Nan choked out the words. She tucked her knees to her chin, shaking.

Tears streamed from Maeve's eyes. "Stay put for a minute while I have a look around."

She stepped over to the letter. The crematory ash had worked to null the scribing, but the paper was now completely covered with ink; Maeve couldn't see the scriptomancer's scribing—just like the last two letters. Whoever scribed them all must have been purposefully working the scribings to destroy the paper to keep their true handwriting a secret.

Maeve turned to Nan. "What did the letter say?"

Nan swallowed and winced. "Only one word: 'leave.'"

A shiver raced down Maeve's spine.

"I think it would have killed me if you hadn't dusted it with ash," Nan said.

Maeve hugged her arms around her chest, feeling the same dread she'd felt in Alewick when she worried that someone might recognize her and hurt Mr. Braithwaite's business, but tenfold. It wasn't an inksmithy that she was risking this time.

She squeezed her eyes shut. Two weeks. She had two long weeks to wait until Claryman returned from the south.

Two weeks would mean more Oxblood letters opened by people she cared about—innocent people. She couldn't stand to see Nan or anyone else hurt. She wouldn't.

She had to leave.

Nan stood up slowly, leaning heavily on her bed. "I think my tailbone is done for," she said, then pinched a wet section of her shirt and made a face. "It looks like someone doused my blouse with a bucket of blood. This will take all night to scrub out."

"Mix a spoonful of turpentine with small thistle and a few drops of fletching oil, then let it soak overnight. The ink should rinse right out tomorrow morning." Maeve rattled off Mr. Braith-waite's recipe, then tossed her saddlebag on the only part of her bed not splattered with ink. She pulled a few smaller items from her dresser and stuffed them into the bag, not bothering with her unwieldy suitcase.

"What are you doing?" Nan asked.

"Going south. To stay with my sister for a little while until I sort some things out. She has a terrible case of gout, and she wrote a few days ago that she needs me." Maeve said the first thing that came to her. "I'll be back in a couple of weeks. If you see another blank envelope sitting around while I'm gone, rip it up immediately. Understand?"

"Rip it up? But . . . we need to tell someone."

"*No*," Maeve said. If Nan told the wrong person, she'd be putting herself in grave danger. "If anyone asks, pretend it was me who read the letter, then tore it up before anyone could see it. Tell them I left to visit sick family. Promise me, Nan."

225

Nan appeared thoroughly confused, but she nodded.

Maeve exhaled. "I swear to you that I'll explain everything when I return."

If she ever returned. Right then, it wasn't looking promising.

Maeve took a second long breath and swallowed back a wave of guilt. It was mixed with other tangled emotions that she had no time to sort through. She locked them tightly inside her chest where they would just have to remain. It was time to run away again. She tossed her saddlebag over her shoulder.

"What should I tell Tristan when I see him?" Nan asked.

Maeve's heart lurched. "Tell him I'm sorry about losing his keys."

The opening reception for the Scriptomantic Exhibition will be held on Midautumn's Eve at Alban Hall, located in the New College of Language and Linguistics in Barrow. There will be music, refreshments, and performances to kick off the weeklong exhibition. All parties involved in planning are encouraged to attend.

M aeve dragged her fingers over the words "all parties." She had touched the flyer so many times that it was beginning to fuzz.

Someone beat on her door. "Dinner, Isla!" a woman's gruff voice shouted from the other side, followed by the clink of plates and flatware.

She waited a moment so she wouldn't have to make small talk, then opened the door to a small cup of watery stew sitting at the threshold. Her stomach growled. It could've been gray jelly, and she would have slurped it down. She brought it inside her tiny room—the smallest room in any boardinghouse in east Gloam. It was the only thing she could afford on such short notice.

After covering the cost of the room, there were no leftover shills to do anything for the past two weeks but walk the city aimlessly, with endless time to think about every letter, every drop of Oxblood ink. Tristan.

She didn't know what to say to him if she ever saw him. How could she explain any of this without telling the truth?

That thought terrified her. Tristan lost his mother to Inverly. If he suddenly learned that she was Jonathan Abenthy's daughter, he wouldn't be able to look at her. He would hate her, and she was coming to realize that she didn't want him to hate her. What she wanted more than anything was for him to leave her head. It was near impossible though, especially when her dreams liked to feature him as well.

She scrubbed her palms across her eyes. Tonight was not about him. It was about her father's roommate.

It was about finally getting the truth.

Maeve washed her face in a chipped basin and braided her hair. A few curls sprang up beside her cheeks, but it would have to do. Not knowing when she'd eat again, she forced down the disgusting soup and went over the flyer for the Scriptomantic Exhibition. Then she slipped on her courier's cloak, checked the fresh traveling scribing she'd penned earlier, and left.

It took her an hour to walk to Blackcaster Square, where she tucked herself inside the cloud of protesters and waited. When a group of couriers came through the Post's gate, heading for the north entrance of the square, she quietly slipped inside their ranks. Nobody questioned her with her courier raiment. She was able to get inside the station and over to the black stone wall within minutes.

She whispered her name against the wall. A courier door appeared.

"Where's your letter?" an older man called out from across the room.

"Oh drat. It's in my pocket," Maeve said with a shrug, and stepped into Barrow.

The scribing brought her to the mouth of Drummond's Close, a five-minute walk to the College of Language and Linguistics.

Snow fell in wet flakes as Maeve found her way through the gate that led into the college, then spotted a banner marked with the Post's pigeon hanging above the entrance to one of the larger buildings called Alban Hall. She hurried up its icy steps and brought her hand up to knock, but the door opened before her fingers touched the handle.

A woman in an elegant black evening gown and feathered headpiece peered down at her. She had a slight sneer to her upper lip. "Are you lost?"

"I'm here for the reception."

"You are?" She smoothed a curl hanging across her collarbone with a gloved finger.

"Pardon us," someone said.

A pair of men came up the steps, then slid around Maeve, tipping their top hats to the sneering woman. One man shrugged off his cloak inside the door, revealing full evening attire.

Maeve was merely dressed in her courier's uniform.

"Tonight is formal attire," the woman said, looking her over. "Which committee are you from?"

"I—I think I've made a mistake," Maeve said, then darted down the steps and around the side of the building, searching for another entrance.

"Ho there! If you're with the troupe, you better hurry. Fenella has her head screwed on sideways tonight," someone called out—a lanky man with a short beard and small row of gleaming bangles in each of his ears. He pointed to a parked wagon where a few people in tweed coats milled about. A side door to Alban Hall opened, and they all rushed inside.

"I will hurry. Thank you," Maeve called to the man, not knowing what he was referring to, nor caring. She ran through the door, to a stifling, packed room with people in makeup and various stages of dress.

A man in an undershirt and breeches slapped a powder puff against his hair, sending up a plume of talcum. Maeve coughed and covered her nose and mouth, weaving past him, then around a woman painting rouge across her lips. A line of men along the far wall were warming up their vocal cords, just like the students would in Inverly.

An interior door hung a few paces away.

Maeve started toward it, until a man stopped her with his arm. "Nobody goes through that door unless they're in costume." His eyes fell on her cloak and narrowed. "I don't recognize you. Are you singing later, or are you with the other talent?"

"The other talent," Maeve said. Her singing might get her booted from the premises quicker than anything else.

"Then you'll get dressed over here." He walked Maeve to an adjoining room filled with men and women in stage gowns sewn with globes and quills, their faces powdered with gold dust. "Another girl for you, Fenella!" he shouted.

Fenella couldn't be more than fourteen, but she clamped Maeve on the shoulder with her tiny hand and shouted shrill orders to a sweaty man twice her size to have a scriptomancer costume pulled or she'd "knock him a good one." The man scurried away and returned with a low-necked gown covered with frothy ruffles and a lace-up corset that was meant to be worn on the *outside*.

"That's underwear," Maeve said, scarcely believing her eyes.

230

"It's your costume, and if you want 'a get paid at the end of the night, you'll shut it and put it on," Fenella said.

Maeve glanced back to the door that she'd come in through. It wasn't too late to run. But then an inner door opened, and she caught a sliver of a dark wood room with university faculty milling about in long plum robes.

There were answers through that door.

She wrenched the costume from Fenella's hands. "Where do I change?"

Fenella led her behind a curtain, and Maeve slipped on the ruffled dress, relieved the long sleeves covered the traveling scribing at her wrist. There were no pockets anywhere on the dress, so she balled up her clothes with her letters inside and tucked them down her saddlebag, which she hid beneath a sideboard.

She took a step from behind the curtain and felt a breeze. The ruffles parted for a slit that crested her thigh.

It was wholly indecent. Maeve's neck and back blazed hot with embarrassment, her fingers furiously pinching the skirt closed.

Fenella slapped her hand away. "Don't tug yer skirt, or it might rip. I'm assuming ol' Monte told you what to do when you get out there?"

"I have a terrible memory. Mind going over it?"

Fenella groaned but told Maeve that she was to walk the reception and dust passersby with "that arcane magic stuff" in the form of a pouch of gold powder that smelled like used socks. And no "yapping with the misters"—whatever that meant.

Maeve caught her reflection in a dressing mirror and froze at the sight of her red curls slipping free of her braid.

Searching the racks of costumes, she found a veil headpiece delicately embroidered with beaded inkpots and stars and put it on. It was translucent, but it hung past her collarbone and would cover her face enough.

"Is the next group ready?" Fenella shouted to the room.

Maeve's stomach flipped over with nerves, but she got in line behind a few others and followed them into the reception, clutching a pouch of gold powder between sweating palms.

Her eyes watered at the cloud of pipe tobacco wafting through the air.

The room was dim and swathed in caramel leather and dark wood. Thick furniture sat beneath hanging banners for the exhibition. Ladies and gentlemen in evening wear milled about, sipping from snifters and fluted glasses.

There was no one she recognized from the Post, and only one person in a plum robe. But she doubted Fion Claryman was a gray-haired woman with large earrings. Judging by the smaller size of this room, there had to be many other rooms to search through inside this building.

Maeve followed the lead of the actors in front of her, stepping with toes pointed, smiling. A round of applause went up as they all circled the room and blew gold dust from their palms.

Three actors dipped through a side door, and Maeve followed them into a glass-walled solarium where a large group in plum faculty robes stood around a refreshments table.

The other actors moved on to an adjoining room, but Maeve hesitated. Her legs felt molten as she moved toward the table. Everyone looked her way, of course.

Not sure what to do, she put up her hands, mimicking Molly Blackcaster's pose on top of the ink fountain.

A man cleared his throat, while a woman beside him whispered, "The House of Ministers paid for that? She's vulgar."

Yes, I realize, and it wasn't my choice, she thought to herself, while she sweated like a pig as more murmured comments were flung about.

She scanned across the faculty, but how was she supposed to know who Fion was without asking? This was a dreadful idea. She lifted the satchel of gold dust to douse them all and make for the door, then froze as a shorter man in a robe poured himself a snifter of amber-colored liquid.

At the sight of him, it felt as though her entire world shifted, spinning on its axis before coming to a grinding halt.

She knew him.

His deep-set eyes were now surrounded by wrinkles, and his hair had gone as white as pounce. He was much shorter than she remembered, but she was probably a whole hand taller than she'd been in Blackcaster Square that day he pulled her though the Written Door to Leyland minutes before it was burned.

This man saved her, then left her beside the milk bottles on the front stoop of the Sacrifict Orphanage.

He met her eyes for an instant, then looked away.

"What do you think, Fion? Shall we go find the others?" someone asked him, pulling him toward another door.

Fion. Of course this was Fion. Heavens, if this was her father's roommate, he must have known exactly who she was that day in Inverly.

Maeve strode toward him and tapped him on the shoulder. "Professor Claryman?"

He met her eyes for the second time. Still no sign he recognized her.

"Can I help you?" he asked, sounding confused.

His voice—his voice was exactly the same.

Her throat closed, and all the words she'd scripted out for this moment fled her mind completely.

He blinked at her, his brows tightening a small amount. He dabbed a handkerchief to his forehead. "I think I might need some air," he muttered, then left the solarium.

Maeve counted to five, then followed through the same door, into another dark wood room filled with people in evening dress, along with a few faculty in plum robes.

Fion wasn't one of them.

"Can you tell me where I might find Professor Claryman?" she asked one of the faculty members sipping from a flute off to one side. "He left a handkerchief on a refreshment table, and I'd like to return it."

"I believe he left out that door."

The woman pointed to a small door hidden in the woodwork.

Maeve walked through it, to a narrow hall. She flipped the veil off her face and rushed down to where the hall abruptly ended at a larger door that had to lead outside, judging from the dusting of fresh snow on the threshold.

There was no time to retrieve her cloak. Maeve held her breath and pushed the door open, stumbling into a wall of falling snow. It soaked into her thin costume slippers instantly.

"Fion!" she cried out, dragging her feet through a nearby thicket of winter oaks, their bare branches scraping her arms.

One snapped behind her.

A hand took her shoulder, and the cold edge of a blade slid against the side of her neck.

"Why are you following me?" a man's ragged voice spoke into Maeve's ear. She caught the flicker of a plum robe in the periphery.

"Are you Fion Claryman?"

The knife dug deeper. "Who sent you?"

"I came on my own."

She hissed as the blade slid into her flesh. A warm trickle ran down her throat. "That hurts."

"Yes, I bet it does. Prove that you're alone, or I'll cut deeper."

"I—I don't know how to prove anything."

"I think you do." The knife slid along her skin, opening it with a thin sting. More blood spilled out.

"*Please.* I saw your name on the flyer for the exhibition and only hoped to speak with you—without a blasted knife shoved down my throat!"

"Then tell me who you are, and I'll consider your request."

Her teeth gnashed together. "I'm the girl you saved from Inverly, you heathen."

She spat the last words.

He released her, and she staggered forward, clutching the gash on her neck. Her palm came away bloody. She turned to face him.

Professor Claryman stared at her, open-mouthed. "Impossible. But you can't be . . . Jonathan's Maeve?"

Her name spoken so freely startled her. She gave a nod.

He stumbled backward a step. "When I saw you inside, I thought I had met you before, but I wasn't sure with your veil, however—" He searched her eyes. "You look exactly like your mother. I cannot believe I didn't see it right away."

Maeve was already on the edge of hysterics, but at the mention of her mother, tears stung her eyes. "You knew my mother?"

"Aoife attended an upper school writing program with me and your father. That was before your father and I applied to the College of Scriptomantic Arts together." He puffed out a wintery exhale. "Aoife was a hotheaded one. When I introduced her to Jonathan, she demanded he marry her before the month was up, then she forced me to the church to bear witness."

Her father never spoke of his wedding. Aggie only ever told her that it was quick, and her mother didn't invite her. Yet this man had *witnessed* it. He had to know more than she originally thought.

"I g-got your letter a few weeks ago," she said, her teeth beginning to chatter.

"I wondered if you would," he said. "Nearly seven years ago, I made the trip to Edding's Close, like I promised in that letter, and you weren't there. I always wondered if the letter had gone out or if it had been lost in the chaos. I tried to hunt it down, but never found anything. Then I had to leave suddenly, and it was too late."

"Suddenly?"

He pressed his mouth shut.

It took everything inside of Maeve to keep from grabbing his shoulders and shaking the answers from him.

She stepped closer. "You said my father was innocent. I want you to tell me why you think that, so I can clear his name."

He barked a laugh. "That's a tall order."

"But is it possible?"

"Perhaps."

Perhaps wasn't what she wanted to hear, but it would do for now.

He pocketed his knife, then handed over a handkerchief to wipe the blood on her neck.

A pair of students trudged by, kicking up the fresh snow.

Professor Claryman stepped closer. "It's not private here. We should talk more in my office."

Maeve was instantly wary, but she'd come all this way. And an office seemed much warmer than her current predicament. Cautiously, she followed him across the grounds, then inside a tall gray building to a small office where an oil lamp was already lit, a fire turned to embers in a hearth. Certificates filled the wall stretching from the hearth to where a large scriptomancy worktable covered with inks sat in the corner.

The professor stepped to a sideboard and poured himself a glass of dark liquor, taking down half in a single swig. The remaining liquid sloshed around his glass. His hands were shaking.

Fion was short and stocky, with legs like tree stumps, but he trembled like a dead oak leaf in a winter gust. "Now would you explain to me how you're part of a Barrow acting troupe?" he asked.

Maeve lifted her chin. "I'm not the one who owes anyone any answers."

"Very well," he said in a short tone. "What should we discuss first?"

"Inverly. What happened?" He was there, after all. He'd saved her.

"You don't waste time, do you?"

"There's no time to waste."

He took another sip of his drink and stared at the remaining liquid as he spoke.

"When the Aldervine took over Inverly, your father knew he didn't have long to get you out—maybe a handful of minutes. He wanted to go search for you at your aunt's, but he worried that the two of you had gone shopping, so he showed me a sepiagraph of what you looked like and described your hair color, then had me look for you around Blackcaster Square."

His words cut straight to her heart. "My father went to search for me?" She always thought he'd abandoned her to the vine.

"Of course he did. But we were finishing up a long lunch just west of the square when the Aldervine got in. It shocked us both. There wasn't enough time to do much searching."

Her pulse thrummed in her veins at the words coming from the professor's lips. "But if my father was eating lunch with you that whole time, that would mean . . ."

"Yes, he certainly didn't travel somewhere that day and bring the Aldervine back to Inverly. He'd been with me that whole morning."

"Then why didn't you say something?" When the professor was silent, anger erupted inside of her. "You took me to an orphanage and dropped me off with a horrible woman who whipped my fingers and locked me in a barn for days," she said, and he flinched. "The least you can do is tell me the truth now."

Fion frowned. "Did she? I'm sorry to hear that, but I had no way to know that would happen. Kirstine was different when we went to school together."

That took her aback. "You knew Headmistress Castlemaine?"

"She was your mother's great friend. I trusted her to take care of you."

Maeve felt as if the ocean tides were rising around her, and she was a wave away from drowning in them. This man had too much knowledge about her past—things she was desperate to know. But she had to remind herself that this conversation wasn't about her mother. "Why was my father framed?"

"If I tell you any more, it puts you in danger."

He was a little late for that. "Go on."

Fion swirled his glass. "Your father—he told me one night that he was working on a special scribing using ideas that he found in journals left over from the scriptomancers of Molly's day. He worked on it relentlessly, writing down everything in this funny little journal that he kept hidden from everyone. I only saw it because he would write down things in our room late at night." Fion's eyes remained bleak, but he gave a chuckle. "The journal looked feminine for a man, with a tracery of silver roses around the cover."

Maeve's breath caught in her throat. She remembered that journal—she'd picked it out for her father when they went shopping a few months before she lost him. She loved gardens and flowers and thought the roses were pretty. "What did my father's scribing do?"

His expression turned grave. He pulled a handkerchief from his pocket and dabbed his forehead. "I don't know the specifics, but your father told me that it made scriptomancy completely safe for the scriptomancer."

"But isn't that what crematory ash is for?"

"Yes, but your father said his scribing was far superior. It allowed scriptomancers to scribe on whatever medium they wished, using any advanced technique they wanted to try—techniques the stewards themselves are afraid of using. All without anything affecting them. With no fear of getting hurt."

"So no turning into worktables?"

"Exactly. That and much more."

"And you think this scribing had something to do with my father being framed for Inverly?"

"I'm sure it did. The week after Inverly everything was a blur. I was not well, as you can imagine. Then I was forced to move out so the constabulary could search our room. I watched some of it. They tore through everything, even slitted Jonathan's mattress down the middle, pulling out the stuffing. One of them asked me about the rose journal—if I had seen it anywhere. But your father had kept that journal a secret. He never showed it to anyone."

"Then why was the constabulary looking for it?"

"I don't know if even they knew. I think someone wanted the journal and used searching our room as an excuse to get their hands on it. I had such a strong feeling about it that one night, I decided to write down everything I suspected. I put down my thoughts about the journal, everything Jonathan told me leading up to Inverly, and my full account of the events of that day—why I was convinced that your father could never have released the Aldervine. I planned to bring it to the authorities the next morning. I went to sleep with the pages of notes sitting beneath a book on my desk. When I woke up, the notes were gone. A letter sat in their place."

Maeve shivered. "What kind of letter?"

"One that still haunts me. It warned me to never tell anyone any of it. I would have shown the letter to someone, but it went on to list some information regarding something foolish I did when I was an apprentice."

"What?"

"I'm certainly not telling you that," he snapped. "Just know that it was an indiscretion that I am not proud of—something that would cost me a great deal if it were made public. The letter gave me two choices: have my secret indiscretion revealed, or resign and take a position here. I chose to resign, of course. Onrich Byrne was in charge by then and wrote me a glowing recommendation."

Maeve straightened. "The Postmaster sent you here?"

"He certainly tried, but this college wouldn't take me unless my name was left off all public information about the investigation. They didn't want Abenthy's name associated with any new professor."

That was why he wasn't listed in any of the press from Inverly.

"I stayed at the newly formed Otherwhere Post in Leyland for a few months, traveling back and forth between the Post and the college, waiting for the school year to start. Then the week before I was to move here for good, I received a letter from Kirstine Castlemaine explaining how you ran away, that you were trouble. It mentioned something about a barn."

"Yes, there was a barn involved," Maeve said in a flat tone.

He nodded and scratched behind his ear. "Your father made me promise in Inverly that if I found you and he didn't make it out that I would watch out for you. It was the last thing I said to him."

Tears flooded Maeve's eyes. "So you wrote me that anonymous letter."

He wrote it using university supplies and posted it from Barrow because he traveled back and forth. Everything made perfect sense now.

"Yes. I was foolish and thought that I could meet you in secret and leave you with a bit of hope before I stopped visiting Leyland for good. But you never showed up, and I moved here. I thought that would be the end of everything, but it was far from it." Fion paused, seeming to consider his next words. "I still receive threatening letters every so often."

"Who's sending them?"

"Someone more dangerous than you know."

He walked to a writing desk and dug around a bottom drawer, pulling out a folded paper.

Maeve backed away. "If that's one of them, you can toss it on the fire. I don't want to touch it."

"It's not," he said. "I wrote this one myself. I planned to give this to you at Edding's Close." He handed it to her.

It was a simple folded paper that was sealed like an envelope, the glob of white sealing wax gone yellow with age.

"What is it?"

"A written account of right after your father left me standing in Blackcaster Square in Inverly. I thought Jonathan was foolish for trying to find you at his flat—it was blocks away from the square, and the Aldervine had already grown over a nearby building— so I followed him, thinking I'd have to drag him back. Jonathan ducked through Edrick's Close, but the vine grew over the alley's mouth after he went in, blocking me. I was forced to run around it, to the other side. That's where I found him on the ground."

"The Aldervine pricked my father?"

"No," he said, and downed the rest of his drink. "Your *father* was lying in a pool of his own blood, his neck slit open from ear to ear."

Maeve gave a strangled gasp. "He was murdered?"

"Without a doubt."

She braced her hands on a nearby chair to keep herself upright.

It felt as if a cloud had opened above her head, dashing rain against her shoulders, battering her, hollowing her out until she was nothing but a husk. Then as soon as the feeling came, it was washed away by a wave of bright hot rage.

The word "murderer" had been written across more walls and doors and sepiagraphs than Maeve could count. And she'd believed it that whole time. When it was a lie. When her poor academic father was the victim. Someone had murdered him and framed him. But the worst of all of it was this person had made her hate him for seven whole years, until she hated every speck of her own face that resembled his, until she believed evil ran through her own blood and corrupted her.

Maeve wanted to run outside and shout about her father's innocence, and shout it to herself most of all.

Claryman gestured to the sealed paper loosely clasped in Maeve's hands. "I scribed that so you can see everything for yourself."

She looked down at the paper. "It's a memory scribing?"

He nodded.

Maeve was suddenly glad she never read Claryman's anonymous letter until recently. Seeing her father murdered in a memory scribing when she was twelve would have driven her to worse choices than she'd already made.

"I'll read it later," she said, folding the paper and tucking it up her sleeve.

There was no way she was about to read a memory scribing in front of him; there was something off about the man—something she didn't trust. But if the memory scribing was real, it could be the proof she needed. It wouldn't tell her who had killed her father, but it could spark an investigation at the very least.

"I took care to make sure there was nothing on that page that will implicate me," Claryman said. "And if I learn that you showed that to another soul or tell anyone about me or my association with your father, then I'll make sure that your name gets out. If something happens to me, you better believe the same will happen to you. Understand?"

Maeve nodded, eager to get away from here. Then she remembered something.

"Whatever happened to the rose journal with my father's scribing? Did the constabulary ever find it?"

It had to be important if the person who murdered her father had wanted it so badly.

"No. I found it in your father's hiding spot beneath the floorboard under his worktable in the Scriptorium, then got nervous and hid it deep in a library and never went back for it."

"Which one?"

"The Second Library."

Of course it was that one.

"If you go searching for it, it had 'The Silver Scribing' written across the cover. That was your father's name for it."

S now tumbled down in heavy clumps. It swirled over buildings and through the bare trees and covered the cobblestone walks. In the gray-green light of the moon, it resembled a blanket of ash.

Maeve trudged through it, shivering in her wet costume slippers. Before she lost all feeling in her toes, she pushed inside an empty lecture hall and sank to her knees, her chest heaving with sobs.

She was pathetic—worse than a faucet—but at least she hadn't come away empty-handed.

Dread swept through her as she took out Claryman's memory scribing and placed it before her on the cold stone floor. If his account of events was real, she could pay a visit to the authorities tonight.

Maeve felt for her ash satchel. Her fingers grazed bare neck. Her ash was inside her saddlebag, tucked in that dressing room in Alban Hall, along with the rest of her warm clothing. As tempting as it was, she wasn't foolish enough to read Claryman's scribing without ash.

Her fingers flexed against the paper.

Did his account of her father's murder even matter? A normal person might bring this to the constabulary and beg for protection, but she was Maeve Abenthy. Her word was as good as mud. Without the rose journal to bolster the account, the constabulary would assume she wrote everything herself. They'd lock her up while they investigated, and the very person sending the Oxblood letters could lash out and destroy the rose journal. It was the one piece of evidence that connected everything. It even connected her father to Cathriona—and to her murder.

Yes, if her father was murdered over this journal, there was a good chance that Cathriona didn't kill herself with the Silver Scribing like Tristan believed, especially since her father's scribing was meant to keep someone safe, not kill them.

There had to be something in that journal that got them both killed—something Maeve wasn't seeing. If she could get her hands on it, she could investigate.

Tristan would know where it was kept.

Maeve held her bottom lip between her teeth. Tristan deserved to know the truth about the Silver Scribing. They could find the rose journal together and bring it to the constabulary . . .

An image of Nan's toes scraping along the floorboards flashed in Maeve's mind. If Tristan helped her, and the wrong person found out, his toes could be scraping the floor next. But would the Postmaster be cruel enough to hurt his own son?

Yes—yes, he would. Tristan barely made it out of Inverly, after all. His father had to know he was there.

No, she couldn't involve Tristan. It was too risky. She was on her own from this point forward.

With effort, Maeve forced her numb feet to carry her outside. She still had her room at the boardinghouse in Leyland for a couple more nights. Enough time to think through how to get her hands on that journal.

But she wasn't going anywhere clothed in veritable underwear. Shivering from the cold, Maeve made her way to Alban Hall, slipping inside through a different back entrance. Pulling the veil over her face, she ran through a long hall to a high-ceilinged ballroom strung with banners emblazoned with the Post's pigeon.

Tables were adorned with delicate floral arrangements and faceted crystal decanters that shivered in the soft string music of an orchestra. People in evening wear sipped drinks, while a group of actors stood along a raised dais in the center, blowing puffs of gold dust from their palms.

Maeve started across the floor, then halted.

A small group of Barrow ministers in their decorated scarlet coats stood beside the Postmaster, all deep in conversation. Blocking her path.

Somewhere in the back of her mind, Maeve knew she should hide. But at the sight of Onrich Byrne, her mouth tightened, and her fingers curled into fists. *You did it, didn't you? You murdered my father. Cathriona. You destroyed an entire world so you could have that cold, sterile office all to yourself.* If Maeve had a knife, she'd be half inclined to slit his throat and be done with it.

No, killing him was far too kind a punishment for what he deserved. She wanted him to feel as she had for the past seven years: to live in hiding, afraid of his own shadow. She wanted him to feast upon the rats of Stonewater Prison for the rest of his endless, torturous days.

Then a breeze skated across her leg, reminding her of her lack of clothing, the eyes on her.

The other actors were close by. Maeve walked to the dais and leaned against the platform's edge, hoping to fade in with the group until the Postmaster left.

But then doors across the ballroom opened and more people streamed in, forcing the Postmaster and the ministers nearer.

Mere feet away.

Maeve tucked her chin to her chest so her veil slid forward, gathering in front of her face.

"I can't believe I allowed you to hire all these musicians," Onrich said to someone. "We wouldn't stand for it inside the Post."

"A little music is good for the spirits, Onrich," said a minister. "You deserve it after that wonderful surprise of the sepiagraph exhibit of the restoration work. This year's exhibition will be the best yet."

The Postmaster nodded. "I think the people of Barrow are finally coming around to trust us when we say that we're working toward repairing the Written Doors."

"And hopefully by next year's exhibition, we can announce that your son here has taken up the task himself."

Maeve stiffened.

"I wouldn't go quite that far," a sharp voice retorted.

She tilted her head and could make out Tristan standing off to the side, not five paces from her. He was dressed in a fine tailcoat and an elegant burgundy waistcoat with burgundy gloves to match. A sleek crow feather was tucked into the band across his silk hat.

He was, without a doubt, the most dashing man in the room. Maeve could barely believe her eyes; there was nothing unbuttoned or askew on him, save for the swath of unkempt dark hair that stuck out from his hat.

He was far too close.

Her heart thrummed inside her chest, but there was nowhere to hide.

Clapping broke out as a man on the dais began singing, the others joining.

Her mouth went bone dry.

She had thought they were actors, but no, they were the *singers*. One of them nudged Maeve's shoulder with her toe. Twice. Did they think she was a singer as well? Surely not.

Her worst fears were answered when another singer gripped her hand, heaving her up onto the dais. They all began clapping and undulating their bodies, and Maeve wanted to die right there. She nearly did, but with the Postmaster nearby, she forced her arms above her head and moved her hips from side to side like the other singers, pointing her toes, prancing across the platform like a naked chicken in a Midspring parade.

Tristan wasn't paying attention, but others were. Then the woman beside Maeve hit a high note, and the entire ballroom looked over.

At her.

Tristan turned as well. Maeve felt his eyes travel up her legs, over the curve of her waist. For a delusional moment, she thought he might not look any farther up—*prayed* that he wouldn't—but then his gaze caught hers from beneath the veil.

He tensed, his eyes darkening.

She dropped, and scurried backward through the singers, then halted at a godforsaken refreshment table blocking the back of the dais.

A few people noticed her crouched and pointed, whispering.

The Postmaster started to turn. Before he could notice her, Tristan grabbed his father's shoulder and said something into his ear. The Postmaster nodded, then stalked toward a door on the opposite side of the ballroom, away from the dais.

Tristan—he had helped her.

249

He started toward her, but she didn't want to talk to him now. Especially now.

She scrambled to the floor, then pushed through the crowd, around to the back side of the ballroom and into an adjoining chamber with several smaller doors. What was this place? Some hellish maze? She picked a door in the center, then found herself in a room stacked with vases and tables. A slant of moonlight spilled from a window near the ceiling. A closet.

Her fingers fumbled over the door handle, but there was no interior lock.

The handle turned, and Tristan stormed in, shutting the door behind him.

Maeve backed away until her legs hit a table, but he didn't come toward her. He unbuttoned his jacket and tossed it at her head. "Cover yourself."

Shame flooded her.

"It's a wonder you still care about my modesty after ogling me on that dais," she snapped, shrugging the jacket over her shoulders.

"Every single lewdster in that ballroom was ogling you on the dais." His eyes darted to her wrist. "How are you in Barrow?"

"I used a traveling scribing. Obviously."

"And how in the worlds did you learn it?"

His sharp tone made her teeth clench. "From Molly Blackcaster's ghost. Bring her an offering of biscuits and mushed peas from the mess hall, and she'll do whatever you ask."

He wasn't amused.

"Fine," Maeve said. "I got one to work my first week at the Post."

That caught him off guard. "You're adept at the traveling scribing?"

"Good gracious, no! At playing knucklenook."

He gave an exasperated sigh, then stared at her in a way that made her feel as if her skirt were slitted to her chin. "Where in seven *hells* did you disappear to for two whole weeks?"

"Tristan—"

"Where?"

"The south. Visiting a dear sister."

"Ah, yes, the infamous sister with the raging case of gout, whom Nan told me about at length. I knew the moment I heard that sorry story that it was a lie." His jaw flexed, his expression fiery. Dangerous. "Are you even capable of telling the truth?"

She winced as the words sliced right through her stony exterior like a hot knife through wax, needling until she couldn't stand the feeling anymore. "Very well. If you must know, I used the last of my money to rent a room at a stinking boardinghouse, waiting for tonight. Then I came here looking for answers about my letterwriter."

His eyes shot wide. "And?"

He expected her to tell him all about it? Her mind went blank because she didn't want him involved. It was a mistake to mention anything.

"I—I learned that I still have a bit of work to do before I find them," she said with what she hoped was a convincing shrug, then debated tearing around him and making a run for it, but an idea struck her. "This is admittedly strange." She picked at a loose thread on his jacket. "But as I was walking through the reception, I thought I saw a few bookcases filled with journals. It made me think of that journal Cathriona used and how dangerous it might be. Is there any chance the journal could have left the Post?"

His eyes hardened. A shadow chased over his features, and she felt awful—truly awful—for bringing it up, but she had to know.

"I believe the journal is still in my father's office."

Maeve tried very hard to keep her composure. "Your father's office?"

"He's the one who confiscated it."

Of course he was. And unless he'd already destroyed it, that rose journal was likely still inside his office, waiting.

She had to somehow steal it.

Her stomach twisted at the thought, and she gripped her belly.

"Are you all right?" Tristan rushed forward and took her hand, then jolted. "You're colder than an ice cube." Was she? "Come with me."

She tried to pull her hand away, but he wouldn't have it. He dragged her from the closet and into a nearby room—a small, sweltering library, where a fire crackled in a small hearth, tossing firelight against the pristine spines of hundreds of linguistics books.

"Warm yourself," he ordered, dropping her before the fire.

Maeve considered running, but even she wasn't foolish enough to run when she could barely feel her feet.

She sank to her knees, letting blessed heat soak into her freezing limbs. Tristan didn't utter a word. He was probably waiting for her to explain herself and this sorry situation.

As if she could.

For a brief moment, she considered telling him part of it—enough to ease his mind and perhaps help her get inside his father's office—then immediately dismissed the idea. She couldn't tell him anything that might put him at risk. She had to somehow get her clothes and find her way to Leyland on her own.

It took several long minutes, however, before all the feeling returned to her appendages, then another handful where she stared at the flames, pretending to still be cold to save herself from having to face Tristan.

He was silent through it all, but she felt him behind her like a second fire licking at her spine. When she could no longer delay the inevitable, she shrugged off his jacket and turned, bracing for a fight.

He blocked the only exit.

"This reunion has been nice and all, but I really must go." She motioned to the door at his back, afraid of her heart if she stepped any closer.

"You'd leave again, just like that?"

Of course she would leave. Leaving was the grand design of her life. The sun set, the sky was gray, and Maeve left.

"Please let me go."

"Funny, I don't particularly feel like it at the moment." He leaned a shoulder against the door and draped a lazy wrist over the handle. "I looked for you in the most ridiculous places, you realize? I even found myself inside a pantry stocked wall to wall with canned legumes. Then a week went by, and I thought you'd fled for good. And now you expect me to simply scoot aside because you asked nicely?"

"I could be mean about it if you want."

His chin slanted, tipping a dark lock of hair across his spectacles as he stared at her lips for a prolonged moment. "I don't know why, but for some unfathomable reason, after everything you've put me through, I want . . ." he started, then huffed a humorless laugh. "I'm certain that if I finish that sentence, you'll disappear into thin air."

She shivered.

He ran his hands against his mouth and came toward her in

a flash, halting so near that she could feel heat rising from him. Her fingers curled inward, pressing tight against her palms to keep from accidentally brushing him.

He slid the veil from her face. "You've been weeping."

"From sheer delight at seeing you."

She attempted to skate around him, but he snatched her right hand and pressed his thumb over her sleeve, against her pulse. Directly above her traveling scribing.

Panic swamped her. She tried to pull her hand away. "Don't look at it."

He held firm. "Stop your squirming. I'm not going to peek, even though I'm *extremely* tempted at the moment. I want you to tell me your first name right now."

"So you can hunt me down as soon as I leave?"

"So I can write to you."

That took her aback. "You wish to send me letters?"

It sounded preposterous, but his expression remained serious.

Dear god, he *was* serious.

"Why not?" he asked. "I know you're going to disappear again, whether I like it or not, and it's been a long time since I've been able to be candid with someone else, and I don't want to lose that. I want to write to you. It doesn't have to be anything monumental, and only when I'm feeling a burst of inspiration that can't be sated by drowning myself in wine or another tedious book. And if you're inclined, you can write me back about how terribly you miss my brocade vests." He shrugged. "Or not."

He truly thought her a fool.

"Once you have my name, what's to stop you from hunting me down?"

"Nothing," he said. "Yes, hunting you down *is* certainly enticing, but I swear to you now that I'll never use your name to track you. Without your permission, of course. I'll always post the letters I send."

"But how can I ever know that for certain?"

"You can't. You simply trust."

He must have sampled a few too many drinks from the refreshment table if he expected her to trust him enough to hand over her name. Her!

He released her wrist and took her hand, skating his thumb along her palm. The touch sent tremors racing beneath her skin. "I know that whatever happened to you makes it nearly impossible to trust completely, but I don't believe you can trust someone all at once anyhow. I think trust is built in small increments, like the words of a scribing, piece by piece, until you know someone fully. I'm probably a massive wagtail for thinking this, but I believe that you could begin to trust me."

The earnestness in his tone had her considering it.

Before Maeve came to the Post, trust was a word so far removed from her vocabulary that it almost sounded foreign, but things had changed. She was loath to admit it, but she did trust Tristan. Probably more than she'd trusted anyone since Inverly.

But that trust would mean nothing if he discovered who her father was—

And things had shifted in the last hour. Dramatically. Her father was innocent, and she now had a memory scribing to prove it. If Tristan discovered her last name, it might not matter as much. It might not matter at all.

Sending her letters wouldn't hurt him or put him at any greater risk so long as he didn't tell another soul, and there was nothing to stop her from believing he wouldn't.

Yes, he would keep her letters a secret, wouldn't he? Just as he'd kept her a secret. She trusted that.

She never thought anyone would want to send her a letter, but now that she knew he did, she imagined herself opening one. Reading it, then tucking it at her hip.

The thought grew until she wanted it more than she was afraid of it. She was badly damaged and afraid of everything, but perhaps—perhaps she could be brave enough to give him this small piece of her.

Her first name. A single word.

"You promise to never use my name to track me?"

His eye flashed. "Never."

"Swear it."

"Very well. I swear it upon all the rabid mice in the worlds."

She choked on a laugh while her tongue turned to liquid between her teeth. If she spoke her name, that was it. She couldn't take it back. She would never be this same person again.

It was good, then, that she didn't want to be.

"It's Maeve."

His eyebrows drew together. "Maeve?" he repeated, slowly, as if tasting the word. "Of course you're Maeve," he said again, this time with wonder in his eyes. "It's a pleasure to finally meet you."

"It's a pleasure to meet you too."

M aeve stepped into Leyland with unease gnawing at her stomach and the barest hint of a smile tugging at her lips. She wasn't sure she would ever get over the shock of what Fion told her about her father's death, but speaking with Tristan had made it all bearable. More than bearable. They planned to meet up in a few days, where she just might give up another secret.

Her smile grew at the thought, while snowflakes drifted down on her cheeks. Leyland was much snowier than Barrow. The streets were difficult to traverse, even with her own boots on her feet.

Dreading the idea of going back to the boardinghouse, Maeve ducked inside a tavern and ordered a glass of milk from the barkeep. She took a sip and glanced over at a stack of newspapers. The headline on the front page of the *Herald* read:

JONATHAN ABENTHY'S MISSING ROOMMATE

"Has the milk gone sour?" the barkeep asked. Maeve shook her head and choked the mouthful down.

The article was dated yesterday, written by a Zelda Crawford.

Maeve dragged her fingers over the name—one of the pen names Nan had rattled off in the Groggery.

The article went on to describe the exact setup of her father's room with the sitting room that connected to another bedchamber, then endless paragraphs of speculation about who it might have been and why their name was absent from all articles about Inverly.

Nan must have been working on this that day in the Groggery when she'd hidden her library books in her saddlebag before Maeve could peek. She'd never wanted to publish poetry; she fancied herself a reporter, and Maeve had handed her the most tantalizing story imaginable on a silver platter.

At least the *Herald* was a Leylish paper. Fion must not have seen this yet, but as soon as he got wind of this, he would think it her doing. The timing was too coincidental.

Maeve bowed over the bar top until her forehead rested against the paper, breathing in and out through her nose.

This was bad. Reporters would come for Fion, and he would tell everyone all about her. Her full name. That man in the tracking office would hunt her down immediately, along with every constabulary courier in the known worlds. She'd be arrested by dinnertime tomorrow.

She couldn't remain in Gloam.

Rifling through her saddlebag, Maeve found her purse and quickly counted out the coins Tristan had given her—the entire contents of his pockets. Enough shills for a one-way train ticket south and little else.

She slid from the stool, then hesitated. If she fled this city now, she would be leaving behind the rose journal—her investigation.

The journal's distinctive cover flashed in her mind. It would be easy to find on a shelf, and the Postmaster was likely still at the exhibition until very late.

"Don't you want the rest?" the barkeep waved at the unfinished glass of milk, but Maeve was already out the tavern and turning up the street that bordered Blackcaster Square.

Most of the protesters were gone for the night. Maeve rushed past the few who were left, then up the steep embankment until she came upon Tristan's secret opening in the fence. She slipped through it, into the Post's silent woods.

Icy footpaths made her trek tedious, but she soon found her way to the office building Tristan had walked her through on her first day here, called Amaranthus Hall. She pushed inside to a small front parlor where a worn chaise sat before a cold hearth. An iron poker hung above the mantel.

Maeve dragged the poker down and carried it quietly along the narrow office corridor, checking the cracks below each door she passed for any hint of flickering light, but the offices were all dark; everyone gone for the night.

The Postmaster's office was like the others, with a simple brass handle that was locked tight like everything else inside the school. Maeve brought the poker up and swung it down with all her strength. The brass handle snapped, pieces scattering to the floor. She kicked them to the side and pushed the door open.

The office felt like an icebox. A dark, stuffy icebox.

Maeve opened a curtain, allowing a sliver of moonlight to spill across the large bookcase that took up one wall. There were hundreds of books, but only one shelf of journals. Her fingers worked quickly, pulling out one journal after another, until at least fifty lay piled across the floor, and not a single one with roses.

Where was it? There were no more bookshelves. No journals on the Postmaster's desk. Maeve opened a small closet and found a large, locked cabinet inside that looked suspicious. She ran over to where she'd set down the poker, then froze at the distant creak of a door.

Footsteps were coming from down the corridor.

She tried to shut the office door, but she'd broken the latching mechanism, and it wouldn't close. She couldn't stay here.

Darting into the hall, Maeve turned deeper into the building, rushing past more shut doors until she found one that led to a darkened storage room with walls hung with tapestries. Chests below the windowsills were piled high with scribing glasses and mounds of rumpled papers.

An oil lamp flickered to life.

Steward Mordraig reclined in a rocking chair a few paces away. He wiped at a string of drool from his chin and squinted up at her.

"Is that you, apprentice? What in god's nose are you doing in my parlor? I thought you were visiting a relative in the south."

"I just returned," Maeve said. "I was looking for a lavatory on this floor, and I got lost. I should go."

She turned quickly, knocking a glass cloche off a shelf with her elbow. It hit the floor and shattered. She was going to leave it and run, but perhaps it was best to stay put for a few more minutes, until whoever was in the hall left.

"Goodness, I'm so sorry. I'll help clean it up."

"It's all right," Mordraig said. He slowly pushed himself up and hobbled toward the patch of glass, pulling an emerald feather from the mess.

Maeve had never seen a feather like it. Iridescent fletching sparked with an inner fire.

"Something, isn't it?" Mordraig said.

"Where is it from?"

"Outside the known worlds. Back when it was safe to travel,

scriptomancers came across some interesting variations on our animals," Mordraig spun the feather. "Cows with sleek gray coats. Cats with violet eyes. Birds with bright green wing feathers. There are more historical artifacts in the Library of Forgotten Things, where I stole this feather from. Don't tell anyone." He winked and set the feather on a shelf, beside a few other glass cloches. "It's a pity that most of the animal varieties were lost to the vine."

Maeve glanced to the open door as the voices carried from down the hall. She could make out Steward Tallowmeade's meandering baritone.

She needed to buy herself more time for Tallowmeade to leave.

"Did the old scriptomancers ever figure out where the Aldervine came from?" she asked.

"The vine? Nobody knows exactly where it started. The earliest recordings of it speak of the Aldervine creeping up buildings and winding around fence posts, but that's all," he said, then looked at something behind her.

She turned.

Tallowmeade stood in the doorway, holding the remains of a knob. "Is that you, Apprentice Hill? I thought you were in the south."

"She arrived back this evening," Mordraig said. "What is that?" He squinted at the broken knob.

Tallowmeade held it up. "Someone took it upon themselves to break into the Postmaster's office and sift through his bookcase."

Mordraig whistled. "Onrich will be raving mad."

"Did you see who did it?" Tallowmeade asked Maeve.

"I—I didn't see anything."

He held out his free hand. "I'll need to confiscate your saddlebag."

"What? Why?"

"Because you're here. It's policy when a crime as great as this one is committed."

"I'm afraid he's right, apprentice," Mordraig said.

But the letter from Professor Claryman was tucked in the bottom, right beside her journal. If one of them saw it, it would be worse than if they thought her guilty of the break-in.

She lunged for the hall.

Steward Mordraig swung his cane up, blocking her, but Maeve dropped to her knees and scrambled forward, under the cane.

"Stop her!" Tallowmeade bellowed, but she was already down the hall, out the door.

Maeve made it off the Post grounds, walking aimlessly for an hour in the freezing snow before she thought to hail a coach. She held out six shills and asked the driver to take her to Dunsmore Station, just south of the city, where the overnight train to the southern coast picked up. He scoffed and said six shills wouldn't get her past Gloam. But she needed the remainder of the coins for the train ticket.

Her legs ached from racing out of the Post, then all the walking. The thin mattress in her rented flat called to her, but if someone met with Fion this evening and learned her name, they might be standing outside her door when she woke, ready to greet her with handcuffs.

"Then bring me to Alewick," she told the driver. Dunsmore Station was only an hour's walk from there.

The cab wasn't any warmer than the air. The seats were sticky and smelled of tobacco and stale sweat. She pinched her nose as they set off over drifts of snow. It clogged the main streets and crusted over the coach's wheels, making the ride painfully slow. They didn't arrive in Alewick until just after ten—long after the last train of the night had already left.

There wouldn't be another train south until first thing the

following morning. At least the snowstorm would slow down the constabulary. If she was lucky, she might still catch the train before anyone found her.

Not sure where to wait out the night, Maeve wandered the streets of Alewick until her feet grew numb once again. Then she turned a corner and found herself in front of the inksmithy.

The shop was shuttered, the curtains drawn on Mr. Braithwaite's second-floor flat.

She slipped her fingers under the base of the doorframe, pulling out Mr. Braithwaite's spare key, then pushed it into the lock, letting herself in as silently as possible.

After the bracing winds, the shop felt like stepping inside an oven. Maeve settled into the worn leather chair in the corner, hoping to doze for a few minutes, but couldn't so much as close her eyes. Her mind kept wandering to that memory scribing in her saddlebag.

Taking a deep breath, she pulled out Claryman's paper then kneeled on the shop floor, placing the paper on the roughened floorboards.

She didn't have the rose journal. If she were caught now, this memory scribing might very well be the only thing to help her. As much as she didn't want to see her father's murder, she should probably give it a read.

Slowly, she opened her crematory ash satchel and placed it beside the paper, then scooted it a few inches away. She would have to be careful with the ash. If she got any on the scribing and nulled it on accident, before anyone else had a chance to see it, she could ruin everything.

She peeled off her sodden gloves. The old white wax seal crumbled as she cracked it, then unfolded the thin paper.

It was dated six months after Inverly, right after she'd run away from the orphanage. The handwriting inside was shorter than expected.

Dearest Maeve,

I'm very sorry that you've been pulled into this situation. Please know I swore to your father that I would protect you. I never wanted to see you harmed, but things don't often work out the way we want, do they? If there was another way to keep you safe, I would have done it already. Now keeping you silent is the best course of action for every party involved. Trust me on that.

—your old friend

The words bled together.

Before she could grab her ash satchel, a sharp pain stabbed her finger.

She lifted her hand in horror.

Ink had burrowed beneath her nail bed in the spot where her finger had touched the paper. She stood slowly, staring at her finger. A foul metallic flavor filled her mouth. Heavy liquid pooled against her tongue that tasted like metal and ash, and her throat burned hot as if a candle were sparking to life inside of her.

She choked and wiped her mouth on her sleeve, and a smear of oily black residue came off. Ink. She tried to scream, but only a muffled scratch came from her throat.

Keeping you silent is the best course of action.

The professor had meant it quite literally.

Panicked, Maeve emptied the entire bag of crematory ash between her lips and forced herself to swallow it down.

The pain in her throat receded, which only made her conscious of how badly the fingers on her left hand stung from where she'd touched the letter. Her thumb had turned black. It was spreading up her hand.

There was no ash left save for a dusty coating on the inside of the satchel, but she plunged her thumb inside of it, swaying at the barest relief, until her stomach cramped, probably from ingesting the ash.

A light flickered on.

Mr. Braithwaite came out in his pajamas. "Isla? Is that you?"

Maeve turned to him.

He staggered at the sight of her. "What is this?"

She tried to speak, but her throat was too ravaged. Ink dripped from her nostrils. It streamed down her chin. She gagged and barely managed to keep herself from retching.

"Demon, shoo!" Mr. Braithwaite shouted, coming toward her. He swung his cane down on her thigh with a crack. He raised it again and jabbed it into her stomach.

"I'm not a demon," Maeve silently mouthed, wincing in pain.

Swiping her mouth, she crouched down and scrambled for her saddlebag and cloak.

Mr. Braithwaite's cane cracked against her back, tearing her blouse. The sharp wood bit between her shoulder blades, and she shook in a silent scream.

Before he could bring the cane down again, she ran out the front door, and didn't stop.

Dunsmore Station was an hour's walk west on a good day, but it would take longer in the snow. The station would have heated lavatories and benches to rest.

Maeve tossed on her cloak and started for it, stumbling over wheel ruts, black ink dribbling from her mouth and hissing as droplets fell against the fresh snow.

The wind picked up. A freezing gust hit her blackened hand, and her eyes watered from the pain. Her body was filled with hot adrenaline. Her mind was sharp. Flooded with fear. She didn't know what that scribing had done, but she knew enough to be worried. She had no more crematory ash, and there was no way to get more without returning to the Post and begging the stewards—and likely being arrested.

She had to keep going.

Using her good hand, Maeve felt her pocket for the lump of a biscuit she'd saved. It was a day old, but she shoved it between her ink-smeared lips, then pulled a glove down over her searing fingers to keep them from freezing off, biting the biscuit against the pain.

She swallowed it down afterward, immediately regretting her decision. Her gut churned from ingesting the ash, and she bent and retched a black puddle onto the snow. Then she forced herself to continue west, through a southern section of the city populated by shuttered factory buildings and little else.

The roads were empty. Desolate. Maeve could barely see anything in the snow. It drifted over her feet, lapping at her legs.

Doubts crept in. She began to wonder if she'd accidentally turned southwest instead of straight west and whether she would make it to Dunsmore Station at all. She didn't recognize anything around her and couldn't feel her feet. Then she turned down another street and halted at a dilapidated barn, its large door hanging open. A shelter.

She hobbled for it, moving as quickly as her half-frozen feet would allow, then slipped past the rusted door. There was nothing but straw and old horse pens long empty. At least it was out of the wind and snow.

Maeve gathered old hay against an interior wall, then tucked herself into the pile. Her hand throbbed, but there was nothing to do but hold it against her chest and shut her eyes.

The night was long. She slept in fits and starts, dreaming of nothing but black sky and frozen ground. Then she eventually fell into a deeper sleep, only to be jolted awake by pain.

An excruciating pain radiated up her left arm.

It left her breathless—afraid to move. She tried wiggling her fingers and managed to wag her thumb. Biting down on her lower lip, she tore off her glove and held up her left hand.

Good god. Blisters lined the pads of her thumb, which was now fully black, along with half of her pointer finger. She brought it to her nose. The skin smelled like ink set to flame.

The saliva soured in her mouth, and she bent and retched again onto the moldering hay, then sat up with a violent shiver.

She had to find help. There was no denying it now.

Clutching her blackened hand to her stomach, she was able to stagger outside, where a stark morning greeted her.

Night drifts had blown a bank of snow against the side of the barn. Her blackened fingers barked with protest as she plunged them deep into snow and kept them under until a blissful numbness swallowed them, and she was able to replace her glove without expiring right there in the shadow of the rotted barn.

Using her good hand, she scooped a handful of snow and pushed it between her lips to soothe her aching throat. Curious at the extent of the damage, she tried to say a few words but could barely speak through the pain.

She had her journal, at least. If her inks weren't frozen, she could always try to communicate by writing. A carriage would come through here at some point. She could write out instructions to take her to City Hospital.

Maeve paused at the thought and glanced down at her left hand curled in on itself.

There was no way to hold a quill to write. If she hadn't dunked her thumb in the dregs of her ash satchel, there might not be a hand at all.

Fion Claryman had tried to silence her completely.

Her teeth ground together, then ached from the bitter cold. This day would kill her if she didn't get somewhere warm soon.

She tried to hurry, but her feet were still numb. Her progress was slow at best. When a carriage finally turned and came up the road, Maeve waved desperately, but it didn't so much as slow down. She considered throwing herself in front of it, but the pain in her hand prevented her from any sudden movements. It ached all the way to her gums. Eventually, it forced her to slow, then sit down hard on an iced-over stump beside the road.

Her body was too tired to remove her glove and check her left hand, but she could feel blisters scraping against the material at her wrist.

Would she even make it to get help? Maybe a constabulary courier would find a corpse instead.

No, they wouldn't find her at all; the tracking scribing didn't work on the dead.

For some reason, Maeve found that funny. Hilarious, in fact. Laughter burst from her ravaged throat until her belly shook from it. Yes, she was certainly delirious.

She stopped abruptly at the sound of more horse's hooves.

Staggering up, she managed to drag her limp body to the middle of the road, where she squinted into the gray winter light.

It was a coach, all right. Large and black, it hurtled toward her, its two draft horses kicking up icy debris.

It wasn't stopping or slowing.

Maeve leapt out of the way before it could hit her, landing on her back on the side of the road.

Unable to move her head, she squinted up at the sky as the morning sun tried its best to scrape through the gray clouds.

She wasn't sure how long she lay there. Minutes? Hours? But eventually, she heard another, smaller noise. The crunch of footsteps over packed snow.

Maeve thought she was hallucinating and rolled to her side, blinking at a polished pair of boots filling her field of vision. An officer's boots? Someone must have tracked her here to arrest her. At least prison would be warmer than this.

The owner of the boots knelt.

"I thought I told you to never leap in front of oncoming carriages," Tristan said.

A wave of relief hit Maeve as sharply as a blow.

Tristan had come for her. Did he track her here? No, he wouldn't have broken his promise. The constabulary had to be searching for her, and Tristan got word and decided to find her first. That had to be it.

She waited for him to mention it, but he didn't. He brought his hand to her cheek and gently tilted her face, his expression carefully blank. "Why, pray tell, is there black ink covering your mouth?"

"A long story," she whispered, then winced in pain.

Biting off his glove, he brought the back of his hand to her forehead and swore. "You're burning up. We need to get you inside."

He gestured to a saddled horse waiting a few paces away. Butternut.

"I'd rather stay put," Maeve whispered.

He ignored her and helped her to stand.

Too quickly.

The world tilted, and she lost her balance, falling against him. Tristan might have said something, but she wasn't sure. Her right ear rung, and her left felt entirely plugged. She peeled off her cloak so the cool air could chase away the heat of her skin. The chill felt divine, until Tristan gripped her left hand.

A scream tore from her ravaged throat.

He took her wrist. She tried pushing him off, but her muscles felt useless.

"I'm not going to hurt you," he said in a clipped tone, and peeled off her glove, drawing in a hiss through his teeth.

The blackened patch had spread to two more fingers and half of her palm. The sight made her drop to her knees.

"Shit," she whispered.

"*Shit* is right."

"It was from a scribing."

"I can see that."

Bending, he put his hands beneath her. She tried to push him away, to stand on her own again. "Stop struggling, you fool."

Maeve felt the ground rush away as Tristan lifted her into his arms and made for Butternut. When the large horse stomped its hooves, she passed right out.

Warm air caressed Maeve's neck as she slowly opened her eyes to a coffered ceiling of rich brown wood. It had to be night; a candle flame flickering in the periphery seemed to be the only light source. Slowly, she trailed a hand along the top of a velvet duvet tucked tightly around her sides, then up over the top buttons of a nightgown, to her bare throat.

It ached from thirst. She needed water. Her fingers raced to pull down the bedclothes. Her *fingers*.

Each knuckle on her left hand was covered with a thick knot of gauze caked in a gray paste. It smelled of antiseptic mixed with pungent herbs and—was that crematory ash? She brought it closer to her nose. Yes, it was ash. At least three satchels' worth. Maybe more, since there was some smeared along her wrist. Her fingers ached a small amount, but nothing like before.

Pushing the covers off her, Maeve swung her bare ankles over the side of a bed so enormous, she had to scoot forward before her toes touched the floor. Her nightgown shifted up, exposing a leg with a long bruise up one side, where Mr. Braithwaite's cane had cracked down.

She ran a finger over the bruise, then up, along the filmy edge of her nightgown.

How she got into said nightgown, she didn't want to think about. There was no sign of her clothes anywhere—

The love letter.

Her leather saddlebag lay tucked beside the bed, her skirt and blouse folded below it.

She lunged toward the pile, regretting the sudden movement when a wave of dizziness took hold. After a few deep breaths, she inched her way to the bag and searched the skirt pockets until the worn envelope crinkled against her palm. She hugged it to her chest before stuffing it back down the pocket. The next order of business was her thirst.

Simple enough, but the room tilted as she stood, forcing her to walk her hands along the wood-paneled wall to the lavatory, where she braced herself against a porcelain sink and looked in the mirror.

The degree of dreadfulness she felt was nothing compared to her reflection.

Her cheeks were as pale as a dinner plate, while her lips still carried a dark tint from the ink. Her hair was the only thing not deterred by the near-death experience. It fluffed around her in a wild tangle of curls.

Maeve rinsed her mouth, then gulped down an entire cup of water. The moment she slipped her fingers from the sink, she lost her balance and fell, landing on her back.

A door creaked open, and Tristan craned over her, shirt rumpled and face covered in days-old stubble. Her heart leapt at the sight of him. "Lo and behold, the great slumberer has awakened at last."

The low pitch of his voice brought back memories of her narrow escape from that hellish barn, how he must have found her using a tracking scribing. Then something new occurred to her.

Fion Claryman had seen Nan's article by now and given up her real name. That was why Tristan had tracked her after swearing he wouldn't. It had to be. He must have believed it was either him or the constabulary, and wanted to get to her first.

But if that were true, he would know whose daughter she was.

Maeve waited for him to volunteer it, but he didn't. Did he not know who she was?

Suddenly filled with nerves, unsure of how to act, Maeve brought a hand to her wild hair. "I must look like a creature from the depths of hell."

"No. *Never*," he said, then brushed a tuft from her forehead. He checked her temperature with the back of his hand. "Still feverish."

"I feel like I may die."

"You almost did die. Twice now in the past three days, if memory serves."

Three days?

He helped her to the edge of the bed, and she sat down hard, facing a small table she hadn't noticed before—with a stack of books beside a crumb-covered plate. Another book sat open on an old club chair.

"My room is down the hall, but you had a most impressive fever and couldn't be left alone for long," he volunteered.

Still no mention of Fion Claryman.

Maeve fixed her eyes on her knees, acutely aware of her thin nightgown, how near he stood. "Where am I?"

"The Widdens' country house."

"Shea's here?"

"And Nan."

Maeve tensed, thinking of the newspaper article.

"Nobody else?" she asked, expecting Tristan to say an officer was downstairs ready to place her in restraints.

His brow furrowed. "It's just us."

That made no sense. She hesitated, then asked, "What happened with the newspaper article—about Abenthy's roommate?"

"The article Nan wrote?"

"Yes. I—I read it right after the exhibition. I guessed it was hers from the pen name."

He nodded. "She's annoyingly proud of it, though we're not allowed to speak of it to anyone because she doesn't want her clandestine activities to somehow get back to a steward. It caused a small stir, and the Post released the roommate's name—some professor in Barrow who ran off before anyone could question him."

Before.

Fion never gave her away. Tristan still didn't know who she was.

"Aren't you curious how I found you?" he asked.

"I already know how," she said, that sting returning. "You heard that I broke into your father's office and hunted me down." *After promising you never would.*

"My father was furious. He sent several people to track Eilidh Hill." His mouth twitched as he said the name. "I heard they found her, and she described meeting you at the testing location weeks ago. They pieced everything together. Then I had to sit through an hour-long interrogation where they questioned me about everything you ever said to me, which wasn't particularly difficult given how cagey you've been. I didn't mention the fact that you were looking for that confiscated journal."

Her eyes snapped to his.

"I'm very curious to know why you risked everything for it," he said.

Of course he was, but she pressed her lips together, reluctant to say a thing.

He'd tracked her.

His forehead creased to a frown. "Very well. Fill me in later if you want. We have time. Several loggerheads at the Post are searching for you, but it's rather difficult to find anyone without a name." He came closer. "I never gave it up."

He seemed proud of that fact.

And it would mean a great deal if he hadn't hunted her without her permission. He had saved her life, but he broke her trust.

"Has anyone thought to come looking for me here?" she asked. It came out sounding harsh.

He noticed. "No one. After word got out about your break-in, I ran into Nan, and she was as worried as I was. I told her that I planned to search for you. Shea—Shea doesn't think very highly of me, but she happens to like *you* for some unfathomable reason, and after I explained why you'd snuck inside the Post, she offered up this house to use in case I found you. Then she invited Nan here to help get over the fact that a criminal mastermind had posed as her roommate," he said with a half laugh. "The stewards sent them with a fruit basket and a bottle of punch and gave them a week off of duties."

A pit formed in Maeve's stomach. Nan cared about her, but what was stopping Nan from turning in another article? What was stopping any of them from running to the constabulary?

"Do Nan or Shea know my first name?"

Tristan gave her a strange look. "Of course not."

A small comfort.

The bed compressed as he sat beside her and lifted her left

hand, unwinding the gauze bandage, rubbing her knuckles gently between his thumb and forefinger. Ash flaked off.

"Where did you get all the ash?" Maeve asked, mostly to keep her mind from dwelling on how near he sat, how her body wanted to lean into him, while her mind warned her away.

"Shea's grandfather was a scriptomancer with the university some forty years ago and kept a worktable in the attic with a large supply of it. It's the only reason you're breathing right now."

That wasn't entirely true. Tristan had played a large part in saving her. She owed him a great debt that could never be repaid. And yet—and yet she wanted to race out the bedroom door.

She must be broken beyond repair to be hurt by such a thing as a boy coming to her rescue, but she couldn't help how she felt. This was her reality, and she was foolish to believe it could be any different.

Tristan took her chin, forcing her to look at him. She flinched. "If you don't tell me what's the matter this instant, I'm tempted to find a piano and make you stand atop it and sing."

Maeve hesitated, then said, "Why did you track me?"

He tilted his head. "Ah. So that's what this is about."

She didn't realize she was crying until Tristan wiped away her tear. His other hand came up and cradled her jaw. Her breathing notched up at the gentle touch, and a sharp wave of desire reminded her of the press of his body in Molly's Keep, the heat of his fingers as they'd stoked across her belly. "I think you should go," she whispered, not trusting herself.

"Maeve—"

"*Now.*"

He gave a single nod, then pulled away and walked to the door.

Halfway through it, he pressed his forehead to the jamb, then turned to her. "The night you disappeared, I rode to the constabulary looking for you and came across a frantic Mr. Braithwaite from Alewick, who said a girl in courier's raiment matching your description had taken off into the snow, that she might be demon-possessed. I rode through the night, searching every roadway until I found you the following morning. Yes, a tracking scribing would have certainly saved me many torturous hours, but I didn't use one because I swore to you I wouldn't."

Maeve stared at him, speechless.

"Now get some sleep. We'll catch up in the morning."

Maeve didn't particularly want the sun to rise. When a bright shaft of light spilled through the drapery, she cursed at it and flipped over, hoping to pretend it was still night for another hour. Her bodily needs, however, had other ideas. Then she smelled something sour and realized the scent wafted from her own skin.

A creature from the depths of hell indeed.

There was no bathtub in her washroom, but she found one situated in the hall lavatory, complete with pearly bars of soaps. She took her sweet time, hissing as the heat from the water seeped into her stiff, aching muscles.

She tried not to think of Tristan yet, which soon became impossible, and she spent the latter half of her bath stuck on the fact that he never tracked her. He'd kept her name from Nan and Shea. He rode through the night and saved her miserable life, then kept vigil at her bedside for days, only to be barked at and thrown out of her room.

He never broke her trust, and he deserved an explanation for what happened.

But she didn't have the rose journal or any proof her father was murdered, only her word, which she doubted was enough to convince anyone.

After Maeve had toweled off and dressed in her laundered clothing, she found that her appetite was the next creature that needed taming, and food sounded much better than wallowing in a bath.

She padded through a maze of creaking floors, past enormous rooms filled with furniture covered in white sheeting, then caught the scent of baking bread and followed it down a small servants' stair to a cheery kitchen encased in windows. Three woodfire hearths sat along a back wall behind two oaken monastery tables that could each easily seat fifteen. A tall, dark-haired woman dressed in slim men's trousers stood beside them, covered with flour and scowling.

"Shea made me finish baking her soda bread so she could clean a few rooms." Nan ripped a heel off a loaf and lobbed it at Maeve.

It hit her in the forehead.

"Ow! What was that for?"

"For disappearing for two weeks, making me lie about it, then scaring me half to death! That bread was a favor. It would have been a hard slap to the face if you didn't look halfway to the grave."

Her roommate rushed around the table and threw her arms around her.

Regardless of whatever Nan wrote, it felt good to see her.

Nan pulled away and held Maeve at a distance. "I honestly thought you would die. Shea nearly called the head doctor at the Post, but Tristan was adamant that we leave him out of it, that you would be arrested if anyone knew you were here."

Maeve searched Nan's face for any clue that she might be suspicious of her, but there was nothing but earnest joy, along with a fair amount of baking flour stuck to her red lipstick.

"You don't know how good it is to see you."

"I think I have an inkling. Here—have a seat. Eat some burned bread." Nan pulled a stool to the counter and heaped a plate with blackened soda bread.

Maeve chewed while Nan spoke nonstop about the past few days, describing at length the struggle it was for her and Shea to get Maeve into her nightgown.

"Don't fret, we made Tristan leave the room."

"Thank you *dearly* for that," Maeve said with a full mouth, then decided it was time to ask Nan about the article. "I saw what you published."

"Did you now?" She grinned unabashedly. "Sorry I kept it from you. I was paranoid of showing it to anyone. Even Shea didn't see it until it was ready to publish. Did you read it? The editor at the *Herald* adored it, but how could he not?"

"So that whole time you were never working on poetry?"

"Me? A poet?" Nan laughed and slapped the counter, sending up a small plume of flour. "The truth is, I spoke with the *Herald* about writing articles before I ever came to the Post, but the editor told me that he simply didn't like hiring women." She rolled her eyes. "He barely gave me the time of day, but that article changed his tune. He still swears to hell and back that he'll never hire me as a staff writer, but he promised to print another article about the Post if I have one juicy enough."

"Do you have one?" Maeve asked slowly.

"Oh dear. You think I'll out you, don't you?"

"It's crossed my mind."

Nan took Maeve's hand. "I won't. Besides, the one article was risky. Steward Mordraig would kick me out immediately if he knew I was behind it, and I'm sure Tristan would only be too happy to turn me in if I did anything to hurt you. He's already threatened it."

"He has?"

"Twice."

Oh.

"Have you spoken to him? He's been beside himself." Nan propped her elbow in the mess of flour, then leaned toward Maeve. "I knew you two had an understanding, but I didn't realize how deep it went."

Maeve's neck burned. "No. I mean, he and I . . . It's nothing."

"*Nothing?* That boy barely left your bedside."

Maeve bit off a piece of soda bread to keep from having to reply to *that*. Her relationship with Tristan was too complicated to explain to Nan this early.

A moment later, Shea burst into the kitchen in a flurry, carrying dustcloths in both hands. "I thought I heard you two in here."

She walked around Nan and pressed a soft kiss to the side of Nan's neck. After which Nan met Maeve's eyes with a secretive smile of her own.

"Why didn't you two come get me?" Shea asked.

"I just came down. Thank you for letting me stay here," Maeve said before there could be any awkwardness.

Shea brushed her off. "No need for thanks. This house belonged to my grandfather, a good man who had the ill luck to be in Inverly that day. My mother can't stand to be here anymore. She says it feels like walking through ghosts—whatever that means." She sighed. "But I like to come. My grandfather always preferred laughter in this house, and turning your back on someone because they're not with you anymore isn't how he taught me to live."

Her words caught in Maeve's chest, and she couldn't help but think of her own father.

Shea took her arm. "Come. I promised Tristan I would fetch you when I saw you."

Maeve's pulse skittered. "Tristan?"

"I'm coming around to him, you know?" Shea smiled. "He's an odd duck, but a loyal one. He has something he's eager to show you in the front parlor."

Nan brought a few mismatched teacups and a jug of juice as Shea led the way through two empty ballrooms filled with slip-covered furniture, to a smaller parlor with burgundy wallpaper, a pair of worn velvet club chairs, and the largest hearth Maeve had ever seen, with a marble stag's head perched at the center of the mantel, meant to command attention. But her eyes couldn't seem to tear themselves from the man standing in front of it.

Tristan's hair was damp from a bath, and he had a small shaving nick on his neck. A gray knit sweater clung to his torso, one side tucked into a pair of low-slung trousers. There was no easygoing humor in his features. He pushed his spectacles up his nose and met Maeve's eyes with a brooding intensity that caused every nerve in her body to swarm to her stomach.

He must hate her after last night, but she didn't know how to turn things back to normal between them. She didn't know what normal meant between them anymore.

Then Tristan reached above the mantel and pulled down a book. A leather journal bordered by a silver tracery of roses.

Maeve stiffened.

"The Silver Scribing" was penned across the front.

She hadn't seen her father's handwriting in seven long years, but she knew it almost better than her own.

Tristan turned the journal, a grim set to his mouth. "I haven't opened it. In all honesty, I never wanted to see this again, but since you risked yourself to get it, I decided to give it a shot. My father has a locked cupboard filled with historic books in his closet, and I know where he keeps his keys. This journal was tucked inside."

Without so much as meeting her eyes, Tristan came forward and placed it in Maeve's hands.

She jolted as the cool leather slid against her palms; it felt like touching a piece of herself that had died.

It took all her wits to open it. The old pages felt as thin as onion skin, covered with her father's small handwriting bleeding together like a coffee stain. It would take ages to sort through the entire journal, to understand why her father was targeted.

Maeve shut the journal.

Everyone watched her, waiting for an explanation. What could she say to this?

No lie came. She doubted manufacturing one now would ever be convincing. Tristan would see through it the moment she uttered a syllable. He expected her to lie. As it was, he looked ready to pounce on the first word from her lips.

But even if she came up with a convincing lie, Postmaster Byrne would soon discover the journal missing and suspect that Tristan was involved. That they were all involved.

Maeve's gaze traveled across each of their confused faces as the reality of the situation struck her like a sudden blow. Her friends were now in grave danger because of her, and none of them had a clue.

This was it.

She owed them the truth.

Her fingers grew slick. They slid against the smooth silver roses and flipped the journal over. The initials J.A. were scratched with pigment on the underside. Her breath caught in her throat.

"What do you think that stands for?" Nan asked.

"It stands for Jonathan Abenthy," Maeve said. It felt like she was floating outside of her body. "This is his journal. I know because I picked it out for him when I was eleven. He's my father."

Nan and Shea both turned to each other, while Tristan stared intently at the journal. "But you told me that your father was lost in Inverly," he said.

"He was."

Tristan's jaw clenched and unclenched, and the sight made Maeve's stomach sink farther to the floor. Finally, he said, "Jonathan Abenthy is your *father*?"

"I thought we established that," said Nan.

"This is between me and Maeve," Tristan snapped.

"And me as well," said Shea. "Technically, I'm harboring the daughter of a criminal."

"My father was a good man," Maeve shot back.

Shea balked, whereas Tristan faced the fireplace and tugged roughly at his hair, as if attempting to pull it all out. He wouldn't look at her. He hated her—that was it. Just as Margery at the Sacrifict had hated her. Tears burned the backs of her eyes, but she swallowed them down and tucked her feelings carefully away before anyone might see.

Nan came forward. "I'd like to point out that if Maeve is who she says, she's put herself in more danger going to the Post than she's put any of us in. I think we should all give her a chance to explain herself. There's some burned bread in the kitchen. We could each grab a plate, have a listen."

"Thanks, Nan, but I don't think soda bread is going to solve anything," Maeve said.

"Agreed," Tristan echoed without turning, and Maeve winced.

"For god's sake, at least let her explain things," Nan said.

Right. She could try to explain things. But where would she ever begin? *You begin with a blank page and a single word.* She could hear her father's steady reply, coaxing her, lending her strength. She shut her eyes and pictured a page in her journal. If she were to write her story down, it would begin that moment in Alewick, when the grizzled courier leapt from the darkness and handed her a letter.

"I used to believe my father was as guilty as you all do," she started, avoiding looking at Tristan. "But then I received a letter. It was one of the lost letters from right after the Post opened. The sender didn't leave their name, but they told me my father was innocent, and I had to know if it was true."

"That's why you wanted to search for his room," Nan said.

Tristan glared at her. "*You* wanted to search for it?"

"I—I needed answers, Tristan," Maeve said, utterly failing to keep her voice even. "You know better than anyone how risky it was for me to remain at the Post."

Tristan's eyebrows flickered. He leaned a shoulder against the mantel, looking about as cross as she had ever seen him, no doubt going over their every interaction with new scrutiny—finding more things to loathe.

Nan plopped into a club chair and kicked her feet up on a low table. "So? Did you find out who wrote the letter?"

Maeve's fingers twisted in her skirts. "Yes. It turned out to be my father's roommate. The one you wrote about. I spoke with him."

Nan's mouth dropped open. "You spoke with Fion Claryman? But he lives in Barrow now."

"She's adept at the traveling scribing," Shea said.

Tristan knocked his knuckles against the mantel. "How in the worlds do *you* know that?"

Shea shot an exasperated look at Maeve.

At this point, Maeve wouldn't mind it if the walls grew mouths and finished the rest of the story for her. She wrapped her fingers around the back of Nan's chair to have something to grip as she went over everything Fion told her, nearly word for word: how her father was working on developing a new skin scribing in that journal, how he was murdered in Inverly, how Fion was threatened afterward with letters—the same threatening letters she'd been receiving.

Both Nan and Shea watched her as she explained herself, while Tristan stared pointedly at a spot on the floor.

This next part wasn't going to go over well, but Maeve had to force it out somehow.

She took a deep inhale, then explained how Professor Claryman was convinced that her father was murdered over the Silver Scribing.

Tristan's entire torso flinched.

"I know it's hard to believe," Maeve said. "But I think the same person who killed my father also murdered Cathriona."

"Impossible," Tristan said. "Cath was killed by the Silver Scribing."

"I don't think so." Maeve held up the journal. "Fion said the scribing inside here is used to *protect* scriptomancers from the effects of scriptomancy to a much greater degree than crematory ash, so a person can practice whatever they wish to without scribings affecting them at all."

They all stared at the journal as if Maeve held a bloody lung on a plate.

"Then you should take that journal straight to the Postmaster," Shea said.

Yes, but the Postmaster might very well shove her to the bottom of the abyss before she could get a word in. She opened her mouth to tell them about her suspicions, then hesitated.

"Spit it out," Nan said.

Maeve's heart stuttered inside her chest. She turned to Tristan. "What if your father is behind everything?"

"My father?"

"Think about it. He was my father's mentor. They would have known each other well."

Tristan looked at her as if she were mad. "My father didn't destroy Inverly."

"You can't deny that your father became a hero when the Written Doors were burned. Inverly was the beginning of his success. If the Aldervine didn't come, he would likely still work for an underfunded college in the university."

"So would all the other stewards."

"Yes, but they're not the Postmaster. Tristan, he confiscated the rose journal. It was kept inside *his* office this entire time. If this journal were discovered—if any of this were made public and there was an investigation—your father has the most to lose. You have to see—"

"Enough," he snapped. "Unless you have real evidence implicating my father, you need to drop it now."

His tone was ice cold, and Maeve's stomach sank. Her throat tightened to a knot.

Tristan didn't believe her.

He looked at the floor with a flattened mouth and cheeks reddened from anger—the exact expression Margery wore right before she raised her eyes to glare at Maeve with enough poison to kill a cat, then gave Maeve's secret away to everyone she could. If Tristan looked at her like Margery had . . .

"I think . . . I think I need some fresh air. Pardon me."

Maeve tossed the journal on a side table and ran from the room, tearing down a side hall, to a mudroom filled with coats and men's hunting boots. A door led to a backyard.

Shoving her feet inside the smallest pair of boots she could find, Maeve rushed outside, into the morning snow.

It was deeper than she remembered. Her feet swam inside the too-large boots, and she stumbled around the side of the house, searching for somewhere to hide, then she spotted a small, boarded-up greenhouse against a back fence and barreled toward it. She flung the door open to a wide stone floor stacked with gardening supplies and empty clay pots. It was warm inside from the sun beating against the building. Most of the glass was boarded up, but an open section in the ceiling let in a small shaft of sunlight, illuminating an old stone garden bench near the center.

She started toward it, making it three whole steps before the door burst open behind her. A second later, hands clamped down on her shoulders.

Panic swamped her. She gritted her teeth and twisted, fighting to be free.

"Stop struggling, you fool," Tristan barked. He let her go, and she stumbled forward, then turned.

His face was still beet red with anger. He was breathing as hard as she was.

Without saying so much as a word, he tugged off the old hunting coat that he must have taken on the way out and let it drop to the floor, then pulled his sweater over his head, tossing it away as well. Leaving only an ink-splotched buttoned shirt clinging to his chest.

He began undoing the buttons.

Merciful heavens.

"W-what are you doing?"

"Something I should have done weeks ago," he said through a clenched jaw.

But weeks ago, she'd barely known him.

Her feet were rooted in place as his fingers worked until every last button was undone. He parted the material, exposing a swath of his bare chest.

Small words were written across his skin—the same words she'd noticed that morning in Molly's Keep—but she had a much better view in the dappled morning light streaming in through the greenhouse roof. The words started an inch below his ash satchel and ran across his pectoral muscles, down his abdomen, nearly to the dip of his navel.

"Recognize any of it?" he asked, parting the shirt further.

Maeve didn't dare step closer, but she could see enough of the top sentence and . . . She knew those words. She'd tried to perform a scribing on them many times over.

"It's a coffee scribing."

He gave a bleak nod. "A more complicated version that uses crematory ash mixed into the scribing pigment, so the magic doesn't kill me outright. I have seven total penned across me and have to redo at least one every day."

She didn't understand it. "But you already have insomnia. Why would you scribe yourself with a coffee scribing?"

"I don't have insomnia, Maeve."

"You don't?"

He pushed his shirt open another inch and pointed out two black marks below his heart, each the size of a small thumbprint. "The two spots where the Aldervine got me."

It took a moment for his words to sink in.

Maeve's eyes shot to his. "You were pricked by the Aldervine in Inverly?"

He gave a solemn nod, and she gasped.

"I don't remember much of it, to be honest. I fell asleep and woke up in my father's office covered in a few of the coffee scribings. It was Mordraig's idea. He found me in Inverly during the commotion, and with the help of a few others, he brought me back and thought to save me. This version of the coffee scribing was something he read about in a text from Molly's time, that it could be used as a skin scribing for a deeper effect. It worked. I woke up with a galloping heartbeat and eyes that wouldn't stay shut."

"But you were sleeping in Molly's Keep."

She had witnessed it.

"A body can't live without some sleep. Eventually I fall into a deep bout for an hour or two, but then the coffee scribing wakes me up long before I would ever choose to on my own. The one upside is I can drink as much as I want; wine never affects my mind like it does for others."

Maeve wrapped her arms across her front. "Why are you telling me all of this now?" As it was, his jaw was still tight and his eyes were dark and bleak.

"Because it pertains to my father," he said, and Maeve's spine pulled straight. "He didn't destroy Inverly to somehow get his position. My *father* never wanted that position to begin with."

"What?"

"He turned down the role of Postmaster at least twenty times in the days after Inverly—so many times that stewards still have their knickers twisted about it. My father wanted us to leave Gloam for good, but then the wrong people found out about my affliction, and the House of Ministers threatened to have me confined to a pea-sized laboratory at City Hospital. It's where they brought a few others who were also asleep from the vine."

She had no idea there were others who were poisoned. She always thought that nobody pricked made it out.

"Mordraig tried the coffee scribing on the others as well, but none woke up," Tristan said. "He thinks there were too many thorn punctures on their bodies, but there's no way to know without sending people into Inverly to test the theory, which would be too risky. Somehow the head doctor who was caring for the other victims found out I was also pricked, and he met with the House of Ministers, demanding that I be handed over so he could remove my coffee scribings in order to attempt other experimental cures on me. He wanted to keep me asleep and *poisoned*. And the House of Ministers planned to go along with it so they could tell the public they were working toward a cure. It was before anyone knew about my scribing ability. When I was worth nothing to them."

Maeve listened to every word he said in disbelief. "They wanted to cage you like a rat."

"Yes, and they would have if it wasn't for my father. He was furious at the ministers, but they threatened to take me against my will. So my father made a bargain. He agreed to be Postmaster on the condition they never lay a finger on me, and they needed him. People were hurting, and my father was the hero." He took a small step forward. "Now do you see?"

She did.

The Postmaster had no motive to destroy Inverly. He wasn't behind the Oxblood letters. He didn't kill her father. Maeve was back to having no idea who her tormentor was, and she was going to fall apart because of it. Right in front of Tristan, who still looked at her like he wanted to drag her to the constabulary.

She flipped to face the back wall. "Thank you for telling me that. You can go now."

"Go? Why would I do that?"

"Oh, I don't know. Maybe because I'm an Abenthy who just accused your innocent father of murder. I watched your face as I told you everything and . . ." She swallowed and rubbed her neck. Her godforsaken throat had tightened, and she could barely speak, let alone breathe. "I know you must hate me now, and I'd simply like a little more time before I'm forced to face that fact." *Go*, she willed.

Tristan didn't go. He was silent for a long moment. Maeve tensed when he took her hand, pulling her around to face him.

His eyes were narrowed. He chewed on his bottom lip, searching her face. "Yes—yes, I suppose I do hate you."

His words seemed to make her heart crack wide open, and she nodded and blinked, on the verge of tears. She tried backing away, but he slid his hand against her waist, stopping her. She tensed as he leaned forward and brushed his mouth against the shell of her ear.

She froze.

"I *hate* how your ear always makes me want to do that," he said. *Oh.*

Tristan's words caused a tangle of emotions to flood through her, breaking her further. Heated tears slid against her cheeks and a shudder traveled down her spine as he slid his other hand to the curve of her neck, then moved her hair aside to press a second, slower kiss below her ear.

"I hate how your horrible, delightful little curls hide that spot," he murmured against her skin, trailing his lips along her jaw, up her chin, removing any doubt of his feelings with each caress. "But I hate your mouth most of all because, no matter how hard I try, I can't stop wanting it."

He pressed a soft kiss to the corner of her lips, then pulled back.

Maeve didn't want him to stop. She was trembling like an autumn leaf by the time she glanced up.

Tristan's eyes were bright with something that resembled hunger. Heat rushed up her neck, and she forgot why she'd been so afraid of him moments ago.

"Are you going to disappear on me if I take this further?" he asked.

He thought she would run now? But of course he did; running was all she'd done up until this moment.

Outside, wind swirled over snow and rattled the greenhouse glass, and Maeve had no desire to rush into it. On the contrary, in fact.

She grabbed a fistful of Tristan's shirt. He grunted as she tugged him forward until her mouth hovered above his. There was nothing left between them, she realized. No more secrets. No more lies. Only a sliver of space that frankly needed to go.

Maeve pushed herself up and kissed him. Tasting the salt on her own lips as she pressed herself into him, so there could be no doubt how desperately she *didn't* want to run. The kiss felt too good. Both feverish and soft. She opened her mouth further and tasted smoke and the barest hint of wine against her tongue.

Why had she been so afraid of this? With each press of his lips, it felt like molten wax was rushing through the cracks of her damaged heart, sealing it, flooding her system with a pleasant heat.

"Are you clear now about how much I hate you?" Tristan murmured into her mouth.

Pleasure snaked down her center. "No. Not quite yet. I still need convincing."

Tristan nipped her bottom lip, and tilted, angling to kiss her deeper. Heat shot through her, and her fingers grasped for his hair—for something to grip on to before she floated away. "The bench," she muttered.

He understood, and they stumbled to it, never breaking the kiss. He gathered her onto his lap so she faced him, his hands moving over her in a frantic rush. Touching, tasting. She drew her fingers down his bare chest.

He jolted.

Maeve pulled up and looked from his chest to his face. "Did I hurt you?"

"That depends on your definition of the word," he said between heavy breaths, then cursed and ruffled his hair.

Heavens, she wanted to kiss him again, but she was afraid of accidentally touching something she shouldn't. She brought her fingers down along the open seams of his shirt. "May I?"

When he nodded, she slid the shirt off his shoulders.

The inked paragraphs covered every inch of his chest, filling the spaces between each of his ribs.

He looked like a page in her journal.

"They're something, aren't they?" The corner of his mouth lifted in a sardonic smile.

His muscles twitched as Maeve traced her finger along one scribing that ran across his stomach, then continued drawing a path upward, stopping just below the lower of the two black puncture marks at his heart. "Do they hurt?"

"No, but they're sometimes as sensitive as raw nerves."

"So I should poke one when I'm mad at you?"

It was a joke, but he caught her finger and dragged it toward him, holding it directly above the mark. "Go on if you want."

She touched her finger down. He flinched. It was shockingly cold compared to his heated skin. She moved her finger to the center of the mark and felt his heartbeat, then jerked back.

"They're revolting, I know," he said.

"No they're not."

"Don't you think you and I are past the point of niceties?"

"They're *not*. Why would you ever think that?"

"Cath—" He frowned. "Never mind."

Maeve dearly wished that Cath were still alive so she could slap her across the face. Slowly, she placed both her palms against his chest.

He shuddered. "What are you doing?"

"Showing you how *not* revolting you are." She slid her palms down and spread her fingers lightly over the marks, then began tracing her fingers between lines of text, going over them as if she were penning them herself.

"Are you enjoying yourself?" he asked, then wiped away a stray tear on her cheek.

"Mmm. I think I could do this all day. All night."

"We would eventually freeze to death."

"I already tried that three days ago. I'll be fine," she said, then decided it was time to kiss him again. He seemed to read her mind because he slid a hand around her waist. The other tugged her hip, pressing her against him, fisting her skirt—at her pocket. The love letter.

Maeve felt for it.

"Are you all right?" he asked.

"No."

The letter wasn't there.

Maeve ran to the upstairs lavatory, but the letter wasn't there either. She had taken it out when she'd bathed earlier. It had to be here. Unless someone picked it up.

She raced downstairs, halting at the sight of Shea in front of the fireplace, her hair dripping—fresh from a bath and reading something. She noticed Maeve and held up a crumpled paper. "It was on the lavatory floor just now. I'm assuming it's yours?"

Maeve came forward and snatched it away, smoothing out the wrinkles with her fingertips.

Tristan came into the room, along with Nan. They were all staring at her.

"It's a love letter that my mother wrote to my father," she said, anticipating the question.

Shea frowned. "Sibilla is your mother?"

Maeve blinked, confused. "Sibilla didn't write it," she said.

"Yes, she did. I thought the handwriting looked familiar, so I dug through my saddlebag and found this." Shea pulled a few yellow slips of paper and handed one to Maeve. A request slip from the Second Library. The top half was filled out by Shea, the bottom half filled out and signed by Sibilla Creel. "I thought I recognized her handwriting in the lavatory, but if you look between the two papers, it's obvious."

Maeve held the pages side by side.

Tristan and Nan both came over to have a look.

Maeve wasn't sure how much time passed. "It can't be," she murmured, going numb from shock.

"They could have had similar writing, I suppose," Nan said.

"But that's identical."

The love letter was written in large, rounded letters with de-scenders that looped in perfect circles. She had always thought her mother had the most distinctive handwriting she had ever seen.

"We should still check everything under a scribing glass to be sure," Tristan said.

"There's one in my grandfather's old office." Shea led the way through the first floor to an old worktable in the corner of a library.

Tristan placed both papers on the table, then adjusted the scribing glass overhead to magnify a small section of each paper. He moved his finger back and forth from one paper to the other. "I think the penmanship is identical."

Of course it was. It was painfully obvious.

Sibilla had penned the love letter.

A ringing began in Maeve's ears. Her father told her he ex-changed letters with her mother for years before Maeve was born. That their love story began with ink on paper. *A letter can become an extension of your soul if you will it, a trapped part of you that shakes loose whenever someone reads your words.*

Maeve sometimes wondered if she carried a piece of her mother's soul with her always, wrapped inside the old envelope and tucked flush against her hip bone.

The letter Sibilla wrote.

Not her mother.

Sibilla had given a love letter to her father. By the subject matter, it was most likely given after her mother died. She hoped so, anyway. If it was before—

Tristan squeezed her hand. "Are you all right?"

"I think I might be ill."

"Waste bin's in the corner!" Shea pointed.

Maeve made a dash for it, retching away the scant bit of bread she had eaten earlier. She collapsed against the wall, breathing heavily through her nose. "If this is all a terrible dream, will you let me know when I should wake up?"

"It's not so bad," Shea said, lifting the letter. "This is just proof your father and Sibilla were . . . close once."

"What if she's the one behind the Oxblood letters?" Tristan asked.

"Sibilla?" That was hard for Maeve to believe. She'd helped her escape the library, after all.

Nan came forward. "Our first week, Sibilla tried to open the door to our room."

Maeve looked at her. "What?"

"Sibilla was surprised to see me. Then she said she was lost." Nan blinked and shook her head. "She seemed genuine, so I never thought to mention it."

Heavens, that would have been right before their room was rifled through, when her journal was stolen and left open on her desk for Nan to find.

Maeve turned to Tristan. He'd gone pale. "What's wrong?"

"I had a strange interaction with Sibilla the day after the stewards found Cath dead. She asked which books Cath was looking at. She said she wanted to know so she could mark them as missing since they were all taken for the investigation. That didn't surprise me, but then she asked about other things that might have been on Cath's worktable. She wanted to know exactly what was confiscated, then grew agitated when I told her. I thought it was just a reaction to an apprentice dying, but what if there was more to it?"

"But if Sibilla murdered Cathriona, why would she want to know what was on the worktable? Wouldn't she have seen it for herself?" Maeve asked.

"It's still suspicious," Shea said. "It's a shame that nobody signed their name in that sales ledger."

"What sales ledger?" Tristan asked.

Maeve told him about going to Plume & Pen in Barrow and looking up the sale of Oxblood ink. "There were only two others who bought the ink besides you. One of them signed for the ink using the Post's archivist account, but there's no way to know who used it."

"Yes, there is," Tristan said. He then told them all about an accounting log that his father kept track of. "Any time someone uses one of the Post's credit accounts for purchases, they also have to record their name in the accounting log. Otherwise, the accountants have a conniption, and all hell breaks loose."

Maeve's blood pulsed. "So this accounting log is filled with names?"

Tristan nodded. "Next to exact purchases."

"I had no idea that existed," Shea said. "But I also don't have any access to the Post's bank account. How do you know about it?"

"I use it to shop." Tristan shrugged and leaned a shoulder against the wall. "As long as I add in a few scribing supplies and record my name for the accountants, my father doesn't chew me out quite as much."

"Where is this accounting log?" Maeve asked.

If Sibilla had signed her name when she bought the Oxblood ink, it could prove she had written the anonymous letters. That combined with the love letter would be more than enough to link her to Maeve's father. To have her arrested while the constabulary investigated. To give them time to pore over the rose journal to try to figure out why her father was targeted for it.

"The accounting logs are kept in the Hall of Routes," Tristan said. "Anyone with a courier key can access the vault where they're kept."

"You could go," Nan said to Tristan.

"Yes, I could have, if my key wasn't left somewhere in the Second Library then confiscated until Wintertide," he said, looking directly at Maeve. He turned to Shea. "You're the only one here with a key, I'm afraid."

"Then I'll go this afternoon," Shea said.

Nan stepped to her. "And I'm coming with you."

"No!" Maeve said. She crossed the room and snatched the love letter from the table. "None of you should get involved. If Sibilla is a murderer, she's dangerous. Probably desperate to remain hidden as well."

"Then what do you suggest we do?" Tristan asked, coming to stand beside Maeve. "Sit around and eat burned bread?"

"Why not? Bread is tasty," Maeve said.

He took her chin, made her look at him. "You need to stop this. You're not alone anymore."

His words caused her heart to swell. No, she wasn't alone, but it would break her to see any of them laid out in a morgue next week because of her.

Shea clapped her hands. "I suppose I'll get dressed and head into town."

"And I'll go to the Minister's Office in Leyland," Tristan said. "There's a collection of full statements there from government and university employees who happened to make it out of Inverly that day. I've looked through it in the past out of curiosity. I doubt they'll think anything of it if I ask to sift through it now. If we can place Sibilla in Inverly, it would help our case. At the very least, there might be something hidden in her statement that could implicate her."

"I'll get ready to go too," Nan said, smoothing her shirt.

They were all leaving her?

Tristan turned to Shea. "There's a cemetery situated beside the minister's records building. Let's meet up there afterward."

"And what am I supposed to do?" Maeve asked. "Sit here and hope one of you doesn't accidentally get yourself killed?" She turned to Tristan. "I want to come with you at the very least."

He scratched his head. "You do?"

Of course she did! "Why do you sound so surprised?"

"Because we all rode here on horseback."

THEY DISCUSSED CALLING a coach, but decided it was too risky with the constabulary on the lookout for someone with Maeve's description. If she was going with them, it would be behind Tristan on Butternut, and that was that.

As they prepared to leave, Maeve begged him to knock her out and carry her into Gloam the same way he carried her here. He refused, of course. Maeve waited outside a large carriage house while Tristan went inside to tack up Butternut, then came out a few minutes later without a horse.

"I want you to go inside and lead Butternut out."

She stared at him, open-mouthed. "I thought we were past the point of trying to kill each other."

He slid a hand around her jaw, then brushed a stray curl from her cheek with his thumb. "I think you can do it, Maeve. If you can't, I don't know if I can trust you enough to ride with you all the way to town."

She grudgingly agreed, immediately regretting the decision the moment she stepped inside the carriage house.

Butternut stood in the corner, kicking at the ground.

Maeve's feet moved gingerly over stray straw, careful not to make a sound.

"Hello there, Butternut," she whispered from a few feet away. "I heard you're a dear girl."

Butternut opened a massive black eye and flared her nostrils, spraying a hay bale with her snort. The beast toed the ground, and Maeve stumbled backward, landing on her bottom in a pile of straw. It stuck to her skirts, but she brushed it off and forced herself to stand.

She wished she had a piece of bread with her as an offering, but there was no time to run to the kitchen; Shea and Nan had already left. Tristan would go without her if she couldn't do this.

Her clammy fingers left damp streaks down her cloak. She walked to the wall and pulled down a coarse brush that looked too large for human hair. She had no idea what she was doing, but she held the brush to the horse's chin hairs, cooing, as if calming a baby. It seemed the sort of thing a stable hand might do. She waggled the brush. "If you let me close enough to grab your reins, I'll comb out your tangles and make you look pretty."

"I think if you don't stop this foolishness, I might expire from laughter."

Maeve spun.

Tristan leaned one shoulder against the doorframe.

He walked past her and took Butternut's reins, leading the horse out himself. Maeve stayed a few steps away as he swung up onto the horse's back and reached a hand down.

She stared at it.

"You'll never get over your fears unless you face them."

With a silent curse, she slipped her hand inside of his. He pulled her onto the saddle, directly behind him. Her thighs pushed against Butternut's rib cage, moving in and out with the horse's breath. Slowly, she let herself relax. It wasn't as bad as she was imagining. "I'm on a horse."

"For the second time this week. Although the first time, you were unconscious. I'd say this is a vast improvement."

In the end, it was good they took the horse. The ride to Gloam went by in under an hour. They rode hard across fields dappled by winter sun, until the gray stone buildings of the city swallowed them. Church bells tolled as they made their way up the river of sleet-covered cobblestones, past students in coats and scarves and workers in winter boots and hats. A man darted out of their way with a steaming bun in his fist that should have made Maeve's mouth water, but her stomach was twisted into knots. She kept her hood tight around her face, her hair hidden beneath her courier cloak.

They passed a few officers, but none paid them notice. Every few minutes, however, someone would look their way, or a voice would shout, and Maeve would dig herself into Tristan's back, unable to shake the feeling of wrongness.

"Don't take too long," she said as he helped her down from Butternut, then tied the horse to a block between the snow-covered cemetery and the minister's records building.

"I'll try to hurry, but the last time I sifted through the Inverly records, it took an hour." He smiled at her and smoothed down a wild strand of her hair, tucking it behind her ear.

"Then I'll stay put in the cemetery and try not to get myself in too much trouble," Maeve said.

He arched an eyebrow. "For some reason, I doubt you're capable of that."

⁍

WITHIN MINUTES, THE sky opened. Heavy, wet snowflakes began falling that soaked into Maeve's shoulders. She threw up her hood and traipsed down a gravel path through the cemetery that snaked north, weaving around iced-over headstones and enormous mausoleums probably built to house the remains of families like the Widdens. The dark gray stones pressed around her in the silent snow.

After several minutes of waiting, Maeve caught a movement to her left. The black sweep of a cloak.

"Tristan!" she called out, and ran toward him. But it wasn't Tristan. The figure was shorter, with wide-set shoulders. A man wearing a courier's cloak.

Heading in her direction.

Maeve stumbled backward, searching the gravestones for somewhere to hide. One nearby was larger than the others. She dove for it. Pressing her back against an embossing of doves, she held her breath until she was positive the man had gone. Slowly, she stood up. A courier with a slight double chin and bright hazel eyes stood waiting on the opposite side of the gravestone with a letter in his hand. He held it out for her to take.

He was only attempting to deliver it.

Maeve stared at it. But before she could decide what to do, the courier's eyes traveled from Maeve's cloak to her face and hair, then down to the envelope. It fell from his fingers, landing atop the gravestone.

"I didn't understand the letter, but now . . . You're her, aren't you? You're the girl they're searching for. The apprentice."

Maeve glanced down at the unmarked envelope with dawning horror. This man would have read the content of whatever was inside while he scribed it for delivery.

"Someone help!" he called, but nobody was close enough to hear.

Maeve snatched the envelope and took off running, dipping around gravestones and trees, up footpaths until her lungs burned.

She exited the graveyard and continued racing down twisting streets, not daring to look behind her until she was blocks away and there was no sight of that courier.

Crouching against the uneven stones of a building side, she tore the envelope open, and hesitated. She had no ash. But it didn't matter; if that otherwhere courier had scribed it, it wouldn't hurt her, and she had to know what it said.

She pulled it out and unfolded it to a blocky paragraph in Ox-blood ink, written in such a way that she couldn't tell if it was Sibilla's handwriting or not.

Maeve,

Many people are trying to locate you, which is difficult without a name. But if you're reading this letter, it means they'll have yours soon enough. I would run.

"One ticket south," Maeve said between heavy panting. She slid a hallion across the ticket booth counter at Dunsmore Station—one of two hallions Shea had given her in case of emergencies. She'd used half of the other one to pay for a coach to bring her here as quickly as possible.

The woman working the booth took it. "How far south would you like the ticket?"

"As far south as I can get."

Out of reach of any traveling scribing.

"It'll be the Hollibroath stop then, near the southern seashore."

"That sounds lovely."

Clutching her ticket, Maeve walked the length of the station, her eyes peeled for anyone in courier raiment, for any black courier doors materializing on the station's brick walls.

A traveling scribing could bring you close to a specific person, so long as that specific person remained in the same location for a few minutes and wasn't moving quickly.

It would take that courier time to get back to the Post and round up help. Maeve hoped it would give her enough time before the overnight train came. If she was lucky, she could be out of range of all traveling scribings by later this evening.

Beside her on the platform, a young man carried a leather suit-case, his free hand clinging to a small boy in suspenders and a bright green woolen coat. A pretty young woman ran up to the man and pecked him on the lips, then bent and flung her arms around the boy, nuzzling her face into his cheek.

Maeve's chest tightened painfully, until she was forced to look away.

She could no longer deny the reality of her situation. Traveling scribings didn't work on people riding moving trains. If she could get herself on this train in time, nobody would be able to find her—including Tristan. He would believe she ran away from him again, and he wouldn't be wrong. But what else could she do? If she stayed, she would be caught within the hour. She had to keep moving.

A moment later, a whistle screamed. Maeve clutched the ticket to her chest as the train roared into the station, a behemoth of steam and grinding metal. Its brakes screeched as it came to a full stop along the platform. As soon as the doors opened, Maeve hurried up the steps, feeling her way to her second-class compartment. She managed to get the door open through a haze of stinging tears.

"Are you well, miss?" a man adjusting his suitcase asked from across the aisle.

Maeve kept her head down. "I'm perfectly fine."

She wasn't, however—far from it.

She shut her compartment door and latched it, then fell into the stiff seat and put her face in her hands, gulping her breaths so she wouldn't pass out.

The train lurched and pulled away, relatively quickly, then picked up a gust of speed. As soon as snowy farmland filled the small square of her compartment window, Maeve let herself take a deep breath. No traveling scribing could catch her now.

She tugged her journal from her saddlebag and ripped out a page in order to pen a letter to Tristan that she'd composed in her mind on the way to the station. She would tell him that she was wrong about everything, and her father was guilty all along. Then end it with a stark order to forget about her, to never come looking for her under any circumstance. But as she uncapped her small well of lampblack, the car jostled. She swayed and her hands shook, and she couldn't pour a godforsaken drop of ink.

The Oxblood letter was still balled into a knot in the center of her sweating palm. She unfolded it. A sob hit her chest as she read through it again, then touched her name, written in Oxblood ink across the top.

Her first name.

It was always only her first name. Never her last.

Why hadn't they exposed her last name? Were they saving it? Or was there some other motive?

Maeve sat with that thought. If the person behind this letter revealed whose daughter she was—that it was an *Abenthy* who had snuck her way inside the Post for some malicious purpose—every person in Leyland would be hunting for her now, with vengeance in their hearts. Every courier would have taken today off delivery duties and penned scribings to locate her, but they hadn't, because the letter only revealed her first name.

She couldn't imagine there were more than a handful of people searching for her now, with just her first name exposed.

If it was Sibilla behind it all, she must not want everyone out searching, or for anyone to find her. Sibilla simply wanted her to leave. She'd written it plainly in that letter Nan mistakenly read, after all.

And Sibilla had never given Maeve's first name away to anyone

310

until now—*after* Maeve tried to steal the rose journal. But why was that? Maybe Sibilla realized that she was close to some revelation and grew fearful.

Sibilla hid who she was, just as Maeve did. She hid behind the Oxblood letters because she was frightened of being exposed—as frightened as Maeve used to be. Sibilla must not want any investigation.

The couple of times Maeve had spoken with her, she seemed skittish. If Shea and Nan found Sibilla's name in that accounting log, Sibilla would likely disappear before anyone could speak to her and take away all of Maeve's hopes with her.

Unless she could somehow force Sibilla to talk.

Maeve pictured the moment in Shea's parlor when she'd confessed who she was. She had feared speaking her name, and yet her friends were all eager to help her. They listened to her story and believed it, despite having no conclusive evidence. Despite her last name. They *believed* her.

What if she told others?

Maeve pulled her lip between her teeth. Sibilla would never suspect that she was foolish enough to tell her story publicly, but what if she did? What if she used herself as leverage to get Sibilla to tell her the truth?

An idea struck Maeve suddenly.

She lurched upward, staggering from her seat, and flung her compartment door open.

"I need to get off! When is the next stop? I need to get off!" she shouted, frantic.

"You'll have to wait another thirty minutes," a man said from somewhere down the aisle.

Time slowed to a flicker. Maeve turned.

Tristan stood in the doorway between train cars, a bright sheen of sweat glistening above his spectacles, his jaw as rigid as she had ever seen it. He must have tracked her here, and she wasn't mad about it in the least.

He shut the door behind him, then stalked forward and took Maeve's shoulder, tugging her into her compartment, sitting them both down. He took her face between his hands. "I've never performed a tracking scribing nor purchased train tickets so quickly in my entire life. Maeve, I thought—" He swallowed his breath. "I thought you were gone. I thought someone had taken you and run off to god knows where. I thought . . ." His expression darkened. "I thought I had lost you forever. But then the tracking scribing led me right to the train station." His sharp eyes pinned her. "Were you running again?"

The way he asked it without any emotion sent a tremor through her.

Maeve was a sodding mess with a red nose and tears streaking her cheeks, but she pressed her forehead to his. "I was scared, Tristan, and made a horrid mistake. But I promise you—I *promise* you—that I'm never running again."

"You have to understand how difficult that is to believe." He searched her eyes. "Why did you run?"

She handed him the crumpled letter.

"An otherwhere courier delivered this right after you left me."

Tristan sat back in the seat, scanning over the words with a tense set to his mouth. He understood the implications of her name.

"You should have gotten me immediately."

"Yes, I should have." She realized that now. "But I panicked and thought if I stayed put, a courier door would have appeared and someone would have hauled me away. I read in the *Scriptomancer's Companion* that my chances are better if I'm moving."

He nodded. "You have to remain in roughly the same general location for a few minutes before a traveling scribing can bring someone close enough to you to get a tracking scribing to work. Ten to twelve minutes, give or take."

That meant if she moved somewhere new every few minutes and stayed far away from every scriptomancer trying to track her, she could go undetected. She could wander around Gloam for hours if she was quick enough. If she didn't stop to rest or sleep.

It could give her enough time.

"Were you able to find anything on Sibilla?" she asked.

"Yes," he said with a small curve to his mouth. "She'd left a statement. Apparently, she'd visited Inverly the day the Aldervine came, then made it back through the station just before chaos erupted."

"She was there," Maeve said.

"She was. And she could easily have lied about the exact moment she returned to keep from being questioned further."

Sibilla was in Inverly right before the Aldervine was unleashed.

"Maeve?"

Maeve realized she'd gone quiet. She cleared her throat. "I'm going to speak with Sibilla."

Tristan wasn't amused. "Surely you can't be serious."

"I've never been more serious. Sibilla will run if anyone else approaches her. She'll run and take away my chance of uncovering the truth. I'm sure of it. And for some reason, she doesn't want me discovered. Otherwise, she would have given away my last name." Maeve gestured to the letter. "I believe she's desperate for me to leave, which I'll promise to do as soon as she talks."

"Have you forgotten that she likely murdered your father?"

"Yes, I know. But I have an idea to get her to talk without hurting me."

He raised an eyebrow. "Does it involve you dressing as a scantily clad scriptomancer?"

"It involves Nan and her contact at the *Herald*. I'm going to write an article that tells them everything: about my father's rose journal, how it's connected to Cathriona, the things we've discovered today, every single Oxblood letter. All of it. Then if Sibilla doesn't give me answers, I want it to print." She gave a shrug. "Or maybe I'll have it printed anyhow. It's about time the truth was out."

His mouth was set in a flat line, but he nodded. "It would certainly confuse people."

"I know."

"And prompt an investigation."

"Yes."

"But it could also go badly and anger Sibilla, and she could hurt you anyway."

Maeve exhaled. "That's always a possibility."

"Or she might not tell you anything."

"Also a possibility. But if she's going to speak with anyone, it's me. She'll have to, otherwise the article will run."

Tristan was silent for a long moment. "And what if it still doesn't work out?"

"If that's the case, I'll sneak away and hop on a train south, then write you devastatingly heartbroken letters from the middle of a garden somewhere," she joked through a wavering voice, knowing full well that if she planned to confront Sibilla, it would have to be at the Post, where there was little chance of escaping afterward.

Tristan understood the implications as well, but he gave her a somber smile. "And after reading each of your letters, I'll compose the melancholiest piano music you've ever heard, which I'll make sure to play in the middle of the night while drowning away my sorrows with expensive wine that has no effect on me."

"It's a deal."

He slipped an arm around Maeve's shoulders and pressed a kiss to the side of her neck. She was half-tempted to tilt up and catch his mouth with hers, but it would only distract her, and she had an article to write.

❧

MAEVE WROTE FOR a solid hour while the train sped south. When they reached a spot that Tristan was certain was out of the traveling scribing's bounds, they changed trains and returned north.

The Dunsmore Station was busier than when Maeve left. Tristan took Maeve's hand and wove her through the crowds of people, to where Butternut was tethered to a horse block. He climbed onto the horse's back then swung Maeve behind him, and they made for the graveyard before a traveling scribing could latch on to them.

The snow was falling, and it took longer to get there than expected, but they spotted Shea and Nan standing just north of it, eating fried fish from newspapers.

"For a moment we thought you two had decided to go on an extended vacation," Nan called out, waving them over.

"Where are your horses?" Tristan asked, searching the streets.

"Couriers needed them to haul some mail in from Blackcaster Station, so we left them at the Post and took a coach here an hour ago," Shea said. "Where have you two been? It's past dinnertime."

"We hit a bit of a letter-shaped snag." Tristan quickly explained their little tour of cramped train compartments.

Maeve showed them the crumpled Oxblood letter. "My name's out."

Nan shot up, looking around them—probably searching for a courier door to appear, just as Maeve was.

"We have a few more minutes," Tristan said, then slid off Butternut, helping Maeve off as well. "Did you two find anything?" he asked.

Shea pulled a scrap of paper from her bag and handed it to Maeve. A yellowed sepiagraph of her father standing beside an oak tree on the Post's grounds. A soft smile dimpled his cheeks. It took her breath away.

"I found it buried in Sibilla's office," Shea said.

Maeve straightened behind Tristan. "You searched *Sibilla's* office?"

Shea didn't seem too concerned. "We thought it might be helpful after we found her name in the accounting log."

Maeve drew in a sharp inhale. "Good god."

"Indeed," Nan said. "O.P.A.A. was Sibilla. The minx purchased that bottle of Oxblood ink the day we started classes."

Then Sibilla must have seen Maeve arrive and went to Plume & Pen to buy the ink, then came back and wrote Maeve that first letter, recording her name in the accountant log, believing nobody would think to look it up. Sibilla was behind everything this whole time.

It was clearer than ever that Maeve needed to speak with her. She needed a confession. Tonight.

"Why do you look like you're about to jump out of your skin?" Nan asked her.

Because she felt like it. She shifted her weight between her feet, bouncing on her heels. If she didn't move soon, she might burst into pieces. "I'm going to speak with Sibilla and get her to confess."

The girls both gasped and looked at Tristan. He merely nodded.

"I know that I likely won't be able to leave after I speak with her, but if I get a confession, that won't matter." Maeve turned to Shea before anyone could interrupt her. "Can you return to the Post and keep watch outside of the Second Library?"

"To do what?"

"I need to know if Sibilla leaves. I'll be there within the next couple of hours."

"But how on earth do you plan to walk inside the Second Library when the Leyland constabulary is hunting for you?" Shea didn't look convinced it was possible. "There were groups of officers at the Post. Now that they have your name, you won't be able to get close without someone following you with a tracking scribing."

Maeve knew that. Getting herself inside the Second Library was the one thing she hadn't figured out.

"You need a diversion," Nan said. "Something to distract all the officials for a little while. Something bold, like one of us running naked."

Maeve shook her head. "Nobody's running—"

"I'll do it!" Nan volunteered. "I always wanted to go for a swim in the ink fountain."

"It's the middle of winter, for goodness' sake," Maeve said.

"I have an idea." Tristan picked at a splotch of ink on his cloak. He'd been unusually quiet this whole time. Everyone looked over at him, but his eyes were trained on Maeve. "There's an advanced scribing I know that's tricky to pull off, but I think it would create a nice diversion. It'll take a little while to prepare."

Maeve's mouth parted in disbelief at his words, and she stepped toward him. "Tristan, I don't expect you to do that—"

"Yes, yes. I know. But then you rode all the way here on Butternut, and I figured if the girl who was afraid of horses could sit on one, the boy who was afraid of scribing might somehow get his sorry act together." He ruffled his hair. "Or maybe I won't. I guess I won't know until I try. It's been too long since I've tried."

This wasn't only about helping her; it was about proving it to himself that he could. That he was capable of something other than hurting people. Her heart twisted, and she reached out and squeezed his hand.

"I'll have to go somewhere with a worktable, but I'll be careful," he said. "And I have a wicked little scribing in mind—something I cooked up a long time ago."

"What does it do?"

"That will be a surprise." He pulled out a pocket watch and checked it. "We should all get moving. It'll take me time to get the scribing to take, and you and Nan should get to the *Herald*'s office before the staff leaves for the night."

Nan startled. "The *Herald*?"

Maeve turned to her roommate. "Do you think your contact will be keen for another article this soon?"

"Depends on the article."

Maeve dug through her saddlebag and pulled out the ripped page from her journal, now covered, top to bottom, in a mess of words smudged from the jostling train. Her entire story laid bare.

She handed it to Nan, then caught a movement from the corner of her eye. Not a courier; an older man walking down the street in a butcher's apron over a coat.

Hurry, hurry, a voice echoed in her mind. It was full dark now. A courier's door could appear anywhere at any time, and she would barely be able to see it.

"I'll meet you in an hour at the gap in the fence," she called to Tristan, then took Nan's arm, dragging her along.

"An hour!" Shea called, heading in the direction of the Post.

"An hour," Tristan repeated, climbing onto Butternut. "And don't you dare stop anywhere for longer than ten minutes, understand? That includes the *Herald*'s office. Nan can pick up the slack if it takes any longer than that."

Maeve gave a brisk nod, watching as Shea and Tristan disappeared into the snow-covered darkness.

"Holy hell, Maeve, this is good." Nan held the article inches from her nose. "My contact will eat his tie at the chance to run this."

"Let's hope you're right," Maeve said.

All she had left was hope, after all. Along with the three people helping her now—her friends. It had to be enough.

A bitterly cold wind railed through buildings, churning up snow and stinging Maeve's cheeks. Nan clutched a fistful of her cloak, pinning herself to Maeve's back as they forged through the labyrinthine streets, their misty breaths mingling in the frosty air. The city teemed despite the cold. People wove around them, faces tucked into scarves and fur muffs, but none wore courier raiment; no one had tracked her, and yet the distant sounds of carriage wheels clattering against cobblestones set her teeth on edge.

Faster—go faster, Maeve told herself, keeping up a brisk pace despite Nan's grumbling. Every now and then, Maeve's fingers would twist into knots in her pocket, grasping for the love letter that now lay buried deep inside her saddlebag.

There was nothing to clutch anymore. Nothing left for her to hide behind.

When they were near the south side of the river Liss, Nan pulled Maeve to a stop before a ramshackle stone building with a small sign for the *Herald* in the front window. Fortunately lights still flickered inside. They slipped in through a back entrance, then halted in a dimly lit hall, the walls adorned with old articles. Their dusty frames jostled as the clank and clatter of a printing press reverberated through the building.

The machine was still running, at least. Hopefully Nan was right, and her contact was still here, overseeing everything.

Maeve sucked in a breath and wrinkled her nose, preferring the stark winter winds to the scents of cheap pipe tobacco and old coffee clouding the air.

"I love the smell of this place," Nan said.

"The burnt coffee or the sweat?"

"The smell of secrets buried in the walls." Nan inhaled deeply.

"If you inhale any more secrets, I might have to finish this on my own. Let's go. We don't have much time." Ten minutes would go by quickly. The clock was ticking.

Nan led the way past rooms of chugging machinery helmed by men covered with printers' ink and day-old stubble, then past a room of crates and packing straw strewn about the floor. They halted at the base of an unlit stairwell.

"The reporters all work out of offices upstairs." Nan twisted her fingers together. "Before we meet my contact, there's something I should warn you about."

She seemed nervous; Nan never seemed nervous.

"It isn't a jilted lover, is it?"

There was no time to deal with anything of the sort.

"It's my father."

Maeve recoiled. "You mean your *father* is the man who wouldn't give you a job? The reason you forced yourself to try out for the courier apprenticeship?"

Nan rubbed a hand over her bedraggled hair. "I can't begin to know why my father makes his decisions. I'm fairly certain that he's never liked me much."

"How could you possibly know that?"

"He's told me. Upward of ten times during every visit we have."

"But you're his daughter."

"Yes, and he doesn't care a whit." She offered a nonchalant shrug. "My mother dropped me on his doorstep one day, and that was it. He was stuck with me. I look just like her, you know? Sometimes I wonder if he doesn't like the reminder and guiding me into the apprenticeship at the Post was a way to get me out of his hair." Nan gave a feeble attempt to muster a smile, but her mouth drooped. "He'll be happy we brought him the article, at the very least."

Maeve was tempted to turn around and forget about giving this dreadful man her article, but they were running on borrowed time.

"I think that after tonight, you should find a new editor to submit to at one of the other Leylish papers," Maeve said. "I'll help you. I know some people."

"You do?"

"Not a soul. But I'll do what I can, and I'm sure Shea has some sway." Maeve squeezed Nan's hands. "Now let's go. I have about eight minutes to spare."

They took the dingy stairwell to a second-floor hall lined with offices. Most were dark for the night save for an office at the end with a tarnished brass nameplate affixed to the wooden door. It read MARCUS FERRO in bulbous letters.

The man behind the door had the same dark hair and wide-set eyes as Nan, but that was as far as the similarities went. His gray mustache dropped over a short upper lip that caused his yellow-stained teeth to stick out. A smoking pipe dangled between them. Bags hung beneath his bulging eyes, which didn't so much as look up. They remained trained on his desk—strewn with papers, dirty cups, half-written notes, and a host of uncapped wells of ink that made Tristan seem like a god of tidiness in comparison.

Nan took a long breath, then sauntered inside and sat down

across from her father. An empty cup fell to the floor as she put her feet up on his desk, crossing her ankles.

Without removing an eye from his writing, Marcus Ferro shoved Nan's feet down. "If you haven't brought me an article, I don't have time for you."

Maeve came to stand behind her and pulled the article from her saddlebag, clasping it to her waist as she watched the second hand tick away on the small silver clock behind Marcus's desk. Five minutes. Then they would leave.

She cleared her throat.

Marcus dragged his eyes up. "Who the hell are you?"

"May I present Maeve Abenthy, Jonathan Abenthy's only daughter," Nan said before Maeve could take a breath.

Marcus blinked, his methodical gaze sweeping over Maeve, assessing her in detail.

She didn't expect him to believe Nan. Even Nan seemed surprised when he rested his elbows on his desk and clasped his hands. "Very well, Maeve Abenthy. What can I do for you?"

"The article you speak of—I've written it myself. I'd like it to run."

Nan turned to her. "I thought you wanted to only run it if you can't get answers."

"I know I said that, but I've decided that I want it to run anyway. If I don't get answers, I'd rather people know the truth. I want the truth out there in tomorrow's paper for everyone to see. Then if Sibilla doesn't talk, maybe someone else will."

"Tomorrow's paper?" Marcus said. "That's a smidge too quick. My typesetter has left for the night with the compositing sticks, and it takes a few hours to prep for anything new. Why don't you two come back in the morning?"

"But couldn't you at least read the article and see what you think?" Nan took it from Maeve's hands and slid it across Marcus's desk.

"All right, then," he said.

He lifted it and ripped it in half.

Maeve looked on, struggling to make sense of what just happened.

Nan shot up. "What was that for? That's an important article."

"I'm sure it was, but I think you should both follow me."

Maeve didn't have a good feeling about any of this, but Nan took her hand and told her not to worry as Marcus led them down to the printing floor.

They passed men in leather aprons and sturdy leather boots pulling reams of paper from the large machinery. More piles of cut papers were stacked against the walls. Marcus took a sheet from a tall stack and handed it to Maeve.

It was the printed front page of the *Herald*. A bold headline read:

MAEVE ABENTHY HAS INFILTRATED THE OTHERWHERE POST

The article described how Jonathan Abenthy's daughter had been living at the Post and impersonating an apprentice for the past few weeks, and in doing so was able to steal dangerous scriptomantic journals from deep within the Post's archives, how the journals contained instructions for scribings deadly enough to kill. It speculated that she was planning something as catastrophic as Inverly.

Panic seized Maeve's chest by the time she read to halfway down the page. This paper would unravel everything that she wanted to print. It would damn her and send every person in Gloam after her, hunting her.

But . . . if she'd left when Sibilla sent the letter earlier—when Sibilla *wanted* her to leave—nobody would be able to find her. And this slanderous article would have made it impossible for her to come close to Gloam ever again. Sibilla had wanted Maeve to run away and never come back, to run for the rest of her life.

"We've already sent cases of the paper to the north side of the city. Merchants should be stocking it within the next hour," Marcus said with a smug expression.

The next hour? It would take her nearly that long to meet up with Tristan.

She glanced around for a clock on the wall. Her time was nearly up; she had to leave, but she *needed* answers.

"Who wrote all of this?" Nan asked before Maeve could get a word out.

"An anonymous source," said Marcus. "I thought it was faked until I received a box of evidence earlier today that's currently on its way to the constabulary."

"What evidence?" Maeve pressed him.

Marcus didn't respond. Instead, he took hold of Maeve's shoulders, digging his fingers into her. She choked at the stink of tobacco on his breath and kicked out, but he was a large man, and there wasn't much she could do.

"Father? What are you doing?" Nan shrieked. She tried to wrench Maeve free. It was useless. Marcus tossed his daughter off in a single heave.

Maeve gagged as he clamped a sweating palm over her mouth

and dragged her along the floor, toward a door in the back wall. A closet by the look of it. Her feet scrambled for purchase, but he was too strong.

"Stop or I'll swing this," Nan said.

Marcus turned around with Maeve still gripped in his arms.

Nan held a metal stool above her head like a club. She was breathing hard. "You have to let her go."

"Get back to the Post, Nanny. You don't belong here," Marcus spat. He spun Maeve toward the door, dragging her. Shoving her. If he forced her inside, that was it.

Nan must have realized it as well because a foot from the door, Maeve heard a *thunk*, and Marcus staggered. His hands slipped from Maeve as he crumpled to the floor. Nan stood over her father with an unfathomable expression on her face, hefting the stool like a billy club.

Maeve dragged in a breath. "I think he's out cold."

"Good. That's what I was aiming for." Nan tossed down the stool. "Though I think I'll have to take my articles to a different paper in the future."

"Yes. I think you will."

Maeve backed away from Marcus's prone form, then heard a shout from across the room. A pair of workers in ink-smeared leather aprons stood at the door. They started toward them. One of the men shouted Maeve's name. He pushed his way past the others. A large man with slicked hair wearing dark slacks and a decorated gray uniform jacket buttoned to his neck—a jacket that Maeve recognized instantly. A constabulary courier, holding a piece of paper in front of him. Letting it guide him. It must be a tracking scribing with her name written on it.

Nan pointed to a small door a few feet behind them. "Go. Get out that door." She ripped the crematory ash satchel from her neck and pinched some in her fingers. "If he tries to follow you, I'll null his scribing. Hurry!"

Maeve staggered backward at the scene. Nan would be arrested for helping her escape . . . But if she got Sibilla to talk, it could all be forgiven.

She would never be able to do anything if she didn't leave now.

The courier started toward her.

Maeve turned and raced for the door. Halfway through it, Nan cried out. Ash plumed in the air, but Maeve couldn't see if the courier's tracking scribing was dusted. There was no time to look.

She hurried outside, gulping in the bitter air, then shot into the back alley, crouching in a shadow.

A second passed, and the door she'd just exited wrenched open.

Maeve ducked down—shoving her body against the cold building side as the constabulary courier pushed his way out the door, searching the darkness.

"Where'd you go?" he shouted, then kicked the ground with frustration. His paper was crumpled in his hand. A hand coated with crematory ash.

Nan had nulled his scribing. He had no idea where she hid.

After a long moment, the courier muttered a string of curses and ducked back inside the building.

At the sound of the door latching, Maeve took off. She raced down the alleyway, then around the adjacent street and across the river Liss in a flash. Gas lamps cast gloomy reflections in the water that might have been pretty to stare at if she wasn't being hunted. But there was no time to catch her breath. Tristan would be waiting, and she had to move.

It took Maeve the better part of an hour to zigzag through the north side of Gloam. She hated running and felt dead on her feet as she rounded each block, but she didn't let herself stop. She kept going, weaving around buildings, then darting through the crowd of protesters still swarming the Post's gate. She passed them by, then scrambled up the iced-over embankment that led to the tree line.

"There you are," Tristan said as Maeve slipped through his secret entrance and onto the grounds.

She'd made it with minutes to spare.

He took her hands. "Where's Nan?"

"Not here."

Mopping sweat from her brow, she quickly went over everything that happened at the *Herald*, including the run-in with the constabulary courier. She then went into detail about the article going out with her name plastered across the top. Many would already be on display by now.

"Did anyone follow you?"

"I don't think so." But she didn't take the time to look either.

"If someone near Blackcaster Square uses a tracking scribing to find you, they'll hit the fence and realize they have to backtrack through the main entrance, which will give us a little time."

"And if they're already inside the fence?"

A somber expression settled on his mouth.

There would be more than a mere handful searching for her soon. The Sacrifict taught her how quickly gossip spread. If the article was truly out, she had minutes. "Were you able to finish the scribing?"

He pulled a thick emerald book from his saddlebag, the ancient cover tattered and stained from years of use. The gilt-foiled title was nearly rubbed away, but Maeve could still make it out.

"*Mythical Beasts of Barrow?*"

"A handwritten book that I was able to write a form scribing on."

Her eyes widened. "Like the book that you left inside the Scriptorium all those years ago?"

"Yes. But this time I made sure to add in enough stipulations that whatever comes out of it shouldn't hurt anyone. Regardless, you're not allowed to open it until it's absolutely necessary. Reading a single word could trigger the scribing." He patted his saddlebag. "This book alone should buy us enough time, but I scribed two more just in case."

Maeve halted in the snow. "Us?"

"If you think I'm going to let you face the woman that killed Cath all by yourself, you're sorely mistaken." His words brooked no room for discussion.

"If you show up, Sibilla might not talk."

"Then I'll keep hidden, but I'm coming with you." He pulled out another decrepit book and tucked it beneath his arm.

Maeve wanted to be angry at him, but she couldn't be. She found herself overcome with relief that she wouldn't have to go in alone.

He tossed her a crematory ash satchel from his bag. "Coat your fingers before you open the book. If the form scribing's manifestation comes too close to you, dust it a little. It should stay back."

Maeve absorbed each word with a growing sense of foreboding. She had been determined only moments ago, but the reality of her situation was setting in now.

This was it. There was no turning back.

Tristan slipped a hand down her forearm to clutch her hand. "If it doesn't work out, I can always bring you socks in prison."

"If it doesn't work out, *you* might be going to prison with me."

"At least I'll like the company." He trailed a finger along the side of her neck, then took her elbow. Together they stayed off the main path and picked their way through the woods until the Second Library came into full view.

Lights were lit behind its glass door. A group of couriers passed it along the path, then a larger group of officers. Another two officers came in from the west, saluting their colleagues. None of them held papers with tracking scribings—yet.

"There's so many of them," Maeve said.

Tristan scanned the area around them. "Where's Shea?"

"I'm here." Shea stepped out from the shadow of a nearby tree and picked her way over to them, her cloak tight around her shoulders. "I thought I was going to freeze to death before you two ever got here." She looked behind them. "Where's Nan?"

"Still with her father. There's no time to explain." Tristan held out a hand. "Your key."

Shea gave him her courier key.

"Here." He dug in his bag and handed her another one of the ancient books, titled *When a Demon Comes to Call.*

"What is this?" She turned it over.

"A handwritten book that I happened to scribe."

"You know how to scribe a whole handwritten book?"

He glanced at Maeve. "Sadly, yes."

Shea opened the cover, and Tristan snapped it shut. "Do *not* open it here. I need you to walk to the other side of the Second Library, read the first page, then drop the book and act frightened. It should get the officers away from the door for a minute or so."

He warned Shea to have her crematory ash ready in case the scribing got out of hand. To not approach it.

"I think I can manage it," she said, then headed for the officers.

"How will we know when she's read the scribing?" Maeve asked as Shea disappeared between buildings.

Before Tristan could answer her, there was a series of screams. The group of officers in front of the library ran in the direction of the noise.

"That's how we know," Tristan said, his mouth flattening.

Maeve took his hand and gave it a hard squeeze. "Nobody will get hurt this time. You said so yourself. In fact, you're preventing others from getting hurt. Now let's go."

Maeve kept her cloak tucked tightly to her head. She ran behind Tristan through the entrance to the Second Library and into the small lobby area.

"Is Sibilla working tonight?" Tristan asked the archivist seated at the desk, a thin shouldered man who took them in with vacant features and the palest eyes Maeve had ever seen.

He picked at his chin hairs that weren't quite long enough to be called a beard. "She's shelving books around floor six below ground," he said, then narrowed his eyes at Maeve. "Him I recognize, but I've never seen you down here before. I'll need your name. I need to check it against our list."

"She's with me, and we don't have time for a list, I'm afraid," Tristan said, then shoved a key in the door's lock.

The clerk's eyes were fixed on Maeve's shoulder. She brought a hand up and winced at the red curl that had snuck out of her braid.

"You're her, aren't you?" he said, standing slowly. "You're the girl everyone is looking for." He shuffled around the desk.

Tristan got the door open, then jerked Maeve through, slamming it behind them until it locked again. The archivist rushed forward and beat a fist against the glass, spittle flinging from the corner of his lip. Maeve thought he would try to come inside after them, but he turned and ran from the library.

"He's going for help," Maeve said.

Tristan nodded into the darkness. "Yes, which means we have less time than we thought."

He held up his book. It was burgundy this time, with a title that read: *The Nightmares of Huber Bramble.*

He placed it on the floor beside the entrance. "Pinch some ash in your fingers and head for the stairs over there. I'll meet you in a moment."

Maeve did as he said, watching Tristan from the corner of her eyes. He held open the cover of the book for a few seconds, then dropped the book and shifted backward on his heels as something dark reached upward from the page. A skeletal hand manifested from ink.

For a moment, Maeve thought it would be another column of ink like the one that nearly choked Nan to death, but this hand was attached to a jointed arm. It felt for purchase along the stone floor, then laid its inky palm flat so it could push itself upward. A sluice of black ink spilled from the book as a skeletal man in a haggard tailcoat and top hat formed above the book, made entirely of ink. He held his head crookedly, a globule of ink flesh hanging in a looping ribbon from his sunken cheek. He moved in a slow rhythm, dragging one foot behind him, leaving a ghastly spill against the stone floor in his wake.

Another hand emerged from the book, this one with four-inch claws that appeared sharp enough to eviscerate flesh.

The manifestations weren't dangerous, but they looked it. They resembled living nightmares.

Tristan caught up to Maeve. "Admit it, I have talent," he said, but his features were ashen.

He must be terribly worried about the scribings hurting something.

"I'll admit to your talent when no officers come after us. Let's go."

They took off down the stairwell, counting the levels as they moved. Maeve held her breath as they passed the entrance to the third floor, where the Aldervine specimen rested behind glass, then down more floors, until they reached a burning torch marking the entrance to the sixth floor below ground. It felt like an icebox. Maeve folded her arms tight across her chest, peering into the dimly lit space, but she couldn't tell if there was anyone there; cavernous ceilings loomed over a maze of shelves that were impossible to see over.

The hollow clatter of a library cart echoed in the distance.

"Hear that?" Tristan whispered.

Maeve nodded, then quietly motioned for him to follow her. They searched the darkened floor for a few minutes but couldn't find Sibilla anywhere. Then the cart rattled again, this time coming from near the stairwell; their expressions tightened as their eyes scanned the floor.

Tristan put a finger to his lips and crept to the end of the aisle, pointing to the direction they needed to go next—the stairs. Maeve came up beside him, halting.

A pair of officers now stood at the stairwell.

"Do you think they're tracking me?" Maeve whispered.

Tristan shook his head. "If they were, they'd be heading in our direction."

"There's another stairwell down that way." Maeve gestured at the narrow stairs she'd used weeks ago—that took her near the room with the Aldervine. "We could make a run for it."

"They'll see us."

He was right.

"Hand me your book," he said, and she gave him *Mythical Beasts of Barrow*. He waved it at the officers.

"What are you doing?" Maeve hissed.

"Giving us a way to escape," he said under his breath, then turned to face the officers.

When the officers shouted, heading for Tristan, Maeve wanted to strangle him.

"I might consider staying back," Tristan called to the officers, his eyes never leaving the book.

The second officer huffed a laugh, but there was a nervous edge to it. "Is this boy trying to bargain with us?"

"I was trying to warn you, but call it whatever you want. It doesn't matter a bit to me."

Tristan opened the front cover of the book. His hooded eyes scanned the contents of the first page, then he dropped the book. The spine cracked against the stone ground, and a rush of oil-black ink as thick as bile spilled from the center, pooling along the floor into a large puddle that behaved like the surface of a lake. Something large shivered and writhed from within it. Ink fingers broke the surface, then floated back down, and Tristan looked like he was about to be sick.

The hellish puddle spread to beneath the officers' feet, then into the adjoining aisles. Tristan inched backward as manifested fingers made of ink slipped up an officer's leg, dragging him down. More black limbs reached from the puddle, wrapping around the man's torso. His hands passed through them like water as he struggled to free himself.

"It's holding them," Maeve said, her eyes locked on the spreading puddle. "We need to go."

Tristan nodded and started toward her, but something sprang from the ink and clamped dripping arms around Tristan's legs. A sinewy black hand slithered over his hip and wrapped around his waist, the manifested fingers drawing trails of ink across his torso.

Maeve doused her hand with crematory ash and came forward.

Tristan shook his head. "Don't. You'll null the entire scribing." He looked from the trapped officers to his own ash satchel still hanging from his neck. "I'll be fine. Find Sibilla before it's too late."

"You expect me to leave you?"

"I'm not particularly thrilled with it either, but we only have this one chance. I'll wait a few minutes then come after you. I promise."

Footsteps echoed from the stairs. Shouting. More officers were on their way, probably led by a scriptomancer with a tracking scribing. Tristan was right; if she nulled his scribing, the officers would be able to walk right through the puddle. But now it served as a barricade created by the one person she didn't want to leave. But Tristan was right—she had to find Sibilla.

Maeve took one last look at him and ran for the second stairwell.

Be quick, Maeve told herself. But her feet felt like lead weights as she raced up another flight of stairs, then down long aisles of books and through rooms she hadn't seen the first time she was here. There was no sign of Sibilla, so Maeve searched the next floor, breathless.

A cart rattled, and footsteps clicked against the stone floor. Maeve flew around an aisle toward the sounds, then skidded to a halt.

Sibilla stood between two large bookshelves, a sorting cart beside her, her frail arms clutching her chest. She held her long gray apron crumpled in her fist as her body trembled. Her face was ashen, and Maeve had to remind herself how dangerous this woman was.

"What are you doing here?" Sibilla asked, her words laced with apprehension.

She must not have expected Maeve to remain in Gloam and seek her out.

Maeve's pulse thundered in her ears. She took a slow step forward, wishing she still had one of Tristan's scribed books with her. "I'm here because I want the truth."

"I don't know what you're talking about."

"Oh, spare me your lies. You know exactly who I am, don't you?"

Her mouth pinched, then flattened. "Yes," she admitted. Her bottom lip began to tremble, then her eyes glassed over, and a glistening tear spilled down her cheek. Maeve couldn't tell if Sibilla's reactions were real or an act. "I would recognize you anywhere. You look nearly identical to Aoife."

"Do *not* bring my mother into this," Maeve snapped, pulling her spine straight as fury built inside of her, fueling her. "I'm sure you're more than aware that people are hunting me. I don't have much time. I know my father was innocent, and I want you to tell me what happened." *And especially how you were involved*, Maeve thought, but didn't voice it yet.

She fully expected Sibilla to balk at her request, so it came as a surprise when Sibilla nodded. "Very well."

"You'll tell me everything?"

"I suppose you deserve to know. But afterward, I want you to leave this place for good. Understand?"

Sibilla said it as if Maeve had a choice in the matter. And she sounded *kind*. Maeve didn't expect any kindness, and it threw her off. "I'm listening."

Sibilla unwrapped her arms and wove her fingers together. "Well, if I'm going to start anywhere, I should begin with your mother."

"My mother?"

"Yes. Aoife was my best friend at upper school, and we remained close. I came to the College of Scriptomantic Arts to work as an archivist right before she died. Aoife suspected her time in the worlds was nearing its end and asked me to check on your father." Her voice faltered. "But your mother was a shining light to all who knew her. It was no wonder that after she was gone, it broke your father. I found him weeping one day. We sat and spoke about your mother for hours, and then I gave him a tour of these archives." She smiled softly. "He liked it down here."

Maeve wiped tears from her eyes, trying to keep her focus. Officers would be coming through this floor soon. She couldn't afford to turn into a puddle in front of this woman before they arrived. "What about the Silver Scribing that he was working on?"

"You know about it?"

"Not much," Maeve said, deciding to keep the rose journal that currently sat in her saddlebag a secret for the time being.

"The Silver Scribing nulled the effects of scriptomancy," Sibilla said. "It made it so a scriptomancer could interact with any scribing. And it worked, Maeve. It worked perfectly. But your father didn't know how to tell the stewards because skin scribings were strictly forbidden. It was written in the college's edicts that a scriptomancer could be sent to prison for even attempting one, along with anyone else that might have helped them. I broke that law when I dug up books for your father to reference—restricted books that needed approval from a steward to even be read. But I was in love." A muscle twinged in her cheek. She looked to the ground. "It's why I can't come forward."

"You're worried someone will lock you up for helping my father with the skin scribing?" It sounded ridiculous considering she was a murderer.

"They will," she said. "They'll take away my position at the very least. This place is home now. There's nowhere else I want to live."

And yet Sibilla was forcing Maeve away from her only home—from everything she had ever known.

Anger lashed beneath the surface of Maeve's skin. It took a moment before she could gather enough composure to even think of continuing with this interrogation.

Then a dark shape shifted behind Sibilla, at the far end of the aisle.

One of Tristan's manifestations had found its way here.

Maeve tightened her fingers around her ash satchel and inched nearer to Sibilla, hoping the manifestation wouldn't come any closer for the time being. She still needed answers.

"Then what happened in Inverly?" Maeve asked in a flat tone. "I know you were there. Your account of Inverly was in the minister's records."

"You found that?"

"Yes."

Her eyes filled with tears. "I was supposed to meet you that day, you know? Jonathan had finally decided that it was time to introduce us. He asked to meet him after a luncheon he'd planned with someone else. He wanted to bring me to your aunt's house."

"He did?"

"Yes. Then the Aldervine appeared before I ever left the station, so I turned around and came right back here."

"You're a liar," Maeve said. "He was murdered a block from the station. You would have had to leave the station to carry it out."

Sibilla's eyebrows drew together. "Jonathan was murdered?"

Maeve stared at her, unable to deduce if she was a wonderful actor or truly surprised to hear of her father's demise. That dark shape was nearly at Sibilla's back.

Biting out a curse, Maeve ripped off her crematory ash satchel. She still had some ash coating her fingers from before, but she upended the rest of the ash into her palm. She was about to throw it when the manifestation crept over Sibilla's shoulder and snaked around her throat, then curled around both of her arms.

It was deep green with waxy leaves and small black thorns running along a lace of stalk. A long, wet leaf unfurled against Sibilla's neck. Black thorns kissed over her skin, drawing blood, until little rivulets streaked her starched apron. Sibilla's irises turned a milky white as it wove around her temple like a crown, piercing her.

And then a tendril of the Aldervine parted Sibilla's pale lips and pushed its way inside of her mouth, then out the base of her neck.

At the sound of Sibilla's body hitting the floor, Maeve staggered to the end of the aisle and retched, then stood and wiped her mouth, looking around her. The shelves were difficult to see over, but she could feel the Aldervine surrounding her, growing over the spines of books, threading its way through pages of ancient parchment, trapping her.

She smelled the same sickly honeysuckle and spring gorse scent from that day in Inverly. It stung her nostrils until the Aldervine's sweet fragrance was all she could taste. If she didn't leave now, she would be trapped inside this place forever.

Maeve picked her way through the darkened aisle, passing patches of the vine growing over shelves, but the back stairwell was still clear. Maeve ran up a flight, coming out on the third floor below ground, right beside the gated room with the glass case.

The gate hung open.

A leafy tendril of the Aldervine curled over a nearby bookshelf, but the entrance to the room was miraculously clear. How was there no vine covering the doorway?

Maeve bit down on her tongue as she picked her way past the gate, wanting to investigate the room. She halted when her foot stepped down on crunching glass. A glittering trail of broken glass littered the floor, leading into the small chamber.

Sibilla could have broken the glass, but how would she have escaped to the floor below without being pricked? If it wasn't her, the person responsible might very well be still inside the room.

Maeve tried peering inside but couldn't see anything. Carefully, she stepped through the doorway, into an empty room. There was no Aldervine anywhere, nor any sleeping bodies. Save for glass debris, the walls and floors were bare, and Maeve didn't understand it. This room should be covered in the vine.

One pane of the glass case had been knocked out. Jagged shards rimmed the opening like teeth.

Maeve stepped toward the broken pane and noticed something on the floor buried in the glass. She knelt and lifted it. It was a strange splinter of wood, one side painted black. There were two more pieces of the painted wood inside of the broken case, along with a puddle of blood.

She swiped a finger near the broken pane, mopping up a fresh streak of the blood.

The person who released the Aldervine had cut themselves badly—probably on the glass.

Sibilla had been clutching her arms, but she'd looked cold and frightened, not bloody. Maeve didn't remember seeing any hint of red on her. Her hands had been perfectly clean—

Her hands.

Maeve splayed her fingers. Ink was embedded beneath her nails from penning the article. Scribing pigment still stained some of her fingers. Calluses and blisters ran up her thumb and index finger. They always looked a wreck, but never quite as much as when she practiced scribing. All scriptomancers' hands looked the same—but not Sibilla's. There were no lampblack spatters on her delicate fingers, no scribing pigment, no calluses or blisters. Her hands were pristine. Because they were archivist's hands.

The revelation felt like a sudden snap of cold. Sibilla wasn't a scriptomancer. It was the only explanation.

She didn't scribe the Oxblood letters—she didn't know how. And she certainly didn't break the pane of glass and release the Aldervine, nor did she kill Maeve's father. Which meant someone else did.

Someone else who was willing to murder to protect themselves. Judging from the puddle of fresh blood, they were still inside the library now.

Maeve pulled a quill knife from her saddlebag and ran outside of the room, crying out when she nearly stumbled into a length of the Aldervine that clung to a bookshelf. A tendril moved toward her arm, then stopped and moved away. It must not be able to sense her.

That was a small measure of relief as she backtracked to the stairs. She took them up to the first floor, halting at a figure cloaked in black blocking the top of the stairs.

Her heart sailed to her throat. "Tristan?" she whispered.

The figure remained eerily silent. Was it an officer? Maeve jerked when she noticed a tendril of Aldervine crawling along the stair's handrail. More had grown over two of the steps below her. She couldn't backtrack.

She rushed forward and raised the knife, hoping to knock the man down, but he shifted away from her hand, gnashing skeletal teeth.

One of Tristan's scribing manifestations.

Maeve opened her left hand. It was still coated with crematory ash. She dusted it at the form scribing then pushed past it without waiting to see if it dissolved or not. She had to get out, but the floor was a maze of the Aldervine mixed with toppled books. She raced down one aisle, then turned up another, coming to a grinding halt at a pile of bodies.

Limbs and feet and arms were tangled together beneath a pulsing growth of the Aldervine, lacy tendrils weaving over their faces. They were all officers of the constabulary. The man nearest her still had his eyes wide open, the irises white. Chests rose and fell in a steady rhythm.

Maeve felt her gorge rise again, but she forced herself to search the pile for Tristan. He wasn't there, though. If he were pricked, hopefully the coffee scribing would at least keep him awake long enough to get through the lobby. He could have somehow made it out. She refused to believe anything else.

The thought kept her moving.

She backtracked down the aisle, then raced for the door separating the library from the front lobby. She opened it and slammed it shut behind her. But when she took a few steps forward, she heard a rustling sound coming from above her and craned her neck to look up.

Tendrils of Aldervine covered the entire ceiling like branching fingers.

The dark green leaves shivered as Maeve stood utterly still beneath them. The last door was only a few paces away.

Holding her breath, Maeve took the chance and walked beneath the canopy of vines quickly, until she reached the glass front door.

A large group of officers gathered a short distance beyond it. There were more lights bobbing in the trees, but no sign that the

Aldervine had gotten outside, no sign anyone outside realized the danger they were in.

Slowly, Maeve gripped the door handle, then let go when a tendril grew down from the ceiling, moving along the top of the doorframe. It twisted its way along as if trying to feel for a way out. It would escape if she opened the door now—and destroy everything she loved.

She couldn't leave.

Maeve thought she heard her name and pressed her forehead to the glass, searching the darkness. Shea came running for the library's entrance, her hand raising toward the door handle.

"No, Shea." Maeve shook her head. She gritted her teeth and threw her weight against the door, bracing her fingers on the handle at the same moment Shea tried to turn it.

Maeve pointed to the ceiling. "The Aldervine!" she screamed.

Finally, Shea looked up and noticed the vine crawling over the ceiling. She jerked backward, her eyes snapping to Maeve, filling with tears. "*The Aldervine?*" she mouthed.

Maeve gave a furious nod. "I'm not the one who let it out," she shouted, but Shea touched her ear and shook her head.

Nobody outside could hear her through the glass.

Shea waved at two more figures racing toward the door. It was Nan and Steward Tallowmeade. Nan's hair was down, her clothes disheveled and sweat-stained. She must have run across the city all the way here. Tallowmeade was usually a breath of calm, but even he looked agitated, his light brown cheeks spotted with red. Both his long hands were wet with ink and dusted with crematory ash.

A grouping of officers ran up behind him, followed by Postmaster Byrne himself in all black. Mouths fluttered, and pupils swelled as every last person noticed the Aldervine across the ceiling.

At the sight, a few officers ran off into the night. Tallowmeade, however, stepped toward the glass and leveled a finger directly at Maeve. He shouted something that Maeve couldn't hear. Postmaster Byrne shouted as well.

Murderer! World killer! she imagined them chanting.

Maeve shook her head with vehemence and mouthed out that she didn't do it, but it was no use. They couldn't hear her, and she would never attempt to open the door to explain herself.

She sank down to the cold floor and tucked her knees to her chin, feeling impossibly powerless. There was no amount of shouting that would change what Tallowmeade or the Postmaster or those officers thought of her. It was a waste of her precious time to even try. Her fate was sealed. Everyone in the worlds would always think she was no different than her father.

A hysterical laugh bubbled from her lips. Let them think whatever they wanted of her. She knew that none of it was true. She was Maeve Abenthy, someone who fought for the things that mattered until her knuckles bled and her hands were stained with ink. The worst part of it was she knew that she could be so much more.

Maeve turned her hands over, taking in the blue veins on the insides of her wrists.

She once thought evil lurked there, waiting to show itself. But there was no evil, only pure potential running through her as thick and powerful as the arcane magic hanging in the air. Potential that could be shaped into whatever she wanted.

At distant shouts, Maeve looked up.

Everyone behind the glass had backed away, pointing down.

At first, Maeve thought they were pointing to her, but a tendril of the Aldervine had spread to the floor, a pace away from where she sat. It grew along the seam at the base of the door—a seam that appeared larger than the other seams.

An opening.

If the vine got out, Leyland would be lost.

Maeve's heart stuttered. The person who released the Aldervine was trying to be rid of her the same way they got rid of her father. They probably planned to pin everything on her as well. After the *Herald* article, it wouldn't be a stretch. It was clear that some outside thought she released the vine.

But she had come too far to sit back and allow others to make up her legacy for her. This was her life. She knew exactly who she was now, and she wanted everyone behind the glass to know it. To *see* her.

Maeve wrapped the edge of her cloak around her hand and tried to grab the Aldervine, but she couldn't get a good enough grip. Out of time, she flung the cloak away and grabbed the clump of the Aldervine with her bare fingers, ripping it from below the door. She pressed her legs along the door seam, hoping it would be enough. The Aldervine was sticky to the touch, but she hurled it across the floor in a fierce toss. It hit the ground and curled into a tight ball, like a wilting rose. A moment later, the vines above her thinned, the ceiling clearing out until the room was nearly free of the vine. It felt like a miracle, until she noticed a throbbing in her hand.

She held it up.

Six overlapping black marks kissed her palm like thumbprints. They smelled sweet, like the vine itself, and oozed with a dark green liquid mixed with her blood. Heavens, it was a ghastly sight.

Her eyes grew heavy. Her body flooded with the sensation of

stepping into lukewarm bathwater. Her vision blurred, but she squinted her eyes, straining to see through the haze as something shifted across the room—at the entrance into the library.

The door opened. She caught a flash of spectacles and dark hair as her eyes drifted shut.

"What did you do?" Tristan asked, pressing a palm against her cheek.

"I stopped it from getting out," Maeve whispered, and fell fast asleep.

Maeve dreamed of a slow chill that turned her bones to icicles, of mildewed barn wood digging into her nail beds, of a horse's enormous eye finding her in the quiet dark, pinning her for hours while her breath came up short in her lungs. She thrashed and tossed then calmed as the dreams shifted to warm parchment and dust. She dreamed of honey-clove wood polish against her tongue, her red curls skimming over a soft pillow. Of melancholy piano notes melting in and out in shallow waves. A dark voice pleaded with her to wake up, wake up, wake up. "Please wake up," it coaxed against her ear.

Let me sleep, she wanted to shout, until a burning sensation behind her lungs forced her eyes to open wide.

Her heart raced like a small bird trying to escape its cage, while the rest of her body felt drugged and lethargic. The edges of her vision were still sleep blurred. She blinked until her eyes cleared, focusing on a yellow candle flame guttering on a nearby table—in a room she didn't recognize.

She could tell she was on a bed because it compressed beside her. A finger swept her hair from her nose. "Maeve?"

"Is this a dream, or did we both die together?" she asked Tristan, then winced at her aching throat.

"Neither one, I'm afraid," Tristan said, drawing his knuckles along her cheek. A torturous shiver rolled through her that seemed to grind her bones; her skin felt far too sensitive. And her left hand . . . good god, it smarted.

The Aldervine.

Everything rushed back to her in an instant. They must still be somewhere in the Second Library, probably trapped here for all eternity. But at least they were together, and Tristan had his writing kit with him.

Maeve flexed her fingers. The six punctures felt like teardrops of ice against her palm.

"Hold still. I need to finish fixing a word here." Tristan slid one of his hands up her bare shoulder.

She was only in her camisole. She tensed as the thin tip of a quill moved along the top of her shoulder, spreading cool ink.

"That tickles," she said, squirming.

"If you don't hold still until the ink dries, I'll make sure to put the next one across your forehead."

Tristan must have finished with her shoulder because she felt him draw very near and blow the wet ink for far longer than ink took to dry.

"Is that necessary?"

"Very," he said quite seriously.

He traced a finger along the shell of her ear. He hadn't stopped touching her since she had opened her eyes—a fact that she was not mad about.

"How do you feel?" he asked.

"Like I could fall fast asleep and run a race at the same time."

"It's the coffee scribings. I've been adding them slowly—only one a day, so as not to shock your system."

"How long was I asleep for?"

"A little under a week in total."

A week underground in the library? Maeve slid around to face him.

Candlelight spilled out in silver waves behind his head, giving him a ghostly aura. He was freshly shaven, but his silk shirt was horribly rumpled and filthy with ink, then cuffed above his elbows. He tucked his quill behind one ear and corked the vial of open ink beside him on the bed.

The bed itself looked more like a scriptomancy worktable than a bed. Tristan was surrounded by quills and wells of pigments and endless vials of ink—some uncapped, others used up and tossed aside. The duvet appeared bruised by all the spills.

Maeve didn't care about the mess because Tristan was here, awake. The sight of him sent a sharp wave of longing racing through her, accompanied by a sudden need to rise up.

"I think I need to leap," she said, clambering up to sitting much too quickly. Her thighs cramped and she leaned into Tristan's chest.

He hooked his arms around her. "Leaping will come later. Your muscles are probably sore from disuse," he said. He took her arm and ran a gentle finger down her elbow, inspecting it.

His handwriting covered every inch of her left arm, from her wrist to her shoulder.

"There's six coffee scribings, if you're curious."

"Oh my god."

"You were comatose until I finished the fourth. There was a moment when I thought you'd never wake, but then you began talking at the fifth. I don't know who Headmistress Castlemaine is, but remind me to make her read a nasty sense scribing if I ever see her."

"You're too late. She died a few years ago."

"What a shame."

"I know. If she were still alive, I'd be tempted to do the same thing myself."

Tristan shifted her arm over, running his thumb along the inside of her elbow over a few Old Leylish runes. Maeve considered grabbing his collar and pulling her mouth to his, but she forced herself to look away so he could at least finish first.

She took in the room. It was small and well appointed, with a tiny window in the corner that looked out to a stone courtyard. They were above ground. "Unless you've done some decorating, this doesn't look like the Second Library."

"I pulled you out."

Maeve froze. "What about the Aldervine?"

"It's still inside. My father hired a team of metalsmiths to reinforce the exterior door with layers of silver. There are several people stationed outside of it now, keeping watch. But so far, it hasn't grown back inside the front lobby."

Maeve could still picture that lobby perfectly, with the Aldervine retreating from the ceiling. She looked above her, half-convinced she could see it now, hiding in the shadows. "Where are we?"

"Inside a room in the basement of Amaranthus Hall."

"Where the stewards keep their offices?"

"There's been talk of moving you to a government facility in Gloam proper, but you're to stay here until they decide what to do with you."

"I didn't let the vine out."

"I know that. Others believe it as well, especially after Nan, Shea, and I told our sides of the story. But there are some that need more convincing and many who are ready to hold you accountable," he said.

"Including all the stewards?"

"Mordraig wants you released, but the others are stone-faced about the subject. Especially my father. Then there's that box that Nan's father brought to the constabulary."

Maeve had forgotten all about the box. "What was in it?"

"I don't know exactly. The ministers have it locked away. Supposedly it's filled with stolen books from Molly's day, along with a number of dangerous pigment ingredients labeled with your own handwriting." His mouth drew into a frown. "It's a shame we never found Sibilla. Part of me was tempted to brave the library a second time to pull her out."

"You wouldn't be able to wake her up. She's dead."

Tristan dropped her arm. "You mean you saw her?"

Maeve explained how she found Sibilla all by herself on the floor, then spoke with her before the Aldervine got her. "She didn't do it. She didn't even know my father was murdered in Inverly. It was someone else," Maeve whispered. "They broke the Aldervine out and left before anyone noticed."

"Then they'll be brought to justice," he said, though he didn't sound as convinced as he had before the library.

Maeve felt it as well—as if the truth were falling through her fingers like a fistful of ash.

He took her hand and turned it over, stroking along the top. It was the lightest touch, but she felt it tingle up her arm. She reached out and ran a finger over Tristan's shoulder.

Her sensitive fingertips couldn't seem to stop touching him. She slid a hand along his shoulder and neck to his ear, then ran a fingertip along his eyebrow and sighed. "Why does touching you feel so . . . good?"

His mouth twitched. "It's the coffee scribing in your system. Your nerves will calm down in a few days."

She didn't want this to calm down. Her breath hitched when Tristan brought his hand up to skim along her jaw. Then he traced her bottom lip with his thumb. Her lip was more sensitive than her fingertips, and her breathing notched up at the touch. He jerked his hands away.

"Did I just burn you?"

"Nearly," he said, his hands at his sides. "All I want to do is kiss you right now. It's a bit of a struggle, in fact."

Heat rose up her back, racing over her neck and chest. She pressed toward him. "Why don't you?"

"Because I'm afraid that once I start, I won't be able to check the rest of your coffee scribings before your guard kicks me out."

"I have a guard?"

"You have six."

As if on cue, someone pounded on the door. "Are you almost done in there?"

"I need another minute with her," Tristan called out. He finished checking Maeve's arm, then slipped his hand around the back of her neck. Of course the moment their lips touched, the guard beat the door again. Tristan pulled away and pressed his mouth to a spot on her shoulder between lines of ink. "I'll be back later to check the scribings. Try not to smudge them."

After he left, Maeve curled up on the bed and tried to sleep, but she wasn't remotely tired. She was, however, terribly thirsty, but there was no lavatory or water save for the glass Tristan had used to clean his quill.

"I need a drink of water," she shouted to whoever was guarding her, but the door remained shut.

Perhaps her guards were hoping she dropped dead of thirst.

To take her mind off of her parched throat, Maeve cleaned up Tristan's mess, then sorted a stack of dusty linens that she found in a closet. Her mind soon wandered back to the Second Library, the broken shards of glass covered in blood, the strange chips of wood along the floor.

There had to be some clue she wasn't seeing. Something that didn't fit.

Maeve longed for a blank page of her journal to work out her thoughts, but Tristan had taken all his writing supplies with him.

She lay down and shut her eyes, picturing that room with the blood and glass. There was no sleeping person inside it. There was also no speck of the Aldervine, even though the vine had covered nearly every bookshelf on that entire floor.

It should have been inside that room as well. There should have been a body there. And why would the person behind everything risk their life to unleash the vine?

Unless they weren't risking their life.

What if they had a method to protect themselves against the Aldervine? Something that they used to escape, so they could blame everything on her? They could have used the same method to protect themselves in Inverly. But what was it? Who were they?

She felt the answers were staring at her in the face, but she couldn't quite see them.

Maeve thought through everything else she saw after she left Sibilla. The ink manifestation, the pile of sleeping officers, the lobby with the Aldervine crawling across the ceiling while everyone outside shouted and pointed. Then that last moment when she grabbed the clump of the vine in a fit of desperate anger and threw it. It had hit the ground and curled up like a wilting flower. The vines across the ceiling all fled the room at the same moment. Right after she touched it.

Her eyes snapped open.

She sat up and lifted her left hand to the light. It was bruised along the side in a mottled mess of yellowish green.

She curled her fingers. Days had passed, and yet thick half-moons of gray dust still clung beneath each of her nails. Crematory ash.

She'd upended her entire ash satchel into her left palm when she thought a manifestation was about to attack Sibilla. The ash still coated her hand when she grabbed the Aldervine. Then immediately afterward, the vine looked wilted. It was the same moment the rest of the vine across the ceiling disappeared from the lobby.

Maeve's spine pulled straight, picturing the vines covering the bookshelves. When she was running through the library, the Aldervine never came close to her, had it? Sibilla and the officers were covered in it, along with probably everyone else who was inside that library, but she had been spared. So had Tristan, who also had crematory ash on his fingers to stop the manifestations.

Crematory ash must somehow affect the vine. It was the only reasoning that made any sense.

She had to tell someone.

She shot to the door and rapped her knuckles against the ancient wood as loud as she could. There was a shuffling of feet, but nobody answered.

"Please!" Maeve called out, then winced at her parched throat.

"It's about the Aldervine. I need to speak with Steward Mordraig immediately. It's a matter of utmost importance."

He would know more about its origin and how crematory ash might affect it, and she didn't trust the Postmaster or any of the other stewards enough to call them. Mordraig's cluttered sitting room was in this building. He might be close by.

The guard didn't respond, but about twenty minutes later, voices came from outside her room. The door hinged open, and Steward Mordraig stood there in his raiment with a mischievous smile plastered on his face. "Maeve Abenthy, how does it feel to be the most infamous apprentice in all the worlds?"

"Not as well as expected," she said, then coughed.

She sounded like a croaking frog.

"God's nose, woman, don't you have water in there?" He sniffed and peered around her little room.

"I asked for some an hour ago, but nobody brought it."

He turned to the pair of officers hovering about ten paces down the hall, glaring at her. "How dare you all," Mordraig said. "This woman saved Leyland from the Aldervine, and you repay her by refusing water? She's coming with me straightaway."

As Mordraig led Maeve down the hall, one of the officers held up a hand. "Sir, we're supposed to watch over her. Postmaster's orders."

Mordraig sighed. "There's already five more of you louts stationed at each exit. I don't think our Onrich will mind if she goes up two mere floors for a few minutes to have a blasted drink of water. I'll return her shortly. Use the time to eat a biscuit if you want. I don't care. If Onrich has a problem with it, tell him to take it out on me."

Clapping his hand over Maeve's shoulder, Mordraig shuffled her past the men, then up the stairwell and down the long hall to his sitting room. His rocking chair still sat in one corner, the rest of the room as cluttered as she remembered.

He poured a large glass of water at a sideboard and handed it to her. She drank the entire thing in a matter of seconds. "Thanks. I was thirsty."

"It would appear so." He took the empty glass. "Now, why did you call for me? Out with it."

She wiggled the fingers on her left hand. "This hand was covered with crematory ash when I touched the Aldervine. The moment I threw it, it shriveled and shrank away." She coughed again, wincing. "Do you think there might be something to it? What if the Aldervine is affected by crematory ash?"

Mordraig scratched his jowl, his small eyes glittering behind his spectacles. "*That* is certainly worth some digging. Come. Make yourself comfortable while I have a look through my storage room. I might have a journal or two that can give us some answers." He shuffled unsteadily from the room.

The sitting room smelled as musty as it had the last time Maeve was here and was infinitely messier. There were a couple of chairs, but her nerves didn't let her sit. Then she caught a movement from the shelf filled with glass cloches. The emerald feather wasn't there, but that wasn't what caught her eye. It was a trapped drear moth.

She wandered over and watched it move its wings for a minute beneath the glass. It had a pattern to how it moved that felt manufactured, like it was somehow made by human mechanisms and not nature. That must be a product of the scribing.

It made her curious, and Maeve lifted the lid, hoping to inspect it, then put it back before Mordraig returned. The moth fluttered around her fingers, then landed on her knuckle.

Up close, its wings shone a deep, iridescent blue. It hopped along her finger for a moment, then fluttered off, leaving a splash of deep blue ink in its wake—just like in Molly's Keep.

She brought her knuckle to her nose and tensed. The ink smelled sharp and sweet, and Maeve caught the scent of henbane and hawthorne, then honeysuckle. All scribing herbs she'd learned about in Tallowmeade's laboratory.

Honeysuckle was a scribing herb, and so was spring gorse—the two strong scents wafting off the Aldervine. They were scribing herbs.

The vine could have simply smelled like scribing herbs, but the fact that it reacted to crematory ash made her wonder if there was more to it.

Maeve took in the drear moth fluttering around, weaving through the air in a looping pattern that looked like words, as if it were mimicking someone's hand penning a scribing. She shut her eyes and pictured the pattern of the Aldervine across the ceiling of that library lobby. It had looked like a pattern of woven lace, but it could have been mimicking words as well.

She brought her left hand up and turned it over, inspecting the faint yellow-green mark along the side of her palm—the mark she'd assumed was a bruise. But she didn't bruise easily, and all her bruises faded to purple over time. This was different. Slowly, Maeve brought her hand to her nose and inhaled. A week had passed, but she could still smell the sharp scent of honeysuckle and spring gorse, then . . . Was that henbane? Yes, it was. Then the barest hint of amaranthus.

All scribing herbs.

Heavens, the mark on her hand wasn't a bruise, but an ink stain. The Aldervine had left behind a godforsaken ink stain on her skin—a stain as ancient and near-permanent as the one left behind on her knuckle from the drear moth.

Maeve felt her world sharpening to a point. If all of this was true, it meant that the Aldervine was made by a scribing. It had to be. That was why it reacted to her crematory ash on her fingers, why she was able to wander through the library without it wrapping around her like it had with Sibilla. Mordraig had said the first sightings of the Aldervine spoke of it growing up buildings and fenceposts. It grew first in cities, and not in nature, because a *scriptomancer* must have created it.

Its poison must work in a similar way to the scribing that blackened her finger, but probably much stronger, given that it took Tristan six coffee scribings laced with crematory ash to wake her up.

The Aldervine was made from scriptomancy.

The truth sent her reeling. She stumbled backward until her legs hit Mordraig's rocking chair and she fell into it, suddenly feeling dizzy, thinking.

She imagined her journal spread before her, with all the elements of her mystery written out with lines drawn, connecting them. And her father's notebook . . . Her father's notebook sat squarely in the center.

The Silver Scribing.

If it nulled the effects of scriptomancy, it would likely render the Aldervine's poison harmless as well. She wouldn't need a dozen coffee scribings if she used it. She wouldn't even need one. The Aldervine would become as harmless as the thorns on a rosebush. Anyone who wished could use the Silver Scribing to walk into Inverly whenever they wanted. If there were people left alive, her father's scribing might even be able to wake them up. It changed everything.

She had to tell Mordraig immediately.

Maeve felt shaky on her feet, but she walked across the sitting room, then through the doorway Mordraig had gone.

"Steward?" she called out, but he didn't answer.

The hall led her past a smaller room with an enormous scriptomancy worktable covered with ink splatters and quill shavings. Four separate scribing glasses were affixed along the edge with unpolished brass clamps. Crumpled papers were strewn about the floor in messy heaps, and Mordraig's black cane was tossed on top of it all.

The sight jarred her. Mr. Braithwaite always asked her to fetch his cane, and she never minded because he used it like a third arm, to help him stand and move around. Mordraig moved similarly, so it was a shock that he would leave his cane here.

She lifted it and saw why; it was cracked down the center, the end broken off. A sharp chip of something had embedded close to the splintered edge. She dug it out with a nail.

A sliver of glass.

The cane fell from Maeve's fingers. She backed away, her stomach sickening as the truth stared back at her.

She had to find the ink.

Maeve listened for footsteps. When she didn't hear any, she stepped around the scriptomancy worktable, where a large shelf of ink hung against a wall. There were over a hundred bottles haphazardly shoved on top of one another, some stamped with flourished manufacturer's labels, some hand labeled.

Her fingers worked fast, picking through the bottles. The dizziness she felt in the sitting room came over her again, and her hand slipped and knocked over a bottle of lampblack. It rolled to the edge of the table and fell before she could grab it, shattering against the floor with a loud crack.

Maeve halted, listening.

Her breath was sharp in her lungs, but she didn't hear Mordraig anywhere.

She kept searching, picking through bottles. Where was it? Finally, behind a row of empty wells, she pulled out a bottle with ink that looked black at first glance, until she tilted it to the light.

A deep, glittering red color coated the inside of the glass.

She ran her thumb along the word "Oxblood" handwritten with thick, swooping letters on top of a label that read: PLUME & PEN, THE LARGEST INKSMITHY IN ALL THE WORLDS.

Her vision blurred for a moment, likely from the adrenaline

surging though her system. She blinked her eyes until it cleared, and she could see clearly, then froze at the sound of footsteps.

Mordraig passed by the open doorway to the room, carrying a large stack of books in his hands. He didn't notice her.

Maeve's muscles bunched; she wanted to run, but she forced herself to wait a minute until she was sure Mordraig was gone. She slipped from the room, moving deeper down the hall, through an open doorway which led to a much colder hall.

A thin dusting of snow coated the stone floor below an open window.

Maeve stepped to the window and glanced down along the sheer side of the building to a small snow-covered courtyard.

Her vision grew fuzzy again, then doubled. Maeve gripped the windowsill, blinking, until her vision cleared slightly. But it still wasn't normal. It looked as though she were staring through a bottle, the walls around her pressing in. Almost—almost as if she'd been drugged.

The glass of water.

Footfalls clicked along from somewhere down the hall.

Maeve tried walking, but she stumbled over her feet. Her limbs grew heavy, and that *tap-tap* of footsteps grew louder. She had to hide.

A few small oak doors lined the opposite wall. Closets. Maeve opened the first, then reeled backward at the pungent reek.

Her hand flew to her nose as she slowly propped the door open further. A fly buzzed out, circling around her. She swatted it and peered into the darkened closet, at a figure in a plum robe slumped against the back wall. Fion Claryman—or what was left of him. Dried blood matted the side of his head, as if something had hit him with a blunt force. His face—

Maeve pinched her nose hard to keep herself together.

"There you are." Steward Mordraig came around the corner.

She listed heavily to the side, clutching the closet doorknob to keep herself upright. Barely. Her muscles were numb. If the doorknob wasn't there, she'd be on the floor.

"You murdered him—as soon as Nan's article ran in the *Herald*," she said, remembering how Fion had disappeared. "You murdered him just like you murdered Cathriona."

Mordraig didn't deny it. In fact, he looked smug. Pleased with himself.

Now he was going to do the same to her.

Run, run, run, her mind screamed. She pushed away from the closet door and took a few steps, then stumbled and fell to her knees. Her mind still felt razor sharp, but her body was failing her.

"W-what did you put in my water?"

"Something that should kick in fully in another few minutes. If you try to scream, I can always shorten that time." He touched his cloak at his hip.

Maeve's eyes widened. He must have a knife.

He leaned against the open window, tapping his fingers against the sill.

Tears clouded her eyes. She couldn't move, but she still had enough of her wits left, and she wanted to know why he was doing this, to understand how someone could be so evil. Her mind spun in circles from all the information she'd uncovered in the past half hour. The murders. The Oxblood letters. The truth of the Aldervine. The ink staining her hand like an old bruise. It took effort, but she dragged it up. Wiggled her fingers.

Mordraig glanced at them and pursed his lips.

"You knew, didn't you? You knew the Aldervine was made with

scriptomancy this whole time," she said, but he remained silent. "If you're going to kill me anyway, you can at least talk to me until then. Unless you truly don't know anything . . ."

"Of course I know what the Aldervine is, apprentice," he said, taking her bait. "Molly Blackcaster discovered its origin long before me and left a diary that's been handed down from each steward of apprentices to the next for centuries, so we're aware of the grave nature of our teachings. It goes into great detail about the magnitude of destruction the vine caused in other worlds, then Molly's ordeals in Leyland up until she created the Aldervine specimen in the Second Library."

"Molly Blackcaster *made* that thing?"

"To study it and test theories, apprentice."

His gaze shifted to something in his left hand. A pocket watch. Was he counting down the seconds until Maeve's heart stopped beating?

"What theories?" Maeve pressed. Mordraig was passionate about scriptomancy and teaching; perhaps that passion might get her answers. Perhaps the drug would take too long to kick in and she could somehow escape with those answers. It was a long shot, but she had to try. *Tell me more*, she willed.

He gave an impatient sigh. "Molly wondered if she might go from world to world cleaning up the vine, then realized there simply wasn't enough ash."

"Because the trees harvested for ash only grow in Leyland," Maeve said, remembering her first lesson here.

His lesson.

"My, my," he said. "What a good memory you have. There were even fewer trees back then. It would take all the ash in existence to even attempt to clear one world of the vine. It was then that

Molly decided to preemptively save our three worlds from ever being infested by putting a moratorium on the old ways of traveling and create the Written Doors." His mouth flattened. "She was nearsighted in that regard; those doors were *death* to scriptomancy."

His eyes burned with a cold fury as he said it, and his fingers continued to drum. He checked his pocket watch again.

Maeve's heart thumped. "But . . . I don't understand. Why were the Written Doors so terrible for scriptomancy?"

Mordraig considered her. "The Written Doors did away with the need for scriptomantic travel," he said simply. "Without the need for travel, our art became a novelty, which the university board liked to remind me every year when they voted on our budgets. Then one year they held a vote to decide on whether to dissolve the College of Scriptomantic Arts entirely and archive our libraries. I was there. I watched people get up and put little scraps of paper that decided the fate of magic in a chipped bowl! It didn't pass, but only by a *single* vote. The former Minister of Communication gloated that he proposed the idea, so I was forced to slip poison into his tea to make sure he never made such a decision for all of us again."

"Forced?" Maeve couldn't believe she was hearing this.

"I'm not an evil person. I don't do any of this because I want to, apprentice. I do it all because it's necessary. Because I signed a sacred oath penned by Molly herself when she created my role centuries ago, to uphold her ideals and do everything in my power to keep scriptomancy *thriving*. Revered. And I've followed that oath damn well, if I say so myself. To the best of my ability." He gave another small smile.

It made her want to retch.

Good heavens, Mordraig believed killing that minister was his stewardly duty. He was unhinged.

"The day of that vote, I realized the Written Doors had to go," he went on. "It was the only way for travel to begin again. For scriptomancy to become *important* again."

That didn't add up. "But the doors didn't burn until much later."

"Yes, I couldn't simply torch the Written Doors in my pajamas one night, now could I? There would be investigations that would jeopardize my oath to Molly. I needed a reason big enough that others would see burning down the doors as necessary."

"Unleashing the Aldervine."

"Exactly." Another smile curved his mouth. "There's an edict kept at the station, written by Molly herself, that states if the Aldervine ever popped up in one of the known worlds, the doors were to be burned immediately. I knew that if I could bring a small enough piece of it over, it would create a panic and ensure the doors were torched. Then afterward, I could nullify that small piece of vine with ash. It was a solid start of a plan, but it was still too risky. Molly wrote about how crematory ash repelled the vine, but stepping inside a world infested with it?" He shook his head. "Even with the coffee scribing, enough puncture wounds could send me to sleep, which would have put everything at risk. I already accounted for a few necessary casualties, but—"

"*Necessary?*"

"I'm not vain enough to think my plan foolproof," Mordraig snapped. "But my *plan* was never to destroy Inverly, apprentice. Only the Written Doors."

"I find that difficult to believe."

"Yes, you would, wouldn't you? But it's the truth. Destroying an entire world filled with innocents isn't exactly my flavor of tea. I certainly don't take pleasure in that part of duty. I taught classes and sat on the idea of using the Aldervine for years. Then I grew close with your father. He was a brilliant scriptomancer in his day—one of the best. Adept at the traveling scribing, though he never got a chance to use it, sadly." Mordraig gave a thin smile that twisted Maeve's stomach. "I asked him to be my successor. The next steward of apprentices."

She had no idea.

"But he didn't want to be a steward," she said. He'd fought with Aggie over it on his last night at home. Her father must have been referring to Mordraig's offer that night—an offer he refused.

"Your father and I argued about it," Mordraig said. "He told me that a stewardship would take too much time away from scribing. And to help convince me how precious his scribing time was, he showed me what he'd been working on in secret."

"He showed you the Silver Scribing."

"Yes."

"And it was the answer you'd been waiting for," Maeve said, understanding everything. "To keep you safe while you brought the vine to Inverly." It was easy to fill in the blanks.

"Indeed. The only flaw in my plan was how quickly the Aldervine spread." His mouth turned down. "I never thought it would take off like it did, just like I never wanted to frame your father, but Inverly was a disaster. I knew that people would need someone to blame."

Maeve's bottom lip drooped to one side, but she gritted her teeth against the sensation and glared up at him. "So you murdered him."

"Jonathan was another necessary casualty," he said with no hint of remorse. "I thought the vine had already finished him off, but he had the Silver Scribing drawn up his arms."

Yes, her father did.

Maeve pictured their last night together, when she'd noticed the moth hole on his cuff after she'd touched the fresh writing on his forearm. The Silver Scribing.

"Your father was too smart for his own good. If he'd escaped Inverly, he would have figured out the origin of the Aldervine and given the secret away. I did what had to be done."

Tears fell down Maeve's cheeks, but she felt too weak to brush them away.

Mordraig killed her father because he'd signed some centuries-old oath that he felt duty-bound to uphold, despite slitting throats and stuffing bodies in closets. Because he loved scriptomancy. Except it didn't have to be like this.

"Why didn't you simply give away the secrets? If you feel a moral obligation toward keeping scriptomancy thriving, you could have easily come forward with the Silver Scribing as soon as my father brought it to you. *You* could have figured out a way to open travel again safely."

Maeve could see it perfectly. Blackcaster Station encased in glass like the Aldervine specimen in the Second Library. Cases of crematory ash at the ready. It might have been impossible to clear all the worlds of the vine, but with enough ash, you could clear one or two. Then plant more trees. Get more ash.

"The College of Scriptomantic Arts could have become invaluable because of you," she said.

"True. But the Otherwhere Post is much more valuable, apprentice. We control everything; the House of Ministers, the university board . . . They might still believe they hold power, but they all do what we say because we train their couriers. We allow their constituents to communicate with their loved ones.

Scriptomancy was always the most powerful tool humanity had, and now everyone knows it to be true because they must depend on it."

"So what happens when Tristan figures out how to repair the Written Doors?" Maeve asked.

She didn't want to hear his answer, but she needed to hear him say it.

Mordraig scratched his chin. "A tricky thing to say. I want to see what the boy can do before I make a judgment."

"To see if he'll also be a *necessary* casualty?"

"Hopefully not, but who's to say?"

Maeve wanted to end him with her own two hands, but her limbs had other ideas.

She lost her balance and collapsed onto her side on the cold stone floor. "You murdered innocent people to save your position," she spat.

"I did what was required to save scriptomancy, Miss Abenthy. There's a difference."

Mordraig was entirely convinced that he was in the right, which made him all the more dangerous. But there was nothing she could do to warn others; her body was useless.

He checked his pocket watch.

"How much longer?" Maeve asked.

He didn't answer. He tucked the watch away and came toward her. "I hoped I wouldn't have to kill you, truth be told. I like your spunk, and I don't want to suffer through yet another investigation like after Inverly. Ah, well."

Mordraig pushed his hands beneath her arms, shoveling Maeve upward. She tried to shake him off her, but it was pointless.

"If you're planning to put me in the closet with Professor Claryman, you won't get away with it," she said. "There were guards who watched me come in here with you."

"True. But none of them will be surprised when you attempt your escape, only to have a little tumble."

Mordraig slid her limp body along the wall until frigid air brushed the back of her neck.

The window.

"Don't worry, apprentice. My drug will have you lose all consciousness in the next few seconds, and you won't feel a thing."

A drug—not poison.

Maeve's vision darkened at the edges, but she forced her eyes to remain open—willed them with all her might. It helped that her mind still felt sharp. Awake.

The coffee scribing.

Tristan had said wine barely affected his mind. The coffee scribing must be helping her resist the effects of Mordraig's drug, just as it did with alcohol, and Mordraig must not realize it. He expected her to pass out.

It was an effort, but Maeve turned her head to the side until cool winter air rushed against her cheek.

Black courier cloaks fluttered in the distance—close enough to hear a scream.

Mordraig had threatened to hurt her if she screamed. But it was only a threat, she realized. He didn't want this to look like murder.

"Help!" she screamed at the top of her lungs. It came out shrill and loud, like a bell carried on the wind.

"*Quiet,*" Mordraig snapped.

As if she would go quietly. "Someone help me!"

Maeve's limbs were useless, but her throat worked well enough, and she screamed and screamed.

Mordraig tore off his cloak and stuffed a section into her mouth, muffling her.

His shirtsleeves were rolled beneath it, his forearms covered in a skin scribing more intricate than the coffee scribing. The same scribing written along her father's arm all those years ago.

Scriptomancy was her father's life's work. The thing he loved most in the world, besides her, and the Silver Scribing was his greatest achievement.

Maeve felt a fierce burst of pride at what her father had accomplished, at the man he was. But mostly that she was lucky enough to be his daughter.

The scribing was beautiful.

It was the last thing Maeve saw before Steward Mordraig shoved her out the window.

Two days passed before the first letter was slipped beneath Maeve's hospital door.

Dearest Maeve,

If you wake without anyone at your bedside and happen to read this first, know that the stewards wanted you confined to the infirmary, but Nan and Tristan pitched a fit and had you brought to a room in Leyland's City Hospital. You're in the Widden wing, if you haven't already figured that out. You can thank my darling grandfather yet again.

You're also probably wondering what is happening, and so are we! The stewards and the constabulary have been ever so cagey. Nobody knows what took place in Mordraig's quarters before your fall, and Mordraig swears up and down that you jumped. None of us believe him, of course. Tristan has been studying your father's Silver Scribing and thinks Mordraig knows more than he says to such a great degree that he's put up a fuss about it with the House of Ministers. They might open an investigation tomorrow and at least search Mordraig's room. Tristan mentioned something about working on a door for the ministers if they do what we ask. Though

I'm not sure what that entails. Hopefully it's a metaphorical door to answers!

I'll write more when I can. Please don't die in the meantime.

Yours in wondrous health,

Shea Widden

Maeve,

You horrid, horrid roommate. Please consult me first the next time you decide to toss yourself over a windowsill. All kidding aside, you need to hurry up and heal. I know Shea wrote two days ago, but so many things have happened in the past few hours that it deserves another letter. The constabulary searched old Mordy's room and discovered a corpse! They won't tell us who it belongs to, but it was enough to arrest Mordy while they investigate. Then an hour later, we got a visit from a researcher with the university who talked our ears off. Tristan took them a sample of Mordy's writing the day after your fall, along with Sibilla's entry in that accounting log. The handwriting was purposely made to look different, but they determined it was still Mordy's hand that signed for the Oxblood ink. Can you believe it? He bought that blasted bottle of ink and wrote the letter that choked me. I think once the constabulary sees the chirographer's report, old Mordy will start to talk. I can feel it.

Miss you dearly,

Nan

Maeve,

I bet you never expected two letters from your dear roommate in a matter of hours, but the best thing happened. They've arrested Mordy! He confessed to killing Fion Claryman. That's right, the

*body in Mordraig's room belonged to poor Fion blasted Claryman.
The same man who nearly killed you with that letter. The constabulary interviewed all of us immediately, and they now know how
Fion connects to everything. The only bad news is Mordy still won't
tell anyone why he did it, but fingers crossed that a few days in
Stonewater will get him talking.*

*Oh! I nearly forgot the best part. When the news broke about
Fion, my lovely father called me in about your article that he'd
ripped in half. He wanted to print it, given what's come to light.
I said fat chance in hell, then snatched it and walked four blocks
and handed it over to the editor-at-large for the Gloam Times. Tristan and I added a section at the end explaining what happened in
the Second Library and how you kept the Aldervine from escaping.
Word is starting to spread about it, and we wanted to make sure
you get credit for that foolhardy move you did tossing the vine with
your bare hand. The article is running tomorrow with your name
printing across the top for all to see. Except for you, I guess. Don't
die on us.*

Yours always,

Nan

*P.S. Now that your name is in the paper, I have a feeling you're
about to receive an avalanche of letters wishing you well. Good luck.*

To Miss Abenthy,

*I'm writing you from where Eamon Mordraig is being held. After
reading your article in the Times, I felt obliged to say that I believe
your version of events. Eamon Mordraig has said several alarming things to my guards, and I'm of a mind that he should not be
allowed to leave this prison. I plan to write a longer explanation*

for the constabulary, but I've heard the rumors that he may have pushed you out his office window, and wanted to send you this note of reassurance in case you were worried.

Kind Regards,
E. Graham
Head Warden, Stonewater Prison

Dear Miss Abenthy,

I am penning you this letter as the Postmaster, but also as Tristan's father. I wanted to give you an update myself as something monumental has occurred. The constabulary has located a diary belonging to Molly Blackcaster buried in Eamon Mordraig's things that tells the origin of the Aldervine, mainly how it's an advanced form scribing. After the discovery, I visited Mordraig myself, alongside a few other ministers and stewards, and showed him the diary, and it seemed to break open something inside of him. He confessed to everything, including pushing you from the window. He even confessed to releasing the Aldervine into the Second Library and lining the exterior with crematory ash as soon as he saw you go inside. He said it would have been better for everyone if you were blamed for it all, which, of course, was grievously alarming. The most shocking part of this is he asked to be made an advisor on the future of the Otherwhere Post now that the truth of the Aldervine is out in the open. And he believed I would somehow snap my fingers and make that happen.

I'm telling you all of this so you can see the horror that you helped contain. You, Miss Abenthy.

Tristan tells me that you're making good progress and can sit up on your own. I'm sure you must think that I worry about my son and wish for you to pull through for his sake, but that is not the case.

I worry about Tristan, of course, but I also know how badly people need heroes. And I believe you have more than earned that title. Along with my deepest respect.

When you are recovered, I would like for you to pay me a visit. I was close with your father once, and I have a few anecdotes from our days together that I think you would like to hear.

Well wishes for a speedy recovery,
Postmaster Onrich Byrne

M. Abenthy,
On behalf of the House of Ministers, I would like to extend my sincerest gratitude for everything you have accomplished. It takes great bravery to face an evil like the former steward Eamon Mordraig. If you are ever inclined to run for public office, I would be honored to have you on my team. Regardless of your political aspirations, we will discuss your future in the worlds as soon as you are well and able.

My deepest regards,
Ailbeart Cunningham, Leyland Minister of Communication

Maeve,
I have to run deliveries this morning, but I will be there as soon as I can.

Yours always,
Mr. Tristan

A loud crack of thunder rattled through the hospital's stone walls, sending bottles of tinctures clinking, rattling the shelf of medicinal instruments along the far wall. Maeve folded the letter from Tristan, then placed it at the top of the growing stack of letters at her bedside table, straightening them before they had a chance to topple off.

Not that it would make any difference.

Letters were scattered everywhere in the stark room. They were piled against the walls, their corners curling against one another, as if from the weight of all the sentiments. They were shelved like books in the wormwood shelf opposite her hospital bed. A pair of clerks from the Hall of Routes had carried in four wooden crates to help Maeve find her way through the jumble, but they were already overflowing, letters spilling to the worn tile floor.

At least the scents of parchment and sealing wax masked the resinous odor of the healing rub the hospital clinicians insisted she reapply hourly. Day after day.

She glanced out the hospital window to a narrow view of a bleak Leylish courtyard. She waited patiently for something green to push its way through the rain-soaked earth and give her a bright spot of color to focus on besides the brown ground. But you couldn't rush a seedling, just as you couldn't rush the knitting of bones.

Sixteen weeks had passed since Mordraig had thrown her over the window ledge. The fall cracked nearly all her ribs, shattered her left foot, and snapped the radial bone in her right arm. The coffee scribing in her system kept her conscious through it all, which was a blessing and a curse. She was able to swing out her arm as she landed, protecting her head from the worst of the fall, and the snow helped to cushion her as well. The clinicians believed that if it were summertime, there was a good chance she wouldn't have made it.

But she pulled through, and now the truth was out in the open for everyone to have.

Maeve didn't think she could be any happier in her discoveries, until a few weeks into her recovery, when a constabulary courier delivered a box of her father's effects that they'd confiscated during their initial search of Mordraig's quarters. It was filled to the brim with years of her father's journals. When Maeve first paged through them, she gasped in surprise when letters spilled out— love letters written by her mother that her father had tucked away within the pages.

Her heart ached thinking about them, but she wouldn't let herself cry over her parents anymore. She'd cried enough over her father as it was. Now she simply wished she could tell him everything.

Already, his work was gathering excitement across Leyland and Barrow. Ministers were in talks with various organizations. There were ideas already being tossed about now that a cure for the Aldervine's poison existed.

Maeve wished her father were still here to see how important his work had become. More than anything, she hoped a guard rubbed it all in Mordraig's face while he sat in his bare cell in the lower level of Stonewater Prison.

A familiar vibration hummed from the wall across from her hospital bed. A moment later, a strange black door appeared and opened. Tristan stepped through, wearing a new shirt covered in ink splatters.

He was soaked through from rain, his dark hair damp. He shook it, and it fell into dripping curls around his ears. The chill spring air had turned the tip of his nose bright pink, and his fogged-over spectacles sat crookedly across it. Maeve imagined if she rested her fingers against his jaw, it would feel the same temperature of fresh snow.

He paused at the foot of her bed and took her in, his mouth curving. "How do you feel?"

"Awful, as usual. But watch this."

Maeve swung her legs down from the bed and pushed herself up, walking unaided for the second time that day.

Her legs wobbled, and she caught herself on the writing desk that Tristan had brought in, stocked with a stack of fresh leather journals and an assortment of left-handed quills. Of course one of those quills happened to be the left-handed swan quill Tristan had gifted her in his room, with the drip of silver along the fletching that ended in a ruby. As soon as Maeve discovered it sitting on her hospital desk, she took a quill knife and carved the tip.

The quill felt lovely to write with. But there was only so much she could write in a journal each day, only so many hours she could sit and stare out of a window at a patch of mud.

Already, she longed to feel paver stones beneath her feet and breathe in fresh air and sunshine. Most of all, she longed to write the traveling scribing on the inside of her wrist again.

She pushed herself from the writing desk. Holding out her hands for balance, she made it the rest of the way across the floor to her little window—something she wasn't able to do yesterday. Tristan watched her with shining eyes.

"You're walking on your own," he said. "How it that possible?"

"Legs." Maeve kicked one. "And muscles and sinew, and probably a small portion of my brain."

Tristan arched an eyebrow dramatically. "There are some who would argue that gravity might have something to do with it as well."

He came forward and brought one hand to her ribs, feeling along them slowly. She gasped and squirmed.

"They're still sensitive?"

Yes. They certainly *were* sensitive, but the sensitivity she was experiencing had more to do with the feel of his fingers pressed against her than any tumble through a window.

They broke apart as the door to her room creaked open. A clinician in a white starched apron over a gray gown popped her head in.

"Time to administer your rub," she said, then noticed Tristan. "Oh, dear me, you have company."

"Yes. Company who has stepped through the fabric of worlds to pay me a visit. I would appreciate it if you left me alone for a moment," Maeve said.

"But your rub—"

"I think my bruises can have a little patience for a change."

The clinician's cheeks pinked, and she curtsied quickly.

As soon as she dipped away, Maeve turned to Tristan. "That's it. I need you to help me get out of this room today. In the next hour, in fact. I'll give you a whole hallion if you help me escape before another clinician comes to prod me again. Two hallions, even."

"You have two hallions?"

"No, but I can pay you in other ways." She drew a finger along his jaw, torn between kissing him and escape.

He caught her finger and pressed his mouth to it. "Tempting, but I'm actually here to free *you*."

Her eyebrows drew together. "You are?"

He ran his hand down her right sleeve. "May I check it first?"

When Maeve nodded, he brushed her hair aside and slipped her hospital gown down her shoulder, pulling out her right arm, inspecting the fresh coffee scribing she had written along the inside of her elbow that morning.

Tallowmeade was kind enough to send over a lotion he concocted from crematory ash and a blend of herbs that took away the stinging cold from the puncture wounds against her palm. Until the stewards figured out the logistics of the Silver Scribing, the coffee scribing still counteracted the black marks on her left hand.

There were estimates about how long it would take to have the Silver Scribing ready to test. Some gave it a month or more, but as soon as it was deemed safe, the stewards promised to call her first. Tristan was ever so slightly bitter, which she made sure to tease him about.

Once he was satisfied with her coffee scribing, he stepped to the small chair on the other side of the room and collected a few books he'd left yesterday.

He'd sat there nearly every night for the past few weeks, reading aloud from an endless array of the ghastliest novels; he had horrid taste in books. She would curl into his lap and try to listen to every word, but it was difficult to be so near to him without skimming her fingers beneath his shirt hem. He would put on a serious face, of course, and pretend to read for another few chapters before giving up entirely.

Maeve felt heat rise in her neck, thinking about those long nights. It was astounding what one could accomplish with a little creativity and no need for sleep.

She caught his hand, pulling him in for a slow kiss that soon left her breathless.

"We should probably stop this," he said into her mouth.

"That's a terrible idea. Why?"

"Because otherwise we'll be here all day and night and possibly the next day. And if I remember correctly, you wanted to leave not two minutes ago."

For a blissful moment, Maeve seriously reconsidered her need for escape.

"Then there's the little matter of my father . . ."

She pulled away. She hadn't yet spoken to the Postmaster, but she kept his letter near her bed and liked to read it from time to time. "What about him?"

"I told him that we would pay him a visit together before luncheon. There should be a coach waiting outside the front of the hospital now." He slipped his arm across her shoulder. "I'll help you walk out, so long as you promise me one thing first."

He sounded grave.

"What is it?"

"That you won't leap in front of the coach."

〜

BY THE TIME they made it out the door, their driver was tapping his toe impatiently. It took longer than Maeve would have liked to get off the front stoop and into the cab, but both Tristan and the hospital staff helped. Tristan climbed in beside her, and the coach rolled northward, across the river Liss, then up the twisting university streets, until they reached the road surrounding Blackcaster Square.

"Look at that." Tristan pointed.

A large white banner was unrolled across the front gate. On it were printed updates from the Postmaster himself.

There was a note about the Second Library and how it was officially cleared of the Aldervine, a few of the survivors had awoken with the coffee scribing, then a larger message from the Minister of Agriculture. He was working with the Post to plant a new forest of white elm trees to harvest for crematory ash in the farmland west of the city.

It went on to explain that as soon as the Silver Scribing was figured out, there were plans in place to send a team of scriptomancers into Inverly armed with the scribing and a large amount of crematory ash, to see if they could slowly beat back the vine and wake up survivors.

For the first time in seven long years there was a stir of hope permeating the air around Blackcaster Square. There were still protesters, of course, but the messages had shifted to demanding timelines and more detailed plans about Inverly.

Soon, Maeve thought to herself. They would all get answers soon.

The coach veered north, through the Post's main gate, then through the forest of oak trees now covered in bright green buds nearly ready to pop with all the spring light streaming through the canopy. They finally rolled to a stop outside the same lecture hall Maeve had visited her first day here, where she had been given the memory scribing.

"If your father makes me read a memory scribing, I will never forgive you," she said as Tristan helped her step from the coach.

"I promise you it's nothing like that."

She halted. "You know what this is about, and you haven't told me?"

His mouth curved. "It's a secret."

"You know I don't like secrets," she hissed.

That made him burst into laughter, and he took her hand, running his thumb along her palm. Together they went inside, then descended the stairs toward the pit of the stage.

Maeve was surprised to find the lecture hall as empty as it had been on her first day at the Post, save for a row of people in the front.

The Postmaster sat beside Steward Tallowmeade and three Leyland ministers in decorated waistcoats.

"Here she is," Tristan said, then left her there while he stepped down and flopped against a chair. She glared at him, and he cracked a smile.

"Maeve Abenthy," said Postmaster Byrne. "I have called you before us to declare that you are officially invited to join the ranks of otherwhere couriers."

She wasn't expecting that. "You're making me a courier?"

"We've already made you a full-fledged courier, but whether you choose to accept the office is up to you. However, that's not the sole reason I asked you here." He steepled his fingers. "Next year, we're planning for a new division of the Otherwhere Post that will begin traveling beyond the bounds of the three known worlds to seek out information that might help us repair the Written Doors more quickly. Given your proclivity for the traveling scribing, I would like you as a member of that team. Along with my son."

Maeve was speechless.

"You don't have to decide anything now. In fact, take as long as you would like to think it through. It's a great decision and not one to take lightly. It comes with many risks, but we all thought that you might be up for the challenge."

Maeve nodded, her mind already spinning with possibilities.

She would take her time to think everything through first, but she knew she wanted to go. As it was, she wanted to race back to her hospital room, crack open a journal, and make a list of all the new things she wanted—everything she'd dreamed of experiencing over the years but never thought possible because of her circumstances, then other experiences she hadn't dared to dream about before. Then she would figure out how to go about doing everything on that list.

She curtsied to a line of ministers and stewards, then started toward the steps to take her off the stage, but the Postmaster held up a hand.

"One more thing," he said.

He stood from his chair and approached the stage slowly, holding out something that caught the light from the gasolier overhead. It glimmered like a coin in the sunlight as he placed it in the center of her palm.

A courier key.

"I think you've more than earned it," he said.

"I'm in complete agreement with you on that." Maeve slipped the key down her right pocket, against her hip bone.

42

Afternoon storm clouds crested the sky as Tristan and Maeve exited the lecture hall. He took her hand and threaded their fingers together, then helped her walk to a winding footpath that curved around a building. Not a moment later, someone shouted Maeve's name from a distance. A tall woman with a dark head of hair came loping up the path. Maeve expected Nan to stop, but she kept racing forward and plowed straight into her, throwing her arms around Maeve's shoulders, knocking the wind out of her in a single wallop.

"She might not be covered in bruises, but she's still healing, Nan," Tristan said, nudging her roommate off.

"Oh dear. Sorry about that." Nan backed enough away that Maeve could get a good look at her.

The hospital staff didn't allow for many visitors, though Tristan had snuck Nan in once. But that was weeks ago now, when Maeve could barely open her eyes through the bruising.

"Did you use an inkwell to wash your clothes?" A splatter of lampblack ran down the front of Nan's blouse.

"Oh, drat. It is rather soiled, isn't it?" She wiped at her front, which did nothing. "I spilled it this morning at the Groggery and haven't had a chance to change. I'm working on something."

"An epic poem?" Maeve asked.

Nan wrinkled her nose. "A gossip sheet."

Maeve sighed. "Why does that not surprise me in the least?"

"I know, right? I pitched the idea to the stewards, and they were as nervous as newly birthed foals, but they eventually caved to my whim after I explained to them the benefits. I'm penning *the* official gossip sheet from inside the Otherwhere Post, with scintillating details of couriers' lives."

"So long as none of your gossip is about me," Maeve shot back.

"I wouldn't dare," Nan said with a devious smirk.

Maeve didn't believe her at all. "Is it going to be printed here on the grounds?" She pictured the flyers pinned up in the mess hall's entranceway.

"Goodness, no. I already have a verbal agreement with the *Times* to run the first few pieces in their Sunday paper. Second page. And so long as the stewards get an opportunity to check over the sheet before it prints, they're fine with it. After everything that happened, they said they plan to make transparency one of their new ideals. I didn't think they had it in them."

"That's wonderful news." Maeve was thrilled for Nan, and also wary.

Nan leaned toward Tristan. "Did you already show her?"

"Not yet," Tristan said, his eyes narrowing at Nan. "I was about to until you nearly ruined the surprise."

"Show me what?" Maeve asked.

"You must let me come. Please." Nan bounced on the balls of her feet. "I'm already writing all about it for my gossip sheet."

That was it. "If you write about me one more time, I will set your paper on fire then sprinkle the ashes over you while you sleep. Are we clear?"

"There's the attitude I've been missing these past weeks." Nan grinned. "Let's show her, shall we?"

Nan covered Maeve's eyes with her hands, while Tristan took Maeve's elbow and helped her to walk. After a minute, Maeve could tell she was standing in the central courtyard by the way the wind blew through trees and the feel of uneven stones beneath her feet.

"Is this really necessary?" Maeve said, trying her best to pry Nan's hands away, which only made her press harder. "You'll blind me before I see anything."

Someone else ran up. "Has she seen it yet?"

It was Shea.

"Unless you think I'm some special human with the ability to see through flesh, I have not. Now, I demand to know what in the worlds you all are hiding from me!"

The moment Nan dropped her hands and Maeve saw what they were speaking of, she staggered backward, nearly falling to her bottom on the uneven pavers.

Tristan caught her. He placed his palms on the sides of her waist, steadying her. It wasn't nearly enough.

"Don't go fainting on me," he whispered against her ear.

"I'm not the fainting type." Maeve stepped forward and placed her hands on the lip of Molly Blackcaster's fountain, staring up at the smaller statue that now stood beside Molly. A man with a soft fall of hair and large dimples and piercing eyes that Maeve would recognize anywhere.

Her father had never worn a courier's cloak, but his statue wore one. The hood was down, the edges flaring out behind him as if caught in a Gloam storm. His shirtsleeves were rolled to his elbows, the Silver Scribing tracing a path along both of his forearms.

The likeness was startling.

"They commissioned it the week after Mordraig was sent to Stonewater," Tristan said. "Before Mordraig confessed to everything. They had enough evidence, and they all knew Jonathan and believed us when we told them your whole story. The statue was a unanimous vote between the stewards, if you can believe it. And now the ministers want to foot the bill and take credit for it. It's incredible, really. They never care about anything on these grounds, but they see the importance of this. Though I think this statue here is the least they could do."

Her father would have been overjoyed to see this statue, and perhaps a little embarrassed as well, considering the artist took a few liberties with his musculature. But it was him staring down at her now, his mouth drawn in concentration, his foot mid-step as if he were walking across worlds.

Maeve had never felt prouder to be an Abenthy.

"He's a hero," Tristan said.

That he was.

Maeve didn't realize she was crying until Tristan held up a handkerchief. She took it and scrubbed her eyes until they stung.

Tristan turned and said something to Shea and Nan. Whatever it was, the two women hurried away. As soon as they were gone, Tristan put an arm around Maeve's shoulders. "There's something else I want to show you."

"I don't think my heart could take another surprise like this."

"I promise the next one won't make you weep. If it does, that's your own fault."

She didn't believe him at all, but she trusted him implicitly, and let him help her walk all the way to his room at Hawthorne House.

He stepped inside first and ran to the window, opening his

heavy curtain, filling the room with daylight. Dust motes shimmered like specks of arcane magic in the air.

The room was rearranged. A modest scriptomancy worktable now took up the entire corner beside Tristan's upright piano. The bookshelves were all still there, but the leather settee was gone, replaced with two smaller chairs that faced a rather large bed.

Maeve stepped to it and ran a finger along a tracery of leaves carved into the wooden posts. They weren't the Aldervine's serrated leaves but resembled a garden of wildflowers sprouting along the wood, weaving upward to where a simple canopy was strung with small bundles of drying scribing herbs.

She imagined herself lying on this bed, asleep, with Tristan's arms draped loosely around her waist, her head pressed into the crook of his neck while her palm covered the top of his chest, rising and falling with his steady breath.

"It's a shame the stewards don't think they'll have the Silver Scribing ready to attempt for another month," she said, playing out the simple fantasy in her mind.

"It is a shame," Tristan said, then pushed his spectacles up his nose. "Which is why I decided to take on the task myself. I figured it out last night."

Maeve turned to him. "You figured out my father's journal?"

He unbuttoned his cuff and rolled up his rumpled shirtsleeve, revealing exquisite lines of text that shimmered silver in the sunlight streaming from the window. She'd seen it on Mordraig's arm, but in Tristan's handwriting, it looked even more beautiful.

"There's a small amount of crematory ash mixed with the original text's ink. It was tricky to get the right amount. I had to test it on parchment for several days first, but I eventually gathered enough courage to try it on my arm, and it worked better than

I hoped." He brought his hands to his collar and unbuttoned his shirt, pulling apart the material. "See?"

She did.

The two black puncture marks surrounding his heart had disappeared.

The truth felt like a quill had pierced open her own heart, and she swiped at her eye. "You promised this wouldn't make me cry."

"Yes, but I lied." He brushed a soft kiss along her lips. "Now, Maeve Abenthy, come and have a seat by my worktable and roll up your sleeve."

ACKNOWLEDGMENTS

A number of people warned me that second books are difficult to write, but I didn't believe it until I experienced it firsthand. Through it all, one thing remained abundantly clear: I would not have made it through this process without a small village of the kindest, most wickedly smart people helping me along the way.

To my editor, Gretchen Durning: You saw my vision and sprinkled it with your fairy dust and helped make words held together with scaffolding and duct tape turn into the story it was meant to be. Thank you for your editorial brilliance and tremendous kindness. I'm endlessly grateful that I get to work with you. To Hillary Jacobson and Alexandra Machinist: What can I say? I have not one but two of the most thoughtful and wise agents on the planet helping me. It's often uncomfortable and takes quite a bit of trust to hand over creative work to be judged and shaped, but I never have any fear that I'm in the wrong hands. Thank you for listening to all my strange ideas and fighting to make this impossible dream of mine come true. Thank you as well to everyone at CAA who touched this story, especially Lauren Denney, Josie Freedman, Berni Vann, Sarah Mitchell, and Filipa Vaz.

To design and cover geniuses Jim Tierney, Kristie Radwilowicz, and Theresa Evangelista: Thank you for conceiving the perfect package for this story. If you can't tell, I adore it. To my incredible team at Penguin—Alex Campbell, Rebecca Aidlin, Natalie Vielkind, Madison Penico, Rye White, Miranda Shulman, Amy White, Sola Akinlana, Krista Ahlberg, Marinda Valenti, Abigail Powers,

Alicia Balderrama, Sarah Liu, Olivia Russo, Deb Polansky, Shanta Newlin, Emily Romero, Christina Colangelo, Bri Lockhart, Alex Garber, Felicity Vallence, Shannon Spann, James Akinaka, Jen Klonsky, Jocelyn Schmidt, and Jen Loja—thank you for helping to make this story shine brighter than I ever hoped. I'm honored to work with all of you. To my foreign publishers: Thank you for allowing this story to travel nearly as far at the couriers in its pages.

Elizabeth Runnoe, you're the first person I text when I get stuck. This book would not be the same story without your brilliant advice, and I would not be the same writer without your friendship. Thank you for all the frantic calls and reads. Now let's do some writing sprints! Lyssa Mia Smith and Anna Mercier, you both came into my life at a time when I was in desperate need of a group chat. Thanks for letting me nerd out over ideas and vibes. Sovanneary Sweere, thank you for the long walks and friendship.

To Renee Kallio, cheerleader extraordinaire: Thank you for being a great friend throughout the journeys of both my books. Yes, your name is first in this paragraph. That means you win. Thank you as well to Angie Beckey, Jenny Pinion, Lena Luckritz, Emily Lane, Denise Lorenz, April Smasal, and Tim Blevins for all the continued support. Your friendship means everything to me. To Joanne Torres and Amanda Clark: Thank you for the coffee catch-ups, T-shirt recos, and your ever-fabulous input on book covers. To Anthony Nemcek: Thank you for the boat rides and unwavering enthusiasm. To Janelle Erickson: Thank you for always finding time. To the Boelkes: Thank you for your excitement.

A massive thank-you to all my other friends who've supported me throughout this incredible ride. Please keeping doing the thing. I can't wait to see it. To my fellow authors who have read and blurbed and shared and boosted this book: Thank you from the bottom of my heart. To my readers: Thank you for all your posts and texts and art. It's impossible to respond to each message, but I see them, and they mean the world to me.

To my family in Arizona, Minnesota, and Milwaukee: Thank you for everything. To my ladies, Caren and Jessica: Thank you for the wine chats and for being calming constants in my life. I love you all!

Eric, once again I could not fathom doing this work without you by my side. I can't possibly fit how grateful I am for everything you do into a small paragraph, but know that I appreciate and love you.

And finally to Casey McIntyre, who was one of the first people to get a draft of this story, thank you for crossing paths with me. As long as I live, I will never forget that short, reassuring email you sent to me in early '21 when I was struggling—when our relationship was new and you didn't have to send anything. You were a shining presence with the coolest hair. I miss you.

KEEP READING FOR A PREVIEW OF
ANOTHER DAZZLING DARK FANTASY
BY EMILY J. TAYLOR

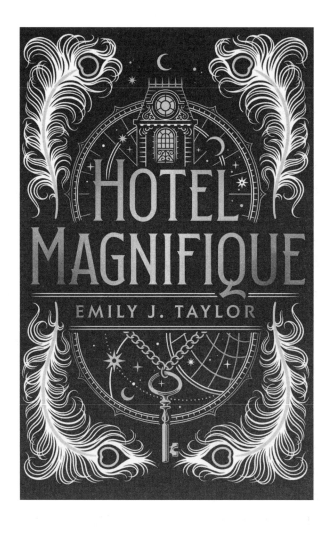

The *New York Times* bestselling fantasy novel
also available from Pushkin Press

PROLOGUE

The courier was given a single instruction: deliver the boy before the stroke of midnight. Simple—except, usually, she delivered packages during the day, not little boys in the dead of night.

The job paid handsomely, but that wasn't the reason the courier agreed. She took the job because she was curious.

She wondered why a well-to-do couple came to her of all people. Why the boy's father refused to write the address down and instead whispered it into her ear, why the boy's mother wept. Most of all she wondered who might receive this boy, considering the delivery location was not a home, nor an address to any physical structure, but the space in between two—an empty alley on the other side of town.

The boy seemed ordinary enough, with unblemished copper skin a shade deeper than her own. However, he hung his head as they walked, as if the thick night air pressed upon his shoulders.

The courier thrust her lantern at the gloom, beating back shadows with a growing sense of unease. Her grandfather's stories came to her: whispers of magic hiding in the corners of the world, and young children met with terrible fates.

She was too old to believe in stories, and yet she quickened her pace.

One block from their destination, the boy dragged his feet. Gripping his bony shoulder, she tugged him down the final street, and halted.

The alley was gone. A strange, slender building stood in its place, squeezed into the narrow space, fitting in seamlessly with the crumbling structures on either side.

A figure peeled away from a shadow near the entrance.

The courier drew the boy behind her. "Are you the person I'm supposed to meet?"

Whoever it was raised a slim object. A blood-red taper candle flared to life, illuminating a young man's blue eyes and pale face.

The courier searched for a match to explain the flame; no one could light a candle from nothing. Unless—

Shimmering golden smoke billowed from the tip. It spilled onto the street, snaking around the courier. Tiny globes buzzed and flickered like fireflies or dust motes catching moonlight. Or something else. Scents gusted by: peppermint oil, then burnt sugar, as if caramel were bubbling too long on a stove, followed by a whiff of citrus left to rot.

The man strode through the golden smoke and took the boy's hand, like a father would do. For a brief moment, the boy stumbled, unsure, but then he *willingly* walked with the man toward the narrow building.

The courier clutched her chest and felt her heart pound in an erratic rhythm—harder than it ever had before. This was all wrong. She lunged to stop the man, but golden smoke twined around her ankles, restraining her. She opened her mouth to scream, but no sound escaped her lips, not even a whimper.

Her hands wrapped around her throat as the man halted at the doorway of the building. She watched in horror as he smiled, sharp-toothed, then brought his striking face level with the boy's own. "Come along now," he said. "I have the perfect job for you."

The man opened the door and jerked the boy inside.

The moment the door shut, the smoke dissipated. The courier strained until she could move her feet. She hurled herself toward the building, skidding to a stop as the entire thing vanished before her eyes, leaving nothing but an alley covered with overgrown weeds and cast in shadows.

1

I often heard my sister before I saw her, and tonight was no ex-
ception. Zosa's supple voice spilled through the open window of
Bézier Residence, sounding so like our mother's—at least until she
began a raunchier ditty comparing a man's more delicate anatomy
to a certain fruit.

I crept inside, unnoticed in the crowd of boarders. Two of the
younger girls pretended to dance with invisible partners, but every
other eye was fixed on my sister, the most talented girl in the room.

A special kind of girl rented rooms at Bézier Residence. Almost
all worked jobs fitting of their foul mouths: second shifts as house
grunts, factory workers, grease cooks, or any number of ill-paying
positions in the vieux quais—the old docks of Durc. I worked at
Tannerie Fréllac, where women huddled over crusted alum pots and
wells of dye. But Zosa was different.

"Happy birthday," I shouted when her song ended.

"Jani!" She bounded over. Her huge brown eyes shone against a
pale, olive-skinned face that was far too thin.

"Did you eat supper?" I'd left her something, but with all the other girls around, food had a tendency to disappear.

She groaned. "Yes. You don't have to ask me every night."

"Of course I do. I'm your big sister. It's my life's greatest duty."
Zosa scrunched her nose and I flicked it. Fishing in my sack, I pulled
out the newspaper that had cost me half a day's wage and pressed
it into her palms. "Your present, *madame*." Here, birthdays weren't
dusted with confectioners' sugar; they were hard-won and more
dear than gold.

"A newspaper?"

"A jobs section." I flipped open the paper with a sly grin.

Inside were advertisements for jobs in fancy dress shops, pa-
tisseries, and perfumeries, positions that would never belong to
a thirteen-year-old who didn't look a day over ten. Luckily, they
weren't what I had in mind.

Skipping past them, I pointed to a listing that had appeared in
papers across town an hour ago.

The ink was vibrant purple, like Aligney blood poppies or crushed
amethyst velvet. It stood out, a strange beacon in a sea of black and
white.

The girls crowded around us, and everyone leaned in as the purple ink winked with an iridescence that rivaled polished moonstones.

No address was given. The legendary hotel needed none. It appeared every decade or so in the same old alley downtown. The whole city was probably there now, already waiting like fools for a chance at a stay.

Years ago, when the hotel last made an appearance, the majority of the invitations were delivered beforehand to only the wealthiest citizens. Then, the day the hotel arrived, a few more precious invitations were gifted to random folk in the crowd. Our matron, Minette Bézier, was one of those lucky few.

That midnight, the guests stepped into the hotel and disappeared, along with the building. Two weeks later, they famously stepped *back*, appearing in the same alley from nothing but thin air.

My fingers twitched and I pictured cracking the seal on my own invitation. But even if we were fortunate enough to win one, we'd still have to pay for a room—and they weren't exactly cheap.

Zosa's brows drew together. "You want me to interview?"

"Not quite. I'm going to interview. I'm taking *you* to audition as a singer."

It had been four years since I'd taken her to a singing audition— the first one hadn't worked out in our favor, and I couldn't stomach going through it again, so we didn't try for more. But today was her birthday and this was *the* Hotel Magnifique. Everything about it felt different. Perfect, somehow. "Hotels hire singers all the time. What do you say?"

She answered with a smile that I felt in the tips of my toes.

One of the older girls shoved a lock of greasy blonde hair behind her pink ear. "That advertisement is a tease. It would be a miracle if any of us got a job."

I straightened. "That's not true."

She shrugged as she turned away. "Do what you want. I wouldn't waste my time."

"Think she's right?" Zosa asked, her delicate mouth turning down.

"Absolutely not," I said, perhaps too quickly. When Zosa's frown deepened, I cursed silently and dragged my thumb along our mother's old necklace.

The worthless chain was Verdanniere gold, rigid as steel. Maman always joked my spine was made of the stuff. I often fumbled for it when I needed her guidance with Zosa. Not that she ever gave it; dead mothers weren't any good for guidance.

"The hotel wouldn't run an advertisement if no one had a chance. Tomorrow, we'll show them what we've got. When they discover how brilliant we both are, we can kiss this place goodbye for good."

The thought felt like a bright coal smoldering in my chest.

My fingers trembled as I straightened one of Zosa's dark curls like Maman would do. "Let's show the advertisement to Bézier. She'll know more about the hotel than anyone here."

Zosa nodded, eyes gleaming. I plucked the jobs section from her fingers and took off. Girls raced behind me up two flights of stairs to my favorite room, the third-floor sitting room that used to house sailors before Bézier bought the building. It was stuffed with shelves of antiquated ocean charts and atlases for far-off places I'd often page through.

Bézier sat before her fire, stockinged feet propped on a window ledge. Outside, rain battered the port of Durc, turning the city I hated into a wet blur.

Her mouth pinched when we all streamed in. "What is it now?"

I handed her the page of newsprint. Purple ink caught the firelight and Bézier's pale face slackened.

"Is something wrong?" asked a girl behind me.

Bézier glanced above the hearth to the decade-old sheet of parchment sheathed behind glass: her invitation. In the low light, the purple ink shone with the same iridescence as the advertisement. "Hotel Magnifique is returning, I see."

Another door opened and a few stragglers squeezed in, jostling for a look.

"I've heard the guests sip on liquid gold from champagne flutes for breakfast," said a girl in back. More girls chimed in with their own rumors.

"They say the pillows don't have feathers, they're all stuffed with spun clouds—"

"Heard each night, you cross the world thrice over—"

"And all their fancy doormen are princes from some far-off land—"

"Bet they give fancy kisses, too." A girl with beige skin and ruddy cheeks made a vulgar gesture with her tongue. Thankfully Zosa didn't notice. Instead, a grin split her face.

Shame there was no way to know if the rumors were true; guests signed away all memory of their stay upon checkout. Besides luggage, the only thing guests returned with was a feeling of devastating happiness. Bézier once admitted to icing her jaw from all the smiling.

Curious, I glanced at Bézier. Her eyes had grown misty, as if the hotel returning somehow sparked a memory. I opened my mouth to ask about it until Zosa slipped in front of me. "Did you ever see the maître?"

The maître d'hôtel was the proprietor and as famous as the hotel itself.

Bézier nodded, smug. "The hotel came once when I was a young, pretty thing. The maître had the brightest smile I'd ever seen. Positively gleamed greeting the crowds. He plucked a flower from the air and tossed it to me." She pretended to catch a tiny bloom. "The thing smelled like blueberry pie then dissolved to nothing in my fingers. Over a decade went by before the hotel came again, and when it did, the maître looked exactly the same."

"Wearing the same clothes?" someone asked.

"No, you ninny. He *looked* the same. Same face. Same charm. Hadn't aged, not a day. Makes sense, I guess. He is the greatest suminaire in all the world."

Girls gasped at the mention of a suminaire: the old Verdanniere word for *magician*.

Outside of the hotel, a suminaire was the most dangerous thing in the world. Magic was said to build in their blood during adolescence until it flared out in an uncontrollable power, with the potential to hurt—or kill—anyone who happened to be near them at the time.

Some said it poured from a child's nose into a dark cloud.

Others said it looked like pitch-black fingers clawing up a child's throat. And there was no way to tell a normal child from a suminaire before their magic flared.

There were rumors of what to look out for, of course. Outlandish things like craving blood or tongues turning black. There were even children said to come back to life after a fatal wound only to discover they had magic in their blood. But no one could prove it.

Whatever the case, magic was so dangerous that for centuries in Verdanne, children suspected to be suminaires were either drowned or burned to death.

But inside the hotel, magic was safe. It was well known the maître somehow enchanted the building himself, allowing the suminaires he employed to perform astonishing feats without harming a soul. Nobody knew how he'd done it, but everybody wanted a chance to see it firsthand.

Before anyone could ask another question, Bézier clapped her hands. "It's late. Everyone to your rooms."

"Wait," I said. "Do you remember anything now that the hotel is back? Is it as magical as the rumors?" As soon as the words left my mouth, I felt silly for asking.

Bézier, however, didn't laugh or think it odd. Instead, she glanced at her old invitation wistfully.

"I'm certain it's more," she said with a bitter note. I'd be bitter too if I couldn't remember the most exciting time of my life. She tossed the advertisement in the fire, then stumbled back. "My god."

The paper caught, burning pink, then green, then crimson, turning the hearth into a dazzling display of rainbow flames. The flames shot higher, raging into the chimney, creating a more arresting sight than the storefronts of boulevard Marigny.

"It's *magic*," Zosa whispered.

My neck prickled. There was a reason Hotel Magnifique caused gasps and goggling. Normally, magic was rare, dangerous, and to be avoided at all costs. But somehow, inside that hotel, it was the opposite, and tomorrow we might finally have a chance to experience it ourselves.

TEEN AND YA FICTION

Available and coming soon
from Pushkin Press

HOTEL MAGNIFIQUE
Emily J. Taylor

BLADE OF SECRETS
MASTER OF IRON
DAUGHTER OF THE PIRATE KING
DAUGHTER OF THE SIREN QUEEN
VENGEANCE OF THE PIRATE QUEEN
THE SHADOWS BETWEEN US
WARRIOR OF THE WILD
Tricia Levenseller

BEARMOUTH
Liz Hyder

ECHO NORTH
Joanna Ruth Meyer

THE BEAST PLAYER
THE BEAST WARRIOR
Nahoko Uehashi

GLASS TOWN WARS
Celia Rees